# Torn Apart

BY THE AUTHOR OF

From Within

# Torn Apart

## Book 1 of Convergence

J. M. Riddles

Cover Design by Seventhstar

ISBN: 978-0-9994476-0-4
ASIN: B07586TV6Y

Library of Congress Control Number: 2017915731
J.M. Riddles, California City, CA

jmriddles.com

Dedicated to my wonderful nerdy husband, Dickie, and my two best friends who have supported my writing through all the years; Natalie and Kat. I love you guys.

# ACKNOWLEDGEMENTS

I want to thank everyone who beta-read the first drafts of this story for me and especially those who helped me with my summary because, for me, there is no pain greater than having to summarize my work.

Special thanks to my two best friends, who are like the sisters I never had, and who have been with me through all the many years of my writing and have offered unconditional love and support. Kat, thank you for all the times you've ever helped me edit. Natalie, thank you for suffering through the more risqué chapters of my work. I'd like to promise you there won't be more of them, but there will probably be more.

Lastly, I would like to thank my husband, Dickie, who has supported me during this entire project. He has been my rock during all the years we have been together, and I know he has always been happy to see me write. He always has a million ideas for me, and he's always loved discussing my work with me. I know he wants all the credit, but I will at least say, yes, you helped push me along…a little.

# Torn Apart

By J.M. Riddles

## PROLOGUE – RETURNED FROM THE DEAD

It had been seven long years since she last saw the two trees that stretched as giants beyond the forest canopy. Their mighty boughs swayed gently in the soft summer breeze. Time had decayed the structures that adorned those trees. Vines grew through the little window holes, and slippery moss had overtaken the steps they had carefully constructed. The world they had once built for just the two of them.

Forts - not tree houses. They did not play house like normal children, for they had never been like other children.

She looked at the tree that had once been her fort and then over to the tree that had once belonged to him. His had withstood the ravages of time somewhat better than hers, and she smiled as she remembered him teaching her how to build her fort and at how exasperated he would get at her lack of skill.

She had not come to relive childhood memories because some were too painful to bear. She had come in search of the tear. She had tracked three demons for the past four days, hoping they would lead her to the source. She had already killed two and couldn't afford to let the last one get away.

Suddenly she had found herself in familiar surroundings. An inexplicable grip of nostalgia possessed her, and she began wandering – searching.

She felt a painful ache in her chest as she walked towards the tree that had once been his fort, and her hand instinctively clutched at the icy blue crystal hanging from her neck. She circled the base of the mighty tree and found the worn ladder. Some of the wooden steps had rotted off, but most appeared intact and still sturdy. Not being able to climb with her spear, she left it at the base of the tree along with her light travel bag. Even without a weapon, she was far from defenseless.

Carefully, she tested each handhold and foothold as she pulled her way up. When she finally reached the top and looked around, a flood of vivid memories from her past caused her breath to hitch in her chest. The little wooden door was missing, torn from its hinges, but the walls remained. The old boards groaned beneath her feet, but she was impressed with how structurally sound they still felt. The thatched roof had long since blown away, revealing the swaying branches above. She looked out the window that faced towards her own fort and remembered the way they used to bicker over the rules they made for the games they played. Both tree forts were just close enough to where they could throw things through each other's windows and heckle each other with ease. She smiled again, but the pain in her heart only increased.

1

The happiest years of her youth were gone. He was gone. She had lost everything that day - her best friend, her mother, her home. Her eyes burned with unshed tears as she struggled to fight back the memories of the day the ritual failed.

Something buried under a pile of dead leaves in the corner caught her eye, and she reached down to pick it up.

It was an earth-colored pottery bowl. It had a few chips but was still intact. It was the bowl they had used to mix the herbs she had to drink, the potion that temporarily masked her human scent. They were not allowed to be together. She was a human, and he was a wolf - a lycan. If he returned to his pack smelling like a human, they would have forbidden him from ever seeing her again, but for years they had played together in secret. They had let no one stand in their way.

This time she couldn't hold it back. It hurt too much, and the bowl trembled in her hands as tears rolled down her face.

She was so distracted, so lost in her painful memories; she hadn't sensed that she was no longer alone until the wooden floor groaned beneath her.

A moment of terror gripped her as she spun around and saw the large and menacing form of a therian male. He was poised as if to strike, the claws of his powerful hands pointing at her in threat, and he was baring his fangs. His eyes glared at her.

His eyes.

The moment they locked eyes with each other, they both froze.

His eyes were a vivid and icy shade of blue, which stood out starkly against his deeply tanned skin, and his ears were long and pointed. His dark brown hair grew untamed past his shoulders, and his face looked rugged and wild. He towered over her in height and was very broad and muscular. He was mostly clad in leather and fur and wore only a light amount of armor. Despite his fighting stance and hostile expression, his wild face was oddly handsome, as most therians were wont to be, but it was his piercing eyes that struck something inside of her like a thunderbolt – those eyes. She could never forget them.

The moment she looked deep into those piercing blue eyes, a small gasp escaped her, and the bowl slipped from her fingers and shattered to pieces at her feet.

"Varg?"

His expression changed subtly. He had been startled by the way she looked at him. Did he know her? He had been hunting a demon that posed a threat to his pack when he picked up the scent of a strange human in his territory. He followed the scent and instantly flew into a rage that any human would dare to trespass, not only on his territory but in one of the few places he held sacred. He had seen the spear at the base of the tree and stealthily climbed with the aid of his powerful claws. He would allow no one to trespass, but there was something strange about this human's scent – almost familiar, but not.

Her back was to him when he first saw her, and he distinctly picked up the scent of tears. He had too much honor to kill like a coward from behind, so he purposely leaned into a weak floorboard to gain her attention. When she spun to face him, something caused him to stay his hand against her. She had long golden hair that was worn loosely except where it was pulled back from her face. She was tall and wore the white robe of a priestess, a robe that was snugly fit but designed to allow the wearer freedom of movement for combat. She was beautiful, especially for a human, but there was something familiar about her face, something odd about the way she looked at him with her hazel green eyes still wet with tears. She looked at him as if she knew him – but it was impossible.

And then she said his name.

"Varg? It is you!" she said and approached him without fear. He stood motionless in confusion.

"You're alive!" she cried while throwing her arms around his neck in a tight embrace.

He stood motionless and tense against her as she laid her head on his chest and new tears flooded her eyes. Eventually, she sensed his confusion and pulled back, but she didn't entirely remove her arms from around his neck.

"Don't you recognize me? It's me, Halea!" she explained while looking up into his startled face.

"Impossible," he said in a whisper. "It can't be."

She gently disentangled herself from him and stepped back. "Have I changed so much that you can't even recognize my scent?"

He leaned into her until his nose came close to where her neck and jaw met and gently inhaled her scent. He could faintly hear her heart and pulse begin to race at his intimate proximity, but instead, he focused on the many notes of her scent as they tripped across his memories.

There!

The Halea he had known was a young girl - a child. The warm scent he breathed now was that of a woman; more matured, anxious, and fertile, but buried beneath all of that was the one scent he had memorized since he was a boy, and it had not changed.

He pulled back to look into her face. "Halea…it is really you!" he cried while snatching her into a crushing embrace.

She wrapped her arms around his waist and wept again in joy and relief.

"I thought I lost you! I thought you had died with your people the day the city was destroyed," he spoke into her hair as he held her close.

"As soon as it appeared, I was taken to the Citadel with the rest of the priestesses. We received news that the lycans were destroyed when the great convergence tear opened, but I didn't want to believe them. It took me almost a year to return, and when I did, I tried looking for you. I went to your den...there was nothing left. Everything had been destroyed; only bones and the shattered remains of what your people had built…and then I found this," she said, reaching into the front of her robe and lifting the blue crystal she wore around her neck. It was the same shade of blue as his eyes.

He recognized it the moment she held it up for him.

"I lost it that day. Many of my pack were slaughtered. I wanted to look for you the moment the great tear opened, but father needed me to help lead the survivors to safety. We fled deep into the mountains and have only just recently returned. I went to the ruined city, hoping that you could have survived, but no one could have survived what happened in that place."

Already she wanted to forget that terrible day that was again threatening to resurface in her mind. She reached up and gently touched his face.

"What happened to you? You're all scruffy now. Where's that skinny little wolf I used to know? Seriously, how'd you even fit through that door?" she teased with a smile.

Oh yes, he knew that smile.

He chuckled in a deep voice so unlike the one she had once known

"What happened to me? What happened to you? Wow…you've changed…you look beautiful," he said, trying not to blush or let his eyes wander too much. She had certainly matured in all the best ways. He had thought she was beautiful when they were still kids, but now she was a grown woman, and every inch of her seemed to be calling for his attention.

She beamed at his compliment. She couldn't help but notice that he had grown ruggedly handsome in the past eight years, but she decided to shift the topic away from appearances as she didn't want to feel awkward with the man who had once been her closest and dearest friend.

"I'm a priestess now. That's why I'm here. A tear has opened," she explained.

"I figured one couldn't be far. The demons are growing in number again. I was hunting one when I found you. Halea…" he said, suddenly changing the subject. "What happened? I know you don't want to talk about that day…I can smell your anxiety, but please, I need to know. What went wrong? What happened at the Citadel?"

She inhaled deeply and once again felt the pain in her heart. She did not want to relive those memories, but for him, she would.

# CHAPTER 1 – WOLF BOY

"Can I play too?" she asked as the children outside the city walls picked opponents for their wrestling games.

It was a beautiful morning, and her grandfather had decided to spare her her lessons for the day at her mother's behest.

"She should have time to be a child. Let her play," her mother had pleaded to her cleric father-in-law. Theia doted on her only child, especially after the death of her husband. Halea was all she had left. She had hoped to give her child a happy, ordinary life, but destiny had not worked out that way. Halea had been born blessed by the Goddess, Tiamet, the world dragon of creation.

No one knew which children would be blessed or why. Theia was distraught to discover that her daughter had been given the light of Tiamet. When she grew up, she would be expected to serve the Goddess. She did not wish the life of a priestess for her child, but Uro had explained that the Goddess had her reasons for choosing Halea, and it would be unwise to deny her daughter the path Tiamet had laid before her.

Theia had brought her daughter to her father-in-law in the holy city of Ruinac by the sea as soon as she discovered her daughter's gifts, and Uro had convinced her to stay and make their home in the city with him, where Halea could be raised in the ways of the Goddess. Uro had lost all of his children, and Halea was his only surviving grandchild. While he loved her, he was strict with her when it came to her training. Halea was all he had left and Tiamet's greatest gift to him.

He had watched her stare wistfully out the windows that morning, and it did pain him to see his grandchild so lonely. She was only ten years old, and she longed to play with children her own age. When Theia had pleaded with him to allow the child to play, he couldn't deny her after he saw the hopeful gleam in the child's eyes. But he doubted she would be gone for long. He knew that other children shunned her.

"Sure!" replied one of the girls, her chestnut hair bound in short braids.

"No! Not her!" interjected one of the bigger boys. "She's one of those freaks that pray to the dragon god. She hurt Ben the last time we let her near us."

Ben stood back from the others, looking solemn and nervous.

"I said I was sorry. I didn't mean to hurt him!" cried Halea.

The gifts of Tiamet would someday serve to make her a powerful warrior against the forces of Chaos, but in the meantime, they made it difficult for her to fit in. She was much stronger than most children her own age and much faster, but the most formidable of her gifts was the power to purify.

5

"You get out of here! We told you last time we don't want you around!" shouted another boy who picked up a rock and threw it at her. Halea easily dodged the stone, but when the others joined in, she was soon injured when one of the projectiles struck her painfully on the arm, causing her to cry out. While Halea was hurt and distracted, another girl took the opportunity to shove her from behind, causing her to fall hard on her hands and knees.

Painfully she pulled herself up, turned, and ran away as they shouted taunts after her. Her grandfather had told her most people feared what they didn't understand, and there were very few who understood the ways of those who were blessed by Tiamet. She did not understand how a blessing could feel so much like a curse.

She ran away from the city and into the forest. She did not want to go home. She did not want to see the sadness and disappointment in her mother's eyes again. Her mother so desperately wanted her to have friends, to be happy, to fit in. The only thing that hurt worse than her loneliness was her mother's pity, and at that moment, she couldn't bear to face it. She made up her mind that she would hide in the forest until sunset, then later return home to her mother and pretend that she had a lovely day and for once had made a friend. She would make something up. She would have to.

She slowed down a little as she made her way deeper into the forest. She was getting tired, her hands and knees stung from where she had skinned them falling, and her arm ached terribly. She knew she should not go too deeply into the woods. There were dangerous wild beasts within, and worse – therians.

Despite the warnings, she had always dreamed of exploring the forest. It looked so lush and green as she would stare from her window over the city wall. Birds were singing as she passed through the trees and the fragrance of flowers filled the air. The warm sun filtered through the leaves, casting dancing flecks of light wherever she turned. The longer she walked, the more she began to forget the pain in her arm and the stinging taunts of the other children. Here, she felt at peace.

Whenever she saw a rabbit, she would follow it until it dodged into its hole. She would watch the squirrels until they ran up the trees and chattered down at her from above. She roamed and laughed and forgot, if only for a moment, everything she had left behind.

And then it occurred to her – she no longer knew the direction home.

Her heart pounded in her chest as panic welled up inside of her. How could she have let it happen?

Once again, she began to run, looking for anything familiar that might indicate the direction home, but the longer she ran, the thicker the trees became, and the more desolate she began to feel. She slipped on the soft moss and fell hard on her hands and knees, reopening her scrapes. She tried to wipe her sweaty hair out of her face with her grimy hands and calm herself, but the panic within her was reaching a frenzy.

And that was when she heard the growling.

Her heart nearly stopped as she turned her head to the side and found herself staring directly into the eyes of a wolf.

It wasn't very far away, and it was crouching low to the ground, growling at her and baring its gleaming white fangs. Slowly she turned her body from where she was still kneeling and crept backward. The wolf's growls grew louder, but it remained still. Ever so slowly, she rose to her feet, never for a moment turning her gaze away from the threatening beast. Its mesmerizing eyes were a shade of blue as cold as a winter's sky, but its fur was brown and shaggy.

Then, it was gone.

In its place crouched a young boy. He appeared to be close to her in age, perhaps a year older. His thick brown hair was strewn wildly around his head, and as he jumped to his feet, he revealed a wiry frame clad in strange furs and animal skins. But his eyes were unmistakable, the same startling shade of blue as she had just seen in the wolf.

"If you come one step closer, I'll kill ya! I'll bite your head off, I will!" he shouted while frantically pacing a short distance back and forth and never taking his eyes off her.

It was then that she noticed the strange markings upon one of the trees. She knew those runes.

"Are you stuck?" she asked.

"Did you do this? I bet you think it's funny. Well, when I get out, you'll be sorry! I'll eat you!"

Suddenly the last of the panic and fear dissipated from her, and she found herself beginning to laugh. She tried not to laugh too hard, she could tell it was making the strange boy furious, but there was something so surreal about the entire situation that she couldn't help herself.

"Oh, you are dead meat, human!" he threatened as he paced even faster, glaring at her the whole time and snarling, which revealed his sharp fangs. She observed that his ears were long and pointed, and instead of fingernails, he had claws, and they looked rather sharp.

"Don't be mad at me! You're in a barrier. Clerics and priestesses use them sometimes to prevent demons from passing through."

"I'm not a demon…you…stupid girl!" he retorted in frustration.

"Are you a therian?"

Therians inhabited the wild places, and they could come in many forms. They were the immortal descendants of the ancient gods, and as such, they were powerful and dangerous. Therianthropes possessed some of the qualities and gifts of whatever animal deity they descended from. They appeared as mostly human and often attractive as a means of drawing in their prey, but most possessed the ability to transform into beasts.

Therians and humans did not often get along. There had been many wars waged over the ages, over territory, resources, or just to survive. Most therians had no qualms about killing and devouring humans; they were the predators, and the weaker humans, their prey.

"I'm a lycan!" he corrected.

7

Lycans were therians who descended from the ancient wolf gods. They shared many similarities to common wolves, and that knowledge did not comfort her.

"I guess they work on therian…I mean, lycans too. How did you get in there?" Halea asked.

"I was scouting from up there," he said, pointing to a large mossy boulder behind him.

She giggled before realizing it, and he shot her another deadly glare, but she couldn't help it. It was clear that he had slipped on the slimy moss from high above and landed right into the barrier. He could have just as easily walked into it, but the fact that he fell into it from above was particularly comical to her. It was hard to not laugh at such a mental image, and she wished she could have seen it with her own eyes.

Apparently, he guessed her train of thought and growled. It was the distinct growl of a beast and not the imitation sound a child would make. It snapped her back into the reality of the danger of her situation. While he appeared to her as just another child, which put her off her guard, she had to remember he was still a therian, and he could, and probably would carry through with his threats.

"I'm sorry. Please, don't be mad. It's not my fault there's a barrier. I didn't do it. I…I might be able to get you out, though."

He quieted down but was still regarding her with his cold and angry eyes.

"I'm going to be a priestess for Tiamet when I grow up. My grandfather is a cleric, and he taught me how to read the ancient language and even some easy spells. I might be able to break this barrier, but if I get you out, you have to promise me you won't try to eat me once you're free."

He frowned.

"Well, do you want out or not? You're not my problem. I can just go home!" she bluffed despite having no idea of how to get back, but he didn't know that.

She noticed him sniffing at the air, and she wasn't quite sure what to make of it.

"You're lying to me, human! I smell deceit!" he accused.

She hadn't realized the scent of anxiety had risen from her as she lied about her ability to go home, and fearing that he had some strange power to read the mind, she instantly confessed in her guilt.

"Fine! I can't go home! There! Are you happy? I'm lost! I didn't mean to come this far into the forest, and now I don't know how to get back," she shouted while bursting into tears.

He watched her uncomfortably as she buried her face in her hands and cried, the scent of her salty tears reaching his sensitive nose. Of all the reactions in the world, he had not expected her to start crying, and he had no idea how to handle it. All he knew was that it bothered him, and he didn't like it.

"Stop bawling! Geez! Look, let me out of here, and I promise I won't eat ya. Just don't cry anymore."

"What if you kill me and don't eat me?" she asked while trying to dry her eyes. Her grandfather had always warned her that therians were dangerous and not to be trusted. She had no way of knowing if this one would keep his word, and his threatening behavior left her with a lot of doubts.

He seemed to look insulted, as if he sensed she doubted his honor.

His father had raised him with a code that his word was his bond, even if it was given to a lowly human. "I won't hurt you, kill you, or eat you, I swear it. Please…come on. Just get me out of here."

She looked him directly in the eye as he spoke. Would she be able to trust her life to him? He appeared to have finally calmed down, and now that he wasn't snarling at her, he seemed like he might actually be nice. Perhaps.

"Okay, I'll try it, but if I get you out…can you…can you tell me how to get back to the city?"

"Well…that would be extra generous on my part. I mean, I'm already letting you live…"

"Bye!" she said and turned.

"Okay, wait! Stop! All right – fine! You get me out, and I'll let you live AND show you the way home," he amended.

A devilish grin passed her lips, but she made sure to make her expression neutral before turning back to face him.

"Deal! Now give me a minute to figure out these runes," she said as she began inspecting the trees surrounding him.

Truthfully, barriers were not meant to contain therians. Their spell was intended for, and worked best, on beings from the Chaos Dimension. An older and stronger therian would have no trouble breaking through the seals, but a weaker therian child could very easily get stuck. This was a fact she had no desire to mention, as the lycan clearly had a sense of pride, and she didn't want him going back on their deal by angering him again.

She read the dark red markings on the tree and could tell that it was an old trap, probably long forgotten. There would be two places around the trap where the markings would be visible, and the rest that created the perimeter of the barrier would be invisible so a demon could wander unaware into the trap. Once inside, any attempt to escape would result in purification. Purification didn't quite work on therians. Experiencing purification for them could be painful but not lethal.

She placed her hand over the red mark and focused as best as she could with the strange wolf boy staring at her back. She felt tense and prayed she was strong enough to activate the runes. She was not a priestess and was still new to being an acolyte. Her powers weren't mature yet, but she forced herself to concentrate, knowing that successfully freeing this lycan might be her only way home. After a tense moment, the rune began to glow.

"I did it!" she cried with glee.

"All right!" replied the wolf boy, who immediately ran forward.

"Don't!" she shouted, but it was too late. He walked straight into the barrier. A blinding white light flashed, and there was a sizzling sound as the lycan screamed out in pain.

9

He lay prone on the ground, and steam was slowly rising from him. At first, she thought he might be dead, but then he slowly began to move, and she heard him groan.

"You're dead, human!" he threatened in a weak voice.

"I'm sorry! I tried to tell you '*don't*!' I wasn't done yet. I only activated the first rune. There's one more I have to find and activate. It's not my fault you were impatient."

"You are a terrible priestess!" he said as he sat up and dusted himself off. The steam was gone, and despite the initial shock and pain, he seemed no worse for wear. She suspected it wasn't the first time he walked into the barrier. He must have discovered he was trapped somehow. The thought of him being shocked multiple times threatened to make her burst into laughter again, and she bit her lip as hard as possible to control herself.

"I'm not a priestess yet! I'm just a kid, gimme a break!"

He scowled and grunted as he pulled himself to his feet.

"I just gotta find the last rune," she explained while slowly circling him. She could feel the edges of the barrier as she moved around him. It crackled against her skin like static electricity. As she walked, she inspected the trees and the ground. At last, she came to a stop once she had entirely circled the barrier.

"Well?" he asked, clearly getting impatient.

"Uh…I didn't find it," she confessed and tried not to cringe as he growled in frustration. "It should be visible somewhere! I didn't see it!"

"Well, keep looking. I don't want to be in here forever," he pleaded.

"Well, what about you? Do you see any more markings?"

He began looking around inside of the barrier as she tried circling it once again.

"Wait! I think I see something!" he said and pointed to the tall boulder from which he fell. There at the base, faded, but still visible was the other mark.

"That's it!" she cried while approaching and kneeling before it.

She placed her hands in front of the mark and focused all of her energy on activating the rune. There was a strong resistance this time. Her hands trembled with the strain, and soft white lights began dancing at the tips of her fingers. More, she needed more power, but she was giving it everything she had.

He watched as perspiration began to bead on her brow. "Come on; you can do it! Keep trying!" he encouraged.

At last, with a loud crack, the rune glowed, and the barrier snapped. The force of the spell breaking nearly knocked her over and left her feeling a little dizzy from the exertion.

"I think I did it!" she said while leaning against the cold boulder and slowly pulling herself up.

This time he stepped forward slowly, gently extending his hand to feel for the charge. Instead, there was none. "It's gone! Hey, you did it! Great job!" he exclaimed, but when he turned to face her, he stopped short. She looked a little sick. "Are you okay?"

She wiped the sweat from her face, smearing more dirt around in the process, and took a deep breath. "Yeah. Yeah, I'm fine…just tired. My powers aren't very strong, and I think I wore myself out a little."

To her surprise, he started to laugh.

"What?" she asked.

"Your hair!" he pointed.

She reached up and felt that almost all of her hair was sticking up on end from the barrier's charge. It must have looked ridiculous, and suddenly she too was laughing. They stood there laughing together for a little while as she futilely tried to tame her hair, but not much seemed to be helping, and eventually, she gave up.

"Well, you *did* get me out. I suppose I owe you. I'll show you to a stream. If you follow it west, it'll take you straight to the city. They seem to get most of their water from our mountains."

"I hope you guys don't pee in it," she said.

He chuckled at her joke. "Only a little. Come on, human. The sun's already high."

"Halea, my name is Halea," she corrected while following him into the woods.

"I'm Varg, and this is my territory. Well, it's my pack's territory, which means it'll be mine someday. It's not very smart to go wandering around in it without my permission."

"I didn't come cause I wanted to! So can I?"

"Can I – what?"

"Can I have your permission?"

He wasn't expecting her to ask such a question. "Why?"

"Maybe someday I'll want to come back. I only ran into the forest today to get away from the city. Nobody there really likes me anyway," she said the last part quietly, but with his sensitive ears, he easily heard her and was surprised she would confide such a thing to him. It made him feel a little bad.

"As long as you don't go past where the great oaks stop growing, I don't care if you come to the forest. Past that point is close to our hunting grounds and beyond that the den, and it's not like the other lycans owe you any favors."

Her heart swelled with joy at the idea of being able to come back to the forest. Except for the getting lost part, she liked it, and the wolf boy wasn't so bad when he wasn't snapping at her.

"Thank you!" she shouted while running to keep up with him as he hopped over logs and moved through the brush with ease.

They walked in companionable silence for several more minutes. She snatched berries from bushes as they walked along to ease her hunger. Her mother was probably wondering why she hadn't come home for lunch.

"Why were you scouting out here by yourself? Where's the rest of your pack?" she finally asked, knowing that wolves usually hunted in packs. She had been wondering, but it had taken her a little time to muster up the courage to ask.

"Some are out hunting. Most are back at the den today. I just wanted some time alone. Nothin' wrong with it," he explained, and she sensed that he seemed a little defensive, though she had no idea why, so she decided to change the subject.

"Will you come out by yourself again?"

"I can do it whenever I want!" he explained.

Eventually, they reached a shallow stream surrounded by fern patches.

"This is it. Just follow it downstream, and it'll take you all the way back. A wolf could make that distance in no time at all, but, well, you're just a human. It'll probably take you an hour."

"I'm faster than all the other kids where I come from," she defended. Speed was one of the gifts of Tiamet.

"Still not faster than a wolf! You've been dragging the whole way here."

"I'm tired! I did just have to break a barrier. I'd like to see you do that. And I bet I could outrun you too…if I weren't tired. I'd show ya!"

He gave her a strange wolfish grin, exposing the tips of his fangs. "Are you challenging me?"

Varg was a wolf, and what's more, he exhibited all the traits that would someday make him an alpha male. Being the strongest and fastest over everyone and everything was a growing obsession for him, and he was not about to let some human female challenge his dominance.

"Yeah, maybe I am. I bet I could beat ya!" she announced, refusing to be intimidated.

"Fine, human, come back here to the fern patch tomorrow when the sun is high. And don't go tiring yourself out before you arrive. That way, when I whip ya, you can't make any excuses."

She grinned at the invitation. "I'll be here."

~~~☼~~~

Theia stood staring out the front door. Children would run and play past the front steps of their home, but she never saw Halea, and she hadn't come home for lunch. She was beginning to worry. Eventually, she decided to wait inside. Maybe this was a good sign. Perhaps she was finally out somewhere making a friend and having fun like a normal child.

She went to the kitchen and began cutting vegetables for dinner when she heard the front door open and close. Theia immediately put down her utensils and went to see her daughter when she stopped short and gasped.

There stood Halea. The romper she wore that morning was stained, and her shoes were caked in mud. She had scrapes on her knees, a giant bruise on her arm, her hands and fingernails were filthy, her face was smeared with dirt, and her hair was a disaster, but despite it all, she had the brightest smile on her face.

"Halea?"

"Mother, I had a wonderful day!"

12

# CHAPTER 2 – THE ODD COUPLE

Halea was pretty winded. Eventually, she stopped running as she neared the fern patch because she really didn't want to give him any unfair advantages by exhausting herself before they even raced. Her grandfather had delayed her with his reluctance to let her be free of her studies that morning, and so she had no choice but to run the first part of the way there if she wanted to meet Varg at their agreed-upon time.

Her grandfather had assumed she would get rejected by the local children again and she would return home to her usually scheduled lessons for lack of anything better to do. He was surprised when his daughter-in-law informed him that Halea had apparently managed to play with the other children and that she wanted to be allowed to go play again.

While Uro was her master in the ways of Tiamet, he didn't have a say in the rest of her life. Theia maintained the final word when it came to all things relating to the care and upbringing of her daughter. She had seen Halea come home happy for once instead of in tears, and she was not about to let anyone take that away from her. Halea would someday become immortal and have all the rest of eternity to serve Tiamet, but she would only be a child once and for a short time.

Uro was getting on in years and wasn't required to be present at the Citadel of the Sun very often during times between convergences, so it was easy for him to make time for Halea. Uro was growing gray, and his hair was thinning a little in the back, and his eyes were often hidden behind thick spectacles. Despite his advancing age, he still took his duties as a cleric seriously. The primary function of the clerics was to find and train potential priestesses and keep watch over the occurrences of tears and demon attacks. They studied the nature of the Chaos Dimension, which sought to converge with their world, and where, why, and how the tears formed. There were many mysteries they sought to uncover. Hopefully, unlocking the answers would solve the problem that was plaguing their world.

Theia had tried to ask Halea about her day and how she managed to come home in such a disastrous state. Halea seemed slightly evasive, simply stating that they had played wrestling games and king of the hill and that she had taken a few too many falls. When asked if she had made any friends and who they were, again, she seemed reluctant to divulge too much information, just that she had met with a group of children and they had all got along very well, and that she would like to meet with them again the next day. Theia did not want to pressure her too much; maybe her new friendships were on shaky ground. One day the local children might want to play with her; the next, they could be put off by her powers and shun her again. At the time, it was enough for her to know that her daughter was going outside in the fresh air and having some fun like a normal girl, instead of being stuck inside poring over her grandfather's lessons.

"You can train her in the evenings after supper and let her have the day to play," she had told Uro.

"For now, I suppose Halea may use her day as she pleases, but next year when she turns eleven, she must begin combat training, and for that, she will have to devote more time," he argued.

"If all goes well, we can settle on a healthy balance for her when the time comes," conceded Theia.

Halea was relieved when she had finally been allowed to leave and was careful to make sure neither her mother nor grandfather saw her exit through the city's main gates. If they knew she intended to meet a strange therian alone in the woods, they would never let her go. She had thrown on a pair of short trousers, a comfortable gray tunic, and some boots which would be more suitable for running through the woods than the shoes she had worn the previous day, and she made sure to tie her hair back.

She was incredibly disappointed when she finally arrived at the fern patch and didn't see the wolf boy.

"You're late!" spoke a familiar voice, and she was surprised to turn and find him standing right next to her with a wolfish grin on his face.

"*Uh-oh, he is fast*," she thought, hoping she wouldn't make a complete fool of herself. If she weren't a worthy opponent, maybe he wouldn't want to waste any more of his time with her.

"It took a while for my grandfather to let me go, then I had to sneak out of the city, but I'm here."

"Good. I was about to give up and go home. Here, drink this," Varg said as he shoved a strange-looking container at her. It appeared to be a small hollowed-out gourd with a cork sealing the opening.

"What's this?" she asked, taking the container from him.

"It's what we lycans drink when we're hunting or fighting other therians, so they can't get the jump on us by picking up on our scent. It temporarily makes you smell like earth and trees. I reeked of human yesterday after leading you out here. I had to bathe and rub myself over with strong herbs before I could go home, just to get the stink off. If my pack knew I let a human so close to our territory, I'd be in big trouble, and you'd be in even *bigger* trouble."

Varg also didn't want his pack, and especially not his father, to know that he fell into a human trap and had been unable to free himself without the assistance of a human. He would never get over the shame if others found out.

"I do *not* stink!" she argued defensively. True, that day, she had been sweating like a hog, but she was pretty sure she hadn't smelled so bad that even he could smell like her. She hadn't even touched him. "I didn't even get that close to you."

Varg could tell he stepped on a sensitive nerve and contemplated twisting the knife but instead decided to explain. "Everybody has a scent; you, me, everyone. Most

14

therians have powerful senses, and lycans, in particular, have a very powerful sense of smell. Just because you didn't get near me doesn't mean your scent wasn't still there, it was faint, but it was there. If my father found out I was near a human yesterday, he'd have skinned me alive. If you want to race me today, you better hide your scent before you start sweating again."

Truthfully, her scent wasn't so bad. Varg had picked up the scent of humans before, and he hadn't liked it, but her scent was unique and not at all unpleasant. He had actually been surprised when he finally saw her walk into the fern patch. The day before, she had looked a wreck, but today she had cleaned up considerably, and it gave him the opportunity to study her appearance. She was thin and gangly with golden dark blond hair, which she had pulled back from her face. She actually wasn't too bad looking for a human girl. She had big hazel green eyes, and now that her face was clean, he could see a light scattering of freckles across the bridge of her nose and cheeks.

Halea still felt insulted and wanted to argue, but she also didn't want to have to go home and make up a story about how the city children had decided they didn't want to play with her after all. Reluctantly she pulled out the stopper and sniffed the liquid inside. It smelled herbal but not too strong, and she thought she detected a hint of mint.

"Is it safe? I'm not a lycan. What if it poisons me?"

Varg hadn't thought about that. Could humans drink those herbs? There weren't any negative side effects for lycans, but maybe it wasn't safe for humans to drink.

"Try a tiny sip first and see what happens," he suggested.

Varg could smell her anxiety rise as she slowly lifted the container to her lips and took a small sip of the herbal potion. They stood there for a tense moment and waited.

Halea was surprised that the strange potion tasted oddly nice. There was definitely a mint flavor and a complimentary spiciness that she wasn't familiar with. "How did you get this?" she asked.

"I stole it from Batsuba, our healer. She has lots. She won't miss it."

"Well…so far, I think I feel fine. I'm not dead, at least."

Varg leaned a little closer to her and sniffed the air. "Your scent has decreased a little. I think it'll work."

Feeling more assured, Halea gulped down the last of the potion and handed him back the container. "What about now?"

Varg sniffed her again, this time coming closer, the closest Halea had ever been to him, which made her a little nervous, but the potion worked rapidly, and he seemed to not even notice that she had blushed a little at his proximity.

"Your scent is completely gone now," he assured. "The effects last for about a day, so we have plenty of time."

"Good! I'm ready to race," she said with a grin.

Varg led her a short distance through the forest until they arrived at their starting point.

15

"The trees aren't so close here, plenty of room to move. You'll have to cross a couple of small brooks and a large fallen dead tree, but beyond that is a little clearing with two giant trees that are very close together. You can't miss them. Whoever gets to those trees first is the winner."

They stood side by side and faced the path, and Halea seethed at the cocky smile Varg wore while stretching. He genuinely seemed to be looking forward to this, and she wanted to wipe that smirk right off his face. She was already faster and stronger than most humans, even grown humans, by quite a bit, all thanks to being born blessed by the Goddess, and as she would grow older, her strength and speed would continue to increase. It was a gift that amongst her own kind had caused her more grief than joy, but perhaps being pitted against a therian, she would finally be on even ground.

"Ready, set, go!" he called, and they were off. Neither was entirely sure of what to expect from the other. Needless to say, Varg had completely underestimated his human opponent. He was shocked when she sprinted ahead immediately for the lead, moving so quickly she almost became a blur even to his keen eyes. No, she was not at all an ordinary human.

Varg increased his speed, dodging past trees and leaping over obstacles with graceful ease.

Halea could sense him gaining on her as she leaped over the first brook in one swift bound and landed with a crouch that cost her only a little speed. Her heart was pounding in her chest, and she cursed the fact that being shut in so much had probably drastically hurt her chances of winning. Though naturally fast, she was certain regular practice and exercise would have made her even faster, whereas the lycan lived in the woods and was probably free to run every day.

As they approached the next brook, Varg managed to catch up with her just as they were leaping over the water. She frowned as he flashed a smug smile, showing his bright white fangs, but neither slowed down. The fallen tree was just ahead.

The fallen tree was a higher jump than expected, and Halea cursed as Varg sailed over it with ease while she had to scramble for a foothold to get over the top. Now he was breaking ahead of her. She was gasping for air, but with one final burst of speed, she managed to come up close behind him. He didn't look back as they were quickly approaching the two giant trees.

At last, Varg surged forward and touched his goal at the base of the great tree, and he was surprised again as he heard Halea quickly come in behind him and reach the other tree. It had been a very close race, but Varg had won.

Halea was exhausted and gasping for breath, and her heart was still pounding from the rush. She noticed that Varg also seemed pretty tired as he struggled for air and wiped the sweat from his brow.

Halea dreaded when he would finally catch his breath and imagined all the bragging and taunting she would get - and she was right.

"Ha! I win! No puny human can outrun a wolf." Varg stopped briefly to suck in another much-needed breath of air that went in with a wheeze. "Told ya," he added.

Halea glared at him. She hated to lose, but lose she did. Varg had won fair and square, and though she hated to admit it, she had to. Even though he was insufferably cocky, she wanted to come back to the forest and didn't want him to dislike her, so she decided to be the gracious loser.

"Yeah, you win. I'm impressed. Not bad for a mangy wolf."

Perhaps not as gracious as she had initially intended.

Instead of taking it as an insult, Varg just laughed, which somewhat ended in a cough as he was still catching his breath.

"I guess you're pretty good for a puny human. I race my pack brothers, and nobody else has ever come that close to beating me, so you probably are faster than most wolves. Don't feel bad; it's just that nobody can beat me."

He had a strange and insulting way of being comforting, but Halea recognized that Varg was paying her a genuine compliment, and considering his crass mannerisms and overinflated ego, that was probably as much as she could hope for.

"You have brothers?"

"Pack brothers, not blood brothers. I have no blood siblings, but everyone is one big family anyway when you're in a pack. Everyone is your brother and sister."

"That sounds really nice," Halea replied, feeling a lonely ache inside. All she had were her mother and grandfather. She thought it must be nice to have people who weren't technically related but who cared about you as if you were a real family member.

"Pack loyalty is everything. We always take care of each other and protect each other. That's how we all survive. My father is the supreme pack leader, not just of our pack but also of all the packs in the surrounding territories. Each territory has a leader, alpha males and females of course, and they all must submit to my father, who is alpha even above them."

"So, they're like lords, and he's a king," she deduced.

"In a way, but kings inherit their crowns, a Wolf King has to fight to win his. My father is training me to be a powerful alpha someday like he is. If he died, all the most powerful alphas from all the territories would come together and battle each other, and whoever is the strongest and most powerful is the one who becomes the supreme alpha and gets the right to carry the Great Fang and whatever pack they originated from would become head-pack."

"The Great Fang?"

"It's a divine weapon, a sword bestowed upon the supreme leader, the Wolf King, by the ancient wolf gods. No one but he can wield the Fang. It works only for him and has great power beyond just being a blade."

Halea had only ever heard of one other holy weapon, and she wondered how powerful this Great Fang really was.

"That's why when I grow up, I have to be the strongest, fastest, best hunter, and best warrior that my pack has. There may be a day when I have to fight to take my father's place."

"Lycans are immortals, though. You should have a long time to prepare and get stronger," she offered.

A sad look passed over Varg's face, and Halea was surprised when he turned away from her.

"Not that long," she heard him say, almost to himself.

Halea quickly realized she had touched on a sore topic and decided to bring them back to the present.

"I have to get stronger too. A priestess has to battle demons and close tears; that's why I'm stronger and faster than other humans. When I become a priestess, I'll be immortal as long as I swear myself to Tiamet. In another year, my grandfather will start showing me how to fight. I'm kind of looking forward to it, though I don't know if I'll be any good at it."

Varg considered her words carefully for a moment before he spoke.

"I can show you how to fight. My father has already started my warrior training. I can show you what I know so far, and we can practice with each other."

"You'll help me?" Halea asked in shock. Was he really proposing to train with her? Only the other day, he saw her as his enemy. But what did she think of him? She knew Varg had a big ego and that he was way too cocky, but there were little moments of genuine kindness too. Her grandfather and mother had led her to believe, with the exception of Lord Anshar, that all therians were evil and nothing but a danger to humans. But Varg seemed different. She suspected that underneath his crass tough-guy exterior, there was a gentle and noble side to him, and she was lonely for a friend.

Varg wasn't entirely sure why he offered to help her. He paid his debt. He owed her nothing. Future priestess of Tiamet or not, Halea was still a human, and he was still a lycan. His father and the elders of his pack had always instilled in him the idea that humans were beneath lycans, they were prey, they were weak, they were the enemy, but when he looked at Halea, he did not see an enemy; he saw a lonely girl who needed someone. Maybe it was the future alpha in him, but he liked being needed, and even though he had only known Halea a couple of days, he was surprised to discover that he genuinely enjoyed her company. She was feisty, and he always liked feisty. It gave him a challenge and forced him to be better. His pack brothers and sisters were rarely a challenge for him anymore. Halea seemed intelligent and driven, and he admired those qualities. Even though they were both still children, they both knew what they wanted when they grew up, and they both seemed willing to work for it. Since his mother had died in the winter, Varg had taken to spending as much time as he could away from his pack. He loved them all. They were all still family to him, and he would never entirely be a lone wolf, but things had changed between him and his father, and more and more, he felt the urge to be away. When his father was not training him to be a warrior, he preferred solitude. It may have been going against everything he was taught to believe, but he liked Halea, and he did not mind the idea of becoming friends with a strange human girl.

"Sure. You can help me train too. You are fast, and if you're as strong as you say you are, you should be able to hold your own in a fight. I spend a lot of time away from the rest of the pack these days, so I have time to kill. Might as well do something fun."

Halea wanted to ask him why he seemed to be avoiding his own pack. Hadn't he just said they were all like family to him? Why would he want to stay away from something like that? She sensed there was something he was keeping inside, but she chose to be patient. She could tell he wasn't entirely ready to be open with her, but she decided to just be grateful and take the friendship he was offering.

"Okay, that sounds great. I would like to get a little stronger…and a little faster. Not to mention I'm all for any excuse to come to the forest. I like it out here. I'd live in a tree if I could," she said with a wistful smile.

Varg smiled as well. The forest was his home, and for reasons he didn't understand, he felt pride in knowing that his domain impressed her so much.

"Some wolves do live in trees. We make our homes in trees and caves, both natural and carved out of rock in the mountainside, anything that keeps us close to nature. I know a bit about how to build a house in a tree. It's not hard."

"You can build a house in a tree? Wow!"

Varg smiled again, he did love impressing people, and he particularly enjoyed impressing Halea. "We're not just wild beasts, ya know. We've got our own craftsmen, and some are very skilled builders. I could build a house right in that tree," he said as he pointed to one of the two tall giants they had used to mark the end of their race.

Halea suddenly had an idea. "Why not two? See, they're right next to each other."

"That's not a bad idea, but I have one better. Instead of a tree house, why not forts? If we put a fort in each tree, we could have battles."

Before they knew it, they were sitting there making plans and drawing diagrams of their designs and ideas in the dirt with sticks. The sun was beginning to sink in the sky before they even realized how long they had been playing.

"I better go. I promised mother I'd be home in time for supper."

"When will you come back?" he asked.

"My mother is okay with me coming out any day as long as I'm home in time for supper and my evening lessons with my grandfather," Halea explained.

"My father is taking me hunting tomorrow, but we can meet here the day after that. Come in the morning."

"I'll be here," she agreed.

That evening Halea ran home the happiest she had ever been. She had finally made a friend.

# CHAPTER 3 – FRIENDS

Varg remained downwind. He watched the buck standing with its does in the distance, its ears perked for any sounds of danger and occasionally lifting its head of massive antlers and staring off into the trees, but it did not sense the lycan who stalked in wait. Varg, too, was being watched. He had to take down his prey quickly and efficiently - he was being tested.

When the moment was right, he moved in for the kill.

The massive buck was taken down without even being given a chance to flee. Its end was swift and relatively painless. Covered in blood, Varg howled the call of his triumph and heard it answered in the distance. Soon his father was by his side.

"A good kill, very clean," praised his father, though his voice came off emotionless.

He should have been happier to see his son hunt so well. Someday Varg would be an excellent provider for their people, but Bledig could barely stand to look at his son. He especially couldn't bear to look into his eyes - *her* eyes. It wasn't that Bledig did not love his son, far from it. His son was his reason for living, his only reason now. He would not fail him. He would train him to be an alpha male and a great warrior, but for Bledig, there was no more joy in the world.

Varg offered the bloody heart in his hands to his father; his head bowed low in respect to his alpha in a sign of submission.

"No, this is your kill. You've earned it," spoke his father as he effortlessly hefted the buck's carcass over his shoulder to carry it back to the den. All the pack would share the meat, and on their return, his son would be praised by everyone for his hunting prowess - praise, which he rightfully deserved.

Honored by his father's gesture, Varg began to eat the heart, still warm and dripping with blood. The hearts of their prey were one of the most delectable parts of any kill and a right usually reserved for alphas and hunters who drew first blood. Yet, what should have been a moment of sweet victory, turned to ashes in his mouth.

Gone were the days when his father would raise him onto his shoulders with pride. Gone were the days when he would listen to his father's booming laugh and see his smile as he looked at him. Gone were the days of his father even looking at him. Everything had changed. Everything had grown cold.

They returned to the den, and that night there was a feast held in honor of Varg's successful hunt. The other lycan cubs, Varg's age and younger, all looked up to him, and their respect did much for his pride and ego. He still enjoyed their company and always would. His pack would always be important to him, but he couldn't shake the black cloud that hovered over his heart. His father was nowhere to be found.

They sparred together that morning before the hunt, and Varg had done well. If only for a moment, it had almost felt like old times again. He wanted to learn to be a great warrior from his father. He wanted to spend time with him like he used to, but he knew in his heart, nothing would ever again be the way it used to be.

~~~✦~~~

Halea was up at dawn, even before her mother. She hastily packed a lunch big enough for two, shoved an apple in her tunic pocket to eat on her way out, and slapped some jam on a piece of toast, which she gnawed on her way to the front door when she heard her mother's voice.

"Halea?"

"I'm going to go play with some of the other kids today. I figured I'd take a lunch cause we'll be way out on the north side of the city. I'll be home in time for dinner, though," she explained.

"Your friends are up at this time of the morning?" her mother asked suspiciously.

"Well...it'll take me time to get over there. I don't want to be late," she added. Her mother knew very well that if Halea wanted to get to the far side of the city, she could do it in a minute flat. There was something off about daughter's behavior, but then again, her daughter had never been able to socialize like a normal child, and in the past few days, Halea was the happiest she had ever seen her. She had tried asking her about her new friends again, but again it seemed as if there was something Halea wasn't telling her, and a mother can always tell when her child is up to something. There was a nagging feeling that Theia could not shake, but she decided to be patient and let her daughter go as she pleased. She didn't have the heart to steal her joy away. If Halea was happy and safe, that was all that mattered.

As soon as Halea was outside her home, she strolled at a casual pace past her street and into the market square. She didn't want her mother seeing her head toward the gate or going anywhere too fast, considering the flimsy excuses she had to come up with, but this morning it would not be so much of an inconvenience. She had a special errand to run before she would meet with Varg.

Eventually, she found her destination and walked inside of the carpenter's shop, and approached the carpenter who was working a tabletop with a planer. The smell of shaved pine and oak filled the air with a pleasant aroma. He looked up curiously as the young girl entered. "This isn't a place for children," he told her.

"I would like to buy some nails, please," she replied and reached into her trouser pockets and pulled out some coins she had been saving from when her grandfather paid her for doing chores in his home. There hadn't been anything she wanted or needed before that day, so she had just held onto her money.

"Someone repairing something at home?" he asked.

"Oh, no, they're for me."

~~~✦~~~

When Halea finally arrived at the two great trees, she was shocked to find a huge stack of lumber waiting for her.

"Well, did you get them?" asked Varg, who sprang up suddenly and startled Halea so badly she nearly spilled the bag of nails.

"Stop doing that!" she barked, but Varg enjoyed the reaction he received from her and just laughed.

"It took me all morning to get this out here. I had to get up before dawn. I even saved any unbent nails I could find."

There was a half-built abandoned tree-dwelling not far from his den. It was halfway complete when the lycan building it had been killed by bear therians who were out fighting to obtain new territories. There was a small group of them, but the lycans had rallied and slaughtered them for their trespass. The skirmish had cost the lives of several lycans. The home was incomplete and left to the elements. No one had ever bothered to tear it down, but the wood was still in good condition, and seeing as no one wanted it, Varg helped himself by removing as many boards as he could pry loose and carried them off into the forest. Varg was immensely strong for a child his age, even strong in comparison to other lycan cubs, so carrying large loads of wood in his arms over a long distance hadn't been a problem for him, though it did take him several trips.

"Well, I was able to buy a whole bunch of nails, so we should have plenty...I think." Halea really had no idea how many nails it would take, but the sack felt heavy, and that reassured her. "What about tools?"

"Got em!" Varg replied while hefting out a wooden box for her to see and opening it to reveal a saw, a hammer, and many other tools that Halea couldn't really identify, but they looked impressive.

"Won't they be missed?"

"My father hasn't used these in ages, and I'm sure he has no intention of using them again anytime soon. I'll put them back before he even notices they're gone."

Halea downed more of the herbal potion that would mask her scent, and they began by working on what would be Varg's fort, using it as an example of how she should make her own. Varg carefully showed Halea how to measure the boards and secure them in place, and she helped him with the hammer wherever she could, but she could tell she was out of her element when it came to construction.

"I'm starving, time for lunch. Want me to catch you a rabbit?" he offered.

"I packed enough lunch for us to share. You don't have to bother," Halea offered, not entirely sure how she felt about his strange but generous offer. She opened the basket and showed him the contents, but he wrinkled his nose at what he found.

"Is this what humans eat?"

"Well...yeah."

"Where's the meat?"

"There's some chicken in the sandwiches," Halea replied, but she was certain that with his nose, he could smell it, so she wasn't sure what he was getting at.

"Ugh, cooked meat! Is there a famine in the city?"

"No."

Lycans liked their meat raw. Fresh meat was a sign of prosperity. If they had more meat than they could eat, they would store it deep in the earth in small rooms filled with ice cut from the surfaces of rivers and lakes in the winter, which they packed with dried straw or wood shavings to help keep it from melting. The only time they ever cooked meat was when they smoked it for long journeys if fresh meat would not be easily obtainable. They could eat vegetables and grains and enjoyed some fruits, but they generally reserved doing so for times when meat was scarce.

"No thanks, I'll go catch something," he said and dashed off into the woods.

Halea sat and ate her sandwich and wondered how long it would take for him to catch something or how long it would take him to prepare it. She at least wanted to finish one fort before the day was through, and they still had a way to go.

She was only halfway through her first sandwich when Varg returned carrying a freshly killed rabbit and two squirrels.

"Want me to start a fire while you skin them?" she offered.

"No thanks," he replied while tearing the skin off the rabbit in one swift expert motion, and she watched in horror as he dove right in.

She supposed she should have expected as much, Varg was a wolf after all, but it was still a little hard to watch him tear the flesh off the small animals with his claws and teeth while the blood dripped all over his hands. Having completely lost her appetite, she put away the rest of her sandwich.

After Varg finished his meal, they resumed working on the fort. It was starting to come together nicely, and they were both getting excited about their results. By the end of the day, the first fort was nearly complete. They were tempted to stay longer to install the roof and finish the final touches, but the sun was setting, and Halea had promised her mother she would be home in time for dinner.

Varg walked with her back to the stream by the fern patch as they discussed ideas for her own fort. Halea had insisted on doing the majority of the work on her own, with only minor help or input from him because she wanted the opportunity to prove that she had learned something that day and that she could do it too. Though she secretly knew she had signed herself up for disaster, she was determined to see it through. She didn't want him to be better than her at everything.

Halea stopped at the stream and rolled up the sleeves of her tunic to wash her hands and arms, which were dirty from a hard day of climbing a tree and getting sap all over them. There were still a few splinters in her aching fingers.

Varg noticed the bruise on her upper arm, the same bruise he had seen the first day they met. Did humans take so long to heal? Lycans, like most therians, could heal from most wounds very quickly. Even terrible bruises would fade in less than a day. Wounds that would be lethal to a human were barely more than a scratch to a therian. He stared at the ugly mark on her arm. It had been swollen and a dark shade of purple when he first saw her, now it had faded to a sickly dark yellow. He wasn't sure why but suddenly, a flash of anger passed through him.

"Who did that to you?" he asked, and Halea was surprised to hear a little venom in his voice.

She quickly rolled down her sleeve and looked away from him. "It's almost gone. It doesn't matter anymore," she said, trying to avoid the subject, but Varg was having none of it.

"Tell me," he said, in a voice that was more of a command than a request.

"They threw rocks at me…the other kids. They don't like me," Halea answered while struggling to keep from choking up as her eyes grew moist.

Varg could instantly smell the tears forming, but it only made him angrier. "Why?" he asked, struggling to understand how anyone could do that to her.

"Being blessed by Tiamet makes me strong…too strong. I got to play with them once. We were playing tag and this boy…Ben…he was It, and he was trying to tag me. I shoved him a little so his hands wouldn't touch me…and he fell hard…really hard. He hit his head and started bleeding, and he wouldn't move when everyone tried to get him up. The adults came running, and people were screaming at me. His mom was crying, and they took him to the healer. He woke up eventually, and I guess he's okay now, but since then, none of the other kids want me around. Even the grownups don't like me much. They're afraid I'll hurt them. I didn't want to hurt Ben. I didn't mean to push him so hard. It was an accident," she said and sniffled, but it was no use; the tears were rolling uncontrollably down her cheeks as she was forced to relive that day again in her mind. She quickly turned her back to Varg, feeling ashamed to look so pathetic in front of him.

Halea felt a gentle touch on her shoulder, and when she looked up, Varg was staring at her with his bright blue eyes. The anger was gone and in its place was a look of pain and sadness. "I'm sorry. You can shove me all you want. I don't break so easy," he offered.

She smiled a little, the tears stopping at his kind words. "I'm glad I met you, Varg. You don't seem to mind that I'm a freak."

"You're not a freak! And I like being friends with you. You're way more fun to hang out with than the rest of the cubs in my pack."

"We're really friends?" she asked, not sure if she could actually believe her ears. She had been so lonely, so desperate for someone to understand.

"Of course! I don't care if you're a puny human. Come back tomorrow, and we'll start on your fort."

"Thanks, ya mangy wolf," she said with a smile, which he returned, flashing his gleaming white fangs at her.

~~~✧~~~

Varg woke up earlier than expected, but he was too excited about the prospect of meeting with Halea and working on another fort to sleep in any later. He was curious to see how her fort would turn out after everything he taught her the day before, and he decided to finish the last of the work on his own before she arrived.

The moment he picked up her scent on the wind, he rushed to greet her.

Halea was surprised at his progress but not displeased. He would help her with her own roof when the time came, so there wasn't any harm done because she hadn't been there to see him install his.

24

"Isn't someone going to find out if you keep giving me so much?" she asked when he gave her the scent masking potion again.

She did have a point, a little here and there wouldn't be missed, but as much time as they were spending together, and with as much time as they intended to keep spending together, Varg knew Batsuba eventually would become suspicious.

"I'll have to ask our healer how to make it for myself. It won't be easy, we lycans can't really lie, and she'll want to know what I want it for."

"You can't lie at all? Not even a little?"

"Maybe humans don't realize it, but anxiety and fear have a very noticeable scent, and when people tell lies, they often get anxious. Sometimes their heartbeat and pulse will even speed up. I suppose if you're really good at always telling lies, you can do it without letting off any physical signs, but most people get at least a little bit nervous in a lie. We lycans learn early not to bother lying, especially to grownups."

Halea finally understood how he had figured out that she didn't know her way home the first day they met, and she was relieved he couldn't actually read minds. A sudden flash of guilt gripped her. She had been telling some real whoppers to come out to the forest without her mother finding out what she was up to, and she couldn't shake the dread that someday her deceit would catch up with her.

"What else can you tell by smelling someone?"

"Just when bitches are in heat," he replied bluntly.

Halea's mouth hung open in shock at his candid answer, and her face burned bright red. *"What a vulgar thing to say!"* she thought, but she reminded herself that Varg wasn't a human and clearly lycan society operated under different customs and ideas than the ones she was raised to accept. It was a little too much for her young mind to wrap around at the time, so she instead swiftly changed the subject.

"Let's work on my fort now!"

Varg wasn't at all sure what he said to earn that reaction.

~~~~◊~~~~

Halea did her best with the techniques that Varg had shown her the other day, but she could tell her structure was coming together with far inferior quality. Varg tried helping her and showing her the right way, and she could tell that she was frustrating him, but she was determined to do her best. When he offered too much help, she couldn't help snapping at him. "I can do it!"

"Okay, okay," he conceded and proceeded to watch her boards go up with a few too many gaps in them, and some at not entirely straight angles, but she was determined to mostly manage on her own, and he at least admired her perseverance, though not so much her craftsmanship.

By the time the day was through, Halea's fort was only half-finished, and she was terribly disappointed. Her finger hurt from where a hammer smashed it, but she had managed to stifle a yell when it happened, so Varg wouldn't know what she had done. She was afraid he would laugh. She had also earned twice as many splinters as the day before, and she didn't at all like the look of what had been built so far.

Varg could sense her disappointment, but he chose not to tease her about her work. He may have been a bit crass and even hot-tempered, but he was always hyperaware of the feelings of others. He possessed a level of sensitivity that he had picked up from his mother, and he had a bad feeling that if he said something to hurt her feelings at that moment, she would most definitely cry, and he did *not* want that.

"It's fine. It's just not finished. When it's done, it'll be great. I have combat training with my father again tomorrow, but the day after that, we'll meet here again, and we'll finish it for sure. You'll see; it'll be a great fort."

"Don't forget to learn how to make that potion," she reminded. His words gave her a small surge of optimism. Maybe the fort was still salvageable.

<center>~~~⬡~~~</center>

Batsuba looked up as Varg climbed the steps into her tree. She knew full well that he had been nicking the potion that masked scents, but young male cubs were always up to some shenanigans, so she had decided to mostly ignore his transgressions. He had masked his scent to swipe the potion from her stores, but she had eyes and knew every single herb in her pharmacopeia and especially when one went missing.

Batsuba was ancient, very ancient. Being lycan, she only appeared to be in her mid-twenties by human standards, yet one only had to look into her mysterious black eyes to know they were in the presence of someone who had seen many ages come and go. Her hair was as white as snow, and her nose was sharp, and her mouth always set in a serious frown. Despite her imposing presence, Varg had always been fond of Batsuba. She seemed stern, but there were little moments when he could get a glimpse of a caring heart, perhaps the same caring heart that led her to pursue the path of a healer so very long ago. She was also fond of the young wolf cub, and quite a lot of that stemmed from the fact that his mother had once been one of her apprentices in the healing arts.

Valria was a warm and caring lycan woman who always devoted herself to others. Her eyes were the same piercing shade of blue as Varg's, and her hair had been long and raven black. Batsuba could see much of Valria when she looked into the boy's eyes. She had been there and helped with the delivery the day Valria gave birth to her son, but she had delivered just about every cub ever born in that pack, including Valria herself. Generations born. Generations died. Batsuba carried every memory of every life created and lost within her. To her, life was always precious.

"Greetings Batsuba," Varg offered respectfully to his elder as he entered her home.

"And what brings the son of Bledig to my humble home?" she replied, skipping the pleasantries and getting right to the point.

Varg could smell his own nervousness, but he hoped Batsuba would only interpret it as him being uncomfortable in the presence of an elder.

"I uh…I want to learn to make a potion. Can you help me?"

"It wouldn't happen to be for scent masking, would it?" Batsuba asked while giving him a knowing look.

"*Damn it!*" he thought.

"Uh…yeah…that one," Varg replied while trying not to look her too directly in the eye, which did nothing to help his situation.

26

"I see. And what, pray tell, does a cub need such a concoction for?"

Varg reeked of anxiety and nerves. Sweat started dripping down his brow, and he blinked a little too fast as it dripped into his eyes. His mind was racing, scrambling. What should he say? What would she believe? Only the truth, he concluded.

"Just makin' some mischief, nothing too bad, I promise. Just a bit of fun," Varg replied while finally managing to look her in the face.

It was the only right answer. A sly smile grew on the old healer's face, revealing the tips of her fangs.

"Just like your father when he was your age. Always up to something. Very well, come over here, and I'll show you the herbs that are needed."

~~~~☼~~~~

Combat training with his father had not lasted long that day. Varg could tell that once again, his father was not entirely all there with him in his mind, though he seemed no less efficient in training. As soon as their sparring was over, Varg rushed to get as far away from the den as possible. He couldn't bear how cold it felt whenever his father was around. Didn't his father understand? He missed her too.

Soon Varg found himself standing before the two great trees. It felt lonely to be in that place without Halea.

Varg felt terrible that her fort hadn't come together better, and he was afraid she would be hard on herself the next day when she came to see him again. He decided if he made a few adjustments, perhaps she wouldn't know.

He crawled up into her fort and began working. Pulling out crooked nails and reinforcing poorly attached boards. He even straightened and adjusted some of the structural pieces in the places where she would be least likely to notice the minor changes. From the outside, it would still mostly look the same, but it would be far sturdier now. At least he wouldn't have to worry about it falling apart on her.

The next day when Halea arrived, they began work again. She seemed a little less irritable as they worked and more willing to let him lend a hand, of which he was thankful, and he tried very hard to not boast about the quality of his work, which wasn't always easy because bragging was in his nature. Together they managed to finish her fort and even install the roof, with a bit of time left over to spare.

"Well...it's ugly, but I guess it'll do," she conceded.

"Meh, looks don't matter, as long as it's sturdy."

"I'm not so sure about that," she replied doubtfully.

Varg tried to suppress a smile. She could never know.

They sat together in her finished fort and came up with ideas for a few more additions and some of the combat games they intended to play. Now with the forts done, Varg could show her how to fight as well.

"I managed to get Batsuba to teach me how to make the potion. Now I don't have to steal it anymore."

"How'd you manage that?"

"I told her I wanted it because I was up to no good."

"And that worked?" she asked in shock.

27

"Guess the old woman understands kids better than the other grownups do," was all he could answer.

"Will you teach me?"

Varg sat in silent hesitation for a moment. "Well, I dunno. We lycans don't like giving all our secrets away. Humans could use that stuff against us."

"Varg! How can you think I'd do such a thing?" she asked, genuinely hurt by his lack of trust. True, they hadn't been friends for very long, but she had hoped he thought better of her than that.

"It's not that!" he quickly defended, realizing he had said everything all wrong. He did trust Halea. He wasn't sure why, but he did, and he didn't want her to think that he didn't. "I'm sure you wouldn't do that, but I'm not so sure about other humans. If I show you, you have to swear never to reveal the potion or how to make it to anyone."

"All right, I swear it," Halea offered without hesitation. Varg had tried to amend himself, but she still felt the need to prove her trustworthiness.

"I'll teach you tomorrow. We'll need a bowl to mix the ingredients in, and I can pick the herbs on my way here."

"I think I can find something to put them in," she offered.

The next day Halea found an old ceramic bowl gathering dust in one of her mother's cupboards and brought it with her to the fort. Varg showed her how to mix the potion, and he was glad that she seemed to have the knack for it. He was confident she could even make it on her own if he weren't around to help her.

Over the next few weeks, they would meet regularly at the great trees. Varg showed Halea some of the hand-to-hand fighting maneuvers his father taught him, and he was impressed that she seemed so willing to learn. She was quite strong for a human girl, just as strong as some of the other cubs from his pack that he wrestled with, though not as strong as him. Her speed gave her a distinct advantage. They had many more races. Some days he would win, and some days she would win. They were constantly trying to figure out who was the fastest, and they were always challenging each other and bickering about it.

They played rough games, and she got knocked down a few times and often had to go home to explain away bruises, cuts, and scrapes to her mother. Halea was a little younger than Varg, and she didn't have his healing abilities, and he had no desire to hurt her. In fact, he felt terrible every time he did so accidentally, but Halea always brushed it off and came back for more, and no matter how hard she would fall in their matches, she never cried.

They added more modifications to their forts, such as trap doors, rope ladders, zip lines so they could swing from one fort to the next, and eventually, they even built catapults. They would often get into small skirmishes where they would launch old rotten fruit, or in Varg's case, the occasional dead squirrel, into each other's windows.

"Why haven't I seen you as a wolf since the day we met?" Halea asked Varg one day as they were lying in the tall grass resting after another round of combat training.

"This form is more convenient. It has a lot of advantages, so most lycans spend the majority of their time looking humanoid, but some lycans choose to spend almost all their time in their wolf form too. To each their own, I guess. I don't think you'd want to fight with me in my wolf form," he explained with a chuckle while imagining what that would be like.

"Why were you a wolf that day? Why transform at all?"

"Freedom! Being the beast within is…it's being free," he struggled to explain. It was hard for him to explain to a human what the difference was, but he knew it in his soul. Being the true wolf had some physical disadvantages, but transforming was the freedom to become one's true self, to let the wild instincts take control. All therians had their inner beast.

"You seem pretty free now," she said, clearly not understanding but trying to sort it out. "Varg," she said while sitting up to see his face. "Don't be mad. You don't have to answer, but why do you spend so much time with me? I mean, not that I don't like being friends with you, I really do, but you at least have friends back home. People that care. You can tell me if something's wrong. You can tell me anything," she offered. He had heard her pour out her heart about being ostracized by the other human children. He knew her loneliness and what brought her into the forest that day, but she still didn't understand what had brought him there. She wanted to offer him the kind of support he had shown her. She wanted him to be able to confide in her, and she knew there was always something there, some pain beneath the surface that he was keeping from her. Whenever she would ask him questions about his home or his father, he would grow quiet and aloof.

Varg let out a sigh and closed his eyes as his neck muscles grew taut, and she instantly regretted asking. She was about to drop the subject when he finally spoke.

"My mother died last winter. A snake therian. They're usually solitary, but they were in a group. My mother had been gathering bark for Batsuba near the borders of our territory, and I guess she got too close to their stronghold. One attacked her and bit her…he poisoned her…he…dragged her back to the other snakes," he struggled to explain, and for the first time, Halea saw his eyes grow moist with pain. She had never seen him cry. "My father sensed her pain through their bond and followed her scent until he found where they had taken her. He was too late. She didn't make it," he stopped for a moment and closed his eyes again. She could hear him breathing heavily, and her heart ached for causing him to relive such painful memories. "That was when my father flew into a blood rage. It's when a lycan lets the true beast within take over completely. It's when we are at our most dangerous. Everything is instinct, and that instinct is usually to kill. Kill until we have spilled every last drop of our enemies' blood, and only then is the beast satisfied. He slaughtered them all for what they did to her."

There was another moment of silence, and Halea realized she was shedding tears on his behalf.

"I'm sorry, Varg," she whispered.

"Since then, nothing has been the same. I used to like spending time with my father, but now he's changed. He barely speaks. He never laughs. He devotes himself to the pack and to training me, but it's like he's gone, and all that's left in his place is some stranger. When he's away from the den, I don't mind being there so much. I can

29

spend time hanging out with the other wolf cubs, but if he's there, I try to avoid him. Unless he needs me for training, I stay away. I think he prefers it that way. I don't think he cares about me anymore, so it's better for me to come out here."

They sat in silence for a long while, watching birds fly overhead and feeling the summer wind dance across the grass.

"What's a bond?" Halea asked though she hated to bring it up. She didn't want to ask, but something inside her didn't want to let it go. She had dredged up enough suffering for him for one day.

"Bond?" he asked while sitting up and stretched a little. His eyes had dried, and he seemed a little more composed. "Oh, that. Well, they were mates. Mates just have bonds. Don't human mates have bonds?"

"Humans don't mate. We marry. So, a bond is when people love each other?"

"No. Well, yes…and no. I dunno! What are you asking me for? I don't have a mate!"

She giggled a little at his reaction. "Sorry."

They were both glad to feel the tension lift between them.

"Hey, Halea…"

"Mmm?"

"Thanks."

~~~✧~~~

She was seriously worried. For over a month now, her daughter had been disappearing, and she had never once seen her outside with any of the other city children. True, Halea was the happiest she had ever seen her, but something felt wrong, and she couldn't put her finger on it. That morning after Halea left, Theia sat alone in her kitchen, sipping a cup of tea and having an internal monolog about whether or not she should find out what was really going on. By noon she had made up her mind. She was going to look for her.

Theia walked down the streets observing the local children as they ran and played. Occasionally she would ask them if they had seen Halea. Some said "No," some asked, "Who's Halea?" The more Theia walked and asked, the more her sharp stabs of panic increased with every block she explored. She finally made it to the far end of the city, where a group of children was playing a sports game in an empty dirt lot.

"Have any of you children seen Halea?" she asked.

"We don't play with that freak," one of the boys shouted. The rest of the children erupted into jeers and laughter at his declaration.

The next morning, Theia waited until she heard the front door close, announcing that her daughter was once again going out for the day. She immediately jumped up and ran outside to follow her. To avoid being seen, she stayed far behind and observed as her daughter casually strolled through the streets, swinging her lunch basket along as she went. That was when Theia noticed her daughter was making a strange turn, like she was doubling back, heading towards the city gates. She stayed on her tail and continued to watch. Halea spoke to none of the other children as she went, and they all ignored her. Then she observed as her daughter strolled right

30

through the main gates of the city and out beyond. Theia was forced to stop at the gate. There would be nowhere for her to hide should her daughter look back. She saw her daughter use her inhumane speed and race off into the tree line at the edge of the forest that bordered the land around the city, and then she was gone.

Theia immediately panicked. The forest was dangerous! Was that really where her daughter had been spending all of her time? There was no way for her to follow, and she was forced to turn back.

Later that evening, Theia sat at the dinner table, waiting for her daughter to come home for supper. She was usually always on time, and if she was late, it wasn't by very much. What was she doing? A mother should know the whereabouts of her child. Was she a bad mother for having let this go on for so long? Every day that Halea went into the forest, she could be killed, and what's worse, Theia suspected she wasn't out there alone. Who was she spending her days with?

"Mother, I'm home," she heard her daughter call, followed by the sound of the front door closing.

"Welcome home," she replied and watched as Halea went to pump some water to wash up before she joined her at the table.

"Did you have a nice day?"

"Yeah, we had a lot of fun. We were playing slap ball," her daughter replied.

"Halea…I think it's time you tell me who this "we" is," demanded her mother coldly.

Halea's eyes widened in a look of discomfort as she slowly lowered herself into her seat at the table. "Just some kids from the north side of the city. That's where we were playing…"

"You were not!" her mother barked.

Halea was not used to her mother having such a stern tone, and her heart began to race. She had been found out.

"I went to the north side of the city yesterday. You weren't there, and the other children who were out playing explicitly said that you were not with them, ever."

Halea watched her mother's hand tremble as she reached for her cup of tea and took a large gulp.

"You went into the forest this morning…I saw you. I want the truth, all of it. No more secrets. No more lies."

Halea was in a panic. She could feel her world shattering all around her. Tears began to well up in her eyes, but she had to tell her mother the truth. There was no lie left that could save her. Varg told the truth to Batsuba, the healer. Maybe if she explained that Varg wasn't dangerous and that he was her friend, she could make her mother understand that everything was all right and there was nothing for her to worry about. She took a deep trembling breath and blurted the truth.

"I ran into the forest one day after the other kids picked on me. I met a wolf, who wasn't really a wolf, he was a lycan, but he's a kid, like me, so he's okay. We spend all day playing and having fun. He doesn't care that I'm a freak. I don't care if he's a therian. He wouldn't hurt me. If he wanted to hurt me, he could have a long time ago, but we're friends, and…he's my friend," she finished lamely and shook as tears streamed down her cheeks. She could tell by the horrified look on her mother's face – it was all over.

"Go to your room, Halea," spoke Theia in a tone both low and firm.

"Mother, it's okay…"

"It is *NOT* okay, Halea. None of this is okay! You ran into a forest filled with beings that want you dead! They eat humans! I don't care if he didn't kill you - he's a therian! A dirty shifter! They are not to be trusted, ever. Just because he hasn't killed you yet, doesn't mean he won't. A beast like that can turn at any moment. Well, it's over. You are never going to see that boy again!"

"He wouldn't hurt me! He wouldn't!" Halea tried to defend, but it was over.

"Go to your room and stay there!" her mother commanded in a tone of voice she had never heard her use before. Stricken, Halea ran to her room and slammed the door behind her.

Theia's heart was breaking as she heard her daughter's sobs from within her room. It was better this way.

# CHAPTER 4 – WOLF CRY

Where was she? She had always shown up before. Varg slowly ambled along the stream that led towards the city of Ruinac. He wouldn't go all the way. He never went that far; it was too close to human territory, but he was hoping he would pick up her scent along the way, at least some sign that she was coming. He could faintly detect her scent from the last time she passed that way, the scent was a few days old and fading, but it was hers. She would always drink the potion upon arriving at the forts, but he would get a good whiff of her before she did. He had grown to like the scent of his human friend. Her scent, before it faded, was a marker to the start of their day, and every morning he waited impatiently for it to reach him on the wind, and his heart would leap for joy because soon she would be near.

Varg sat by the stream the whole day waiting for Halea to come, but she never appeared, and eventually, as the sun began to set, he was forced to return to his den. That night he felt absolutely miserable. What happened? Did he say or do something to upset her? Sure, they squabbled the last time they played because as they were sparring, she managed to knock his knees out from under him and take advantage of a good choke hold. He had argued that it was unfair, with him calling her a puny human and her calling him a mangy wolf, but that was all in good fun, and they had gone back to playing as if nothing happened. She was smiling when he walked with her to the fern patch. She always smiled at him when she said goodbye. Why hadn't she come?

But Halea did not come the next day either, or the day after that, or the day after that. He would sit within the trees as close to the border of the forest as he comfortably felt and watch. His lycan eyes could see easily from far away. Way out in the distance was the city, and beyond, in the sea, stood the Citadel. But no matter how long he waited, Varg never saw Halea, and every night that he returned home, he felt as if his heart was being crushed. Something had gone wrong.

She would come. She wanted to come. They were friends. She would have at least told him if she never wanted to see him again. Wouldn't she?

He had lost focus, and it cost him dearly as his father's strike knocked him painfully to the ground.

"You did not adjust your stance, Varg. Focus!" his father barked. They had been training for most of the morning, and Varg could not pay attention. What if she was out there right now? What if this was the one day she decided to return and he wasn't there to greet her, and she would turn around and leave, never to return?

Bledig could sense his son was distracted by something, but distractions would have to be set aside when he became a man. An enemy wouldn't be so understanding. When you were fighting for your life, you couldn't afford to be anywhere but in the present, a fact that he was struggling with himself at times since the loss of his mate, and so he had shown Varg no mercy that morning.

Varg was sore and irritable by the time his father ended their lesson. It was noon, and he wanted to escape into the forest when some of the other lycan cubs stopped him.

"Varg, we're going to go chase after a lynx that went up the east slope. Come with us," called Faolan, who was a couple of years younger than Varg, with forest green eyes and light blond hair.

"You haven't been on a chase with us in ages," added Aatu, who was a little bit older than Varg but had already accepted Varg as the alpha of their peer group. His hair and eyes were brown, and he was usually level-headed and good to have around.

Varg usually made time for his pack brothers on the days when he trained with his father because there was no hope of seeing Halea on those days anyway. He did care about his pack brothers, but they offered him no challenge, as he had long since established his dominance among them, and they were not *her*.

With them also was Bardolph, who was closest to Varg in age. His hair was a slightly darker shade of brown than Aatu's, but his eyes were a warm amber color. He looked up to Varg greatly and probably missed having him around the most, but unlike the others, he knew that Varg sought solitude ever since his father's grief had changed him. He was wise beyond his years and understood that Varg was dealing with the loss of his mother and his father's grief in the manner that worked best for him. He did not hold Varg's aloof behavior against him.

"You mean I chase it, and you idiots just follow me around? No, thanks. I'm too sore after training."

"Let's take a swim in the lake instead; if your aching bones can handle a little water," offered Bardolph.

He couldn't keep making excuses. Training days were the days he usually tried to make time for his lycan friends. He agreed to join them at the lake, but as they went on their way, he could feel the wolf within him crying out in pain.

~~~✧~~~

It had been nearly a week since Theia discovered the truth of her daughter's whereabouts. Uro came that first evening to give Halea her lessons, and Theia had sent him away by telling him that Halea had come home ill and that she had probably picked up a sickness by playing with the other children. She had kept Uro away every day since. She wasn't sure why, but she didn't want to tell her father-in-law what Halea had actually been up to – not yet.

Halea had cried nonstop since she had been forbidden to see the lycan. Most of the time, she refused to come out of her room, but Theia could hear her soft sobs from within. Halea would only come out for meals, meals she refused to eat. She would merely pick at her food, take a few bites, then drag herself back to her room again.

34

Theia was torn. Her daughter went from the happiest she had ever seen her to the most miserable she had ever seen her, and deep down, Theia couldn't shake the feeling that she had been too hard on her. She had to constantly remind herself that she was doing the right thing. Halea would never be safe with a therian. They were predators. Even though the Goddess had blessed her daughter with special gifts, she was still human, and humans and therians did not mix.

Inside her room, Halea lay with her back to the window, her pillow moist from crying. Was Tiamet punishing her for lying? Usually, the Goddess did not concern herself with petty things such as sins. The only real sin was not to work towards the preservation of life and the elimination of Chaos.

She had finally found someone who didn't hate her for who she was and who took away the aching loneliness. She had finally found a way to be happy, and it had all been taken from her.

Not having the chance to say one final goodbye to Varg was the thing that hurt the most. What if he thought she didn't like him anymore? What if he thought she was angry with him for something?

That night Theia tossed and turned in bed. She had hoped her daughter would get over her disappointment, but it was clear that nothing for her would ever be the same again. Theia had heard the way the city children spoke of her daughter.

*We don't play with that freak!*

What was left for her, an unhappy childhood of musty tomes and shattered joys? The other children had made it quite clear that they would never accept her, but Halea had said that the lycan did.

*He doesn't care that I'm a freak.*

Was that true? Why would a lycan child make friends with a human girl? Though Theia knew in her heart the same truth all the children in the city knew, Halea was not a regular human girl. The Goddess had made her strong, and she would grow stronger yet. Could humans and therians really not get along? She knew of only one other therian who had a peaceful relationship with humans; Lord Anshar. But Lord Anshar was a direct descendant of Tiamet, and humans were under her protection because they honored and served her. Other therians had their own gods and allegiances. Lycans, in particular, were known for being vicious towards humans and having no compunction towards killing or eating any unfortunate enough to cross their path.

Halea had spent a great amount of time in the presence of this lycan. He had plenty of opportunities to harm her, and yet, he never did. Had they really played together as equals? As regular children would? Were lycans even capable of such behavior?

At last, Theia sat up. There would be no sleep for her. She eventually got up and made her way towards her daughter's room. There was silence inside, and she contemplated turning back, but she heard the soft sound of a sniffle, and so she knocked.

Her daughter was silent for a moment, but eventually, she replied, "Come in."

Halea watched her mother enter her room with a dim lantern which she set on her bedside table.

Theia sat beside Halea in her bed. She could still see tear stains on her daughter's cheeks, even in the poor light, and it crushed her as a mother to see her baby in pain.

"Tell me everything," her mother said.

And so, they sat together through the whole night as Halea explained exactly how she had met Varg in the forest. How he had acted that first day, versus how he changed over time. She told her of their games, of their forts, of him teaching her to be strong and to fight, assuring her mother that he never hurt her and that her grandfather would probably give her way worse when it came to combat training in the coming years.

Halea did not mention how powerful his sense of smell was, for then she would need to explain the potion, and she had given Varg her word that that would remain a secret, and it was a promise she was not going to break, but everything else she told her mother.

By the time the glow of the sun began to peak over the horizon, Theia was feeling better about what her daughter had experienced out in the woods.

True, lycans were still dangerous, but it was only one little boy who apparently wanted a friend just as much as her daughter did. He could be dangerous, but he chose not to be. Maybe some therians were more civilized than she had imagined? Or perhaps it was just the innocence of children, too young and uncorrupted by the ways of the world to understand hate or prejudice, but instinctually understanding love and friendship instead.

Theia was still scared. She couldn't help it as a mother. Halea's life would always have some element of danger. She knew one thing for certain now; her daughter unequivocally trusted that lycan boy, and after hearing her talk about him, she felt herself trust him as well, even though she had never personally met him. She could finally see that perhaps he genuinely meant Halea no harm. Perhaps it was wrong to take away the only friend Halea had.

At last, Theia sighed and ran her hand through her daughter's hair, gently combing out the knots that she had developed from restlessly rolling in her bed.

"Halea, I want you to be happy. I want you to have friends. I also want you to be safe. If you truly trust this boy, if you're certain you aren't in any danger out there, then you may return to the forest."

"You mean it?" she asked, jumping up to look her mother in the face.

Theia nodded her head and smiled at her daughter's enthusiasm. There was the Halea she had been missing.

~~~✕~~~

Varg ran through the woods, the trees speeding past him in a blur as the wind howled in his ears. He needed to feel the earth under his feet. He needed to be free of everything, but he couldn't shake his sadness even as the wolf.

He didn't want to return to the forts. He didn't want to see them empty again and be disappointed, but in his wolf form, he ran on instinct, and the beast would not be denied.

36

As he ran towards the great trees, the wind changed direction, and that was when he picked up her scent.

Halea.

~~~☼~~~

Even though Halea hadn't slept that night for staying up with her mother, there was no holding her back from setting out as soon as she dressed. She was worried, though. She disappeared without a trace for a week. What if he didn't come to meet her? He probably wasn't expecting her anymore.

She sat on the ground away from the great trees so her scent wouldn't contaminate their forts in case Varg came back. She wasn't ready to drink the potion yet. Maybe he would pick up her scent and find her if she waited.

She sat there through the whole morning. The sun was reaching its peak in the sky, and still, he had not come. Was it too late? What if he never came back to that place again? What if he never even cared if he saw her again? The warm sun was making her drowsy as she sat in the grass waiting. Eventually, she closed her eyes and lay back in the grass. She would stay there until nightfall if she had to.

She must have dozed off without realizing it, but something suddenly startled her out of her sleep. Some wild beast was licking her face!

Halea jumped up, startled, and almost had a heart attack at the sight of a wolf nearly on top of her. It gamboled about excitedly. But her panic erased the moment she recognized the unmistakable icy blue eyes.

"Varg? Geez, you scared the hell out of me!"

The wolf transformed, and there crouched Varg.

"You came back!" he shouted while leaping at her and nearly crushed her in a hug.

Halea didn't hesitate to return the gesture. She thought she had lost him forever.

"I'm sorry, Varg. I didn't want to be away. My mother found out."

They sat down in the grass, and she explained all that happened between her and her mother. In the end, she was able to set aside all of his fear and doubts. Best of all, she would no longer have to hide her whereabouts from her mother. Her mother would not tell anyone her secret, not even her grandfather.

"I missed you. It wasn't any fun without you," he confessed.

"I missed you too, but it's okay now. Nothing will ever separate us again," Halea promised.

# CHAPTER 5 – THE DEMON IN THE WOODS

Ami dashed through the trees in pursuit of the demon that had escaped her. A tear opened near a village, and the beings that spilled out from the Chaos Dimension had slaughtered several humans before she arrived. She had found and closed the original tear, but some of the demons had eluded her. Demons were stronger in number, and without the open tear to send reinforcements, they would run to where another tear was expected to open and wait for the arrival of more of their kind.

The disciples of Tiamet did not entirely know how the demons knew where to expect more openings, they hardly seemed organized, but where demons were allowed to live, more tears would come.

Eventually, she tracked the demon into a small gulch. It was an ugly beast. Creatures from the Chaos Dimension took many forms. No two ever seemed to be entirely alike. This creature had no eyes, and as far as she could determine, no nose or ears, yet it could hear and see. It was bipedal, and its twisted body was a sickly deep gray. Its hands extended into claws disproportionally long for its arms. The only feature of its face was a wide jaw filled with razor-sharp teeth. This demon was more bestial, weaker. The ones more humanoid in appearance were always far more dangerous, but no servant of Chaos was safe from her.

Ami was one of the most powerful priestesses in the service of Tiamet, perhaps the most powerful, but that was an honor few priestesses truly wanted. Spear in hand, she showed her enemies no mercy. She could purify several demons at once with the rush of her purification power, and she was an expert at tracking tears over great distances.

She watched as the demon stood motionless. It was waiting, and she knew it was time to strike.

She leaped from her hiding place and charged the dark creature with a furious jab of her spear, its tip glowing as it amplified her purification powers. The demon, finally sensing danger, dodged and slashed at her with its gleaming claws, which she blocked from tearing into her with the shaft of her weapon. She pulled back quickly as it poised to strike again, this time charging her spear with an even greater level of her power as it leaped in for the attack. She launched her spear with all her strength, piercing straight through the pouncing demon that let out an ear-splitting shriek as it burst into a flame of white light and was gone.

Ami retrieved her weapon and waited. If the creature came to this place, a tear might yet open.

Suddenly, she felt it, a tear. First, it appeared as only a strange flash of purple light, but then the light began to grow and spread, a portal opening into the realm of Chaos. She avoided looking directly into it. Looking into the heart of Chaos had the potential to drive one mad. It was spreading rapidly, and she had to act fast before more demons would force their way through. Quickly, she stabbed her spear into the ground and charged towards the opening. She raised her hands high and called upon the Goddess to give her strength. There was a sound like a clap of thunder as her white light overcame the tear, and then it was gone.

This had been an easy tear to subdue. It was caught early, but the larger the tears, the more difficult they were to close. Some tears could grow so large it would take several priestesses working together to seal them. The largest tear of all, the one that would bring the convergence of the two dimensions, was so powerful only one being could seal it – Lord Anshar. And such a feat could not be done without great effort and sacrifice. The more frequently tears would appear, the more signs indicated that the coming of the great tear of the convergence was neigh.

Ami frowned as she reclaimed her spear. That was the fourth tear that month. They were happening more now, and she prayed the time of convergence was not drawing near, but in her heart, she could feel it coming.

~~~◇~~~

Summer finally came to a close, and the days grew shorter. Halea promised her mother to always be home before nightfall, which meant she had less time with Varg and more time to study with her grandfather, who had finally begun her combat training as she had just turned eleven. She quickly surmised that she hated the coming of winter. Though, when winter finally did come, it did have its benefits.

The forest was undoubtedly cold and stark, and she was not allowed to go out and play in the heavy snow or the prospect of heavy snow, but when she was allowed to venture out, she and Varg had new games to play. They made snow forts on the ground and constructed obstacle courses where they would duck and run and pelt each other with snowballs without mercy. Varg showed her how to make a sled and snowshoes, and together they even found a frozen-over pond and would skid around on its surface. Thankfully, her thick winter clothes concealed her bruised knees, or her mother would have become concerned with how rough she was playing.

Her grandfather had started slowly with her combat training, and he was surprised to discover that Halea seemed to have natural talent. It was as if she already knew how to fight. He concluded that the Goddess had truly smiled upon her. While Uro was advancing in years, he was still strong and fast, and Halea had underestimated him a little at first because she had always just thought of him as her studious grandfather. She was aware that he would teach her how to fight, but Halea had never really imagined that at one point in his life, Uro had been one of the fiercest clerics in the service of the Goddess. In his youth, he had even taken on demons. He had trained many priestesses before her, and he hadn't lost his talent for the art of battle.

Clerics were the non-blessed devotees of Tiamet. Their power was not innate, they could only purify through spells, and they did not possess the ability to close tears. Unlike priestesses, who could only be women, clerics could be male or female, and clerics were allowed to marry and have families, whereas priestesses could not. Clerics were mortals, but they would spend their entire lives answering to the Goddess, the High Priestess, and Lord Anshar.

Halea was faster and stronger than her grandfather, but it was the technique of fighting that he wanted her to master. He showed her the many stances for defense and the powerful abilities of offense. Halea was impressed that her grandfather knew so much. Most of what he taught her she had already learned from sparring with Varg, though she pretended to be new at everything to not rouse her grandfather's suspicion. Surprisingly, he did manage to show her a few moves that even Varg didn't know, and she grinned wickedly at the thought of springing them on her lycan friend the next time they squared off.

Varg was always stronger than her in their training matches, and so she had to rely on speed and cunning to win against him. She was not allowed to use her powers of purification when she battled Varg. Early on, they had set the rule that only physical ability was allowed, though that didn't stop her from occasionally zapping him if he gloated too much.

With the coming of spring, her grandfather progressed her from hand-to-hand combat and into bo staff training. A priestess's weapon was a spear, the conduit of her power. The spear could be charged with purification and thrown with lethal accuracy into any demonic target, but it was most potent while still held in the hands of the priestess who could continually feed her power into her weapon. A priestess could also use her spear for blocking attacks and close-range combat if wielded like a staff.

Halea had never fought with a weapon before and had been rather clumsy at first. Her grandfather was surprised that she didn't pick up the bo staff as intuitively as she had hand-to-hand combat, and he wondered why the Goddess would bless her so much in one area of expertise and not the other.

In time, her grandfather's rigorous training only increased.

Varg, too, was being dragged on more hunts. At first, it had just been his father training him, but once he had established his ability as a hunter, he was expected to participate in hunts like all the rest of the pack. There was also the prospect of an enemy attack. Some lycans who guarded the borders of their territories were reporting increased demon sightings.

There had not been a tear on western lycan territory in over an age. Long ago, they had suffered a priestess to close it, but word was coming down from the high mountains that these disturbances were increasing and possibly migrating further into the western lands than they had for many years.

Bledig was growing concerned with the news of the demon sightings. An alpha's duty was to protect his whole pack from any and all threats. Demons could be easily slain by any therian and often were, but tears were a more significant problem. Bledig had lived through a convergence once before, or at least he had heard about it. The source of the great tear had been far in the east, and all he knew was that it had eventually been sealed, and tears had been of minor concern since. But now, his instincts were on edge, and he sensed danger in the wind.

Varg and Halea were finding it harder to make time for each other, but they did not let it deter their friendship. They always managed to find at least a few days out of the week to spend in each other's company, and while they wished for more, for the time being, it would have to be enough.

"A tear opened near the city yesterday," Halea told Varg as they sat together in his fort, mixing another batch of scent masking potion.

"A tear? This close? Did you get to see it?"

"No. I only heard about it when my grandfather didn't arrive for my training. He was called to the Citadel when it happened. Several priestesses came down from the Citadel and closed the tear, but according to my grandfather, they're getting more frequent and popping up in more unusual places."

"My people are worried about them too. They're usually not a problem in this area. Will they get worse?" he asked. Varg feared for his pack as much as his father, and Halea knew more about demons and tears than he did. He was hoping that somehow, she could reassure him.

"They might. Grandfather hasn't said anything yet, and I've asked. Supposedly when tears become more frequent, it's a sign of a convergence, a great tear."

Varg shivered without realizing it. There wasn't much, if anything, in the physical world that caused him fear, but the idea of a Dimension of Chaos outside of their world filled his heart with a sense of dread. It was something he had no control over, and the feeling of helplessness was deeply unsettling for him. There hadn't been a convergence in several hundred years, but he had heard about them from the elders of his pack.

"But you guys stop them, don't you? The dimensions have always been stopped from converging in the past, or otherwise, we wouldn't be here," he said, more to convince himself than her.

"Only with the help of Lord Anshar, and to close the great tear…a priestess has to die."

"Die? Why?"

"Lord Anshar possesses 'The Blade That Cuts Through Worlds.' It's a divine weapon from Tiamet herself, though I don't know why they call it 'The Blade That Cuts Through Worlds.' It doesn't cut. It closes the Dimension of Chaos, banishing it and making the path between our two dimensions harder to bridge, at least for a few more centuries before it all begins again. But the blade won't work without a sacrifice. Only the strongest priestess may give her life, which charges the blade. The combination of a strong priestess's power, Lord Anshar's power, and the blade is the only thing powerful enough to banish the Chaos."

"What? That's bullshit!" he shouted and jumped up in a rage. "What happens if you become a priestess someday and they kill you?"

Halea was shocked at his outburst. She knew he wasn't mad at her, but she didn't like seeing him upset. "Varg, all priestesses would give their lives to battle Chaos. It's the risk they have to take. If you become an alpha someday, you'd face great dangers, too, anything to protect your people. Besides, if I were to refuse to be a priestess, I would remain mortal and die anyway, but probably just of old age. Not to mention only the strongest priestess is meant to sacrifice her life. I doubt I'd be the strongest. There are quite a few priestesses, and according to my grandfather, none of them would hesitate to give their lives to protect the lives of others. It's just what comes with serving Tiamet."

Varg continued to scowl in anger. He didn't like it, though he couldn't logically explain why it still bothered him. Everything she said was true, and he would never turn against her for pursuing what she wanted out of life. He knew she wanted to be a priestess, but there was something inside of him that bristled at the idea of her being in danger, of her even having the slightest chance of being offered up like a lamb to the slaughter. He just didn't like it.

"Don't worry so much. I still have a long wait before I'm a priestess. They may not even want me if I can't get the hang of my bo," she offered, trying to soothe him.

Halea had brought her bo with her every day since her grandfather started training her. She may not have been the most skilled, but it felt natural to keep it close, and with all the demon sightings, she figured her mother would appreciate her having a little extra protection with her for her long walks through the woods. Truthfully, she was afraid that if the demon attacks persisted or got any closer, that her mother might eventually forbid her from going into the forest.

Varg wasn't much interested in bo sparring with her. Lycans rarely used weapons, instead choosing to rely on their claws and fangs. Some would occasionally use bows and arrows for bird hunting, and his father possessed the Great Fang, but he had only ever unsheathed it a couple of times in his entire life, and only while in a blood rage or a very decisive battle.

Eventually, Varg settled down. He had other concerns for the day than theoretical futures. Today was the day he was going to finally show Halea his den.

They had been talking about it since the end of the last summer. Varg had powerful vision and could see the human city from the forest without getting near it, so he knew at least what one human civilization looked like. Halea did not have his physical ability to see over such long distances, and she was curious to see what a lycan den looked like. Naturally, they had both accepted that she would just never get to see it for herself until the day she stumbled on an item in her grandfather's house as she was dusting – an old telescope.

Her grandfather had done some sea travel in his younger days when he used to cross the sea to find new priestesses for the Goddess. It was nearly rusted from having been exposed to so much salty sea air, but the lenses still worked, and when she asked her grandfather if she could play with it, of course promising not to break it, he eventually relented.

For her to see Varg's den, she had to stay far, far, away. She could not allow herself to be seen or smelled. Even Varg would have to mask his own scent to avoid rousing suspicion. They waited until Varg managed to talk his way out of having to join a large hunting party that would be out for most of the day. The safest time to approach would be when all of the most powerful hunters were gone. They would have to pass through lycan hunting grounds, but he knew for a fact that his father was leading the hunters into the north, so going through the western lands would be relatively safe.

This was by far the most dangerous idea they ever had, and Varg could not deny the anxiety he felt. He had never willingly put Halea so close to danger before, but at the same time, for reasons he didn't entirely understand, he wanted her to see it. He wanted her to see his den and the way his people lived. Lycans were very different from humans, and while they had learned much about each other's people, he still felt like Halea was far from understanding who he really was as a lycan and what it truly meant to live as a wolf. She seemed to have no qualms about accepting him for who he was, but he wasn't sure if she really saw all that was there. Pack life was everything to a wolf, and he wanted her to know that side of him.

After they finished their preparations at the forts, they made their way towards Varg's home. Halea followed closely behind Varg, careful to walk in utter silence, as he had taught her when he showed her how to hunt rabbits in the forest. It was a long walk at their slow speed, but they had to remain quiet and alert every step of the way. Halea kept the telescope, still wrapped in its velvet cloth, clutched closely to her chest. She had strapped her bo to her back for safekeeping.

Eventually, Varg stopped them and signaled ahead. There, before them, was the high ground, the vantage point that was sometimes used by lycan hunters to observe the migrations of the wild game and keep watch over the pack during times of danger. It was a massive jut of land that formed ages ago when the river flowing before it was first forged. Large trees grew all the way to the top, providing them with perfect cover as they made their way up.

Once they reached the top and crouched beneath some dense vegetation for extra cover, Halea removed the telescope from its covering, and Varg indicated where he wanted her to point the lens.

It was then that Halea first saw the wolf den, and she had to remind herself not to gasp in surprise. Varg had described his home to her many times, but she had never truly imagined what she was now seeing through that lens. Most of the caves of the den were masterfully chiseled into the rock of the mountainside. There were ornate carvings in the mountain face that reached as high as some of the towers in Ruinac. Statues, of what she could only assume were great elders or heroes, adorned the many entryways around the mountain. Trees even taller than the great trees in which they built their forts grew all around the base and sides of the mountain, and massive homes of elegant construction nestled in their branches. There were bridges and walkways between most of the trees and from the side of the mountain and into the trees as well. In front of the mountain, at the base, appeared to be a common area where many people gathered around fires. She saw children, wolf cubs playing with each other in rough-and-tumble games, and lycan women carrying babies on their backs as they went about their business. There were some males around, and they looked large and fierce. It was hard to imagine that Varg could ever grow up to look like one of them. She could see lights glowing inside some of the carved caves as she marveled at the ornate stonework.

She felt ashamed, horribly ashamed. She had always imagined Varg as having to live in some dirty, musty, old mountain cave, like a primitive. She knew he was skilled at making things and working with his hands, but she had no idea the extent to which his people had taken their craft. She supposed that when you were immortal, you could find time to make such wonders. She knew Varg's world was still harsh, that pack law was the law of wolves, and that they answered to their instinct above all else, but she never really imagined that there could be more to lycans than the harsh fight for survival.

Varg waited quietly and patiently as he observed her as she looked through the telescope. He was anxious for her reaction. Would she be impressed? Would she be disappointed? He couldn't even risk asking her until they were safely outside of lycan territory, lest they be heard somehow. At last, she lowered the lens and gave him a look of wonder, and he released a breath he hadn't realized he was holding. He would never forget the beauty of her eyes when she looked at him at that moment.

Quietly they turned and started on their way back across the hunting grounds and towards their usual meeting place. Varg's heart was soaring all the way. Once they were safely past the tall oaks that marked the transition of territories, he turned to her.

"So?"

"Wow! No wonder you're so good at fort building!" she exclaimed.

Varg's chest swelled with pride at her genuine praise. "Did you like it?"

"It was amazing! You're so lucky to live in such a beautiful place. Human cities look okay from the outside, but inside they're dirty, lonely places, despite having so many people. Your home…I dunno…it looked like…a home. Like it belonged there. Like you belong there." She couldn't really describe it to him. There were still many things she didn't understand about lycans. Seeing the den had actually raised more questions than answers, but she was glad that she saw it.

As they continued through the forest, Varg suddenly stopped and sniffed the air.

"What is it?" she asked, assuming a deer was nearby or some other prey animal that would usually garner his attention.

"Something strange…I've never smelled it before. Stay close to me," he spoke in a low voice.

She quickly moved in by his side and pulled her bo staff off her back. She still had the telescope in one hand, and her heart began to race. Why was Varg acting so on edge? Nothing had ever harmed them in this forest. Very few predators dared to come near the lycan territories.

Rapidly, he shifted himself on his feet, and she could tell he was listening for something, something she couldn't hear. She wanted to ask him what it was, but she knew she had to stay quiet. A deep growl rumbled through his chest, an inhuman sound. She clutched her staff tighter until her knuckles turned white and darted her eyes around them. Something had to be close.

Suddenly, something came crashing through the forest, and even she could hear it heading their way.

"Varg?"

"Run!" he commanded, and they took off into the trees.

Terror gripped her. Whatever was after them, it was gaining on them. Whatever could be so fast?

Her heart raced in her chest as she and Varg kept pace with each other. She could hear trees crashing behind her and the sound of heavy feet pounding after them.

"Don't look back!" he called.

Instinctively they ran for their forts, perhaps they could climb to safety, but they never made it that far.

"Halea, look out!" Varg shouted, and she felt him push her to the ground as some large form sprang up from behind them and smashed into him.

She felt stunned for a second. She had fallen hard, and the telescope had broken beneath her. She looked up in horror; some strange creature had Varg pinned beneath a tree. It appeared to be a quadrupedal beast, with short, stocky legs covered in scales, each foot ending with two massive claws. Heavy horns adorned its large head that curved out and back in towards each other. It had no eyes, but its massive jaws were snapping at Varg, who was pinned and using all his strength to push back against the creature's horns which were bearing down on him.

With her staff still gripped firmly in hand, Halea quickly jumped to her feet and sprang forth.

"Halea, don't," cried Varg, but she would not leave him to die.

Halea felt her powers of purification surge forth, and she attacked the creature with all her strength, striking down her staff with all her might. She managed to knock the beast away from Varg and burn a hole in its side where her staff made contact, but she had only made things worse, now the creature was furious, and it was heading straight for her.

Varg immediately leaped into action and jumped onto the beast's back, slashing furiously with his claws. The creature's strange black blood began to spurt into the air as it tried desperately to shake the lycan from its back, but Varg would not let go.

Her purification powers were not strong enough yet. She was still just a child, and she had no proper conduit to channel what little power she did have. Real priestesses used spears with shafts of steel because metal was a perfect conduit for their power, but her staff was only a practice weapon made of wood that could barely conduct any power at all.

Suddenly it dawned on her – the telescope!

It was broken and bent, but the elongated metal pieces were all she needed. She prayed to Tiamet to give her strength, and her powers flowed through her, her hands glowing white as the light poured from her into the metal.

"Varg, pull its head back!" she shouted.

He could see her holding the glowing object in her hand, and with all his strength, he grasped the thrashing beast's horns and pulled its head back as far as he could, causing the monster's mouth to open in a protesting roar. Halea rushed forward and lodged the telescope down the creature's throat, and quickly jumped back again before one of its strange claws could slash her.

It let out a terrible high-pitched shriek, and Varg tumbled off just before the beast burst into a strange white light, and then it was gone.

Halea sat on the ground, panting, and shaking all over. Varg immediately rushed to her side. "Are you okay?"

She sat there in a state of silent shock. He wrapped his arms around her, and she turned and buried her face in his chest – he had almost been killed.

"We're safe now. It's gone," Varg assured her.

"A demon," he heard her say in a shaky voice.

She knew it the moment her staff struck.

"Yeah, not bad considering you're not a real priestess yet," he said as he rubbed her back to comfort her.

They sat together for a while longer until eventually, she stopped shaking, and her heart slowed to its normal pace. Varg was relieved when he felt her finally calm down. He had been worried too. She had taken a terrible risk in trying to save him. She could have been killed. That thought alone shook him in a way that he never felt before, and he held her tightly to comfort himself just as much as her.

He walked her home, further downstream past the fern patch than where they usually went their separate ways. After what happened, he was on high alert, constantly sniffing the air and listening for any unfamiliar sounds. Everything seemed peaceful as it had once been.

"Varg, thank you for saving me," she told him as he finally stopped before going too far towards the edge of the forest.

"You saved my ass too. We're a damn good team. I wouldn't be alive either if it weren't for you. Sorry about the telescope. Your grandfather won't be too sore, will he?"

"Oh, he'll be pissed. He'll take it out of my allowance by making me dust his house from here to eternity," she said with a smile.

Varg smiled too. He was glad to see her coming back to herself.

"What are you going to tell him?"

"Not sure yet. Dropped it in the street, and some horses ran over it? Stolen by vagrants? Pawned it to buy a dress? Nah…he wouldn't believe that one at all. Don't worry, I'll think of something."

~~~☼~~~

Maven felt dread as she entered the castle. She had not seen him in several years, and she hated that it was bad news that brought her to his home that day. But the time had come, the signs had been read, and there could be no denying it any longer.

One of his servants announced her as she entered the massive library where he stood alone next to the fireplace. He had his back to her as he studied something in his hand.

"High Priestess Maven, my Lord," the servant said with a bow, and he closed the great doors, leaving them alone.

Her heart fluttered as he finally turned to face her, carelessly placing a book onto the mantle. She quickly dropped to one knee and bowed her head.

"Is it in the signs?" he asked, in a voice both smooth and deep.

"Yes. The tears are too many to ignore. They seem to be moving as well - as if they're congregating in the west," she answered while raising her eyes to look at him.

46

Lord Anshar did not know if there was any sentience to the dimension of Chaos, but he couldn't shake the suspicion that the next convergence was trying to place itself near the Citadel of the Sun, the holy pinnacle of worship for the followers of Tiamet. Was this a strategy? He hoped it was just a coincidence.

Maven filled her eyes with him. It had been too long. Lord Anshar was tall and fair, with long flowing hair of palest silver and eyes that matched. Like many therians, he possessed claws and fangs, though he never harmed humans. He wore armor when called upon to do his duty, but here, in his home, he appeared more relaxed in dark trousers and a white linen shirt. The Blade That Cuts Through Worlds hung dormant above the mantelpiece.

Maven had been the High Priestess for nearly an age. It was a position earned by seniority, not power. Whichever priestess was most powerful was destined for the blade. She had lived to see four convergences in the past, and soon she would see her fifth. Her hair was wavy, long, and dark brown, bound in a thick braid that trailed down her back. Her eyes were dark brown and piercing, and her lips thin and serious.

She watched him silently contemplate the meaning of her information. She thought she saw a momentary flash of pain or sorrow cross his face, but it quickly fell away and was replaced by his usual stoic mask.

"My Lord, will you come to the Citadel?" she finally asked, not being able to bear the silence anymore.

"I will come. Now go and prepare the clerics for my arrival," he commanded, and he heard her let out a sigh of relief.

"Thank you, my Lord. Everything will be ready for your arrival," she said but stopped as if there were one more thing she wanted to say, but she hesitated and turned to leave instead. Maven wanted to tell him how she missed his presence at the Citadel, how she had every faith in his abilities, but she could never be so forward. Lord Anshar was the grandson of the Goddess Tiamet, her hand upon the world, a demigod, the wielder of The Blade That Cuts Through Worlds, guardian of the dark mirror, and their hope and savior against the Chaos. She worshiped the ground that he walked on, yet compared to him, she felt as though she were nothing more than the dust beneath his feet. No one was worthy of such a being, but she couldn't help what she knew in her heart. She would do anything for Lord Anshar.

Once the High Priestess left, and the doors had closed behind her, Lord Anshar turned his eyes back to the fire. Another convergence. Another sacrifice. How many innocent people had died at the hands of demons since the tears began to increase in number? How many more would perish before he could seal away the dark dimension? The signs were in place, but the convergence could still be a year or more away. The exact time was hard to predict, but he felt it deep inside. He didn't need a priestess to tell him it was coming; he could feel it in his bones. He would prepare the disciples for the coming war ahead at the stronghold of the Citadel. He would lead them through this crisis, and he would watch many fall and die. He would fight back the darkness, and in two hundred years or so, it would only return again and again. He would look into the eyes of the priestess who sacrificed herself to protect their world, their dimension, and he would be forced to cut her down. He had done it too many times, and their eyes all haunted him, all begged him to save their world, but the world was never truly saved. The cycle never ended. He couldn't end it; he could only delay it. But he wished to end it; he wished to break the cycle.

# CHAPTER 6 – GROWING UP

Summer came and went. Halea never told her mother about the danger they faced in the woods. Demon attacks had become more common, but the tears that appeared were close to the priestess's stronghold in the city of Ruinac, and so they were swiftly dealt with, if not for that, Halea's mother would have forbidden her from ever going past the city gates.

Theia was forced to concede that her daughter was growing up. She had watched her practice sparring with her grandfather and marveled at the power of her child. Someday she would be a warrior for the Goddess, and already she could see that her fate to serve was sealed.

Autumn came along with Halea's twelfth year, and her grandfather was pleased with her growing skill with the bo staff, soon she would be given her first spear. Every day he watched her strength and speed grow, along with her powers of purification, and he could not have been more proud.

Varg, too, noticed that she was growing more powerful, and he was grateful, for he was also changing and becoming stronger with every passing day. By learning new combat techniques from her grandfather, Halea had won more sparring matches against him than his alpha pride wanted to admit, but truthfully, he loved that she challenged him. No one near his own age challenged him the way she did. She forced him to be better at everything. He lived for the days when they could be together and hated every moment that they were apart.

Winter was the hardest to endure. There were many heavy blizzards that year, and it seemed the season lasted far longer than it usually did. The days when they could see each other grew few and far between until at last spring came.

Halea ran barefoot through the stream that flowed through the fern patch. The rocks felt smooth and polished under her feet. The water was ice-cold from snowmelt flowing down from the mountains, but she didn't mind it at all. She hadn't been able to see Varg in over two weeks, and she was anxious to return to the forts but also dying to enjoy every aspect of her day in the forest after such a long and grueling winter. She reached the area where the stream began to bend away from the direction she wanted to go and stepped out to dry her feet in the grass. As she stood there wiping the droplets off her legs, something in the water caught her eye, and she went back to see what it was.

There in the bed of the stream gleamed a beautiful crystal of clearest icy blue. It stood out brilliantly compared to all the duller, more rounded stones in the water, and she wondered if it had washed down from the mountains. She plucked it out of the water and held it up to the sunlight. It was then that she realized she had seen that exact shade of blue somewhere before – it reminded her of Varg's eyes.

She tucked the stone into the pocket of her short trousers and made her way toward the forts.

Halea started out early that morning and was the first to arrive, so she quickly drank the potion they kept in a cache box at the base of the trees and then went into her fort. She reached into a pile of animal skins that sat in the corner and pulled out a couple of long thin cords of leather and began to weave them into a complex braid. She bound the blue crystal with the woven cordage and admired the necklace she made. It was then that she heard Varg call up to her from the base of the tree.

"Sorry, I'm late!" He entered the fort and sat next to her. "We had to gather extra wood for pit fires since all our stores of wood have been depleted from the long winter. Eventually, I pawned the work off on my pack brothers."

"Bet they love ya for that," she said with a laugh.

"What's that?" he asked of the wadded cord hanging from her hand.

She smiled sweetly and told him to close his eyes. He gave her a look of doubt but eventually complied. She leaned over him as she placed something over his head, and for a moment, he could feel her warmth close to his skin, and suddenly his face flushed red. When he opened his eyes, he found a blue crystal around his neck and raised it in his hand to look at it.

"I found it in the stream this morning. I wanted to give it to you. It matches your eyes," Halea said with a smile.

He looked from the gleaming stone to her smiling face and was filled with joy to know that she thought of him. He wanted to give it back to her so she could always look at it and be reminded of him, but he could tell she had worked lovingly to weave the cord and surprise him, and he would not be ungrateful.

"Thank you. It's really cool. I usually don't see stones like that this far west."

He wasn't exactly sure when or how it happened, but somehow, he felt different around Halea now. She was taller, slightly less gangly, her hair was growing even longer, and the freckles on her face were beginning to fade away. Sometimes when she looked at him with her beautiful eyes, his heart leaped a little in his chest. Sometimes when they sparred, and he grappled with her, he didn't want to let go. Sometimes when he touched her, his hand would linger for just a moment too long. He thought about her almost every moment they were apart, and every night before he would see her again, he could scarcely sleep for excitement about the coming day.

His body was also changing; his voice fluxed between boyhood and an occasional deeper tone that resembled his father's voice. He was growing taller with slightly more defined muscles, though he was still a bit scrawny. New hair was sprouting around his groin, and his body was beginning to feel strange urges that he was not accustomed to.

The other lycan cubs close to his age were starting to notice the young females of the pack in a different way. The scent of their ovulation was beginning to become a distraction.

50

Only one female garnered such a strong reaction from him – but she was still a girl, and worse, human.

Varg was becoming a young man. He could not help the way his heart would jump whenever Halea came near. He couldn't help but become distracted watching her sometimes as she spoke to him, and only half paying attention to what she had to say. He couldn't help inhaling her scent just a little too deep whenever she arrived at the forts before she drank the potion. He ached to hold her hand. He longed to stroke the softness of her hair. He craved to have her eyes upon him at all times. And it was becoming maddening because it was wrong.

She was a human, and he was a lycan. Being friends was one thing. No one could take that away from them, but for someone who would eventually become the future leader of his pack, he couldn't see how more was possible. True, a leader has supreme authority; even if the others in the pack don't like his decisions, they must obey. Technically, he could have any mate he wanted, as long as they wanted him. But wolves did not mate with humans. It was simply not done. Besides, Halea would someday become a priestess. She had to in order to become immortal. If she didn't, she would grow old and die, and he would live on forever, without her. She had explained to him that priestesses were not allowed attachments. They were forbidden to fall in love, marry, or have families, because they were required to devote themselves to Tiamet first and always. A priestess could decide to give up being a priestess to pursue those things, but she would lose her immortality by rejecting the path of serving the Goddess. He did not want to see Halea grow old and die. He did not want to deny her her desire to be a priestess. He knew it meant the world to her and that she had spent almost her whole life preparing for it. He could not have what he wanted from her. All he could have was her friendship, and for him, that would have to be enough.

~~~◇~~~

Ami stood her ground, with Bree and their newest priestess, Samesa, to either side of her. The tears were appearing all over the western lands, and they had rather hoped they would not have to deal with the therians that inhabited those places, but the tears could not go unsealed.

Ami was tall and muscular, with dark hair cut short and emerald-green eyes. To her right stood Bree, who was slight and frail in comparison, her long wavy hair a light shade of blond and her eyes were sky blue, but despite her delicate appearance, she was one of the fiercest priestesses in the service of the Goddess. With them was Samesa, who was new to their order. Samesa had journeyed far from the southern lands, and her skin was almost as dark as her hair, which was very curly and pulled back from her face by several strategic braids that wrapped around her head. Her eyes were also dark, and her smile enchanting. She wore her priestess robes double-layered, with long sleeves instead of the conventional half sleeves as the others wore. She was used to a warmer climate and could never acclimate to the northern lands' constant chill.

Before them, a fierce lycan glared, clearly the alpha leader of the pack, and close behind him were many of his strongest warriors. It hadn't taken them long after

51

crossing the border into their territory that they were discovered, and their presence challenged.

"Leave or die," commanded their leader, who emitted a low, threatening growl.

"If we leave, it is you who will die. Hear this now; the great convergence is coming! I'm sure you've noticed demons from the Chaos seeping into your territories. More tears will come. They must be sealed. We have no desire to linger on your lands or involve ourselves with your people, but we must fulfill our mission. We ask you to allow us to enter your lands, unharmed and unhindered until the convergence has passed, and then we assure you, we will gladly leave."

Bledig scowled at the three human priestesses before him. It had been almost an age since priestesses entered lycan territory, long before even he had been born. It was true, though. Demons were appearing more frequently within their lands. They managed to slay every one they found before any pack members could be harmed, but their numbers were always increasing. It was only a matter of time. The news that a convergence was soon to appear sent a chill up his spine. What if it came close? What if it happened in the west this time? He was reluctant to take the lives of the few who could truly stop it, but that didn't mean he was pleased with the idea of humans being anywhere within his territory.

"When will the convergence come, and where?"

"We don't know the exact time or place, but signs lead us to believe that it may not be long, and unfortunately, it may be quite close," replied the leader of the three priestesses.

Bledig grunted and scowled. Lycans were very straightforward people; they did not like vague answers.

"I wish to consult with the elders and other pack leaders before I grant you permission to enter our lands. We western lycans have not suffered humans to enter our realm in a very long time, and it is not something to be granted lightly. Return by the next moon. You will have your answer."

Ami bowed her head in a sign of respect, and together, she and the other priestesses turned and dashed back into the woods.

It was time to call a wolf gathering.

~~~⛌~~~

It had been almost a week, but eventually, lycans from the other territories began to arrive in great numbers. This was Varg's first wolf gathering. The wolf packs rarely converged unless there was a significant danger or an important matter to be settled. When packs arrived for a gathering, they brought as many able-bodied pack members as possible, but they did not bring every pack member, some could not make the journey, such as mothers with young cubs, and many would also remain to guard their den and defend the territory.

Varg and the other cubs watched with wide eyes as strange lycans they had never met before appeared and were welcomed into their den. So many new arrivals kept things very interesting for him and the other young lycans.

Faolan, in particular, seemed excited about the prospect of meeting new females in their age group. Wolf gatherings were a time for every lycan to gather, not just the elders and leaders. It was also for families who rarely saw each other to reunite and for young people from different packs to meet prospective mates outside of their usual pack circle.

Varg grew weary of hearing his friends go on and on about females all the time. They seemed to think of nothing else, and the arrival of so many more young lycans made their banter particularly grading. What's worse is several new females seemed to have taken a fancy to him, and he wasn't sure how he felt about it. The lycan girls he knew from his own pack admired him, but they had grown accustomed to his aloof behavior. They were hoping that with age, he would eventually take an interest in one of them. The new girls were less patient and converged in small groups, and whenever he would walk by, they would stare and giggle and blush. As a young lycan male who could someday grow to be an alpha, the attention wasn't entirely unappreciated, but having appraised all the new girls, he concluded that there weren't any that he was particularly interested in. Some were quite pretty, but in his eyes, none could compare to Halea.

From the eastern pack arrived Otsana. She was the same age as Varg, with full round lips, flowing chestnut hair, and dark blue eyes that grew black when her mood shifted. Her father, Ethelwolf, was the alpha of her pack, and she was the alpha of her peer group. The moment she laid eyes on Varg, she began to pursue his attention relentlessly. Though he was still quite young, she could see the great potential in him. He was already taller than the other lycan males his age and even a few older than him, and his clear visage of dominance thrilled her to the core. Someday he would surely be a great alpha leader.

"Varg, may I join your group on the hunt today?" she asked when it had been announced that a hunting party was being assembled and that Varg would be participating. So many visitors would greatly tax the local game, and far more hunting parties would have to go out and span further distances to keep such a large assembly of wolves fed for the duration of their stay.

"Do whatever you want," he replied while brushing off her hand that had been trying to grab his. Every time she approached him, she would try to grab his arm, lean on him or put her hands in his hair. Lycans were very physical when it came to showing affection, and it was clear to everyone that Otsana was doing her best to stake a claim on the young male's attention. His rebuffs did nothing to discourage her.

Later in the evening, when Varg returned with the hunting party, there was another flurry of excitement. The northern pack had arrived, and word was spreading like wildfire - a human was with them.

Varg ran to the common area to see with his own eyes. A human? Why? How?

A large crowd had gathered, and he observed as his father sat with the leader of the northern pack, exchanging casual pleasantries. They would not discuss the problem that assembled them until everyone arrived. He looked at all the new faces, and then, he saw her – a human woman. She had dark coppery red hair and eyes as black as night. Her nose was thin, and she had many freckles, even though she was no longer a child. Her face did not betray fear to be surrounded by so many lycans, but he could smell some anxiety coming from her. Everyone was staring and talking about

53

her in hushed tones, some were curious, and some were angry. Eventually, Varg noticed a powerful-looking lycan male was standing next to the human woman with his arm wrapped protectively around her.

Was she his prisoner?

He was shocked when his father seemed to pay her no mind and continued to devote his attention to the northern leader.

It wasn't until the next day that he finally found out the truth. The human woman was mated to a lycan, the male who had guarded over her that night.

Everywhere he went, people were talking and making crude remarks.

"Didn't anyone ever tell him you're supposed to eat your food, not play with it?"

"Perhaps he went to eat her and got too excited."

The news struck him like a thunderbolt. A human was actually mated with a lycan! But how? His mind reeled with the implications. He desperately wanted to ask his father about it, but his father had no time for him since the gathering began, and so he went to the wisest person he knew.

"How did he mate with that human woman?"

"How? Why, Varg, I thought you were old enough to know how coupling worked," laughed Batsuba, and she watched the young lycan cub blush red before her.

"No, not that...I mean. She's a human...he's a lycan...I thought...it's not possible," he babbled.

"It's possible, but it is also incredibly rare. Therians have been known to take humans as pets, though they usually kill them when they're done having their way with them, but every once in a rare while, a therian will choose a human as a mate. It's not particularly approved of. I'm sure you've heard the mutterings. Most are not happy that Alf mated himself to that human female, but the heart of a lycan cannot be changed, and he would not be parted from her. He was lucky his brother was an alpha and was eventually able to get his way about allowing her to become a part of the pack. He was almost banished, but the woman, Jance, I believe her name is, has a pleasant disposition, and I guess over time, she endeared herself to the pack. Now almost all of them accept her and love her like she was born to them. These meetings are trying, though. While most of Bertolf's pack has accepted her, the other packs still disapprove, and many are still very vocal about it."

"Is this the first time a lycan has mated a human?"

"Actually, no, it's happened before, and who knows, maybe it'll happen again. People will love who they will love."

"But she'll die. She's mortal. She'll grow old and die. What will Alf do when that happens?"

"She is not mortal anymore. Surely you can smell that the decay of death has left her?"

He had been too shocked at the moment and too distracted by Jance's anxiety to pay attention to that detail.

"How?"

"There is a way, a special blood magic ritual that can be performed. The love of a human would be very fleeting indeed if not for such a ritual. This appearance of the human woman seems to have greatly upset you, Varg. Don't worry. Your father knew about her long before they arrived. Bledig has great respect for Bertolf; they are old friends, though he doesn't approve of Bertolf's brother being mated to a human. In fact, he was adamantly against it at the time, but it's Bertolf's pack and Bertolf's choice as to whether or not he would stand by his brother, and so Bledig will no longer speak on the matter."

"He could have. My father is leader even over him. He could have ordered her killed and Alf too."

"Varg, someday when you are older, you'll learn that being a great leader isn't always about getting your way. Alliances and friendships are important, especially among lycans," she reminded him.

Bledig's word was law. He was the supreme alpha and had power over every pack, but he was also a wise and just leader. He weighed every decision he made and always did what he thought was best for everyone. Varg knew his father was a good leader and highly respected, and not just because he was the strongest alpha, it was something he hoped to aspire to as he grew up.

Varg left Batsuba's home that day in a state of shock and distraction. A lycan could have a human for a mate, and there was a way for a human to become immortal outside of being a servant to the Dragon Goddess.

He was still a boy, too young to consider the gravity of such a decision, but someday he would be a grown man. He knew when he was older; he would have a choice to make.

Someday. Perhaps.

~~~☼~~~

At last, all of the pack leaders and elders had arrived, and they assembled in the sacred cave, which was buried deep within the mountain. Its ceilings were high, and there was a phosphorescent glow when lanterns and fires were not blazing, but today everyone gathered in a circle around the main fire pit. Bledig stood before the alphas and elders, his hand tightly gripping the Great Fang that he wore at his side, the symbol of his power and authority.

Varg sat quietly next to Batsuba and watched as his father paced. Normally, Bledig did not include his son in pack meetings, but Varg was growing older, and it was time for him to learn that being a great leader meant relying on more than just claw and fang.

"Friends, brothers, sisters, I have assembled you here because I have grave news. I know many of you are dealing with an increasing number of demon attacks. Some of you have told me of tears opening within your very borders. Some of you have even lost pack members to these demons. We, too, in the west, have been plagued by these evil creatures sent from the Chaos. Not long ago, my scouts and I discovered three humans, priestesses of the Goddess Tiamet, who came to the borders of our lands, seeking permission to pursue the demons and close the tears, but worse, they have proclaimed the coming of a convergence."

He paused, and suddenly, the leader of the southern pack, Rafe, jumped to his feet. Rafe was a large and powerful lycan alpha with jet black hair and eyes. He bowed his head in a sign of submission to his supreme alpha.

"Speak, brother," said Bledig, acknowledging the other alpha's desire to be heard.

"In the southern territories, there are now two open tears. Priestesses have come, asking permission to seal them, but we have refused to let them on our land. They are humans; we don't need their help. We lycans can slay demons on our own, especially if we band together. I think it is unwise to let these human dragon worshippers interfere. How do we know that their very existence does not encourage the Dimension of Chaos? You are extremely unfortunate to be so close to their holy city," he said and then sat down again.

Rafe was older than Bledig, though not old enough to remember the last time priestesses had come to lycan lands to seal tears. He cared deeply for the safety of his pack but was often too hot-headed, and while he respected Bledig as his supreme alpha, he resented him as well. It had been Rafe that Bledig battled to become the Wolf King and wield the Great Fang.

"I hear and acknowledge you, brother," replied Bledig. He could always feel that Rafe wished to challenge his authority. He was consistently the loudest voice of dissent at gatherings. "I do not doubt that a lycan warrior is more than a match for any demon, but lives can, and have, already been lost. Brother Bertolf, please share what your pack has endured."

Bertolf jumped to his feet and bowed in thanks to Bledig for being allowed to speak. "We in the northern mountains have had tears as well. Demons have poured out from the Dimension of Chaos in such great numbers that our strongest warriors are struggling to protect the den. They are also frightening away the herds, and soon our hunting grounds will be barren. I have already let one priestess into our territory. We could not suffer the tear to remain unsealed. She warned us of the convergence as well. If we do not accept their help, we will all suffer."

Rafe jumped to his feet in a rage and addressed Bertolf without acknowledging Bledig or asking his permission to speak again. "You filthy human lovers! Priestesses or not, humans are not to be trusted. They are the cause of all these disasters! Your judgment is clouded because you let your brother rut a human wench."

Bertolf's eyes burned, and he snarled at Rafe. Before the two could collide, Bledig leaped on Rafe in such a swift move that at one moment, he stood there challenging Bertolf, and the next, he was pinned to the ground with Bledig's claws slicing into his throat.

Everyone could feel the tension in the air as Bledig stared at the other male in threat, his growl sending a deep rumbling vibration through the entire cave, his grip tightening with every moment.

Rafe had shown disrespect to his leader, and as the head alpha, Bledig had no choice but to punish him and put him in his place. Such behavior could not be tolerated. An alpha had to maintain his authority, brutally if necessary.

Rafe contemplated fighting back. He wanted to. Everyone could see his eyes begin to glow red with the threat of blood rage, but Rafe was not the stronger male, and he knew it. He had been defeated once before, and like it or not, he had to submit.

After a tense moment, Rafe tipped back his head and exposed his throat further to Bledig in a clear sign of submission, and just like that, it was over, and he was released.

The eastern leader quickly stood and bowed before Bledig, who acknowledged him as though nothing had just happened between him and the southern leader.

"Tears will grow worse with the coming of the convergence. I dislike humans as well, but the safety of my pack comes first. I vote we allow the priestesses to do their duty unharmed. I have lived through a convergence before, as I am quite a bit older than many of you. I remember it well. It happened close to our lands, and if we had not let the priestesses do their job, we would have lost a great many pack members. I say, yes, let them."

"I vote, yes, as well," called Batsuba from where she sat.

Bledig listened to the many voices around him. The overwhelming majority agreed; they would have to suffer the priestesses to enter their lands.

"So be it. The priestesses may enter our lands…all of our lands," he said while shooting a threatening glare at Rafe. "As long as they keep to themselves and close the tears; they may come and go unharmed. Once the threat of convergence has passed, then they must go."

~~~◇~~~

"I do not like this decision," complained one of Rafe's pack-mates as they stood outside after the pack meeting, far away from the others so as not to be heard.

"Bledig's judgment is not to be trusted. He is an alpha with a dead mate. He is no longer whole, and he is not thinking clearly. He is not long for this world. This decision will cost us all. I feel it; he will bring ruin upon us."

"He has given his order. We have no choice," complained the other male.

"If our people survive this, I will soon have my chance again," Rafe replied and swore to himself that someday he would be the wielder of the Fang.

# CHAPTER 7 – ENTER CHAOS

"What's wrong?" Halea asked after greeting Varg at the fern patch, he appeared distracted about something.

"We've received word of the convergence. Did you know?"

Halea sighed and looked down at her bare feet.

"I just found out too. I was going to tell you today, but I guess you heard."

Halea knew of the lycan gathering that had been going on back at Varg's den. Varg hadn't been able to sneak away to see her as much as he liked during that time, but he had managed a few short visits to the forts. Varg knew his father had called for a gathering, but the exact reason hadn't been revealed to him until the night of the alpha's council, though he had his suspicions. Demons had been appearing within their hunting grounds, and everyone was concerned.

"Will they stop it?"

"Yes, I'm sure they will. That's why priestesses exist. They've always stopped it before. There's something else I wanted to tell you. We don't know when the convergence will begin, but when it starts, I must join the priestesses in the Citadel."

"Why?" asked Varg, clearly worried. He did not want Halea near such a calamity.

"I'm not a priestess yet, but these convergences only happen once every couple centuries. Lord Anshar has ordered that I should attend and witness for myself the true nature of what a priestess must battle."

"I don't like it, Halea. Aren't they going to sacrifice someone?"

"Yes. It hasn't been decided yet, but it will be whichever priestess is strongest." She tried to offer him a comforting smile. "Don't worry, Varg. They'll fix this. I'm in no danger. Every cleric will be there, and almost every priestess, and even Lord Anshar."

Varg couldn't shake the deep and unsettling feeling within himself. All his instincts were screaming that something terrible would happen to her, that he might never see her again.

"I can't stay to play today. I just needed to speak to you. The convergence tear is expected to arrive at any moment, and I'll have to join them as soon as it appears. Once this is all over, I'll come back. I promise."

"Halea...I..." he said while struggling to think of something to say, anything to say to make her stay, but there was nothing he could do. "I'll wait for you...no matter how long it takes," he said as he wrapped his arms around her and held her close.

Halea had never had a friend like Varg, and she didn't mind when they would occasionally hug. She knew from him that lycans were quite physical when it came to showing affection, and so she had always accepted it as just one of his ways. She hugged him back, but eventually, she pulled away. She could feel that he was reluctant to let her go.

"Everything will be okay," she told him as she finally turned to leave, and he was left alone to endure the howling of the wolf within.

~~~☼~~~

Lord Anshar stood at the window, watching the sun sink in the west from his vantage point in the Citadel of the Sun. The water sparkled, and the sky took on warm hues as the last of the sun's rays disappeared. Then a strange purple glow appeared, and he heard a loud commotion from outside the great hall, and with his keen ears, he knew.

"Lord Anshar!" cried several priestesses, including High Priestess Maven, as they burst through the doors. He turned to look at them and saw it in their eyes.

"It has appeared. It can be seen from the eastern facing parapet. This is the closest it has ever come to the Citadel. It's floating right over the city," cried Bree. This was not her first convergence, but it was clear that its appearance so close to the Citadel and the holy city had shaken her resolve. He couldn't help but suspect that it was not just a coincidence.

"Then this is where we must make our stand. You know what to do," Lord Anshar said while turning to Maven, who gave him a knowing nod before fleeing from the great hall.

~~~☼~~~

Halea had barely finished her dinner when her grandfather burst through their front door.

"It has come! Halea, we must go," he said.

Halea shot her mother a nervous glance, which her mother also returned.

"It's alright, Halea. Everything will be fine. I'll be here waiting for you," Theia said to try and reassure her daughter, though she noticeably trembled as her eyes grew moist with unshed tears.

Halea jumped up and embraced her mother.

"I'm proud of you," her mother whispered in her ear before finally letting her go and allowing her grandfather to whisk her out the door.

~~~☼~~~

The moment she stepped outside, the convergence tear was unmistakable. Its eerie glowing purple light swirled above the city, and everywhere she turned, people were running and screaming in panic. The streets were utter chaos as they struggled to make their way to the tunnels through the maddening crowd.

The Citadel of the Sun was west of the city, rising out of the sea itself. Its base had been constructed by marine therians ages ago, but no matter how the waters raged, the Citadel always stood strong. Everyone could see it as a shining spire reaching for the setting sun from the walls of Ruinac. There were only two ways to enter the Citadel; one was through a series of long tunnels that were most often used by the clerics and priestesses. They were buried deep below the ocean floor, and so to pass from the city to the Citadel, one would literally be walking beneath the sea. The walls of the tunnel were airtight as they were also constructed by the mer-therians long ago. The only other way to reach the Citadel was by ship.

It would be a very long walk through the tunnels to the Citadel.

Halea kept up with her grandfather, who led her into the echoing darkness. Several more priestesses were making their way to the citadel ahead of them, and it sounded as if someone, perhaps a cleric judging by their slower pace, was coming up behind.

She would have liked to run and get out of there quickly. The dank, windowless walls were making her feel claustrophobic, and there was a strange humming from where the air entered the tunnels through a system of pipes, but she allowed Halea grandfather to dictate their pace.

The sconces cast eerie shadows all around her, and she felt an uncomfortable tension build as she wondered if the tunnel would ever end at all, but at last, they came up into the fresh air at the base of the Citadel.

Halea had never been to the Citadel before; she had only ever heard about it from her grandfather and seen it from the city walls. Tilting her head back just to gaze at the top that could not even be seen above the clouds was enough to strain her neck. Harbored close to where they stood was a beautiful ship with tall white sails. It would have been a breathtaking experience if not for the looming tear spreading behind her in the city. In just the time it had taken them to traverse the tunnel, the tear had grown immensely, and she could see fires in the city.

"Mother!" Halea gasped. She knew that demons would soon be flooding the streets of the Ruinac, and she was almost certain she could hear cries of terror from across the waves.

"Clerics have already been dispatched through the eastern bound tunnels. They will help defend the city until Lord Anshar can close the great tear. Your mother knows to stay inside and lock the door. Have faith, Halea. Lord Anshar will save us," Uro reassured as he watched Halea's terror-stricken face. He hoped he was right.

Uro led Halea into the Citadel and to an enormous spiral of stairs that seemed to rise forever. Suddenly the long tunnel didn't seem so bad; at least it hadn't been as exhausting as the stairway to the top of the Citadel.

At last, they reached the top. The last rays of the sun had completely faded upon the water, and the stars began to glow. It was a moonless night, yet the sky was not dark because growing in the distance, as if the heavens had been torn asunder, loomed the convergence. It had doubled in size since they reached the base of the Citadel, and it seemed to be coming straight for them.

Halea was panic-stricken for her mother as it was clear more fires had taken the city.

"Don't look into it, Halea, and do not focus on the city. You are here to observe the ritual. There is still time."

Halea forced herself to tear her eyes away from the coming of the Chaos and to observe the procession taking place around her. There were hundreds of clerics and

60

dozens of priestesses surrounding a long walkway that led up to a tall man who stood waiting. His hair was long and silvery, and he was dressed in fine gleaming armor and wrapped in a long red cloak. Clutched within his hands was an exposed sword. At first, it was hard for her to get a good look at him because she was so far back, but eventually, her grandfather urged her to move closer, and as she approached, she noticed that he was a therian. His face was noble and handsome, his ears were long and pointed, and his fingers tapered into claws. This was Lord Anshar, the dragon therian demigod who would wield The Blade That Cuts Through Worlds.

A hush fell over the gathered devotees, and Halea turned her gaze away from the therian Lord to behold a priestess walking towards him from across the Citadel. She was tall and strong-looking, with short dark hair and a determined look on her face. Halea could see no trace of fear on this priestess. Painted upon her arms and legs were many runes, and in her hand, she wielded her spear.

If not for the drawn weapons and the looming Chaos, the entire scene could have reminded her of a wedding.

At last, the priestess reached the Lord who stood waiting, and she dropped to her knees before him with her head bowed low.

Another priestess to the right of the Lord, and who wore a more elaborate robe, spoke.

"Ami, you have been chosen. Of all who serve Tiamet, she has blessed you the most. It is your power we require," spoke the dark-eyed priestess.

The strongest priestesses knew who they were, and they all had come to the Citadel to be a part of the choosing ritual that had already taken place. Each of the priestesses had been required to lay their hands upon The Blade That Cuts Through Worlds, and for whichever priestess was most powerful, the blade would glow with the light of purification. Ami had been chosen.

"Will you give your life for Tiamet? Will you sacrifice your blood so that all others may live and that evil may be banished?" asked Lord Anshar.

Ami looked up into Lord Anshar's eyes. It was the look he hated the most – resignation. He hated it because he could smell the fear. He could hear the pounding of the hearts of the priestesses who laid their lives down as a sacrifice. Brave women, all of them, and he hated what he had to do. He hated the hopelessness of it all. But no matter the pain and regret he harbored in his heart, he would fulfill his duty. He would not fail.

"I will die willingly," Ami replied while looking up at Lord Anshar, whose grip on his weapon only tightened.

Ami rose to her feet and took several steps back, and Halea noticed that the priestess was standing over sand that had been poured out over the ground and spread around neatly.

She watched as the priestess chanted in the ancient language and moved her body in a strange ritualistic series of poses. Halea thought the way she moved was beautiful like she was dancing. With her spear, she drew a large circle around herself in the sand. While continuing to chant, she used the tip of her weapon to scribe the sacred runes.

"Look out!" someone shouted, and before Halea could understand what was happening, everyone was running and screaming. Weapons clashed, and people cried out as they were cut down.

Three large tears had burst open right above them, and without any delay at all, hundreds of humanoid demons charged through the dimensional rifts and leaped upon the congregation.

Lord Anshar tightened his grip on his sword as the demons attacked his priestesses and clerics in numbers too great for them to withstand. Even though he needed to complete the ritual, in that one moment, his instinct to protect those around him took over, and he surged forth into battle. A blood rage had taken him, and his pupils became elliptical in shape as he slashed through demons without mercy, but still, they continued to emerge through the tears. He burned with hatred against the Chaos as his many devoted clerics and priestesses were viciously slain. The Citadel was too besieged for anyone to seal the tears.

Ami was forced to stop her chanting and put up her weapon to fight. It was now apparent; it was she who was their primary target. They had come for her. She let out a gasp as one of their dark blades stabbed her in the back, and then another, and another. And soon, she lay on the ground as her blood pooled all around her, and she was gone.

"Halea, run!" commanded her grandfather as he grabbed her arm and dragged her away from the chaos. A massive demon tried to intercept them, but Uro vanquished it with a sacred sutra. Halea wanted to help, to stay and fight with the others, but she didn't have her bo staff with her, and there were just too many demons.

Together they fled down the spiral stairway as demons chased after them the entire way. "Hide!" ordered Uro as they reached the bottom, and he shoved her into the great hall and barred the doors after her.

"Grandfather!" Halea cried while pounding on the doors, but even with all her strength, they wouldn't budge, and she could hear fighting just outside.

There was a crackling sound behind her, and she turned to discover that the oil lamps in the vast chamber had been knocked over, spreading fire over the tapestries. Within the clouds of smoke stood the demon wraith that started the fire - and it saw her.

It leaped at her, and with no weapon to protect herself, she could only raise her hands and call upon the Goddess. Though she had no conduit, somehow, her power was strong enough to injure the demon and send it reeling back away from her. As it began to rise again, she could see its twisted humanoid body and its eerie eyeless face. She quickly rushed for one of the tall iron candelabras and brandished it before her.

The smell of smoke was becoming overpowering, and she could still hear fighting outside the doors. There was no one to help her, and the fire was spreading all around.

The demon leaped at her and she managed to block its claws from slashing into her by putting up the iron piece in time, but she was pinned to the ground. It reached inside its black raiment and produced a dark blade - a weapon from the Dimension of

Chaos. Kicking with all her might, Halea managed to throw the creature off. Before it could right itself, she leaped upon it, pouring all her power through the wrought iron. The moment she made contact, the wraith exploded into a blinding white light.

There was no time to be relieved. There was a deafening crash, and to Halea's horror, when she looked back to the doors, a large structural beam had fallen before them as it smoldered in flames. She was trapped. The fire roared all around her. She could scarcely breathe as the fumes burned her lungs and assailed her eyes.

Terror gripped her as she knew she was about to die within the fire. She would perish there alone, and she suddenly cursed that she hadn't let that demon get her. Surely being struck down by a dark weapon would be a more merciful way to die than to perish in flame. She huddled on the floor, choking, and coughing, and struggling for air, while the heat of the fire threatened to sear her flesh.

Just when all seemed lost, when she was sure her end had come, she heard another loud crash. Her eyes burned and watered so severely she could barely see anything in front of her, but suddenly before her loomed a tall and imposing figure. She instantly feared another demon, but instead, a heavy cloak draped over her entire body, and someone scooped her up into their arms. Blinking rapidly, she faintly made out the gleam of long silver hair.

"Don't be afraid. You're safe, I have you," reassured a deep and melodious voice.

The next thing she knew, she was away from the fire and out in the open night air. She was still bundled tightly in the strange fabric, her savior holding her firmly in his arms. Her lungs ached, and her eyes wouldn't stop watering, but it was then that she knew; it was Lord Anshar who saved her from the flames.

"Load the survivors onto the ship. We must pull away from the Citadel," he ordered as they boarded the vessel. Around them lay many slain demons, clerics, and priestesses.

"Lord Anshar," cried the High Priestess. "Ami is dead!"

"There must still be a sacrifice," he replied.

"Allow me, Lord Anshar, I am now Tiamet's most blessed," volunteered Bree as she sprang forward.

Lord Anshar merely nodded his head. Bree was a powerful priestess, but he doubted her ability to help him subdue the Chaos. Yet, there was no other way.

The ship lurched on the turbulent water, and an enormous rumbling could be heard. "Lord Anshar, the city, look!" cried one of the clerics, and all eyes turned out towards Ruinac. The ground had split open all along the shoreline, and the burning city was crumbling into the churning sea. Massive waves nearly overturned their ship, causing everyone to hang on for their lives. Once the waves settled a little, everyone looked up again and watched in horror as the city was swallowed up by the raging sea, and then it was gone.

Above, the convergence nearly covered the entire night sky.

Halea fell catatonic as she undoubtedly witnessed her mother's death. The image of the city's destruction beneath the looming mass of the convergence would haunt her nightmares for the rest of her life. She would never forget it.

"Halea!" cried Uro as he struggled to make his way towards Lord Anshar as the ship rocked violently. Lord Anshar gently placed the shocked child into her grandfather's arms. Halea did not move or speak; she only stared out where her home had once been.

Uro had managed to fight back the demons. When he saw Lord Anshar leading a small group of survivors to safety, he had pleaded for him to save his granddaughter. Uro had seen the smoke seep from beneath the door, and he feared that he had lost his only granddaughter.

Uro clutched Halea to him and wept in relief at her safety, but he could tell by her silence, she had seen the city fall.

The survivors felt another lurch as the ship's sails billowed in the violent winds that pulled them further out to sea. The Citadel was engulfed in flames as it crumbled into the sea. The holy temple of Tiamet was gone.

Maven helped Bree prepare the runes on her body as quickly as possible. The more powerful the convergence would get, the harder it would be for them to seal it. Once prepared, Bree kneeled before Lord Anshar.

"Will you give your life for Tiamet?" he asked as he drew his sword.

"I will die willingly," she replied, then rose to complete the remainder of the ritual.

Halea watched silently as the priestess danced and completed the circle of runes, which she scratched into the ship's deck with her spear. When she was done, she stood before Lord Anshar again.

"Let my sacrifice be consecrated with blood," Bree said while looking up into Lord Anshar's eyes.

Halea looked into Lord Anshar's face, and she saw it - pain.

It was brief, but she had seen it nonetheless, and at that moment, her heart shattered. Lord Anshar's sadness had broken the final dam that allowed the sorrow to flood into her heart, and she burst into uncontrollable tears. She cried and sobbed wretchedly in her grandfather's arms but never turned her eyes away.

Halea watched as Lord Anshar ran his blade through the waiting priestess. His sword coated in blood as he withdrew it from her still-warm body. Bree let out one final sigh and collapsed onto the ship's deck, her beautiful white priestess robes now stained red.

Lord Anshar raised his sword into the air and called upon the Goddess, and Halea witnessed as the lightning rained down from the sky, and the blade glowed, and the sea roared, and the winds raged all around them, tilting the ship.

He never faltered as he swung his blade across the heavens, and she beheld as gradually the great convergence tear was sucked into a mighty vortex that roared like a thousand hell beasts.

Everyone held their breath, praying it wasn't too late, praying the sacrifice was enough.

At last, when the vortex closed, the sky grew clear, the sea calmed, and the thunder silenced.

Chaos had been banished once again.

## CHAPTER 8 – DEVASTATION

The lycan warriors were quickly overrun with hordes of demons flooding into their territory from where the great tear of the convergence opened.

Samesa and several other priestesses had finally been allowed into the lycan territory to seal the smaller tears. The shifters disliked their presence but, for the most part, ignored them and allowed them to close the tears they found. Samesa was not one of the priestesses whose presence was required at the Citadel the day the convergence began. She watched in horror as the convergence grew and became visible from the skyline above the lycan lands. She was still very young and had only just recently become a priestess. Lord Anshar had wanted her present to witness it with the others because it would have been her first, but priestesses were sorely needed to mend the smaller tears. The High Priestess had pressed her case that there would be more convergences. For the time being, Samesa was required elsewhere.

*"Are all convergences this big? Why haven't they stopped it yet? Did something go wrong?"* Samesa thought while slashing through another demon with her spear. In the distance, she could see the lycans were retreating. Pouring out through the trees, she saw a sea of black beasts and humanoid demons, as many as locusts. Their numbers were too great, and even she was forced to run and take cover in a secluded cave which she sealed with a barrier spell.

"Retreat! Protect the den!" cried Bledig as he and the remaining lycan warriors raced back to their home. Their numbers were temporarily increased thanks to the lycan gathering. The northern pack had already left to return to their home after the council meeting, but the southern and eastern packs had stayed a little longer and rallied around their Wolf King, who brandished the Great Fang. With a single stroke of the sacred sword, a mighty blast would lay waste to over a hundred demons, and he launched countless attacks, yet still, it was not enough. There was no end to their numbers.

Rafe wanted to leave the gathering as soon as the northern pack had gone, but something in his instincts made him bide his time. He had been right. He had warned of the human's incompetence and treachery, and now he felt immense satisfaction in watching Bledig and his pack suffer.

"I warned you, the humans would bring ruin upon us," he gloated disrespectfully to his supreme alpha. "My pack will lose no more lives in this doomed fight; we shall leave. Give up the den. Flee where you can. And may the mighty wolf gods have mercy on you all."

Normally to speak in such a way to the Wolf King would be to sign the warrant for one's death, but Bledig heard Rafe's words and took them to heart with sadness and regret. Ever since the loss of his mate, he had not thought as a leader should. Perhaps he had failed his people? He knew he had failed his son, who was crushed by his distant behavior, and in failing his son, he had failed *her* as well.

"Ignore him; all hope is not lost yet. I've seen the miracle of the convergence being banished. There must be something that's holding them up, but he is right. The den will not be safe. Flee with my pack and me deep into the eastern mountains. It's our only hope now," offered Ethelwolf.

With determination burning in his heart, Bledig raced back to the den with his surviving warriors. "The convergence has come! The priestesses have failed us! Take only what you can carry. We cannot save the den. The demon hordes are coming," he called.

The convergence growing over the horizon caused the remaining lycans at the den to panic and the news that the demon hordes were coming nearly sent them into hysteria.

"Varg?" called Bledig as he desperately searched for his son.

"Father!" replied his son, who came running.

Just then, another small tear opened, and three humanoid demons emerged and attacked. Varg quickly defended himself, but humanoid demons were much more formidable than the bestial kind, and he found himself facing off with a towering wraith that wielded a black blade. It leaped at him, but Varg easily dodged the creature and slashed it fiercely with his claws. A second armed wraith also attacked, and its black blade sliced within a hair's breadth of Varg's throat, and he felt something slide down his chest, but he had no time to see what it was.

"Varg, get down," called his father, and Varg wasted no time dropping to the ground as his father leaped over him and on the demons that he mercilessly tore to shreds.

The tear still glowed ominously, and they could hear sounds in the distance warning them that more demons were coming.

"I need you to help lead the pack out of here. The others and I will hold them back a little longer."

Varg wanted to argue. Halea was still out there somewhere. If things were going this badly for them, the city had to have been destroyed, but there would be no way for him to get through the hordes of demons that stood between him and her, and he was forced to obey his father's command. With a heavy heart and tears forming in his eyes, he nodded and turned to help the others.

The lycan warriors held back the demons as long as they could, but even with the mighty power of the Great Fang, they had been forced to escape and abandon the den. As they fled, many lycans were slaughtered, including Varg's friend Bardolph. Varg hadn't seen him fall in the chaos but he found his lifeless body on the ground as he was forced to lead his people away. He moved to help his friend when he felt Batsuba's hand on his arm.

"He is gone, Varg. I'm sorry," she said.

After sunset, they finally saw in the distance that the enormous vortex of the Dragon Lord had swallowed the convergence. They were relentlessly pursued by demons until they reached the high ground beyond their eastern border. Only then did Varg realize that the blue crystal Halea had gave him had been cut loose by the demon that attacked him. He wished to go back for it, but they all could see from their vantage point that the den had been overrun. He was left with nothing of her now. With a heavy heart, Varg and his father helped lead the remainder of their people deep into the eastern mountains.

~~~☼~~~

Lord Anshar's castle was in Antherose, north of Ruinac, and a day's journey up the coast. The day after the great convergence, Halea watched from the bow of the ship as they sailed into the small port of the quaint seaside city. A little further north of the city, towering cliffs jutted out towards the sea, and at the top of the cliffs sat the castle of Lord Anshar. She had never seen a real castle before. An elegant carriage was already waiting as they stepped down the gangplank. Someone in the city must have seen Lord Anshar's ship coming into port and ordered it for him, though they had not expected him to bring so many clerics and priestesses with him. She could hear him giving orders to a man that had been waiting to fetch more coaches and wagons to help bring the injured, of which there were many, up to his castle.

Halea had cried herself to sleep that night on the ship with her grandfather's arms wrapped tightly around her. Her grandfather had some cuts and bruises, but he had managed to avoid serious injury. Halea was impressed that he had held off so many demons on his own considering his advanced age. Many of the others were severely wounded, and several had died before the ship reached port.

Halea woke at dawn and realized that she had been wrapped in the red cloak of Lord Anshar the entire time. He had protected her with it in the fire but had yet to claim it from her.

Uro watched as his granddaughter silently regarded the cloak while stroking her fingers along the unusual fabric.

"It's made from tufts of fiber that grow from a strange flower that only blooms near volcanoes. It does not burn in fire, nor does Lord Anshar; that is how he was able to pull you from the flames unharmed," he explained.

"He can't burn?"

"He's a dragon. He fears no flame."

Halea remembered the heat as if she were still in it. Lord Anshar's cloak had saved her life. He had saved her life.

Her mind wandered to Varg. Her grandfather had such great respect for Lord Anshar, despite him being a therian. Why was it impossible for him to believe that there could be no other good therians in the world? Being reminded of Varg suddenly filled her with even more aching loneliness. Was he alive? What happened to the lycans? Lycans were so much more powerful than regular humans. Surely, they had survived. She had just lost her mother and she couldn't bear to believe that she might have lost her best friend too.

67

Halea looked for Lord Anshar to return his cloak to him, but he had already disappeared.

There was enough room in a large wagon for them, and when they finally reached the castle, many servants came running to help move the injured. Halea assumed Lord Anshar must have ridden ahead to warn them of their arrival. The castle was massive, with grand vaulted ceilings and beautiful marble pillars. Lord Anshar had lived many ages and amassed much wealth; it was he who funded the servants of the Citadel. Every servant of Tiamet received a stipend from Lord Anshar for their services. At the moment, the place was bustling with healers, servants, and Tiamet worshippers, but what was it actually like the rest of the time? Was it empty? It felt cold, and Halea wrapped the red cloak tighter around herself. She still had not found Lord Anshar, but she assumed he must be terribly busy.

As evening came, things began to quiet down. The injured had been tended to, and Halea's grandfather had left her to herself as he went to a meeting with some of the other clerics. She wandered the great halls and looked up at all the enormous portraits and sparkling glass windows. It was a beautiful place, but so cold. Her heart yearned for the forests around her city, for trees and grass and the songs of birds. At last, she couldn't stand the echoing of her footsteps anymore, and she ran outside.

She hated the immaculately manicured grounds around the castle. She wanted wild, untamed vegetation, but for now, this was the best she could get. She found a gravel footpath and followed it further away from the castle. The moon was beginning to wax, so there wasn't much light with which to see, but the stars offered some faint glow. The ocean waves crashed against the cliffs below, and the sea air was refreshing to breathe again after having spent the day inside the castle. She stopped as she noticed a figure standing near the edge looking out over the sea. She did not want to bother anyone, and she didn't want anyone to bother her, and so she decided to go back when she heard a familiar voice.

"Halea? Your name is Halea?"

Halea quickly turned to the man addressing her.

"Yes, sir…I mean, yes, Lord Anshar," she answered.

Lord Anshar made it a point to know all his clerics and priestesses, and he knew Uro well, and of course, Uro had mentioned, or rather, boasted blatantly, about his talented granddaughter.

Lord Anshar turned from the sea and regarded Halea. Despite the warmth of the summer night, she was still wrapped in his red cloak.

"Were you harmed?"

"No, not at all. I was hoping I would find you. I wanted to say thank you and give this back," Halea said while removing his cloak and offering it to him as she approached.

He accepted it from her, and once again, she saw that small wave of sadness pass over his eyes.

"Who did you lose in the city?" he asked.

The image of the city being swallowed up by the sea flashed before her eyes, and her heart lurched in agony.

"I'm sorry, I didn't mean to…" he quickly tried to amend when she blanched.

"My mother," Halea replied in a whisper as she looked down.

"I failed," he said, and she looked up into his face. "For too many ages, the convergence has come and gone, but it grows stronger, it grows…knowledgeable. It's changing, and we must change too if we are to survive," Lord Anshar said, more to himself than her. She was too young to understand the true nature of the Chaos that threatened their world, though she would know soon enough. Soon it would be her battle as well.

"You didn't!" she argued. "You still sent it away! It's no one's fault the ritual was disrupted. I…I still want to be a priestess."

Even after all she had lost, she still believed in him. She still believed in fighting the Chaos. Perhaps it was the naivety of her youth, but Lord Anshar smiled for the first time in a great many years.

"You still wish to serve?"

"Yes. Someday a way will be found. I know it. Maybe if I become a priestess, I'll live long enough to see it end."

"Then I, too, wish for you to see the end of this. May we all see the end," he said as he walked past her to return to the castle.

"Lord Anshar?"

"Yes, Halea?"

She paused for a moment. This was the great Lord Anshar, a demigod, perhaps she shouldn't ask, but he seemed to sense her hesitation.

"It is okay. Speak what you will."

She swallowed a little and mustered her courage. "You…you don't like it, do you? Having to sacrifice. I just…I thought you looked sad for a moment…I…I don't know what I'm asking, I guess."

*"Stupid. Stupid. Stupid,"* Halea thought to herself. What was she saying? Of course, he wouldn't like killing innocent priestesses. He wasn't a monster.

Lord Anshar regarded her silently for a moment. She had found just the right nerve, but he didn't hold it against her because he knew that it was true.

"No…I have regretted every single one, but there is no choice…until another way is found," he explained. As much as he hated what he had to do in those moments, he would always do it, no matter how it pained him. He was a descendant of Tiamet. It was his ordained duty to protect their world, and he would fulfill his duty, no matter what it cost him.

"I better go back before my grandfather chews me out," Halea hurriedly said as she dashed off back to the castle. She was afraid if she stayed one moment longer, she would open her mouth and say something really terrible, and she could already tell that she had upset him with her question.

~~~☼~~~

The next day Halea sat outside in the courtyard, trying her best not to let anyone see her cry. The loss of her mother was tormenting her. She had not slept that night for nightmares of seeing the city destroyed that plagued her every time she closed her eyes. She wanted to be alone, or at least she thought she did until she saw Lord

Anshar walking down one of the paths in the distance. Part of her wanted to speak with him again; the other part of her said that would be a terrible idea. She wasn't sure why, but she felt that if anyone had all the answers, surely it had to be him. Suddenly she heard a commotion and noticed a priestess running up the path towards Lord Anshar. Halea walked towards them but kept behind the hedges. She was downwind, and she hoped Lord Anshar wouldn't pick up her scent.

"Lord Anshar! I bring news," cried a priestess who Halea noticed had dark skin and soft curly hair. Her robes were dirty and disheveled and stained with what she could only assume was demon blood. The priestess dropped to her knees before the Lord.

The priestess did not wait for Lord Anshar to acknowledge her but kept her head bowed as she addressed him.

"My Lord, almost all of the priestesses sent into the western lycan territories were slain when the great tear opened. Only Kalee and I made it out alive. We barely escaped with our lives."

"And the lycans?" he asked.

"Slaughtered, my Lord. I am certain none survived. The demons were too many, even for therians. All tears were secured. Kalee and I will need to return to finish rooting out the surviving demons, of which there are many. I request all of the clerics that you can spare."

"You will have them. Is there anything else?"

"No, my Lord," the priestess replied before getting up and dashing away.

Halea had heard enough and ran in the opposite direction as fast as she could. She could barely see for the tears blinding her. It couldn't be true. It couldn't!

*"Varg, please be alive,"* she prayed.

~~~☼~~~

Summer ended, and Varg waited in anguish to return. Demon hordes had overrun their lands, and according to scouts, most of what they had once built was destroyed. For reasons they didn't understand, no smaller tears had opened since the convergence was banished. His father had become even colder and more reclusive since that day.

Ethelwolf had kindly offered to take in the refugees from the west for as long as they needed. He would not turn his back on the Wolf King, and he didn't blame him for the destruction that happened, but it was clear that Bledig blamed himself. Rafe's words had been like poison to him. As if he hadn't already been beaten enough by the loss of his mate.

Reclaiming their lands would take years. Often they sent out parties of their best warriors to exterminate as many demons as they could find. They had suffered too many losses to attempt open warfare against them again so soon without risking the blood of more lycans.

Varg lived every day in turmoil.

She had to be alive.

The city had high walls and secure gates. Surely, being under the protection of so many clerics and priestesses, the city had been spared from the destruction? He had to believe that. He couldn't bear to let himself think that Halea could really be gone. Losing his home and seeing his father's spirit further crushed had taken enough of a toll on him. He had become even more withdrawn and took no comfort in the company of his pack brothers and sisters. He couldn't banish the image of Bardolph lying dead; it haunted him every time he closed his eyes. He grew quiet and hardened as he accompanied the warriors on their treks into the west to root out the demon invaders. He relished in the thrill of every one he slaughtered. He was still young, but lycan boys were expected to mature early and contribute. Being with the older and more experienced warriors, helping his pack, gave him purpose. Blood rage threatened him every time he fought, and even though he was not an experienced warrior yet, he was quickly gaining respect from his elders. He would make every demon pay for what they had taken from him, for what they destroyed.

Fall passed into winter, and still, they went out searching, seeking and destroying, and picking off any enemies they could find. It seemed that the remaining demons were directionless and unable to open tears. Their numbers were significantly reduced, but they were still long from reclaiming their lands, and Varg could wait no longer.

One night, when the moon was high, Varg crept away from their camp. His father had led him and a band of their best warriors into the northwestern borders of their territory. He had not personally seen the den in many months but had heard of its devastation. He would try to skirt around the northern border of their territory from where they were camped and move westwards, towards the human city. He needed to see it. He needed to see that it was still there. What he wished to attempt would be dangerous, and he had no doubt that there would be many demons in his way, but he had grown accustomed to battling them and did not fear to go alone. His father and the others would quickly sense his disappearance. They were all using scent masking potion to remain undetected from the demon invaders, and they would not be able to follow him as the snowfall would quickly cover any tracks he left behind. He could return by morning if he ran through the night.

No one questioned him as he walked away from their camp. They were either asleep or assumed he had gone into the thick trees to relieve himself. As soon as he was far enough away, he transformed into his wolf form and ran with all his speed into the night.

Eventually, he heard the howls in the distance. They were calling for him, hoping he would return their call, but he couldn't. He hated to worry his father and the rest of his pack brothers and sisters, but with the scent masking potion, he had the luxury of being able to lie about his whereabouts. He would tell them he went looking for the den. They would understand the need to return home, they all felt empty without it, but he knew he wouldn't escape punishment from his father for taking such a risk and for not answering their howls that night. It was a price he was willing to pay.

As Varg ran through the snow-covered trees and over the many hills, he was able to avoid many demons by merely outrunning them. Occasionally he would be forced to fight, but for the first time in his life, he allowed the beast within to take control.

71

His blue eyes burned red, and his power and strength increased exponentially with every taste of demon blood. He tore into his enemies with claw and fang in a frenzy of unstoppable madness. He even managed to kill several of the more powerful humanoid demons that attempted to stop him. None could stand in his way. He would let nothing prevent him from reaching the western border of their territory - from reaching her.

The familiar scent of salty sea air grew stronger as he went, and at last, he reached the edge of the forest that boarded the coast. He shifted back into his humanoid form and dropped to his knees.

There was no city.

What he saw before him sent a stab of unbearable pain through his heart. The entire city of Ruinac had crumbled. The ocean waves drifted back and forth over what little remained of the once towering spires. The human harbor was completely wiped away by the sea, and far in the distance, where once the Citadel of the Sun stood tall and proud; was nothing. It, too, was gone.

She was gone.

Varg trembled uncontrollably as tears streamed down his cheeks, and he pounded the earth with his fists. No one could have survived in that place. No one.

He let out a long and keening howl into the cold night air.

# CHAPTER 9 – GOODBYE, MY FRIEND

Halea had grown very solemn. Nobody blamed her. They all knew she had watched as her mother died when the city was destroyed. What they didn't know was that she also grieved for the loss of her best friend. She did not want to believe that Varg was dead. Surely, lycans could not be so easily killed? Some, yes, but not all, not Varg. Varg was strong. Someday he would be the strongest lycan of all; of this, she was sure. He could not be among the dead, but her heart ached whenever she thought of the possibility. She had lost everything the day of the convergence. She needed to believe that somewhere he was still out there – alive.

Lord Anshar helped his clerics rebuild their lives within the small city surrounding the harbor, and so Uro and Halea were given a new home. They owed many thanks to Lord Anshar, but none more than when he requested to help Halea with her training.

With the Citadel gone, the castle of Lord Anshar became the new hub for the priestesses and clerics of Tiamet, and Uro had insisted that Halea accompany him whenever he needed to attend to any of his clerical duties at the Lord's castle. All her days had now become entirely devoted to her training, but she didn't mind. She had nothing else. She ended up spending a great deal of her time outside in those overly-manicured gardens. She still preferred them to being inside the castle, where she couldn't shake the feeling that she didn't belong.

Uro knew her pain at the loss of her mother. He had loved Theia too, as much as if she had been one of his own daughters, but he was pleased that Halea had taken her devastation and forged it into a new resolve for her future as a priestess. She no longer dragged her feet when he asked her to spar with him or complained when they went over spells and runes. She was already far faster and stronger than him, or any human, and her ability to quickly master the many techniques that he taught her filled him with pride.

Yet, with that pride came one pain. He wanted her to be a strong and powerful priestess. He wanted her to serve Tiamet and become immortal, but he did not want her to become the most powerful. Her life would be dangerous, but that was one danger he hoped would not be assigned to her fate. His duty would always make him put the Goddess first, but no grandfather would ever wish that on their grandchild, and he knew that it was selfish of him, but he couldn't help it.

Halea's power and skill caught the eye of Lord Anshar one day as he observed her practicing the many intricate stances for offense. Her talent was undeniable, and it

73

had been long since he offered to assist in the training of any potential priestesses, but he felt sorry for the girl. He felt guilty.

He had seen her devastation at the loss of her home and her mother, and he felt personally responsible. He had failed everyone that day. He hadn't closed the great tear in time to save the city, and she, as well as many of the other priestesses and clerics, had suffered loss and pain because of it.

The thing that unsettled him the most was that that young girl knew it. She knew his regret - his doubt. She had seen his pain, and there were many times when he walked the castle grounds and could feel her eyes upon him. When he looked at her, she didn't turn away. She never turned away.

Pity. She pitied him. She was always watching, looking for that one moment of vulnerability, and no matter how he tried, she always seemed to find it. She would be quiet and reserved with everyone, even her own grandfather, but when he was near, her face would light up with a smile, but her smile wasn't entirely genuine. He could see it in her eyes. She was smiling for him, just to make him feel better, but he knew there was no true joy in her heart. She would push aside her own pain just to try and ease his.

He had lived through many ages in solitude, revered as a demigod, a savior, but she did not see him that way. He was no infallible being to her, she saw something in him that was almost human, and she reminded him of it every time he looked at her.

He wanted to run from her taunting, insincere smiles, her kind words, and her gentle ways. He didn't want her pity. He hated it. No one concerned themselves with him beyond his function as the right hand of the Goddess, but she did, and while it bothered him, he couldn't help but be drawn into those false smiles. There were times as he worked with her on her combat technique that she managed to make him forget, if only for a moment, that he wasn't the mighty Lord Anshar, descendant of Tiamet, but just a man. There were times when he smiled with her, and when he did, her smile changed - it was no longer false. The moments when she genuinely pleased him changed her and made her truly happy because his happiness was what she wanted. No one had ever wanted such a thing from him before. No one had ever cared whether he was happy or not, as long as he fulfilled his duty to the Goddess. Yet, despite all that she tried to give him, there was nothing he could ever offer her to ease her own pain, and it only served to increase his guilt.

A year had passed since the day the convergence destroyed the city, and he waited patiently outside for Halea to arrive for her lesson for the day. Uro was in charge of her training most of the time, but at least once a week, he would meet with her to gauge her progress and provide additional instruction.

"You are late today," he commented when she finally came running up the path that led to the grass patch where they trained.

"I'm sorry, Lord Anshar. Grandfather forgot to wake me this morning before he left," she explained while trying to catch her breath. She never bowed before him, a fact that enraged Maven, but he had reminded the High Priestess that Halea was not yet one of them and that she was still a young girl. Though, in the year since the great tear, Halea was beginning to grow into a young woman. Truthfully, he preferred that

74

she didn't treat him as the others did. He should. He should demand greater respect from her and curb her informal behavior, but he could never bring himself to do it.

He could smell deceit from her. Something else had delayed her that day, but not every secret was his business to discover, so he ignored it.

"Did you practice the dragon strike sequence?" he asked, referring to one of the combat techniques he had taught her from the week before.

"Yes, my Lord," she replied with a beaming smile, an honest one. She was usually very enthusiastic to please him as a pupil.

He pulled his spear out of the ground and faced her. Halea raised her own spear and prepared to enter the first stance.

He had insisted she be given a proper spear, even though she wasn't yet a priestess. The weight and balance of a spear were something he wanted her to get used to; it would be her truest ally in the years ahead.

He moved in with a series of quick strikes, twirling his spear so fast that a regular human's eyes would never have seen it, but Halea was ready for him and put up every appropriate block, and much to his surprise, an additional one that he had not taught her. She enjoyed doing such things to him, trying to catch him off guard. It was an antagonizing little game of hers that she loved to play, but he allowed it. Unexpected moves were an advantage, and he did not mind her challenges.

She easily dodged the thrusts of his spear and quickly shifted into the offensive maneuvers of the intricate dragon-strike style. He couldn't hide his slight smile of appreciation as she flawlessly demonstrated the technique, as well as throwing in a few additional strikes based on a modification of the existing maneuvers. He had only narrowly dodged one of these modified attacks when he saw the gleam of satisfaction in her eyes as she watched his stoic composure break ever so subtly under the unexpected maneuver.

At last, they ended their dance-like duel, and he waited for her to catch her breath.

"Almost had you," she taunted with a carefree laugh.

"You did well," he offered, not wanting to concede too much. "Now that you have mastered dragon-strike, we shall begin working on the tiger claw technique."

"Lord Anshar?" she asked, and he could detect the scent of her growing nervous.

He merely looked at her and nodded, giving her permission to speak on whatever was troubling her.

"I…well…I heard Mama Dragon talking to Kalee and Samesa this morning on the way here. They said the demons that invaded Ruinac have been nearly completely subjugated. Is…is that true?"

Though they had lost many priestesses and clerics with the opening of the great tear, the remaining servants of Tiamet had worked tirelessly to exterminate all traces of the evil beings that poured into their world that day. What did not help was the unfortunate knowledge that new tears were once again appearing. Usually, after a convergence is stopped, there are at least a few decades of complete peace without the appearance of tears, but deep in his heart, he knew something had gone horribly wrong.

"The ruins of what remains of the holy city have been completely cleared of any remaining servants of Chaos, and much of the surrounding area has been wiped clean as well," he confirmed.

"I want to go," she blurted.

He felt as if she had shoved a knife between his ribs. Why? Why would she want to return to that place of death? Her mother was gone; she knew this. Seeing her destroyed home would only torment her and force her to relive that day again, and worse, to imagine what her mother's final moments must have been like. How could she not blame him for having allowed that to happen? He should have known the demons would focus themselves on attacking Ami that day. He should have sacrificed her as soon as the smaller tears opened when he still had the chance. He had failed Tiamet by choosing to defend those around him instead, and even in that, he had failed. Ami had been their target, and he should have known. He had long suspected that there was a purpose within the Chaos, and that day proved it.

"There is nothing for you there," he finally replied.

She watched that familiar pained look pass over his face. He did not like thinking about that day. She knew he held himself responsible, and it pained her because she genuinely believed he did all that he could. He had chosen to defend rather than complete the sacrifice because, deep down, he did not like having to kill the priestesses to stop the convergence. Within that moment, protecting life had meant more to him. True, the sacrifice would have prevented even more deaths. It was for the greater good, but such decisions are hard to make in moments of pandemonium, and he had gone with his instinct to protect those around him instead. His choice had cost her her mother, her home, and possibly even her best friend. She should be angry with him. She should hate him for having not put his duty first, but she couldn't. Though he was a descendant of the Goddess, a mighty therian Lord, she knew he was as flawed on the inside as any human. Having spent so many years with Varg, she appreciated that therians had more human qualities and emotions than people realized, perhaps even more so than therians themselves realized. If the attack on the Citadel had not happened, he wouldn't have hesitated to fulfill his duty as expected; of this, she had no doubts.

"I know. I need…closure. I need answers. I never got to say goodbye," Halea explained while trying to fight back the tears that welled up in her eyes, though she wasn't speaking of her mother.

Lord Anshar closed his eyes and inhaled deeply in frustration. How could he deny her? How could he take away her right to know, her right to heal? He owed her at least that much.

Finally, he opened his eyes again. "I will tell Uro that he may be excused from his duties so that he may take you…"

"No!" she interrupted. "Please…I want to go alone. I can take care of myself. The demons have been slain, and if there are any still, I can protect myself. Grandfather would not want me to go."

He suddenly realized why she was seeking his permission.

"Very well, your grandfather will not stop you. If you wish to go, then go, but you must not stay long."

"I won't! I promise! I'll be careful, and I will return."

~~~☼~~~

Halea looked back at the ruined city from where she stood near the border of the forest. She had not come to see that place. She would be happy if she never saw it again. It reminded her of that day, that day that still tortured her every time she closed her eyes. She shuddered at the fleeting thought of what her mother's last moments must have been like in that place, and she brushed a tear from her face, turned her back to her old home, and quickly ran into the woods.

The forest looked wrong now. Flowers no longer bloomed, and many things weren't growing as they once did. She could no longer hear birds singing or see small animals playing as she walked along the stream that led to the fern patch. All of her senses were on high alert due to the unnerving silence. She had managed to avoid encountering any demons on her journey so far, but the threat was still there. She instinctively made her way to their forts. They were abandoned, as she expected, but not too badly in disrepair. It had only been a year, but being there without Varg was causing a terrible ache in her heart. She had to find him, and she knew he would not return to that place.

She went back outside and began gathering the herbs needed to make the masking potion. Once she had everything she needed, she went back into Varg's fort, found the old pottery mixing bowl, and prepared the potion. She would need to go back to his den. It was the only way. They couldn't have all been slaughtered, not all, not Varg! Someone had to still be there - he had to still be there.

Once she was confident that her scent was masked, she began her journey across what had once been the lycan western hunting grounds, but the further she ventured into their territory, the more her hopes were crushed. There were no herd animals to be seen anywhere. Had they all been chased off or devoured by the demons? How could Varg's pack survive without their prey? Surely they had other hunting grounds, perhaps further north? This couldn't be all that was left.

At last, she reached the vantage point, where she and Varg once observed his pack from a distance. She made her way to the top and looked out towards the den.

And she burst into tears.

Without her grandfather's telescope, she couldn't make out many details from such a distance, but there was no sign of movement in the den. It had been so lively before. Now, no fires were burning, no children were playing, and no families were gathered. Several of the mighty trees that once had houses built into them were either cut down or burned to the ground. If lycans were still there, they would have repaired such damage by now. They wouldn't have allowed their den to be in such disarray.

*"No! It can't be! Someone must be there!"* she thought while racing back down the hill and towards the den, not caring that if there were any lycans still around, she would be in great danger to come so close. She needed to believe that perhaps she just couldn't see from the great distance, and if only she got closer, things would be okay.

But things were not okay. Halea knew the moment she reached the den; she was all alone.

She felt something hard under her foot and looked down in horror to find a bone, a humanoid bone, and that was when she truly looked at the ground. Bones of lycans were strewn all around her. She buried her face in her hands and sobbed uncontrollably.

It was true. They had all been slaughtered.

She collapsed in a heap upon the ground and let loose every painful emotion she had been bottling up inside.

He was gone. Varg.

Her mother, her home, her best friend – everything had been taken from her.

She laid there for hours and cried until she could barely breathe anymore for sobbing. At last, she stopped and lay there defeated and weary. Something glinting in the distance caught her eye, and she rolled over to see it better. She crawled to where the strange object lay, and there, half-buried in the dirt, lay Varg's blue crystal, the one she had given him as a present. The weathered cord had obviously been cut. Varg would have never taken it off. She knew without a doubt – he was dead.

She clutched the crystal to her chest as fresh tears trail down her face.

Suddenly she heard a strange sound, a gurgling, growling noise. She looked behind her in time to see a shambling humanoid demon coming her way; its gruesome steely claws outstretched towards her.

Halea leaped to her feet and quickly found her spear where it lay on the ground, and with fury in her heart, she attacked the beast with all her might. But she wouldn't kill it quickly. No, she would make it suffer. First, she slashed its legs out from underneath it. The eyeless wraith howled in pain as it collapsed to the ground, where she stabbed it repeatedly with her spear, refusing to deliver the killing blow and relishing in its agony as it pulled out one of its dark daggers and tried to attack from where it lay. At last, her seething hatred could stand it no longer, and she lopped off its head.

Halea stood there panting and trembling with rage.

This was it. This was all that was left for her now.

# CHAPTER 10 – LEADER OF THE PACK

Varg wasn't punished for the night when he ran into the woods to look for the human city. They had all been worried about him and went looking for him, but when he returned the next morning safely, they could clearly see by the black blood staining his claws that he had encountered many demons that night.

When Bledig asked him why he had run off, he couldn't smell deception when Varg said he returned to the den due to the lingering effects of the masking potion, but he could see the discomfort in his son's eyes as he stared him down.

Varg waited for his father to strike him for his disobedience, but he was surprised when Bledig only turned his back to him and led the warriors back to their temporary home.

Bledig would not begrudge his son for wanting to return to the den. He could never imagine any other reason for his son wanting to disappear into the night, and so he questioned him no further. They had all lost their home, and he knew he would never again return to that place. In the years to come, it would be Varg who would have to reclaim their lands.

Since the coming of the great tear and the day of destruction, Bledig somehow managed to grow even more cold and distant.

Batsuba watched as the young wolf cub grew to mimic his father in his withdrawn behavior. She suspected it was entirely due to him knowing that Bledig would not live much longer and that the loss of his last parent weighed heavily upon his young shoulders. She could not imagine that the true anguish that dwelled within the young wolf lay in more than just the loss of his home and father.

In truth, Varg had already accepted his father's ways, and for once, he understood him. Losing Halea had utterly crushed his spirit. She had been more than just his best friend. He had allowed himself, if only for a moment, to imagine growing up with her and them never being apart. Now that she was gone, he felt as if a gaping hole had opened in his heart, and there was room for nothing else.

He focused himself on becoming a better and stronger warrior under his father's training. He went on every hunting party, especially if they were hunting demons, and as he grew older, he became even more venerated for his value to the pack.

His pack brothers and sisters knew the path he was destined for, and in time, he would be their new alpha. The young wolf cub males all looked up to him and followed his every order. Almost all of the females vied for his attentions, especially Otsana, who took advantage of their temporary displacement to constantly throw herself in Varg's path. The eastern pack had offered them a place to stay until they could reclaim their lands, but Varg hated that they were forced to interact with the eastern pack so much. It was not that he disliked other lycans outside of his own pack; it was that Otsana had set her eyes on him, and he knew she only wanted him because he would someday become a pack leader.

Lycans were not a prudish society. Sex outside of a mated relationship was not taboo, and it was naturally expected that young lycans, both male and female, would sow their wild oats before settling down with their one true mate if they ever chose to mate at all. Lycans did not experience love the way fickle humans did. Once a lycan fell in love, they knew it without a doubt. Their chosen love was the one and only person who could ever be their mate. If their chosen rejected them or died before they could be mated, it was not impossible for that lycan to let go and perhaps fall in love with someone else, but it was extremely difficult, and for some, it could take decades, even centuries, to get over their heartbreak. With a mating bond having never been established, that lycan could live on and perhaps find another, but once mated, there would never be anyone else. The bond between a mated pair could never be broken, not even by death. Unmated lycans, or lycans who were not in love, could couple with each other freely.

Yet, Varg was simply not interested in partaking in the physical pleasures that his peers were beginning to discover amongst each other. Whenever a female would become amorous towards him, he would instantly become uncomfortable, as if he were betraying someone, and would quickly distance himself. His aloof indifference only seemed to further incite the females to pursue him. He and Halea had only been children, and he knew as he grew older, it wouldn't be wise to hang onto a childhood crush.

"She was a human. It would have never worked anyway," he would think.

Someday he would be the alpha male of his pack, and while there were unmated alphas, they were considered *incomplete* without an equally strong alpha female for a mate. Packs always thrived best under the reign of an alpha pair. His childhood hopes and dreams were forever gone, and the day may come when he would have to choose another, but every time he tried to convince himself of this, his stomach would clench, and his heart would ache. Why couldn't he just let go?

The years rolled by, and Varg had finally grown into a man. Powerful muscles and towering height replaced the scrawny frame of his boyhood. He looked much like his father, except for his eyes, and his voice had grown deep and authoritative.

One night, Bledig came to his son, who was sitting outside under the full harvest moon, gazing up at the stars.

"Tomorrow will be the eighteenth year of your birth, and you will be a man."

Varg closed his eyes as his heart wrenched. He had spent the many years since his mother's death dreading this moment. He rose to his feet and faced his father. The pain in Bledig's eyes was undeniable, but also so was his resolve. He, too, had waited long for this time to come.

"I understand, father. I will fight for the right to lead this pack. I will not disappoint you," he promised while trying his best not to let too much of his emotion show. There could be no tears.

Bledig nodded. "The elders will keep the Fang until the next wolf gathering can be called. I am counting on you not to let it fall into the wrong hands."

Just because Varg could become the leader of their pack didn't mean he would be the supreme leader of all the packs until he had challenged the other lycan alphas. Wolf gatherings did not happen regularly, and they could survive for several years without an established Wolf King before the time came when a supreme alpha would need to be decided. When that time came, he had no doubt that Rafe would be his biggest threat. Rafe had once challenged his father for the right to bear the Great Fang and lost, and he would stop at nothing to finally become king. His father had never forgiven Rafe for his defiance on the day of the convergence.

"When the time comes, I will fight to the death. I swear it."

"Goodbye, son. Don't think that I am not proud of you. You have been my only reason for living since your mother died. If you ever choose a mate, no matter what, let no one take her from you," he said as he embraced his son one last time, then turned and walked away into the forest.

Varg never saw his father again.

~~~☼~~~

Everyone knew of Bledig's fate. Many had wept and grieved because even though he lost his desire to lead the pack after the death of his mate, he had done his best and been their king for centuries. All eyes turned to Varg, and he wasted no time stating his intent to lead the pack.

Only two challenged him. One was a lycan male named Hemming. He was only fifty years old, which in lycan years still made him practically a cub, but he was a strong and respected warrior of the pack. Lyall, the other challenger, was many centuries old and had actually been one of his father's oldest friends. Lyall did not really wish to be alpha, but he doubted Hemming would provide enough challenge in battle against Varg, and he knew all too well that an alpha would never truly be respected if his leadership was just given to him. Almost the entire pack had already decided to stand behind Varg and support him in being their new leader, but it was not a democracy. Strength and power were the lycan way, and Varg would have to prove that he possessed the qualities needed to lead his people. Lyall challenged only so that it would not seem that he had earned his position too easily.

As expected, Hemming was no match for Varg in single combat, though the entire pack admired that he had even dared to try. Lyall, on the other hand, was not so easily defeated. Varg had taken a severe injury to the chest that bled profusely during the battle, but it was nothing that wouldn't heal in a day or two. In the end, he pinned his challenger, and Lyall was forced to bare his throat in a sign of submission to his new alpha.

Many from the eastern lycan pack came to witness the choosing of the new alpha, and Otsana was thrilled at knowing that Varg had risen to her expectations. In time a new Wolf King would be chosen, and she knew in her heart that it would be

81

him. He was cold to her and rebuffed all of her advances, but who was more suited to be his mate? She steeled her resolve. One way or another, she would win him.

Varg was one of the youngest alpha pack leaders in over an age, and though his people would obey and respect him, he would still have to prove himself in ways other than strength. Should he prove to be an inept leader, another pack member could challenge him in an attempt to displace him. Once a leader was established, it was rare that any others would try to overthrow him, but it was not unheard of.

His first decision as leader was to announce that he and his pack would be returning to the west. Almost all of the demons were gone, and in the years since, some of the herds had even returned to their hunting lands. It was time to rebuild. He would take back his homeland.

<center>~~~☼~~~</center>

Halea felt her heart pounding in her chest as she put on the white robe of a priestess. It was oddly comfortable, but she supposed it would have to be for what was expected of her. She grabbed her spear and took a deep breath. She turned eighteen in the fall, but now it was winter, and Lord Anshar had finally returned. She had not seen him in almost two years. He had been called away across the sea to supervise the building of a new temple by the clerics in that country. He had also commissioned the mer-therians to help rebuild the Citadel of the Sun, though it would take many years to finish it. Her training was complete. She was ready. It was time for her to take the oath.

A knock at the door caused her to jump a little, though it was only her grandfather.

"I'm ready," she told him through the door, and he allowed himself in. He beamed with pride when he beheld her in her robe. His glasses had only gotten thicker in the past years, but she could still see how his eyes lit up at the sight of her. Uro had waited many years to have a priestess in his family, and he knew that Halea would please the Goddess.

Halea always knew that she would choose to take the oath and devote herself to the Dragon Mother. Her determination to be a great priestess had only increased with time, but still, she was nervous. Once she swore her services to the Goddess before Lord Anshar, she would forever be changed. She would become an immortal and leave her grandfather behind to go out into the great, wide world to battle the forces of Chaos. This was the day she considered her childhood to be truly and officially over.

As she walked with her grandfather through the halls of Lord Anshar's castle, she heard some of her priestess friends running up to her excitedly. In the years of her training since the great tear, many of the priestesses had become her friends. Unlike regular humans, priestesses understood the gifts of Tiamet, for they were all blessed. Halea had grown to care for them all, but no friend would ever be dearer to her than Varg had been.

Uro nodded, giving his silent approval for Halea to have a moment alone with her friends, then he went on ahead.

Kalee fidgeted with joy at the sight of her young friend in a priestess robe at last. "You look beautiful! You could have any man you want looking like that," she teased,

82

causing Halea to blush. Kalee was a fiery redhead with brilliant blue eyes and dimples when she smiled. Kalee was also completely boy crazy. She perpetually acted like a teenager, though she was well over a hundred years old. Kalee had taken many clerics as casual lovers and any regular men who also took her fancy. She was not shy about her many exploits and often teased Halea for still being a virgin.

"What are you saving it for? It's not like we can get married," she would often say.

Priestesses were forbidden from having attachments that would get in the way of their service to the Goddess; love, marriage, or having children were forbidden to them, but sex was not prohibited, and there were spells to prevent pregnancy. It was seen as a bodily need, and as long as no lasting attachments took place, and the priestess never shirked her duty, she was allowed to indulge in the pleasures of the flesh if she should so choose. Kalee was very indulgent.

Samesa gave Halea one of her brilliant smiles that lit up the whole room. Samesa was nearest to Halea in age, and they had grown close since Halea came to the castle. Samesa had no problem in finding men who were more than anxious to get beneath her double-layered robes. Her smile beguiled everyone who looked upon her, and she exuded an undeniable charisma that made Halea feel awkward in comparison.

Some of the young male clerics who frequented the castle had taken notice of Halea in the past years. She was no longer the gangly little girl with the wild hair and a face full of freckles. Her body had filled out voluptuously, her hair had grown long and flowing, and her freckles had almost entirely faded. Mama Dragon took it upon herself to give Halea the talk about sex and becoming a woman that her own mother never got to give her, and of course, the other priestesses were more than willing to educate her. But whenever men approached her, she still had no idea what to make of their behavior. She was aware that some men had grown to desire her physically, and some of these men were quite attractive, but there was a nagging voice somewhere in the back of her mind telling her to avoid them. She couldn't explain why she didn't have the normal inclinations of a girl her age. She simply felt nothing for any man.

"Well, that's good! You're not supposed to feel anything for them. A priestess's duty is to avoid attachments," Kalee would argue.

Despite her friend's encouragement, Halea just knew in her heart; she wasn't ready. Ready for what? Wait for whom? She didn't know, but there was no rush. Perhaps someday, she would give in to the temptations of the flesh, but she would wait until she was ready, and only she would know the time.

"Where's Mama Dragon?" asked Halea.

"She's already in the great hall. Almost everyone is assembled. They're just waiting on Lord Anshar and you, so let's hurry," replied Samesa.

Halea felt another nervous quake inside as they headed towards the great hall. Most priestesses and clerics made a point to attend oath ceremonies, they didn't happen often, and they were always a sacred occasion. The moment she entered the great hall, her friends stepped to the side, and all eyes fell upon her as she walked up the aisle. Before her stood Lord Anshar, dressed in his armor and red cloak, the same way he had appeared on the day when her world was destroyed. She flinched and tried not to remember that day.

Beside Lord Anshar stood High Priestess Maven, her face as impassive as stone. Next to the High Priestess stood another priestess that Halea had only just met, Denji; she had returned with Lord Anshar from across the sea. Her skin was dark but not as dark as Samesa's, and the bone structure of her regal face told of a foreign and far away land. Her eyes and short bobbed hair were as black as ink. She was beautiful, and if not for being a priestess, Halea believed she was lovely enough to be a queen or some other woman of great nobility. Tiamet chose her priestesses from all over the world, and many came from strange faraway lands and exotic places that Halea could only imagine.

Halea looked around and noticed her grandfather standing among the other clerics, and over with a group of priestesses, she found Mama Dragon.

Mama Dragon was only her nickname. Her real name was Sophia, though only Lord Anshar and High Priestess Maven called her by her given name. To all the other priestesses and clerics, she was Mama Dragon.

The cutoff age for swearing the oath was roughly in the mid-forties. Once the oath is sworn and immortality bestowed, it is as if the sands of time stop. Most girls and young women blessed by the Goddess pledged their oath in their late teens or early twenties, but some blessed by the Goddess lived in faraway lands and remote places where the Goddess wasn't even known or worshiped. Such was the case with Mama Dragon. She was raised in a small village in a war-torn country far across the sea. She had always been different and more powerful than other human women, but it hadn't stopped her from leading a full life. She once had a husband and even children. But the ravages of war destroyed her village and took the lives of her entire family, including her oldest daughter, who had been twenty years old and about to be married. In her pain and devastation, she fled, and she had wished for death until a cleric found her and brought her to Lord Anshar. With nothing else to live for, she swore an oath to serve the great Dragon Goddess.

Even though many priestesses were older than Mama Dragon in actual years, none appeared older than her physically. Because of this, she saw the other priestesses, not so much as contemporaries but as children. Often the younger-looking priestesses would remind her of her own lost daughter, so she would dote on them in a motherly and often overly protective manner. On top of her kind and loving nature, she was undoubtedly a fierce and powerful priestess in her own right. Never was she known to fight more viciously than when fighting alongside other priestesses. All of the priestesses loved her because they all knew she would give her very life to protect them. To them, she was Mama Dragon, and it was a name that she wore with honor and pride.

Mama Dragon smiled and winked at Halea as she passed by. No one would ever replace her own mother, but Mama Dragon had been there for her in her times of need. Halea had been a girl when she came to the castle, and Mama Dragon had instantly taken her under her wing.

Lord Anshar watched as Halea came and stood before him, the hilt of The Blade That Cuts Through Worlds clasped tightly between his hands. He had not seen her in the past two years and was surprised she had changed so much in just that time, but he tried not to focus on it. He had a duty to perform.

Halea dropped to one knee before him and looked up into his silvery eyes as he lifted the blade horizontally before her. A flash of dread pierced his heart as he looked into her shining eyes, and he prayed that she would never again come before his blade.

"Will you swear upon this holy blade that you will devote your life to Tiamet, and only Tiamet? Will you serve this world and all life upon it? Will you vanquish Chaos wherever it may be, and if asked of you, will you lay down your life if the Goddess wills it so?"

"I swear upon the Holy Blade That Cuts Through Worlds, my life and soul belong to Tiamet. I will go where she leads me. I will do as she wills. I will devote myself to the Great Mother Dragon, and I will defeat Chaos by her hand," she replied the well-rehearsed oath.

Lord Anshar watched as she reached forth her trembling hand and laid it upon the blunt edge of the blade. At that moment, he felt the power of the Goddess flow through him and into the holy sword which glowed before him. The light spread into the kneeling priestess until she too glowed with the heavenly light of the Goddess, and then it was gone. Her immortality had been bestowed.

"Rise Priestess Halea, servant of Tiamet," he declared.

For the next two years, Halea roamed the land, hunting demons and closing tears, which were becoming far too frequent considering that the convergence had only happened eight years prior. Everyone who served the Goddess had a terrible sense of foreboding, and none more so than Lord Anshar. He made sure to return from across the sea with some of the strongest priestesses he could find, hoping he would not need them but dreading the inevitable. Halea had managed to become undeniably powerful since he helped train her when she was a girl, and it worried him.

He had grown very fond of her while he had trained her. When he was with her, he had allowed himself to be happy. At first, he only did it to please her so she wouldn't try so hard to lift his spirits, but as she became older, he grew to genuinely enjoy and look forward to their time together. Her thirst for knowledge and her enthusiasm to learn everything that he imparted to her was appreciated, but it was the way she looked at him that eventually wore through his defenses. At first, he hated that she looked at him as a flawed creature, as something to be pitied, but in time, he realized that she wanted to see beyond the visage that he wore like a mask. For her, he had become a friend, and he could tell she was trying to let him know that he could turn to her for someone to understand, to listen, to forgive - but that he could not allow. He was the right-hand servant of the Goddess. He could not afford to let emotions or instincts get in the way of his duty. He made that mistake once; he could never do it again.

# CHAPTER 11 – TOGETHER AGAIN

Varg was alive. After eight long years of thinking that she had lost her dearest friend, Halea had found him again, in the same place where they had once played as children.

Varg listened intently as she explained all that happened since the last day he saw her. He told her how he became an alpha and brought his pack back to their territory and of how they had spent the past three years rebuilding their home.

He couldn't take his eyes off her. He was almost afraid to blink for fear that he would wake from some dream. Halea was alive, and she was really there with him once again.

"I'm sorry about your father, Varg. I wish I could have been there for you. If only I had known. If only I had known all along. I'm so proud of you, though," she added with a warm smile. "Finally, the big bad alpha that you always said you'd be. Not that I doubted you, but you were pretty cocky as a kid."

She couldn't get over how different his voice was now, as he laughed a deep laugh at her jibe.

"Cocky? I seem to recall you always going on and on about someday being a priestess. You were pretty sure of yourself for a puny human."

"Like I'd let some mangy wolf convince me otherwise," she laughed.

It felt good to casually taunt her old friend again, almost as if they had never been apart. They stayed together in the old tree fort, catching up until the sun began to sink into the west.

"I didn't mean to return to this place, but I couldn't help myself once I was so close. I was tracking a demon. I think there's an open tear somewhere nearby."

Varg's expression turned hard, and his eyes narrowed.

"I was tracking a demon myself, that is until your scent distracted me. My pack has fought hard to keep these lands free of their filth, but now it seems their numbers are growing again."

"The tears are growing numerous, more numerous than they should be considering the last convergence was only eight years ago. They shouldn't be this frequent again, at least not for another century. We've never experienced anything like this before. As if tears weren't unpredictable enough. I have to find that tear and seal it, or more demons will come. Demons tend to congregate where another dimensional rift is about to appear. I don't know if we were tracking the same demon or two different ones, but I sense this area might be a focal point for Chaos, as it was the last time. I'm sorry, Varg. I'll try to stop it."

"And if they move further into lycan territory?" he asked, knowing full well what would be expected. It was not that he had a problem with Halea coming into his territory; far from it, he would prefer for her to remain close, but the other lycans would not like it. They remembered what happened the last time they accepted the help of human priestesses. If he put her under his protection, none within his own pack would harm her, as none would dare to defy their alpha, but he had no authority over the other packs – yet.

"I hope it won't come to that. For now, I should have no reason to go beyond the boundaries of your hunting grounds."

"What happens if the tears subside after you close them?"

"Then I must leave and continue my duties elsewhere," she replied, with a note of regret in her voice. She wished she could stay as long as possible. Being with Varg again felt like being home, but she was a priestess now. She had sworn an oath to Tiamet to put her duty above all else. She had to go where she was needed, and she couldn't linger where she was not.

It would be better for Varg and his pack if she weren't needed. If the tears could not be purged from their lands, that could pose a serious danger for his people.

Not that Varg wanted demons or tears anywhere near his territories, but he wasn't ready to give Halea up yet. He had only just found her after thinking she was dead. He didn't want to see her leave again so soon.

"I will help you track these demons. It's my duty as alpha to defend my territory," he stated with authority.

Halea's face brightened again. She certainly wouldn't mind his company or his help.

"Thank you, Varg."

~~~☼~~~

The moon was bright, giving her enough light to see as she followed Varg as he ran into the forest. Halea usually avoided tracking demons after sundown as their senses were at their strongest and most deadly in the night. It was best to hunt them in the daytime when they were at a disadvantage. But Varg was anxious to pick up the scent of the trail he had been following earlier that day, and a lycan's eyes could see just as well at night as they could during the day. They could also go as much as two weeks without needing sleep.

Halea didn't complain as they sped through the night, and despite the dark, she was almost positive she saw Varg grinning as she kept pace. They had both grown even faster since their childhood days of racing each other, and she had a feeling that he was testing her, challenging her to keep up.

Varg came to an abrupt halt, and Halea skidded to avoid running into him. He had picked up a fresh scent on the wind. They were close.

She tightened her grip on her spear as they slowly moved through the underbrush, being careful to make no sound.

Varg wasn't usually so patient with his prey, but they couldn't afford to rush out and attack right away. They needed the beast to lead them to the tear.

It was a hideous bipedal creature with a long dragging tail and thick, hulking arms. Its face tapered due to a long snout and a mouth filled with gleaming razor-sharp teeth. It possessed no eyes, yet it stood amongst the trees regarding the space around it as though it were watching for danger. Its wide nostrils sniffed the air, but they were downwind of the creature, and it failed to pick up their scent before it turned and made its way up a slope into a denser part of the forest. Halea was just getting up from where she crouched to pursue it when Varg grabbed her wrist. At first, she was confused, but he motioned with a nod for her to look again. Another shape was moving slowly in the same direction as the other demon.

This demon was far more humanoid and wrapped in a black cloak that flowed like smoke as it moved among the trees. Usually armed with a dark weapon, the humanoid demons were far more intelligent and deadly.

Halea was sure the first demon had been the one to escape her from before and that the tear was very close.

They watched as the demon disappeared over the same slope as the other, and they stealthily fell in behind it. Halea could no longer see where the wraith had wandered, but Varg seemed locked onto its scent, and so she stayed close to him.

At last, Halea could see the all too familiar purple glow in the distance, and her purification powers flared up in anticipation. Surrounding the strange light were far more than just the two demons they had followed. There appeared to be a large gathering close to the tear.

There was no further need for secrecy with the tear located, and they rushed in for the attack. Halea charged her spear with her power and leaped on one of the more primitive-looking beasts, which roared just before it exploded into a blinding white light. Several more bipedal creatures rushed in to attack her, but she easily fended them off and destroyed them with her still flashing weapon.

Varg mercilessly tore into one of the more humanoid demons that dared to challenge him with one of its dark blades, his claws easily shredding the wraith whose black blood stained the trees. Several more of the wraiths sprang in for the attack, and Varg could feel the familiar tinge of red begin to bleed into his eyes, but he fought to suppress it. He had never been in a blood rage around Halea and didn't want to take the chance of her getting hurt while he was in that state. The beast within could be unpredictable.

Halea watched as Varg eliminated several more humanoid demons, showing them no mercy as he viciously tore them limb from limb. A shudder rolled down her spine as she witnessed a side to him that she had never seen. It wasn't that she feared Varg, but she had never seen him behave so brutally before.

Once she was convinced he could hold back the remaining demons, she turned her attention to the swirling eerie light of the tear. No matter how many tears she closed, she could never shake the horror of being so close to one. She could feel it through every fiber of her being, the horrible evil that dwelt within the realm of Chaos. She quickly averted her eyes, trying not to stare directly into the purple light as she raised her hands. This tear was large, but she had sealed worse. She called upon the Goddess's power and focused all her strength on sealing the dimensional rift.

Amidst fighting the remaining demons, Varg was able to look over and see that Halea was facing the tear and that it had become smaller than it was when they arrived.

When by herself, Halea usually had no choice but to eliminate every demon surrounding the tear before she would have the ability to concentrate enough to close it, but she trusted Varg to keep the remaining demons away from her. She wanted to close it before more reinforcements from the Chaos Dimension emerged.

Varg was down to only two more wraiths, which stood before him wielding their dark blades when suddenly his ears detected a strange sound coming from the tear.

Halea was still focusing all her energy on sealing the dimensional rift. It was shrinking and close to snapping shut when Varg shouted from a distance.

"Halea, get back!"

He quickly slaughtered the two remaining demons and raced towards her, but he was too late. Several more humanoid demons sprang forth from the nearly sealed tear, and one leaped towards Halea while slashing its dark weapon. She tried to dodge but wasn't quick enough and cried out as the blade sank into her hip.

Varg watched as she collapsed to the ground, and his eyes burned red the moment the metallic scent of her blood hit him. He dove towards the demon that was raising its blade for another strike. The other demons that emerged quickly scattered, but Varg focused on the one who stood before Halea.

Everything happened so quickly. One moment the tear was just about to close, and the next, Halea had been rushed by demons, and now she lay injured, but before the wraith could strike again, she felt her powers flow through her. She was about to raise her hand to purify the demon that wounded her when she felt a rush of air, and the wraith was gone. She heard a vicious snarl and turned to see that Varg had flown into a terrible rage and was shredding the wraith limb from limb. She almost couldn't recognize him. His features were suddenly so much more wild, and his eyes! The beautiful blue was replaced with a glowing blood red. Even his fangs and claws were longer and more deadly.

When there was nothing left but mangled bones and shredded flesh, Varg threw back his head and let out a primal howl.

"Varg?" Halea called. She needed to bring him back. Whatever gripped him had yet to subside, and when he turned his burning eyes and flashing fangs towards her, her heart almost stopped.

"Varg, it's me, it's Halea. It's okay now," she said in a low and soothing voice. The tear had shrunk, but it seemed stable at its smaller size, and the remaining demons that emerged from it had scattered into the forest.

Varg sniffed the wind. The wolf within him was raging to track and hunt the ones that escaped, but the scent of Halea's blood and fear and the sound of her voice snapped him to attention. He could see the fear in her eyes as she laid there, her white priestess robe stained with blood.

Again, everything happened so quickly. One moment Halea was looking into Varg's burning eyes, and the next thing she knew, he had sprung to her side and scooped her up from the ground. She wanted to protest, but he let out a low rumbling growl, and she could feel the vibration in his chest as he held her close. There was a rush of wind all around her as they sped off into the woods, leaving the tear far behind.

It was hard for Halea to tell where he was taking her at first, but soon she began to recognize familiar landmarks. They had returned to their old tree forts, and she thought that he would, at last, let her go, but he didn't. His eyes had yet to return to normal.

"Varg, I'm okay. Please, I've had far worse injuries," she tried to explain, and it was true. Being attacked while trying to close a tear was a fairly common occurrence, and even the best priestesses could be caught off guard in such a vulnerable state. If he had not attacked that demon, she would have easily purified it.

Once priestesses received their immortality, they also gained the remarkable ability to rapidly heal from grievous injuries. A wound that could take weeks to mend on an ordinary human could disappear from a priestess in a day or two, depending on the severity. They could almost recover as quickly as a therian. This was not the first time Halea had been injured in the line of duty. While she was in pain, the wound was already slowly beginning to close, though it would still need to be tended to.

Her attempts to calm him only caused Varg to growl deeply within his chest in protest.

She needed to reach him. She could tell by the way his eyes darted around and the firmness of his grip that he was protecting her, perhaps from any further demon attacks.

"We're safe. I'm safe," Halea assured while slowly reaching up to touch Varg's face.

The moment her gentle hand brushed against his skin, he looked down as if just noticing he was holding her in his arms.

"Varg, please come back," she pleaded.

"Halea?" he asked in a low tone, far deeper than even his normal voice.

She watched as slowly the red faded from his eyes, and his iron grip began to loosen. He gently lowered her to her feet while still supporting her, so she wasn't standing with her full weight on her injury.

"Varg, are you okay?"

She was surprised when he leaned into her and buried his face in the side of her neck, and she heard him say, in his normal voice, "Forgive me."

Halea instantly wrapped her arms around him, giving him the comfort he was so desperately seeking.

Varg could scarcely remember how they returned to the old tree forts. One moment he was fighting demons, and the next, Halea was in danger; after that, everything had become instinct. He had not wanted to lose control in front of her that way. He had only just barely got her back. Why did he have to show her the worst side of himself? She was a human. What if the true wolf was too much for her? He couldn't bear the thought of her ever being afraid of him, but she had been afraid. The scent of her fear was fading, but he could still detect in on her. Halea was the last person in the world he wanted to scare away. All of his anxiety was compounded by the fact that the wolf was unpredictable. Once a blood rage began, the beast's thirst for blood could have turned against Halea. Such powerful instincts were unstoppable. What if, instead of protecting her, he had mistaken her for an enemy and hurt her? He could never live with himself if he allowed that to happen.

"I'm okay, Varg. You didn't do anything wrong," she said, guessing the nature of at least some of his concerns. When they were still children, he had explained how blood rage was the uncontrollable instinct of every therian's inner-beast, though she had never witnessed it for herself before.

He drew back a little to look into her face, and she could see the last traces of his rage transformation had vanished. His fangs had receded, and his eyes and features were once again normal.

"Halea…" he started.

"Don't! You have nothing to apologize for. Varg, I trust you more than anyone alive," she confessed.

He felt a terrible mixture of joy and shame. His heart swelled with happiness to hear that she trusted him above all others, even after so many years of being apart, but at the same time, he felt crushed. There had been a very real possibility that he could have hurt her. A lycan can turn on anyone in a blood rage, anyone, except for their mate.

"You mustn't. If I ever fall into blood rage again, if I should turn on you…kill me."

Halea's eyes opened in shock. She wanted to argue, but even after all these years, Varg still had that same stubborn expression on his face when he was putting up a block. There would be no point arguing with him tonight, but that didn't mean she was done speaking her mind. Eventually, she would make him understand.

She sighed in resignation and felt the tension in him subside as she let his words pass unchallenged, a fact which pleased the alpha in him.

Halea moved to step back from him when she felt a stabbing sensation in her hip, and Varg could smell fresh blood ooze from her wound. Her face twisted in pain, and he moved forward to steady her again.

"You're hurt," he said, stating the obvious.

"It will heal over by morning, but I have to bandage it to prevent infection," she explained.

A dark blade injury was instantly lethal to a regular human as it was a weapon from the Chaos Dimension, and it could cause a slow and painful death to any therian unless a priestess could purify the wound. The weapons were least effective against priestesses, as the evil poison of the blades would purify on contact with any priestess. For Halea, it was no more dangerous than being stabbed by any sharp weapon, but other minor infections were still a possibility. Even though she could heal from illnesses quicker than regular humans, becoming sick could slow her down and was best to be avoided.

Varg's brow furrowed in worry. There wasn't much he could do for Halea away from his den, and he suddenly wished Batsuba was there.

"I have medical supplies in my travel bag," she explained and pointed to the base of the tree that had once been his fort. It hadn't been disturbed since she left it there that morning. Varg picked her up again and walked her towards the tree's base, where he gently set her down next to her things. She wanted to protest that she could have walked on her own, but he would have sensed she was lying from a mile away.

"I would have camped here for the night anyway. Can you please make a fire and find some more water?" she asked while handing him a partially empty water bag.

Varg accepted the water bag and sped off into the forest. Halea shifted a little to try and ease her discomfort before rummaging through her travel bag and dragging out her medical kit and a few dried food supplies. She hadn't eaten a thing since that morning. It had been a whirlwind of a day, first finding Varg again and then going on a demon hunt, now being injured. Food hadn't even crossed her mind but seeing her emergency rations reminded her that she was starving. She popped a few dried fruits in her mouth and began sorting through some herbs.

Varg returned quickly with the filled water bag and his arms loaded with firewood. She thanked him as she accepted the water, and he set to work on a fire.

She was a little embarrassed. Why did she have to get stabbed in the hip of all places? She would have to open the lower half of her robe to clean and tend to her wound, and while she was never embarrassed around Varg when they were children, it suddenly occurred to her that perhaps it wasn't proper to expose so much of her body, even if he was an old friend.

Varg had his back to her for a moment while getting the fire started, but when he turned around, the blood rushed to his face when he noticed she had partially opened the lower half of her robe. He could see all of one of her long legs and smooth thigh as she used a dampened cloth to wipe away as much of the blood from her skin as possible.

He jumped up and blurted, "I think I'll catch us some food," then dashed off into the forest again. Halea wondered if maybe he had heard her stomach rumbling.

Her wound was deep but not serious. She quickly finished washing it, applied a few stitches and a poultice of herbs, and bandaged it over. She was just finishing up when Varg reappeared carrying a small dead deer.

"Are you okay?" he asked, noticing that she seemed to be done with her bandages, and he felt quite relieved.

"I'll just need to take something for the pain, but I should be well enough to move again by morning. Isn't that an awful lot of meat?"

"This is barely a snack," he said with a wolfish grin. "You rest, and I'll cook some of this for you. Besides, I'm sure if there is any left over, I can dry it, and you can save it for later."

"You? Cook?" she asked incredulously. He had absolutely abhorred the idea of anything cooked when they were children.

His face grew somber as he explained. "There were some hard winters after my pack fled into the east. Having fresh meat wasn't always an option, but we did what we had to do to survive."

Her heart ached when she thought about all that he must have gone through.

Using a few lightweight cooking utensils from her bag, Halea boiled some water to make a medicinal tea to ease her pain while Varg skinned and prepared the meat. While waiting for her food, she used a basic spell to repair her robe and another spell to remove any remaining blood stains. When she was done, it was as if her robe had never been damaged.

As expected, Varg ate his share raw. Halea added a few of her cooking herbs and some dry rations to the meat in the pot and produced a decently flavored stew. She tried offering him some, but he was still just as revolted by her dietary tastes as she was by his.

Varg sat close to Halea as they ate their meal and they talked and shared stories. It felt right to be with her again. It felt as if they had never been apart, and he wished that night could last forever, but he could tell she was growing tired, and she would need her rest to recover.

She pulled a soft white cloak from her travel bag and spread it beneath her, rolling up one end to offer her head a little support from the ground. Priestesses often had to sleep outside in the wilds. Their duties dragged them far and wide, and the luxury of staying at an inn was rarely afforded to them. At first, it had been a little frightening for her to be outside alone at night, but in time she grew to love sleeping under the stars. She would usually put up a barrier around her campsite so that no demons or any other people who intended to harm her could sneak up and attack her in the night. But that night, she didn't need to because Varg was there, and she knew that with his keen senses, nothing would get the jump on them and that he would let nothing harm her.

Varg sat up and watched over her the entire night as she slept peacefully beside him, the light of the crackling fire dancing across her face. He kept his ears perked for the slightest sound of danger and would constantly check the scent of the wind, yet nothing disturbed them that night. He couldn't help gazing at her where she lay. He had missed her so terribly when he believed she was dead and gone. Her absence had left an empty hole in his heart that never fully healed, but now he could howl to the moon for joy.

Familiar feelings he thought he had long outgrown stirred within him. Besides once being his best friend, she had also been his boyhood crush, but he had spent the past eight years trying to convince himself that the fancies of his youth were something best left in the past. For one thing, she had been so young. It would have been wrong to keep thinking of her that way well into his adulthood, yet the Halea who lay before him now was no child.

No. He couldn't. Not again. He had just been a hormonal cub with crazy ideas. She never liked him that way, and he had no reason to believe she liked him that way now. Halea was a priestess. Serving her Goddess was all she had ever dreamed of. How could he ask her to give up everything she had ever wanted just for him? He could no sooner abandon his people than she could abandon her Goddess. Even though he was an alpha and could do as he pleased, he still had to consider his pack's feelings, and he knew they would never accept a human.

She did not belong to him. She could never be his. But she was still his friend, even after all these years, and he would never give that up.

# CHAPTER 12 – A VULGAR DISPLAY OF AUTHORITY

The smell of food warming over the fire woke her. She had plenty of stew leftover from the night before, and it seemed that Varg had thought to reheat it for her. Halea grimaced from the pain in her hip as she rolled over and looked at the massive trees that had once been their forts and noticed the sun was a lot higher than she was hoping it would be.

"Are you still in pain?" Varg asked as he suddenly appeared right next to her.

He had spent most of the morning circling the perimeter and watching for danger, but he rushed back immediately when he heard the rhythm of her breathing in her sleep change.

Even after all these years, he was still the master of making an abrupt appearance, and he grinned at the startled reaction he got from her, but his grin quickly changed into a frown when she winced in pain again.

"It's okay. I can feel it's mostly healed over already, but it is still a bit tender, and I feel a little stiff. I'll have to check these bandages, would you uh…"

"I'm going, I'm going!" he quickly offered. "Call me when you're done, or if you need me," he added.

Halea bit her lip and stifled the desire to laugh at his embarrassment. Perhaps he had seen a bit too much the other night after all, and she couldn't entirely suppress the blush rising in her cheeks.

She quickly opened the bottom half of her robe and inspected the bandages to find that the wound had already fully closed, but it still appeared red and a little raw. She cut out the few stitches she had put in from the night before, with the flesh closed; leaving them in would only cause her discomfort, and she was sure to have an active day ahead of her. She rewashed the wound and applied a mild antiseptic ointment and a smaller bandage. Once properly robed, she stood up. Her hip did feel sore, but as she walked a little circle around the campfire, the tension in the muscles loosened, giving relief to her aching injury.

"You can come back now, Varg. I'm decent," she called, and nearly as quickly as she called him, he reappeared from the tree line, making sure not to startle her again.

She noticed his claws were covered in fresh blood, and she guessed he had caught his own breakfast while waiting for her.

He was a little worried to see her standing and walking again so soon. He didn't want her overdoing it too quickly.

"Are you sure you're okay?"

"Much better," she said, giving him a heart-meltingly warm smile. "I won't feel a thing by this afternoon, and considering how much you let me sleep in, that won't be long to wait."

"Well, you were injured, and I know you puny humans need so much more sleep than us lycans," he replied with a deep chuckle, not being able to resist taunting her.

Halea shot him one of her classic dagger-eyed looks, and his laughter only continued.

She hadn't changed at all.

~~~☼~~~

Halea hadn't realized how useful it was to have a lycan help her track demons. On her own, she had to follow footprints, broken underbrush, or leftover signs of carnage. She was good at what she did, but Varg's sense of smell and powerful ability to hear over further distances allowed them to pick up the trail of at least one of the wraiths that escaped from the tear the night before.

The first thing they did when they set out was to return to the tear and see if any of the demons had returned. The tear still loomed ominously, emitting its sickly purple light, but there were no signs that any of the demons that emerged from it the night before had come back. Varg could tell because their scent was no longer fresh. Halea used her powers and successfully closed the tear, but she was not relieved.

The demons that had escaped, if not found, would bring about more tears. It was only a matter of time, and what was worse, most of the demons had fled eastbound, into lycan territory.

"How many trails are there?" she asked as Varg continued to sniff the air.

"Four, and at least three are heading into my territory," he answered and emitted a low, angry growl.

"I'll help you hunt them," she offered.

"It wouldn't be safe for you to enter further into our lands. I will have to find them on my own. It's not like I haven't tracked and killed countless of their kind before."

Halea simply shook her head.

"This isn't like before, Varg. These are not the same demons abandoned after the convergence. They're here to open more tears. If they open tears within your territory, you won't be able to seal them without my help. I was hoping I wouldn't have to ask you."

He could protect her from his own pack, his word was law, but when humans interfered the last time, a gathering had to be called. He was not the only alpha, and if tears were growing in number, the other packs needed to know, and they would all have to be involved. This put a considerable amount of pressure on him as a young leader. Once an alpha was established, it wasn't necessarily for life. If someone in the pack was powerful enough to challenge him to remove him from his position, they could do it and become the new alpha. A young leader was far more vulnerable to such a threat. He doubted anyone within his own pack would challenge him, but the other packs would only obey a Wolf King, and since his father's death, another had not been chosen. He knew Halea would never harm his people and that she only wished to help, but he wasn't sure how he could make them understand after what happened with the last convergence.

Halea gave him a silent moment to consider her offer. She knew she was asking a lot of him. At last, he answered her.

"Come with me to the den. You will be under my protection. None from my pack will harm you, but I will have no choice but to call a wolf gathering. The other lycans must know of the coming threat from tears, and they must all have a say in how we as a people must deal with this problem. The final say is with them."

"How long can that take?" she asked, worrying about what could happen if they took too long to make the right decision.

"I'll send a runner to spread the message. Once summoned, it can take a week, maybe more if they are coming from a great distance. The decision cannot be made until all have gathered. You'll have to stay close to me once the other packs begin to arrive. I have no control over them, and many of them are very distrusting of priestesses since the disaster of the last convergence. Too many lycans believe the priestesses made promises that they could not keep, or worse, that they brought the Chaos with them."

Halea felt a flush of nervousness at the prospect of such an uphill battle. She expected them to dislike her for being a human, but she hadn't realized the priestesses of the past had left such a bad impression upon the lycans. Most therians disliked humans, but they were at least willing to accept help from the priestesses when it came to sealing tears. She was grateful that Varg was on her side. If not for his trust in her, there would be no hope for any priestesses to seal the tears in their lands, and they would eventually doom themselves.

Varg instantly detected the scent of her growing nervous, and he gently placed his hands on her shoulders until she looked him in the eye.

"I promise I won't let anyone hurt you. I know this won't be easy, and my people won't be welcoming, but I'll do everything in my power to get them to understand that you mean them no harm. Please, just give me a little time."

"I take it telling them that I'm an old friend is out of the question?" she asked with a coy smile.

The scent of her being nervous had significantly dissipated, and for that, he was relieved. He smiled a sad sort of smile.

"I wish I could tell them, maybe if things go well someday, I can, but for now, we'll have to act as if we've never known each other before."

Halea understood. Varg's pack would probably feel betrayed if he let it be known that he had such sympathies for a human, and that fact could put his judgment and his authority into question, and she couldn't ask that of him.

It was probably best that he brought her back to the den. He would otherwise have a hard time explaining why a human's scent was all over him. She hadn't masked her scent at all since she returned, and to be honest, he didn't want her to. Her scent had matured in a way that both soothed and excited him. And the fact that he could smell his scent on her from when he had held her the night before seemed to incite his more basal instincts. He wanted his scent to remain on her, and he wanted everyone to know.

He could easily explain it away with the truth. He found a priestess, and together they hunted demons and tried to seal a tear, she was injured, and he spared her life. It was all the explanation his pack needed, and for now, it would be all the explanation they would receive. The human priestess would be under his protection, and his scent upon her would serve as a reminder of that.

Halea suggested continuing to hunt the demons they had already been trailing before making their way towards the den. The day was growing late already due to their slow start that morning, and once Varg made up his mind to take her to the den, he felt the desire just to go and get it over with. With so many demons loose, he would prefer to have the additional help of his best warriors; they could cover more ground that way.

~~~☼~~~

Aatu and Faolan were waiting at the lookout point. Varg had been gone for nearly two days, and they were debating if one of them should head out to find him.

"He'll come back when he's ready," said Faolan, who knew Varg would often disappear to scout for danger or patrol the borders of their territory. It was part of his expected duty as alpha, and Varg could more than handle himself.

"This seems longer than normal. What if bear of panther therians are trying to encroach on our borders again?"

"Then may their gods help them if Varg finds them," replied Faolan.

"Look, over there!" cried Aatu, as he spotted movement from far along the western border of their hunting grounds.

"See, what'd I tell ya? I knew he'd be back when he was ready." But Faolan stopped short when he noticed two people were heading their way.

Even with their powerful eyesight, it was hard to make out for sure if Varg really was one of the two approaching figures from that great of a distance, so they both raced out to intercept them.

At first, they approached with caution in case they were foes. As they neared and got a better view, they instantly recognized one of them as their alpha, though they didn't have any idea who the other person was beside him. Seeing Varg at least reassured them that it was safe for them to approach and that whoever was with him couldn't be an enemy, so they ran out to greet their leader.

The wind changed direction, and that was when they got a better look, as well as the scent, of the other person accompanying Varg – a human.

They stopped dead in their tracks, dumbfounded and not at all certain if they should even proceed, but Varg spotted them and hailed them over. There was no backing out now.

They walked towards their leader slowly, both feeling very defensive and wary.

They said nothing when their alpha and his human companion finally caught up with them, but they passed each other confused glances.

Varg picked up the scent of their nerves.

98

"All right, you two, calm down. She's not going to bite you. This is a priestess. Her name is Halea. There's been trouble with demons," he explained, trying to soothe the beta males.

"Demons? What kind of trouble?" asked Aatu. Demons had been less of an issue since they reclaimed their lands, but on occasion, some of their hunters would find them sneaking within their borders. They were always quickly slain.

Faolan sniffed the air in the direction of the female human, and he was startled when Varg shot him a deathly glare of warning. Their scent was all over each other, but he knew better than to ask at that moment.

"I'll explain everything when we get to the den," said Varg, and it was clear his voice broached no room for quarrel.

Varg led everyone back to the den. Faolan and Aatu trailed closely behind, dying for answers, but knowing better than to demand them before Varg was ready. They couldn't help but notice the human priestess seemed unusually relaxed in the presence of their alpha, which meant she was either very brave or very foolish.

Everyone at the den was startled when the three lycans returned with the strange visitor, and Halea felt instantly uncomfortable as an awkward silence fell, and all their staring eyes turned to her. Varg could smell the anxiety rising from her, and he ached to assure her that everything would be okay, but he couldn't afford to act too familiar with her at that moment.

"I know you are wondering why I have brought a human priestess to our den. I have spent the past two days hunting demons. Tears are returning to our lands," Varg said and paused, letting his listeners have a moment to mutter worriedly amongst themselves. He could already hear voices disapproving of his decision to bring the human into their home.

Halea was a little startled when he let out a low and threatening growl that instantly silenced everyone around him.

He went on to explain how they had hunted demons for the past two days and successfully sealed a tear, and of how she was temporarily injured, and that more demons had escaped into their territory.

"With the coming of these threats, the other packs and the council of elders must be consulted. I will send for them immediately, but in the meantime, this priestess is under my protection. I will watch over her personally to ensure that she fulfills her duty to seal any tears found within our borders, and I will take full responsibility should anything go wrong. Until the other packs arrive, I will be organizing hunting parties of our best warriors. We must seek out and find these demons and eliminate them before they bring any more tears into our lands."

"Varg, I wish to speak!" called out the familiar voice of Lyall.

Varg sighed, knowing he would not get away with bringing a human into the den without someone wanting to argue.

"Speak, Lyall," he finally allowed.

"If you wish to put this human under your protection until the high council can convene on these issues, then it would be unwise to allow her to interfere until they have decided whether we want her help or not."

"And you would suggest we let our lands become infested with more demons due to open tears in the meantime?" retorted Varg, who seethed with anger to have another male challenge his decision.

"These evil creatures may not have even opened any new tears yet. Perhaps they won't. Perhaps it is she who will bring them. Priestesses are not to be trusted. I was hoping you would learn from your father's mistake."

Before Halea even knew what was going on, Varg had sprung upon the other lycan, and soon they were tearing into each other. Everyone stood back as the two males slashed at each other, and their growls and snarls made many cower in fear. Varg dodged Lyall's fist and easily knocked him to the ground. Once the other male was down, he was quickly pinned, and everyone watched as Varg mercilessly began beating him. Halea felt sick as she watched the other lycan's face get pummeled into a bloody pulp as he struggled to get up, but he could not overcome Varg in his rage.

"Submit!" growled Varg, and Halea heard several other lycans gasp as they witnessed the slightest tinge of red begin to form around the blue of his eyes. Lyall knew he could defy no longer and tipped his head back, exposing his throat in submission. And just like that, it was over.

Whatever protests were left had been thoroughly silenced by Varg's display of dominance.

"Go," commanded Varg, and everyone scattered back to their business as if a strange human and a terrible fight hadn't just happened.

Halea was left alone with Varg, who still appeared a little tense. The display of brutality she had just seen left her shaken. Varg had explained dominance displays to her before. As an alpha, she knew he would be required to violently discipline any who dared to defy him, but this was the first time she had ever witnessed it for herself, and she was trying to come to terms with this darker side of her old friend that she had never truly known.

Varg could sense her discomfort, and shame instantly filled him. It was easy to forget she was human and that his people's ways could appear strange and harsh compared to her own.

"Come with me," he spoke softly to her as he came closer and looked into her frightened eyes. She nodded and followed him.

Varg led Halea up a slope that was cut along the mountainside. There were several large caves, some natural, and others hand-carved out of the rock. She didn't know where he was taking her. She was still in a bit of shock, and so she quietly went along until she found herself inside one of the caves that faced out into the west. Inside it was remarkably nice. She had always imagined the inside of a cave as primitive, but there was beautifully carved wooden furniture and a comfortable-looking bed covered in various soft animal furs. Naturally, there were no windows, but there were heavy iron doors that could close the mouth of this luxurious cave for either privacy or safety in the event of a raid. There was a small window at the top of the doors for letting in a little daylight or perhaps some fresh air. Lycans left their doors open most of the time to allow natural light into their homes and to let their pack members know that they welcomed any who would wish to stop by for a visit as they were very sociable people.

She was vacantly looking around her when Varg took her in his arms and buried his face in her hair.

"I didn't want you to have to see that. I'm sorry, it's just the way we are," he tried to explain. He was tense with worry until she rested her head on his chest, and he could feel her relax in his arms.

"I know. You don't have to apologize to me for what you are. I may not fully understand what it's like to be a lycan, and your ways may seem a little...terrifying...ya know...to a puny human, but I won't judge you for them. I'm sure it won't be the last time you shock me, but that's okay," she said, trying to soothe him.

When she looked up at him with her beautiful hazel green eyes, her pupils growing wide with the fading light outside, he felt something pierce through his heart, something undeniable. Somehow, she was in his arms again. Her heart was beating against his, and her lips looked so warm and inviting. Without even realizing it, he reached out to caress the side of her face. He could hear her pulse quicken at his soft touch, and she was so close.

Halea wasn't sure what was happening, she was drowning in the blue of his eyes, and suddenly she could scarcely breathe. She was spellbound by his gaze as he held her close, and her heart hammered as his face slowly leaned towards her's.

His lips were so close to hers when suddenly he pulled back as if burnt and made for the cave entrance.

"Someone will bring dinner for you. We will hunt in the morning," Varg said over his shoulder, and then he was gone, and she was left standing all alone with her heart still racing and her face flushed red.

# CHAPTER 13 – OLD FEELINGS, NEW FEELINGS

Varg paced alone in his private cave. He wanted to shift into his wolf form and run into the night, but he couldn't. It didn't feel safe for him to leave Halea alone. Even though she was under his protection, he had been challenged once that day already.

"*It can't be! What is wrong with me? What am I thinking?*" he cursed to himself. He wasn't some hormone-crazed cub anymore. He had let those hopes die when he thought she was dead and gone, but now they were returning. Perhaps those feelings had never entirely gone away? He had never allowed any other females to come close to him, yet he could have practically anyone he wanted, but he had never wanted them. Maybe he never forgot the way he had felt for Halea. Perhaps his choice had already been made.

No matter how much she may have grown and changed, she was still Halea. It would be wrong to want more from her than the friendship she had always so openly given. She was a priestess, and he was the alpha leader of his wolf pack, and lycans did not trust humans. How could he expect her to give up everything she had devoted her life to, to be with him? His people would never accept her.

No.

Halea was his friend. Perhaps he did harbor deeper feelings, but he would have to push them aside. He couldn't bear the thought of losing her again, and he would do anything to protect what they still shared together. It was wrong to hope for more. Yet, the very thought of spending the rest of eternity being denied the one thing he wanted most made him feel as if his heart was being crushed.

~~~☼~~~

What had just happened? Did anything happen at all? Or did she just imagine it? The way Varg had gazed into her eyes, the way he held her close, it felt as if - impossible.

She must have misinterpreted his behavior. He had only been worried that he offended her with his lycan ways. That was it, wasn't it?

They had been separated for many years, but he was still her oldest and dearest friend, the first person besides her mother who accepted her for who she was. She owed it to him to accept him for who he was, even if lycan behavior was shocking and cruel compared to the way humans interacted. It was not her place to judge.

Yet, Halea couldn't shake the feeling that it wasn't just his people's reaction to her that caused Varg to run away from her. She couldn't forget the way he had caressed her face and the way he looked at her when he came so close their lips nearly touched. She felt an aching disappointment that he hadn't kissed her, and suddenly she was ashamed. How could she think such things about her best friend? Varg was a lycan, an alpha pack leader; he could never love a puny human. Priestess or not, that's all she was. It was her fate to roam the world alone, battling Chaos, and his fate was to eventually settle down with some she-wolf. That thought made her burn with jealous rage, and again she chided herself for such stupid feelings. She wanted him to be happy. She cared about him more than anyone. When she thought he was dead, it was as if her heart had been torn out. Finding him after all these years made her feel as if all the broken pieces had been put back together again. But nothing could ever be the way it was. They weren't children anymore. He had his responsibilities to his people, and she had her responsibilities to her deity. She had sworn an oath to protect her world and let nothing distract her from her purpose. Once the tears in the lycan territories were under control, she would have to leave their lands, and it could be decades or even centuries before she would return again, if at all. She would have to cherish every moment she could share with her old friend and take comfort in knowing that at least he was alive and well.

It would be better now - wouldn't it?

But she couldn't shake the creeping loneliness that threatened to consume her heart.

Eventually, there was a knock at the cave entrance. The door was still open, and because she wasn't paying attention, she hadn't even noticed anyone come or go, but a tray of food had been left at the entryway, and despite her jangled nerves, she was hungry.

Varg must have told them that she didn't eat like a wolf. There was meat that looked like someone attempted to cook it, but it was still quite rare by human standards, and she wasn't sure she could stomach it. There were also a few vegetables and a couple pieces of ripe fruit. She ate everything except the meat and hoped that it wouldn't be considered an offense. She was already off to a bad start with his people.

After Halea finished eating, she explored her accommodations. It was a comfortable living space, and there was even a stone tub fed with spring water from the mountains. It was a little chilly, but she decided to wash up and inspect her injury. It had finally stopped hurting, and when she removed her bandage, there was only a slight mark remaining, and that would soon fade. She never seemed to carry any permanent scars no matter how severe the injury and no further bandages would be needed.

That night, she tossed and turned fitfully, barely managing to sleep at all.

~~~☼~~~

Varg knocked on Halea's door that morning, and she came out to greet him with a smile, though he could tell she looked a little tired. He was afraid things would be awkward between them, but he was surprised and more than a little relieved when she announced that she was ready to begin the hunt.

He had assembled a small group of his best warriors to partake in the hunt; the rest would remain and guard the den. With demons on the loose, he did not want to risk those left behind.

Since returning to their territory, Varg's pack was once again growing in number. Many new cubs had been born in the past three years, and many females chose not to hunt or fight when their cubs were still so young. While this was good for their numbers, it meant they were more vulnerable.

Halea had been too stressed the night before to look around the den. She had only seen it twice before, once from a very great distance, and the last time, when it had been destroyed. She was pleased to see that in the few years since Varg's pack had returned, they had restored and repaired much of the damage, though there were still small signs of the devastation, such as missing statues and tree-dwellings.

Varg noticed her looking around as he led her out towards the common area. "It's been a busy three years. We've rebuilt much, but there's still a lot of work to do."

When they reached the common area, Halea noticed several families sitting around fire pits, a few grabbed their children and got up and left at the sight of her, but some stayed and subtly, or not so subtly, observed her. She had a feeling this area was usually much more lively than it was at the moment, thanks to her.

Varg was greeted by Faolan, as well as Hemming and his mate Daciana.

"You're coming, Daciana? What about Fillin?" asked Varg.

Daciana was a new mother, and her son Fillin was only a toddler and was still incredibly clingy.

"Mother's watching him. She wanted more time with her grandson anyway, and I want to get out of the den. He's weaned. He'll be fine," she said with a note of defensiveness.

Halea looked over to the area where Daciana had turned her eyes as she spoke and saw a tiny boy being held and fawned over by a woman who looked the same age as Daciana. It suddenly struck her that everyone appeared very young. She didn't recall seeing a single person who looked older than twenty-five. It was then that the reality of being an immortal set in for her. A grandparent could walk beside a grown grandchild or great-grandchild and look like peers of the same age. Having never seen her grandfather as a young man, it was impossible to imagine him without thick glasses and thinning white hair.

Sitting next to Daciana's mother was another woman. Her hair was pure white, and her eyes were as black as coal, and Halea realized this woman was staring directly at her. There was something strange about this lycan woman, something powerful that she couldn't explain. She seemed to be looking straight into her soul.

As Aatu, Ula, and Lyall approached, Halea pulled her attention away from the hypnotizing stare of the white-haired lycan woman.

Halea was taken aback that Lyall would be joining them, and what was even more shocking, his face appeared to have completely healed. Varg had beaten his face to a bloody pulp the night before, yet today he didn't seem to have so much as a bruise, and she marveled at how quickly lycans could heal.

Lyall turned his eyes to Halea with a glare, and she realized she had been staring. Varg had not missed Lyall's reproachful glance, and he fought the urge to growl.

Faolan and Aatu seemed the least unnerved by Halea's presence. They had grown up with Varg, and they trusted him implicitly. If Varg felt comfortable enough to trust this human priestess and bring her to their den, then they were willing to accept the situation. Hemming and his mate were distrustful of the stranger, but as long as she did her task and stayed clear of the cubs of the den, they would suffer her presence. Ula was harder to gauge. She was a tall blond-haired, blue-eyed, lycan woman with many dominant traits. She appraised Halea with a look of contempt but otherwise chose to ignore her. Halea couldn't help but be reminded of her childhood days when the city children didn't want to play with her, and she felt as if she was about to be the odd one out. She had rather hoped she was past that stage in her life.

Nevertheless, her scent betrayed no signs of nervousness or fear, and Varg had no doubts that she could prove his entire pack wrong if only they would give her a chance.

They set out, heading northwest towards the borders of their hunting grounds. Varg was always faster than anyone else in his pack, and the others were amazed that the human priestess had no trouble keeping up with them and even matched pace with their alpha. Once they reached the thicker trees, their party broke up into groups of twos and spread out to cover more ground, searching for the scent of demons.

Halea and Varg paired together and followed along a river's edge. Once they were alone, Varg could speak freely.

"I'm sorry about Lyall. He was very close to my father. They're a lot alike in many ways."

Halea was aware that Varg's father would have never approved of his son making friends with a human girl, so it didn't surprise her that his father's friend would have similar feelings.

"You don't have to worry about it, Varg. I never expected any of them to accept me. I'm just grateful they haven't eaten me alive...yet," she said with a sarcastic grin.

She had just begun to set a trap when Varg bolted upright and faced south with an intense look on his face. He could hear something that she couldn't, so she stopped in the middle of casting the spell for the trap so her words wouldn't drown out the noise. It was then that Halea heard the faint howl of a wolf echoing far in the distance.

"Aatu has picked up a scent," Varg finally explained, and Halea gave up her task, and together they sped through the forest towards the sound of the howls.

Varg and Halea were the first to find Aatu and Faolan, the others had not arrived yet, but even she could hear the howls in the distance signaling that they were on their way.

"There are two trails. They're both heading further into our territory," explained Aatu as Varg came closer to inspect the trail.

Just then, Hemming and Daciana appeared.

"We don't have time to wait. The others will follow. We have to find those demons before they open a tear near the den," ordered Varg as they all raced back into the hunting lands surrounding their home.

The scents were still relatively fresh, but they were dismayed to find that they diverged, with one heading further east and the other moving north.

"Aatu, Faolan, follow the trail that heads north. The rest of us will follow the other scent," commanded Varg.

Their party of four raced through the trees when suddenly Varg stopped them short. There was an unmistakable scent on the wind, demons, and lots of them.

"I think they're trying to ambush us," cried Daciana.

"Well, they don't know who they're dealing with," said Hemming.

Halea knew the increase in their numbers could mean only one thing – a new tear. She gripped her spear and listened as suddenly even she could hear the growling and snarling of the bestial demons coming towards them.

The lycans and priestess immediately attacked the demons that charged through the trees.

Halea had never seen any other lycans fight beside Varg, and she was impressed with how powerful both Hemming and Daciana were as a pair. They fought side by side and were even more lethal whenever they perceived the other to be in danger.

Varg leaped upon a huge beast of a demon with massive horns and a sweeping tail that bore lethal spikes and tore into its throat with his razor-sharp claws.

Halea faced off against several wraiths at once, and despite their flashing dark blades, they all fell as her spear glowed with the charge of her purifying power.

Once Varg finished killing the large demon, he let out a howl, calling for reinforcements. They were still being outnumbered, and they hadn't even reached the tear yet. Just then, two massive wolves sprang into the battle. Halea had never seen wolves so large in her life. They were bigger than horses, and their fangs flashed as they snarled and leaped on the demons, viciously tearing them apart.

"Halea, the tear!" called Varg, and she nodded before slaying one more wraith and running deep into the trees. Varg followed closely behind her, shredding demons left and right.

Halea, at last, saw the familiar glow through the trees, and she was about to approach when several more wraiths barred her way, twirling their dark bladed weapons and snarling with their strange silvery teeth. Varg came in beside her and helped her fight back the humanoid demons defending the tear.

With another slash of her spear and a burst of white light, Halea managed to break through their numbers and quickly made for the tear.

"Seal it. We'll keep them back," called Varg as he jumped between her and the demons that were attempting to swarm her from behind.

Halea could hear the vicious snarls of both demons and wolves as the lycans battled behind her. She had to focus and seal the tear before another wave of demons rushed out. Reaching her hands towards the tear, she called upon the Goddess for her power.

Faolan and Aatu had rushed back the moment they heard the howl of their alpha. They could see that Lyall and Ula had chosen to battle in their wolf forms and that Hemming and Daciana were struggling against the overwhelming numbers of the demons around them. It didn't take long before they, too, were being assailed from all sides.

Ula snapped the head off a bipedal demon and raced towards the tear. She found Varg defending the priestess who stood before the pulsing rift, her hands glowing white. The scent and sight of the strange dimensional anomaly horrified her to the core as if she had looked into the face of evil, and she quickly averted her eyes. She shook her head to free her mind from its dark influence and charged in to help Varg.

"Ula, look out!" shouted Varg, but it was too late. Two wraiths sprang up from behind her. One landed on her back and stabbed her repeatedly with its dark weapon. She yelped in agony and fell to the forest floor. Varg sprang forward and slashed his claws through the wraith, tearing it to pieces, its black blood spraying everywhere. The second wraith moved to attack when Lyall jumped it from behind and bit it in two.

There was a clash as if thunder was in the sky, and then the tear was gone. The lycans slaughtered several of the remaining demons, but many escaped and scattered in all directions.

Halea was slightly tired from sealing the tear, but she quickly ran to the fallen wolf that was bleeding profusely all over the forest floor. Its breathing was labored, and Halea could see that the wounds were great. Suddenly the other wolf sprang between her and his fallen comrade and bared its fangs at her.

"She's been wounded with a dark blade. I have to purify the wounds, or she'll die. Let me help her!" Halea shouted fearlessly in the face of the massive dark brown wolf as he glared at her.

"Stand down, Lyall!" ordered Varg in a booming voice that left no room for argument. Despite how intimidating Lyall looked in his wolf form, he reluctantly stepped aside at his alpha's order.

Halea went to Ula's side, and she could hear a low rumbling growl coming from the fallen she-wolf.

"I won't hurt you. Please understand," Halea pleaded in a gentle voice. Ula quieted her growl, but the whites of her blue eyes showed as the strange human female approached and knelt beside her.

Halea placed her hands into the fur of the she-wolf and was surprised at how wonderfully soft it felt, but she forced herself to concentrate on the task at hand.

The other lycans were soon with them, and they watched as the priestess began to emit a strange white glow that passed through her body and into Ula. When at last she removed her hands, Ula was able to transform back into her humanoid form. She was breathing easier, and the strange dark haze that had appeared before her eyes was fading away.

"I don't have my travel bag with me. Her wounds will still need to be cleaned and bandaged, but she should be able to heal on her own now that the darkness has been banished from her body. Someone will have to carry her," Halea said with authority.

Lyall transformed back into his humanoid self and went to Ula's side and gently lifted her and draped her over his back. Without a word, he sped through the trees towards the den.

"Many escaped," said Aatu.

Varg felt overwhelmed. The way things were going, they'd never seal the tears. He sent a runner to assemble all the packs the first day he had brought Halea to them, and he was beginning to hope they would hurry up and arrive. They were going to need every wolf they had to find and destroy these demons before they were uncontrollable.

Halea was worried too. This was strange behavior. The demons were opening tears far more frequently than they should be, considering how recently the last convergence was. She couldn't shake the terrible foreboding that gripped her. If things continued at this rate, she would have to report to Lord Anshar.

"We will return to the den and begin the hunt again tomorrow," Varg said at last. With one of their pack injured and the day nearly over, it would be best to rest and regroup.

"You guys can go on ahead. The priestess and I will follow," added Varg.

"What does it mean?" he asked Halea, once the others were well out of hearing range.

"Nothing has been right since the last convergence. We shouldn't have any tears at all this soon. It usually takes a couple of centuries for it to get this bad. I think because the wrong priestess was sacrificed, perhaps the dimension of Chaos wasn't sealed properly. I don't want to believe it, but I'm afraid it's coming again, fast."

Suddenly a terrifying thought passed Varg's mind.

"Who will they sacrifice if it does come again?"

It was hard for her to look him in the eye. There were many strong priestesses, many older, more experienced, but she had been well trained, and her powers of purification had grown incredibly strong. She wanted to tell him not to worry, that there wasn't any chance, but there was a chance, and she knew he would not accept it.

Finally, she forced herself to look at him, and she was crushed by the concern in his eyes.

"Whichever priestess is most powerful. There are many of us. Lord Anshar even brought some of the strongest from across the sea. They would have to partake in the ritual of choosing."

"Will you be among them?" he asked as he held her gaze.

"Yes," she finally replied, knowing she could not lie to him.

His face grew angry, and his jaw clenched.

"You would let them kill you?" he said in a harsh tone, but Halea was having none of it.

"Yes, Varg! That is my duty. I am a priestess! I swore an oath to give my life to protect this world, and if I am the one chosen, then I *will* see it through. It is not up for discussion, and don't you give me any of your dominance crap! You may be an alpha, but I am not a wolf, so you can't order me around! We don't even know what's going to happen or when, so just drop it," she shouted.

Varg was stricken. It wasn't that she had never told him off before; she used to give him an earful all the time when they were kids, but this was different. This wasn't childish bickering – her life was on the line. The alpha in him was seething at her defiance, but he forced himself to calm down. She was right. She wasn't a wolf, she wasn't one of his pack members, she was not his mate, and he had no claim to her life, except as her friend.

She could see him struggling between hurt and anger, and she hated upsetting him, but it was his own fault. He demanded it, and she had no choice but to give him the truth.

"Halea," he finally spoke. "It's just that I…"

"Please, Varg. Please, let's just not worry about it for now. We don't know what's really going to happen, so let's not automatically assume the worst. Things could still be okay. Please…I don't want to fight with you, and I don't want to hurt you. I'm sorry," she said before turning to run off into the forest, back towards the den.

He was left behind feeling even worse.

# CHAPTER 14 – IN THE COMPANY OF WOLVES

When Halea returned to the den, she was suddenly self-conscious to arrive without Varg, but she was sure he wasn't far behind. She knew where to find the quarters she had been given, and it seemed it would be best for her to stay there, away from the pack made so obviously uncomfortable by her unwelcome presence.

But she never got that far.

"Human, wait!" called a woman's voice, and Halea turned to notice Daciana running towards her.

"You can call me Halea," Halea said, trying to keep the tone of irritation in her voice down.

"Ula wants you. Will you please go to her? She's with our healer," explained the she-wolf.

"Me? Why does she want me?"

"You're the priestess," replied Daciana matter-of-factly.

Halea allowed the lycan female to lead her along. She noticed as they walked past the common area that more lycans were gathered than the last time she had been there. Their eyes followed her as she walked, and though she didn't have lycan hearing, she could tell there was a lot of gossip about her.

Daciana led her to a large tree-dwelling on the outskirts of the den. Halea admired it because it was far nicer than any tree fort. The structure didn't look out of place at all. It appeared as if it had grown there as a natural part of the tree.

"Go on up. They're waiting for you," said Daciana.

Halea felt a moment of trepidation at the idea of wandering into a strange lycan dwelling. What if it was a trick? She wondered where Varg was all of a sudden and thought perhaps she should wait for him to return before accepting strange invitations.

Daciana must have smelled the tinge of nervousness coming from her.

"They won't bite. Nobody here would dare defy Varg, at least of that you can be sure."

Halea reluctantly ascended the stairway that spiraled up around the base of the tree. If this was a trick, she still had her spear and would make them sorry. When she reached the top, she noticed the dwelling had no door.

"Come inside, priestess," called a female voice that she did not recognize.

When Halea walked in, she saw Ula lying on a bed of furs, and beside her was the strange white-haired lycan woman she had seen that morning. She realized that this same woman must be Batsuba, the healer Varg had often spoken of when they were growing up.

Her face looked young, but there was something uncanny in her dark eyes, some strange presence of power as if she were looking into eyes too wise and knowing for the face they belonged to. It occurred to her that this woman was ancient. This was a being that had seen ages come and go. She recognized this because she had sometimes seen that same look in Lord Anshar's eyes.

Ula was heavily bandaged all over her torso, but she looked relaxed and in relatively little pain considering the terrible injuries she had just sustained.

"Priestess?" called Ula in a low and exhausted voice.

A jolt of pity passed through Halea at the sight of the downed lycan warrior, and she went to her and knelt by her side, resting her spear flat upon the floor.

"Ula, are you feeling any better? I have herbs for pain in my travel bag..."

"I have already seen to her medicinal needs," interrupted the white-haired woman.

Halea decided not to argue, though she felt slighted a little. She only wanted to help.

"I've been better, but I will heal. I wanted to thank you for saving my life today. I thought I was gone for sure when I felt the evil of a dark weapon."

"We lost many of our people to the weapons of Chaos when the convergence happened. We had to flee our lands, and there were no priestesses to help our injured. Even my skill could not save them," added the mysterious healer.

"I heard about the overwhelming hoard of demons that ravaged these lands. I'm sorry there was no one there to help you. Those weapons are instant death to regular humans, but I was able to purify her wounds, and because she's a lycan, there was still time."

"I'm in debt to you. Name anything you wish of me," said Ula, her face growing serious.

"I'm a priestess. It's my duty to protect life, all life. You owe me nothing. All I ask is that you rest and recover."

Ula was going to argue, but Batsuba quickly cut her off.

"Lycans look after their own. All pack are family but owing debts to those who are not pack is difficult."

Halea remembered when she first met Varg, and at least in that instance, she was glad he had felt indebted to her, or they would have never become friends.

Suddenly they heard someone rushing up the stairs into the healer's dwelling. It was Varg. He looked angry and anxious, but his anxiety eased the moment he saw that Halea was safe.

He hadn't been far behind her, but the moment he returned to the den, everyone wanted to speak with him about one thing or another. He was used to it as a leader, but at that moment, he did not want to lose sight of Halea in case she encountered any of the more volatile members of his pack. He was kicking himself for having let her get so far on her own.

Batsuba noticed the alpha male's strange behavior and expression at being reunited with the human priestess, and her eyes narrowed.

Halea knew it wouldn't be good for him to explain such behavior, so she picked up her spear and rose.

Varg turned and went back down the spiral stairs with Halea close behind. They both wanted to speak, but there were too many lycan ears.

"The hunters have brought fresh boar. Perhaps you will eat with the rest of us in the common area tonight," he offered, desperate to kill the silence between them.

"And spoil everyone's food?"

"Actually, it may not be as bad as you think. I talked to many pack members when I arrived before I found you," he said, trying to subtly explain his absence from her presence. "Ula is one of our best warriors, news of you saving her from the dark blade has spread, and Hemming has told everyone of how you sealed the tear. A few doubters are starting to see your usefulness."

"A few is better than none, but it isn't all," she replied.

"Give my people time. Some of us lycans are pretty nice when you get to know us better," he said with a warm smile, and she couldn't help but smile in return.

Perhaps for his sake, she could try to be outgoing.

Lycans were social by nature. Almost all meals were shared with friends and family in the common areas. Even if a lycan was incapable of hunting, they never went hungry because everyone in the pack took care of everyone else. Everyone contributed in one way or another. Some watched and cared for the young when their parents were busy, some specialized in their crafts which were freely given to pack members, and some skinned, cleaned, and prepared the meals. Not everyone was a hunter or warrior, but everyone contributed. There was no money used within their society, though they traded with other therians for things they didn't have the skill or resources to produce on their own, such as textiles or metals.

The fire pits were large circles dug into the ground, and many had smooth wooden benches recessed into them, covered in furs or cushions. Halea liked to imagine how nice it would be to sit around such cozy fires, surrounded with friends and loved ones, all sharing a meal and telling stories like one big happy family. It was a pleasant image, but one that sent a pang of loneliness into her heart.

Varg led her to the largest fire pit. His seat looked the most comfortable, and it was clear to her that nobody else was allowed to sit there, and he motioned for her to sit next to him. Someone lit the fire, and slowly more lycans joined them. Aatu and Faolan were there, and a few lycans she didn't recognize. Hemming and Daciana sat close to her, and she was shocked to see Daciana curl up in her mate's lap. She tried not to blush while noticing that such affectionate displays were also going on amongst other couples. Was that how lycan mates acted towards each other? Varg had once told her that lycans were openly affectionate, but this made her feel like she was intruding on something private, yet no one else batted an eye as if it was the most natural thing in the world.

Across the fire pit from Halea sat Batsuba, watching.

Halea could feel the dark eyes of the healer on her, but she tried not to let it unnerve her. She was relieved when the food was served so she could focus on eating rather than on how uncomfortably out of place she felt. Varg must have sensed her discomfort, and he leaned in to speak softly to her.

"Relax."

"I'm fine," she replied a little too quickly, and he smirked at her obvious lie.

Varg leaned over and spoke to another lycan passing by, but she couldn't hear what had been said.

"I told them to make sure to bring you something other than just meat for your meal," he explained at her curious glance.

"Thanks," Halea replied, being glad that he remembered. The idea of eating raw boar seemed like a salmonella nightmare to her, but at least their stomachs could handle it.

She was handed a plate of lightly cooked vegetables, fresh fruit, and an unusual bread that was still warm but smelled delicious.

Varg watched her take a bite of the soft bread, and her face lit up with delight at the flavor. She was so beautiful sitting there beside him, and he wished for nothing more than to hold her, but he forced himself to snap out of such reveries.

"Do you like it?"

"This is great. I've never had bread this good," Halea replied.

To her surprise, he broke off a small piece of her bread and popped it into his mouth.

"You're right. It is good," Varg said, smiling brightly and exposing his pearly white fangs.

Halea didn't know why she suddenly felt so warm.

No one else noticed his behavior, except for across the fire; Batsuba's eyes widened as she watched her leader's flirtatious display.

A large serving tray of the sliced boar was laid before Varg, and everyone around the pit passed him their plate as he served the meat. He also handed a plate to Halea, but she shook her head.

"A little rare, don't you think?"

"I've got a skewer," he offered and shot her a particularly wolfish grin.

"What?" she asked, her eyes growing wide.

"Right here," he said while pulling out a few sharpened sticks from next to the bench.

"Oh," she said, feeling somewhat relieved.

She skewered the meat and leaned it into the fire and then sat back to watch it cook, though the smell caused her to receive quite a few glances of disapproval.

While Varg was busy discussing the pack's preparations for the coming gathering with the others, Halea took a moment to look around and noticed that Lyall was nowhere to be seen. She tried to casually glance over her shoulder towards the other fire pits to see if maybe he was with another group, but it didn't surprise her that he wasn't there, though it did make her feel bad. She didn't want to create trouble between Varg and his pack.

113

While observing, she noticed that many of the lycan couples, who were in each other's laps, or nearly in each other's laps, were sharing their food from a single plate.

"Is there a plate shortage?" she attempted to whisper while leaning towards Varg.

Varg burst into laughter at her question, which caused most to look their way. Varg had grown to be so serious. They almost never saw their leader laugh or smile, yet he seemed to be candidly enjoying himself in the company of the human woman.

Daciana had heard Halea's question and also found it particularly funny. Lycans shared food from the same plate as their mate as a form of intimacy and flirtation.

"Humans don't share food with their mates?" she asked.

"Well…we cook for each other, I guess, but eating off another person's plate is usually considered bad manners," Halea tried to explain.

"Lycan mates provide for each other and share everything; it's how we stay close," explained the she-wolf.

Suddenly Halea remembered how Varg ate some of her bread, even though she knew he hated that sort of food, and quickly berated herself for reading too much into it.

The rest of the evening went by without much incident. A few lycans actually talked politely to her. They seemed genuinely curious as most had never met any humans, and she found herself answering a lot of their questions.

Daciana, in particular, seemed to take a keen interest in her and her priestess abilities. Halea felt comfortable talking with the she-wolf and no longer detected any animosity.

Varg had to get up and leave her because he had been called away. He had ordered guards to watch the den carefully that night. He was taking no chances with so many demons roaming loose. Hemming, Aatu, and Faolan had gone with him, and there were only women left socializing around the fire.

Eventually, people began to leave the common area and go about their regular evening business. A lycan woman approached Daciana carrying a young boy in her arms, and Halea recognized her as Daciana's mother.

"I can't get him to sleep," said Adolpha, who exhaustedly handed over the little boy before returning to her mate.

The young lycan cub looked extremely energetic, and Halea smiled to see him. He had the same gray eyes and dark brown hair as his mother.

"How old is he?"

"This is his third summer," replied Daciana as her son fidgeted in her arms.

"He looks just like you," Halea said while smiling at the little lycan cub who looked up at her with curious eyes. He was used to being coddled by all the women of the pack, but he had never seen this woman before, and Halea was shocked when he stretched out his chubby arms for her.

"Don't bother her, Fillin. Behave!" scolded his mother, but at that, the boy began to cry while kicking. Exasperated, Daciana set him down, and he immediately jumped into Halea's lap and clung to her robe. Halea could feel his sharp claws digging into her, but she tried not to wince and remained still.

"I'm sorry. He's so spoiled when it comes to attention. If he's bothering you, I can take him away."

"It's all right. He seems willing to be calm now. He must keep you busy," Halea said with a smile.

"Between him and his father, I've got my hands full," she replied with a laugh, grateful that the priestess wasn't offended by her son's behavior. Daciana would have never thought to let a human touch her precious son, but Halea did not seem threatening despite her strange human ways. She had saved Ula's life and fought honorably beside them that day, and Varg appeared to trust her, and no matter her initial misgivings, she trusted her leader completely.

Halea and Daciana sat together before the fire, waiting for the men to return when the healer joined them.

Halea looked up at the imposing she-wolf and put on her best polite smile and greeted her.

"It seems Varg rather enjoyed himself tonight," said Batsuba.

"That's…good," replied Halea.

"You two seem to get along rather well, especially for a lycan and a human."

Halea had the keen suspicion that Batsuba was implying something. She felt guilty, but she didn't know why. They had done nothing wrong. There wasn't anything going on between them, not like that. He was her friend.

"I can't remember the last time I heard Varg laugh like that," interjected Daciana, sensing a sudden tension rising in the air.

"I'm very grateful for the kindness and hospitality I've been shown so far. I'm glad Varg has given me the chance to help."

"Something tells me he is very glad that you're here, unusually so."

Convinced the woman was prying, Halea narrowed her eyes and gave her nothing. There was nothing to give.

"Well, I would hardly want to be on his bad side, now, would I?"

Batsuba was sniffing the air deeply during this exchange, searching for answers hidden beneath deceptions, but this priestess was on to her, and she admired her ability to look her in the eye and stand her ground. Few could do such a thing when she wanted information from them, but the priestess never flinched. Batsuba knew she was staring down an alpha bitch, and she smiled. Perhaps that was the root of why she had earned such attention from Varg. Ultimately, it wasn't her business who Varg decided to have sex with. He wasn't the first lycan to have such unconventional tastes. If he wanted to enjoy the pleasures of the flesh with this human priestess, she wasn't about to judge. Varg was a virile male who could make his own decisions. But still, Batsuba couldn't shake the suspicion there was something more than physical desire between those two, but she shrugged it off. It was impossible. They had only just met, and no genuine connection could be forged so quickly.

"I think I will like having you around, Halea. You certainly make things interesting," said Batsuba with a knowing smile before turning and walking away.

Daciana leaned in close to Halea and asked in a low voice: "What was that about?"

Halea could feel the heat rising in her cheeks, but she offered only a shrug in answer, afraid her own roiling emotions would betray her.

Varg felt relieved the evening had gone so well, relieved enough to leave Halea with the other females as he went to check with the guards posted around the den for the night. Lyall seemed to be keeping his distance, but as long as he no longer acted openly hostile, he felt like Halea would be relatively safe among his pack members.

When he returned to the common area, he was surprised to find Halea holding Daciana's cub, who had apparently fallen asleep in her arms. She looked up at him and smiled at his return, and his heart melted. There was something so picturesque about seeing her smiling before him, holding a child in her arms, and he felt his primal instincts clawing at him from the inside.

"Is everything okay?" she asked.

"Yes. We will resume the hunt at first light," Varg said, and she nodded, understanding that he was trying to suggest she retire for the night. She was tired. It had been a long day, and she had begun to feel oddly relaxed sitting in front of the warm fire. Halea handed the sleeping wolf cub to his mother, who carried him off, and she felt a little sad to let him go.

When she turned back to Varg, he looked at her in a way that made her heart race again, and she hoped that he couldn't hear it over the dying crackles of the fire.

## CHAPTER 15 – YOU FEEL THE SAME

An even larger group of warriors and hunters had been assembled to help with the hunt than the day before. They needed to cover as much ground as possible. Once again, everyone was choosing partners before spreading out across the lycan territory. Several lycans greeted Halea that morning, and she was glad to see Daciana and Hemming were joining the search again. Many were still clearly uncomfortable with her presence, but there was no open hostility, though she suspected Lyall still hated her. When the mated pair spoke to her on friendly terms, Lyall had given a look of disapproval before deciding not to select a partner and vanishing into the forest alone.

Halea set out with Varg again, but after reaching the thick trees, she convinced him to stop long enough for her to set up a barrier trap, much like the one he had been trapped in when she first met him.

"That may not be a good idea. What if one of my pack gets trapped? We're always roaming these hunting grounds."

Halea giggled and confessed the truth she had always spared him. "Only if a dumb and weak little wolf cub wanders into it on accident. A more powerful grown therian could break out. It might hurt a bit, but it'd be impossible for a full-grown lycan to be permanently trapped."

He shot her an angry glare. "Dumb? Weak? Why you…puny human!" he growled and moved to grab her, but Halea playfully dodged him while laughing.

He chased her a short distance through the forest, and she almost would have been faster than him if she hadn't become disoriented about which direction to turn, and before she knew it, he had grabbed her from behind and caged her in his arms.

"Not so weak now, am I?" he breathed into her ear, causing a shiver to travel up the back of her neck. She could feel herself blushing, and her heart nearly jumped into her throat when his nose nuzzled softly behind her ear.

He breathed her in deeply, and he could smell it, arousal. It was only faint, but it was there, and it pleased his alpha male pride. He could feel her heart pounding as he held her tightly to him.

"Varg?" he heard her breathe, but before he could answer her, they both heard it, the howling in the distance.

Danger.

"The den is under attack!" he explained, and they set off with all their speed.

Halea and Varg were the first to return to the den from the band of warriors that set out that morning, and what they found was utter chaos. A tear had opened just

117

outside of the den, and dozens of demons were pouring out. Several powerful lycan warriors were always on guard at the den, but they were completely overwhelmed. One of the tree-dwellings had been set aflame, and lycan women and children were running and screaming in terror and panic.

Varg and Halea immediately jumped into the fight. Unless the demon numbers were subdued, she wouldn't be able to seal the tear. They needed more help.

A huge wolf appeared and barreled through a cluster of demons, ripping them apart, and Halea was sure that she recognized it as Lyall in his wolf form.

Varg was slaughtering demons all around them while shouting for the survivors to take cover.

Halea was about to make a run for the tear when she heard a woman scream.

"My cub! No, please!"

She turned to find a humanoid demon with a small female toddler grasped within its clawed hands. The little girl's mother wanted to charge after her child, but wraiths were attacking her from all sides, and she couldn't get past them.

Halea raced towards the demon, but she couldn't charge her spear while the girl was a hostage. Coming into close contact with purification would be too much for a child that young. She would have to fight the demon without her powers.

The demon looked as if it were about to take a bite out of the screaming lycan child when Halea sprang upon the creature and slashed into it with her spear. Its black blood sprayed everywhere, but it did not let go of the girl. Instead, it only tightened its grip, causing the child to wail in pain. Halea could still hear the mother screaming in terror for her child. Now that the demon knew the priestess had singled it out, it used the child as a shield.

With no other choice, Halea threw down her spear and leaped in, attacking with hand-to-hand combat, which the beast hadn't been expecting. It was unable to defend itself from her furious blows, and it dropped the screaming child, which Halea managed to catch before kicking the legs out from under the wraith.

"Here, give her to me!" a voice shouted once the demon was down, and she turned to discover that Lyall had returned to his humanoid form. Halea quickly passed him the crying child before turning back to the demon, which was scrambling back to its feet. Her spear was nowhere near, but she didn't need it. Her purification power flowed through her as she hit the beast with all her might, causing it to burst into white light, and then it was gone.

As Halea raced for the tear, she noticed more of the lycan warriors had returned and that the demons were being defeated. She raised her hands to the tear and called upon Tiamet for her strength, and with a thunderous crash, the dimensional rift sealed.

"Priestess!" someone shouted, and Halea turned to see Lyall had picked up her spear and was aiming it at her. At first, she felt a moment of panic. She had let her guard down.

"Behind you!" he shouted, before throwing her spear for her to catch, which she easily did, spinning in time to stab her charged spear through one final demon.

Once the battle was over, Varg was quickly by her side. "Halea, are you all right?" he asked in genuine concern.

"I'm okay. What about the little girl?"

"She's safe. No one died, but many were badly injured by dark blades. They'll need you."

Halea nodded her head and followed Varg. Several lycans were struggling to put out the tree-dwelling that was still ablaze, but it was clear that it would not be salvageable. All around her, people were shaken and crying. She even saw that Daciana and Hemming had returned, and they were hugging their son and Daciana's mother, but other than being frightened, they seemed okay. Faolan and Aatu were helping to move the injured, and Batsuba was working diligently on stabilizing the more critically wounded.

"Priestess Halea, may I ask for your help?" requested the old healer. Halea nodded and joined her. Varg wanted to stay close to her at a time like this, but all around him, his people were in need, and so reluctantly, he told her he would return once everyone was seen to.

Halea set to work using her powers to purify the wounds left by the dark blades, while Batsuba bandaged the wounds and administered herbal potions to prevent infection and ease the pain.

"Elder Batsuba and Priestess Halea, please let me be of assistance to you," asked Ula. Her wounds were doing much better, and she could sit up and move, though she was noticeably still in some pain. She had felt particularly helpless when the chaos erupted, and as a proud lycan warrior, that was difficult for her to deal with.

"And have you reopen those wounds? Certainly not, you will lie down until you are well, and only *I* determine when that is," chided the old healer.

Ula looked hurt to be sent away when her pack was suffering, and Halea could sense her disappointment. "You're looking much better, Ula. I'm sure it won't be long," she offered the she-wolf in consolation. Ula gave her a gentle smile in thanks, and for the first time, Halea was able to see past her stern demeanor.

Batsuba told Halea to run along once the last of the wounds were purified. Halea offered to stay and help administer more herbal remedies. She had learned quite a bit about healing herbs from Mama Dragon before becoming a full-fledged priestess, but Batsuba assured her that she had the situation under control.

Halea decided to see if she could find Varg, but she didn't make it very far before a lycan woman came running up to her with tears streaming down her face and a familiar child in her arms.

"Priestess, thank you! You saved her. I couldn't get to her. I tried so hard. There were too many of them," explained the lycan woman, who looked on the verge of hysterics. Her little girl stared up at her mother with wide, confused eyes.

"I saw you doing your best. She's okay now, and that's the important thing. What's her name?" asked Halea.

"Daisy, and I'm Ulrica. I am in your debt. Please name anything you want of me," she offered.

Halea had a feeling she was going to be dealing with a lot of the lycan's strange sense of indebtedness, especially once all those injured by the dark weapons were up and about again.

"There's no debt. I'm a priestess. Protecting life is my job."

"But…"

"Ah, no arguing! The matter is closed," interrupted Halea, sternly, but not unkindly.

"Thank you," replied Ulrica as she tried to dry her face with the back of her hand, her daughter still regarding her curiously.

Varg had seen and heard the exchange between the two women. After Ulrica left, and as soon as he could break away from his duties as leader, he went to Halea and gently placed his hand on her upper arm, trying to offer comfort through physical contact as was customary among lycans. His presence was soothing for her, and she couldn't help leaning into his gentle touch. They were standing where everyone in the pack could easily see their intimate behavior, should they choose to look, but neither cared. It had been a long and tiring day.

Varg was about to speak when they were both interrupted by the sound of Lyall's voice.

"Priestess?"

Halea was surprised that he was speaking to her, at least outside of a battle. He had never addressed her before. She turned to give him her full attention, and she was certain she heard Varg growling low under his breath, warning Lyall not to start any trouble.

Lyall heard his alpha's warning loud and clear, but he had not come to make trouble.

"You fought well today. We would have lost many pack members, perhaps the whole den, if you had not been here. Forgive me…I misjudged you."

Halea was shocked by this concession. She had been convinced that Lyall had been unwaveringly set in his ways, and it made her realize that perhaps, she too, had been too quick to judge. Perhaps Varg had been right. Maybe all they needed was time.

"Thank you, Lyall. I bear no ill will towards you or any lycans, for that matter. I came to help, and I'm glad I've been given that chance," she replied.

Lyall bowed his head respectfully towards her and then towards his alpha before walking back towards the den. Halea let out a small sigh of relief.

～～～✧～～～

That night Varg ran through the woods, allowing himself to take the form of the wolf.

They had accepted her. Human, though she was, his pack had set aside the last remnants of their hatred that day, and he couldn't be happier. He ran through the night, the breeze rustling through his fur, and he stopped to howl at the moon.

Halea had earned her place with his people, and she had always held a place in his heart.

He loved her.

He couldn't help it. Deep down, he had always loved her. He had never stopped loving her, and being reunited with her only reaffirmed what he knew all along. She belonged to him, and he belonged utterly and completely to her. He couldn't live without her again. He couldn't bear the thought of being parted from her.

But she was still a priestess.

He tried not to dwell on that. She loved him. He knew she loved him. He could see it in her eyes when she looked at him, and the way her face would flush whenever he came near her, and he could hear it in the beat of her heart. He had picked up the scent of her desire for him that day. She had to want to be with him as much as he wanted to be with her.

He knew without a doubt – his choice had been made.

The next day the warriors set out in pairs again. Many demons were tracked and slain, but it was clear by the scent trails that there were still more. They found no new tears that day, but with demons still on the loose, it was only a matter of time. Halea set barrier traps in every convenient place she could find, and Varg had ordered more guards to watch over the den while they were away. Many of the wounded were already up and feeling better, and all who were kept asking for the priestess who saved them. Halea was grateful for getting out and helping with the hunt before they had time to descend on her with all their gratitude and indebtedness. Though, she knew she wouldn't be able to avoid their attention indefinitely.

Varg appeared to be acting strangely that day, and she wasn't sure why. He seemed to be watching her extra closely, and he always looked as if he was on the verge of saying something, but he never quite came out with it. It wasn't like him. It was almost as if he was nervous to tell her something, but she dismissed that idea. Varg had always been bold, often blunt when it came to saying exactly what was on his mind. Perhaps whatever was bothering him had to do with the demons or the attack on the den from the day before. He was a pack leader with many responsibilities that she couldn't begin to fathom.

Halea had hoped returning to the den would calm him, but when they finally ended their hunt for the evening, he was more agitated than ever. She wanted to ask him what was bothering him, but by the time she finally decided to ask, they were around far too many lycan ears for her to bring up any potentially private matters. She sat beside him at the fire pit again. Despite the demon attacks and tear threats, the lycans managed to keep up their spirits during those cozy moments of camaraderie as they all shared their evening meal together. Many were more readily including Halea in their discussions, almost as if she were actually one of them.

As Halea had expected, many of the more recovered from the previous day's injured came to her, offering their gratitude. She always graciously accepted their thanks and denied their requests to offer her anything in return for doing, what to a priestess, is only her duty.

Batsuba was not with them at the fire pit, she was too busy tending to the injured, and Halea was a little relieved not to have the strange lycan healer watching her while she enjoyed her meal, especially considering Varg's behavior.

She could feel Varg's eyes on her that whole evening, and when she turned to look at him, he never averted his piercing gaze. Was she doing something wrong? He seemed unusually quiet and intense.

After their evening meal, Varg was called away to meet with the guards keeping watch over the den, and Halea decided that she was a little overwhelmed. She wasn't used to so much attention and so many people talking to her. It was nice, but it left her feeling emotionally drained. She decided to unwind before going to bed by taking a walk towards the lake she had seen earlier that day and practicing her defense formations.

She twirled her spear effortlessly from one maneuver to the next with fluidity as graceful as a dance. She was so immersed in her routine that she hadn't noticed she was being watched.

"Pretty good. Better than the bo staff, as I recall. But what about your hand-to-hand combat?" asked Varg as he emerged from the trees.

Halea was momentarily startled, but once she realized who it was, she eased into a smile at his challenge.

"You know, I don't recall us ever settling which of us was fastest?"

"Then let's settle it," he answered with a wicked grin.

Halea set down her spear and took up a fighting stance when she noticed Varg removing his chest armor. She tried to avert her eyes and not blush. He had fought her bare-chested when they were kids, it had always allowed him more freedom of movement, but his body had been so different back then. He even had a strange new scar on his chest. He definitely wasn't a skinny little kid anymore, and she could feel her face burning red.

*Great, now he has the advantage of distracting me,* she thought.

Varg's smile grew wider as he received precisely the reaction he was hoping for.

It had been years since they last sparred, and they had both learned many new techniques that they hoped would give them the advantage over the other.

Halea made the first move with a false jab, attempting to force Varg into defense, instead, he moved to knock her legs out from under her, but she was too fast and managed to avoid the attack while throwing more jabs and punches his way. She was faster than she had ever been before, and he couldn't hold back the smirk on his face at knowing how powerful she had become. He missed this. He missed having a real opponent who challenged him. The only other person who had ever challenged him and forced him to fight at his greatest potential had been his father. No other woman could ever be as worthy of being his alpha bitch as Halea.

Halea easily blocked his fists and landed a hard hit with her elbow into his ribs, finally forcing him to take defense, but Varg was determined to get the upper hand.

And that was when he punched her in the face – hard.

The blow didn't seem to faze her too much. He made impact with the side of her jaw. It did hurt, but she was so thoroughly immersed in fighting-mode that she had already recovered and was planning her next move when Varg suddenly stopped their fight.

"Halea, I'm so sorry. I thought you'd dodge it. Are you okay?"

She probably could have dodged it if she hadn't been staring at his biceps at that moment, but she wasn't about to admit that.

"It's nothing."

"Let me see."

"It's not a big deal," she argued.

"Let. Me. See. It," Varg said in a commanding tone.

"*Still pushy and domineering*," she thought, but she decided to placate him and moved closer so he could see her face. The sun had already set, but the moon and stars were bright, and she knew Varg had powerful night vision.

When she was finally close, he gently touched the side of her face. She winced a little at the contact, and he cringed, knowing that he hurt her. A bruise was already forming along her jaw, and he was furious with himself for getting carried away. They had always played rough as kids, and he hated to hurt her even then, but now he felt shame deeper than any he had ever known.

Halea watched the easily readable emotions pass over his face.

"Hey, I'm not a softy. If there's a bruise, it'll be gone before sunrise. I can heal now, ya know. So stop worrying. We knocked each other around all the time when we were kids."

"Halea, you know I'd never really hurt you, right? I'd do anything in this world to keep you safe – to protect you," he said while looking down into her eyes as they reflected the light of the stars above. His hand gently stroked the side of her face, avoiding the tender bruise.

He was so close she could feel the warmth radiating off his body, and his pale and mesmerizing blue eyes were filled with passion in the moonlight.

"I know, Varg, you've always made me feel safe."

His other hand grasped her waist, and before she registered what he was doing, he had pulled her into him. She let out a small gasp of surprise, which he quickly stifled as he pressed his lips to hers. At first, she was stiff and unresponsive, but slowly, tentatively, she relaxed against him and raised her hands to rest them on his upper arms. He moved his hand from her face to the back of her head and hungrily deepened their kiss.

His other arm held her tightly against him, and it felt like the world was spinning. She was overwhelmed as he explored her mouth, and there didn't seem to be enough air, but it didn't matter. In that moment, she would willingly drown in him.

One of her hands slid up his chest, and he groaned with desire. He wanted her touch more than anything, and then he smelled it, her arousal. He could feel her breathing heavily and hear her heart pounding as he tasted her, caressing her tongue with his.

She was his. She wanted him. She wanted his touch. She wanted his kiss. Her body was telling him secrets that even she didn't know.

The beast within him raged with primordial needs begging to be satisfied, his instincts threatening to overcome him. He moved his hand down the small of her back and firmly grasped her round ass, pulling her against him – and he knew she could feel him.

She gasped and broke their kiss as something hard began to press against her, and it was all too much too quickly.

"I'm sorry," she mumbled while pulling away from him.

He wanted to hang on. He wanted her to stay, but he picked up the faint scent of her fear, and he knew he had gone too far. He would never force himself on her. He gave his word he would never intentionally hurt her, and he meant it. Reluctantly he released her from his arms and watched her turn and run back towards the den.

He cursed himself for having come on so strongly. He had to remember that Halea was a human, and perhaps they did things differently than lycans. While he felt a terrible aching loneliness at the sudden loss of her presence, he was not deterred. For that one moment that he possessed her, he knew she felt the same for him as he felt for her, and his heart soared. It was only a matter of time before she would be his. He would not give up.

# CHAPTER 16 – CONFESSION

That night, Halea tossed and turned in bed. She couldn't ignore it anymore; things had changed between them. She had always loved Varg but had never thought of him *that* way when they were young. But they weren't children anymore. She couldn't deny the way her heart fluttered when he looked at her with his piercing blue eyes. She couldn't pretend that being close to him didn't give her butterflies in her stomach. She couldn't ignore the way she ached for his touch every time he was near. It felt inappropriate to react that way towards someone who had only ever been a friend. Varg was a lycan and a pack leader; wouldn't he prefer someone of his own kind? Lycan women were all so fierce and beautiful, and an alpha could have his pick of willing partners. Maybe it was just a wolf thing? Maybe there was some lycan custom she had misunderstood?

"*I should have told him to get his own damn bread,*" she thought and buried her red face in her hands as she rolled over and groaned. But deep down, she didn't regret that he had kissed her. Her body burned every time she remembered the way his hands touched her, the way he felt pressed against her, the way his lips left her weak and trembling. She had never felt so much, so alive, in her entire life. But it was wrong.

A priestess could take lovers as long as they didn't become attached, but how could she not care for Varg? Her duties had to come first, and she knew by the terrible ache in her heart that she was already dreading the thought that once her mission was complete, she would have to leave lycan territory and perhaps not return for many years if ever. The thought of losing Varg again after only just having him back in her life made her feel sick with dread.

After many years, decades, centuries, she imagined returning again only to find Varg with a mate and cubs of his own, forgetting all about his old friend. Her eyes welled up with tears. Varg deserved such happiness, but it was something she could never give him, and the thought of being separated and forgotten was tearing a hole in her heart. She was terrified that perhaps she was already in too deep.

~~~☼~~~

Halea came down to the common area for breakfast and was relieved when she didn't see Varg. He was probably deciding which hunters to take and which would stay behind and guard the den. Her heart was pounding in her chest with anxiety. What would she say to him? What would he say to her? Had she upset him by running off? Was he angry with her?

"What's wrong?" asked Daciana, who was feeding her son when Halea joined her, and she instantly smelled the strong reek of anxiety.

Halea cringed. *"Oh, gods, they can smell it. Oh, no, he'll smell it!"* she thought while cursing the lycan's powerful sense of smell.

"I...had some bad dreams, nightmares. All these tears, it's a lot of stress for a priestess."

Halea had already reeked of anxiety, and her heart rate had already been high, so Daciana was unable to detect her falsehood. In fact, it seemed highly believable, it looked like the poor woman hadn't slept a wink, and she couldn't begin to understand what it was like to be a priestess.

"Here," said Batsuba, who had been observing the two young women in their conversation. "Drink this. It will relax you a little," she explained while offering Halea a cup of an unusual smelling tea. Batsuba usually only brewed such a tea for evenings and chose more caffeinated teas for morning consumption, but she could tell the priestess was stressed out the moment she came into the common area.

"Thank you," Halea replied as she readily accepted the pottery cup from the old healer. Drinking something relaxing in the morning after not sleeping probably wasn't a good idea, but she was desperate to calm her nerves before Varg arrived.

Batsuba eyed Halea as she gulped the drink a little too readily, but she said nothing.

Varg found Halea before they were about to leave, and despite her best efforts, he could still smell that she had recently been anxious, and he smiled a predatory smile as he approached her.

Her face suddenly grew pale.

"Everything okay?" he asked in a teasing tone.

"Yeah. Yeah, I'm fine. I'm good. I'm ready. I'm fine," Halea rambled, but he could hear her heart rate quicken at his approach, and he reveled in knowing that he had such a powerful effect on her.

She couldn't gauge if he was angry or not. They couldn't exactly talk about what happened in front of all the other lycan warriors, but there was something about the way he looked at her that let her know the subject would come up the moment they were alone.

Ula had fully recovered from her wounds and was happy to rejoin the hunt. She even offered to be Halea's partner, but Varg told her that wouldn't be necessary, and so the she-wolf had instead partnered again with Lyall. Halea couldn't help but shake the disappointment that maybe partnering with Ula for the day wouldn't have been such a bad idea.

Shortly after the group set out, but before they split up for the day, a runner caught up with them and asked to speak with Varg alone.

"I'll go on ahead. You can catch up with me later," offered Halea, who ran off before Varg could protest. He could simply track her scent. She wasn't going to avoid him that easily.

Halea made it as far as the northwestern hunting grounds, and still, Varg was nowhere behind her. It must have been important business. Perhaps he had even been called back to the den. Whatever the reason, she was glad for any extra moment she could get before having to discuss the events of the previous night. Despite tossing and turning the whole night and running through lycan territory most of the morning, she was still at a loss for what to do or say.

Once she was well alone in the forest, she began setting more barrier traps. She stumbled on several of the traps she had already set, and at least two had managed to successfully capture and purify demons. She could tell by the subtle scorch marks of purification on the ground and trees.

Between her troubled mind and activating runes for a barrier, she was too distracted to sense that she was being watched until it was too late.

Something sprang out of the trees at her and knocked her to the ground. She cried out in pain as a blade slashed down the back of her upper left arm. She was able to knock the attacker away and get back to her feet when she discovered herself face to face with a wraith, its dark blade gleaming in its clawed hand. It sneered at her with its creepy eyeless face.

She had set down her spear to perform the spell for the barrier, and now the demon stood between her and her weapon.

It lunged at her, but she was able to stop its weapon by gripping the demon's wrist and using her own body's momentum to toss her assailant. With the wraith down, she quickly grabbed her spear and finished it as it was rising again for the attack. Her charged weapon caused it to burst into a flame of white, and then it was gone.

Her arm ached painfully where the dark blade had cut her, and she quickly began digging through her travel bag to find her medical supplies.

"Halea?" she heard Varg shout in the distance.

"Varg, I'm over here," she called, and the next moment, he was crouching next to where she sat on the ground with her open bag.

"I smelled blood! What happened? Are you okay?" he frantically asked with a fading trace of red in his eyes.

"One of those bastards got the jump on me when I was putting up a trap. It's gone now," she explained while pressing her hand over her wound to slow the bleeding, the white sleeve of her robe now stained red.

Varg was following her scent when the wind changed direction, and he recognized the smell of her blood. He was furious that he hadn't been there to watch over her while she worked.

"You shouldn't have gone on alone. What if you'd been killed?"

"I'm almost always alone when I'm performing my duties as a priestess. Injuries happen…a lot. They'll happen again when I…they'll happen again," she said, quickly cutting herself off. She didn't want to bring up having to leave someday. She didn't want to think about it.

Varg scowled as he guessed what she had almost said, and it cut him like a knife to think she would even consider leaving him. He couldn't allow it. He had to prove to her that her place was with him.

"It's still bleeding. Here, let me help you," he offered.

Halea's face flushed red, and her heart started pounding. There was no way to get to the injury without pulling herself out of the upper half of her robe, but sadly she needed the help. The wound needed to be stitched, or she would keep losing blood, and it was difficult for her to see behind her upper arm. If she tried bandaging it without closing it, the wound would take longer to heal, and she would weaken from blood loss. If she were alone, she would have to suffer from temporary vulnerability. She had done it before, but it was better to avoid such a situation.

He could sense her hesitation, but he didn't want to force himself on her. He didn't want to make her uncomfortable and frighten her away again. He wanted to prove to her that he could take care of her and that she could trust him.

At last, she turned her back to him and untied the red sash that held her robe closed. Her breasts were bound beneath her robe because the active lifestyle of a priestess required such support, but her breast binding left little to the imagination.

Varg averted his eyes, tempted though he was, and waited until she pulled her sore, injured arm from the bloody, damaged sleeve.

She crossed her good arm over her chest to cover as much of herself as she could and settled onto the ground.

"Everything you need is already laid out," she said when ready.

Varg crouched down close behind her and began washing the wound with the water from her water bag. Even the cool water stung against the pain of the gash, but she gritted her teeth and waited as he prepared the needle for the stitches.

It was hard to stay focused being so close to her. Her scent was driving him crazy, and all he wanted to do was bury his nose into her hair and hold her close. It wasn't helping that he could easily see over her shoulder, and from where he was, the view looked just like heaven. He immediately felt guilty peeking and again tried to pay attention to the task at hand.

Once he started stitching the gash closed, Halea decided to talk to him to distract herself from the discomfort of the needle.

"Where did you go?"

"I had to return to the den. The runner was sent to let me know that the eastern lycan pack should be arriving after sundown. The other packs will not be far behind them. The gathering is about to begin."

He could instantly smell her anxiety again.

"It's going to be okay. I won't let anyone hurt you. Most of my pack is indebted to you. They wouldn't let anyone else hurt you either."

Once the final stitch was in place, he wrapped the bandage around her arm.

"I'm sorry my returning has made things difficult for you."

"Don't say that," he argued, sliding his arms underneath hers and wrapping them around her. Her heart began pounding as he pulled her into him and gently kissed her temple.

"I want you here," he breathed softly into her ear, and she involuntarily shivered. Slowly his lips moved down the side of her face, and with a gentle nudge against her jaw, she leaned her head to the side, giving him access to her throat. His instincts nearly went into overload when she exposed her throat for him. Perhaps it meant little to humans, but to lycans, it was a sign of submission, and from a female, it meant she was offering herself to him.

He inhaled deeply as he tightened his hold on her, trying to remind himself to go slowly with her, but the scent of her arousal was already growing, and the beast within hungered for more.

She shouldn't let this happen. She should turn him away, but the moment she felt his lips exploring her throat, the way his tongue would slide slowly up to the base of her ear, and the way his razor-sharp fangs skated over the surface of her skin, she could only close her eyes and give in. She wanted to be in his arms and feel his touch as his hands explored her body. She wanted to be with him.

When she didn't refuse him, he grew bolder and began to let his right hand wander. She had stopped trying to cover herself with her good arm, and he took the opportunity to move his hand along the small of her waist and slowly up until he cupped one of her ample breasts and gently began to massage it. He could smell her arousal spike, and he knew she wanted more.

Every scent from her was driving him mad. Even the blood from her wound was enticing him. He was almost intoxicated just breathing her in.

Jarringly, he released her and shifted her around so he could pull her onto his lap and have her facing him, and he captured her lips with his own. This time she didn't hesitate and returned his kiss, delving hungrily into his mouth with her tongue and caressing the sides of his face with her hands before letting her fingers tangle in his thick, dark hair, causing him to groan in pleasure. Emboldened, his hands wandered down her back and lower, grasping her bottom. She moaned into his mouth at his touch, and he moved his hands down, even more, to grab her thighs and wrap them around his waist. She could feel him now, his hard member straining against his leather trousers. There was so little between them, and she was growing wet at just the thought of what he could do to her. Her whole body was burning as his hands moved back up, and when she felt his hand wind into her hair, pulling her head back, she gave in as he released her lips only to dive into her throat, sucking her warm flesh and lapping at her with his tongue. She released one of her hands from his hair and let it slide down his chest, but his armor and furs were still in the way. Sensing her desire, with his free hand, he quickly unclasped his armor, breaking contact with her throat only long enough to pull everything off and exposing his powerful chest.

She wasted no time exploring him and letting her fingers glide over every rippling muscle. He struggled to breathe as she left trails of fire wherever her soft hands caressed him, and he could feel himself straining against her as her fingers curiously explored the scar across his chest.

He untied the front of her robe, and she stopped caressing him long enough for him to slide down her garment and free her uninjured arm. He slid both hands beneath her breasts, pushing upwards, and buried his face in her collar. She reached behind herself with her good arm and undid the clasp to her bindings, allowing him to have his prize.

He captured her lips in another deep kiss as he let his hands revel in the feel of her soft skin. He circled his thumbs slowly over her taut nipples, causing a wave of heat and desire to travel to her core, and the extra spike in her arousal was nearly enough to send the red into his eyes. He needed more.

Again, he shifted her, being careful of her injured arm, and before she knew it, she was lying on her back, and he was on top of her, staring into her soul. She reached up and softly caressed his face, and he moved in to place a slow and gentle kiss to her lips.

Her robe had already been removed, leaving her with only her undergarments, and she could feel his hands moving down her body and tugging them downwards. He broke their kiss long enough to reach down and yank off her boots, then pulled her undergarments down past her legs, freeing her from the last of her clothes. She was completely at the mercy of his eyes.

She blushed to be exposed before him, and he predatorily smiled at her shyness before moving back up her body. She suddenly seemed embarrassed to look him in the eye, but he refused to let her be ashamed. She was beautiful, and he would willingly spend the rest of his life doing everything he could to let her know it. He ran his calloused fingers along the side of her jaw. The bruise from the night before was entirely gone. She finally looked at him with her beautiful hazel green eyes. She had always been impressed with the vividness of his eyes, but hers were far more attractive. They were the color of the forest, and when he looked into her eyes, he felt at home. She was everything to him, and she always had been. He gently let his thumb glide across the top of her cheek and was pleased to see a few remaining childhood freckles. He had always loved every freckle on her face. The crystal she had given him so long ago still hung around her neck.

He softly tasted her lips, which she parted for him. She was his. She wanted him as much as he wanted her, and he would do anything to please her. Slowly his mouth trailed down her chin and throat, stopping to lap at her collarbone, causing her body to writhe beneath him. When he moved his hot mouth over her breasts, she let out a small gasp as he hungrily sucked on one of her nipples while gently torturing the other with the pad of his thumb. His sharp fangs grazed her flesh, but he never cut her. Even his claws were gentle as his other hand glided over her body, his pointed fingernails softly raking her flesh but never damaging the skin. His mouth moved from one breast to the other, and she moaned in bliss as the heat grew within her core. The sound of her pleasure was exciting him, but he would not rest until he had shown her what it meant to be loved by an alpha.

He released her nipple and moved lower still, lapping at her navel and raking his claws along her thighs. She gasped when he opened her legs, and her eyes shot open as he nudged his nose into her warm wet heat.

The scent of her arousal was not enough, he needed to taste it, and he growled with pleasure as he ran his tongue along her fold, and she let out a startled moan.

He swirled his tongue around her swollen and sensitive node, and she dug her hands into the grass of the forest floor to keep the world from spinning around her. Barely able to catch her breath, she cried out when his hot tongue moved inside of her, teasing her entrance and thrusting with promise. She could hear his strange inhuman growl of pleasure as she writhed beneath him. She could barely hold still as he tortured her, and she opened her thighs wider for him. His grip on her tightened, almost painfully, but to her, it was bliss.

She needed him. Her body needed him, and the alpha in him was raging to provide. He heard her scream out his name as she threw back her head and her body trembled as he lapped at her juices. He quickly removed all the clothing from the lower half of his body as she lay there quivering and gasping for air before opening her legs again and positioned himself at her entrance.

"Halea, tell me you want me," he breathed into her ear as he leaned over her.

Everything was still reeling around her. When he removed the last of his clothes, she almost gasped. He was so immense. Was she ready for this? This was Varg, her Varg. He was the only one she wanted, but was it wrong to want him? She shook those thoughts away when he spoke his command into her ear. She couldn't lie to him, and he knew it.

"Varg, I want you," she affirmed and gasped as he slowly, gently, began to nudge inside of her.

He could feel the untouched nature of her body, and he stifled a growl of satisfaction.

His. His and his alone. No one else would ever have her, just as no one else could ever have him.

He moved as gently as possible, desperate to avoid bringing her any pain as her body stretched to accommodate him. It took every ounce of his strength to restrain himself. His eyes were bleeding red into blue. She let out a small whimper once he was finally sheathed inside of her, and she trembled in his arms. Her heart was hammering, and she gasped for air.

"Are you in pain?" he asked.

She couldn't speak and could barely think, but she nodded her head 'no' and gently ran her hands along his muscular back. The need was desperately building within her again. She was ready.

He let out a low growl of pleasure as she ran her hands along his body. He could smell her arousal building again, and once more, he found himself struggling to remain in control and not let the beast take over. Slowly he began to thrust inside of her, being careful to give her time to adjust. Her body quaked beneath him, and he buried his nose in her neck.

Nothing else mattered to her at that moment, only him and the way he made her feel. She could tell he was struggling to be gentle with her and that he was dying to unleash his true nature, but she wanted him to let go. If only for that moment, she wanted to give him what he needed and allow him to possess her.

"More, Varg, please," she pleaded, and she didn't have to ask him twice.

At her words, he could hold back no more, and he pummeled himself inside of her with long hard strokes. She cried out in pleasure, and he growled in satisfaction to finally be claiming her.

His. His Halea. She was his love, his life, his world, and he would never give her up. Never.

She cried out for him as he gently ran his fangs along her throat. So close. She could be his for all eternity with only one mark, and the beast within him was raging for him to claim her as his own, but he couldn't, not now. It was not a decision she could regret. She was human and didn't understand what it would mean, and he could never do that to her. There could be no permanent bond if she didn't want it as much as he did, but he would bide his time. He would have her again.

He felt her blunt human nails run down his back, leaving trails of stinging fire, nearly undoing him, but he would not give in until her need was met. She was close. He could feel it. She was gasping for air and writhing beneath him, her body begging for him, needing him, and he would give anything for her.

At last, she screamed out for him, her walls clenched around his shaft, and her body went limp in his arms. With a snarling growl, he released himself inside of her, longing to sink his fangs in, but forcing back the red that was threatening to take over his eyes.

They were both gasping for breath, and he wrapped his arms tightly around her trembling body as he stared into her hazy eyes.

"Halea, I love you."

# CHAPTER 17 – A GATHERING OF WOLVES

She looked back at him in shock. Deep down, she always knew how he felt, but she had tried to convince herself otherwise because it seemed impossible that a human priestess and an alpha lycan could ever be allowed to love each other.

"Varg, please don't. I'm a priestess. I'm not allowed to be in love," she pleaded as her eyes teared up.

His eyes narrowed. "Just because you're not allowed doesn't mean you aren't."

"It's not that I don't want to be with you, but I don't belong here. I'm not a lycan. I swore an oath to Tiamet. Please understand."

He released her and got up and began pulling on his clothes. She felt so ashamed. She had let it go too far. He wanted something she couldn't give him, and now she had hurt him. Varg meant more to her than anyone in the world, and though she couldn't allow the words to pass her lips, she loved him. He was the last person in the world she would ever want to hurt.

She began pulling on her clothes, suddenly remembering the pain in her wound. The blood had already dried and become stiff on her left sleeve, and she would have to clean and repair her robe again.

She heard him sigh and looked up. His back was to her when he finally spoke.

"This is my fault. I know you're not a lycan," he explained and turned to look into her eyes.

"Halea, I love you. I've always loved you. I want you. I want to be with you. I can't be with anyone else because I've chosen you. I don't want to take anything away from you, and I know what being a priestess has always meant to you. It's just that when we lycans know who we love, we love without doubt. Once that choice is made, things move rather quickly. I know this is a lot to put on you so soon, and I'm sorry. I know you haven't even been a priestess for very long, but I will wait for you. I don't care how long it takes; you're my chosen. I can't forget you or just stop loving you. It doesn't work that way, not for us."

She would have preferred it if he had just been angry with her. She wouldn't have blamed him if he had kicked her right out of his territory. But this - this was wrong. What if she never gave up being a priestess? How was that fair to him? And what did he mean it didn't work that way? That couldn't be true!

"Varg…"

"Halea, please. I don't want to lose you. I don't want to frighten you away," he said, interrupting her. "Even if you can't ever love me as more than a friend, please just don't take that away from me."

She reached out for him and wrapped her arms around his waist and buried her face in his chest as the tears flowed down her cheeks. She could hear his heart hammering in his chest, and she could feel her own breaking.

He wrapped his arms around her, desperate for her comfort and terrified that she would turn away from him forever.

"Nothing will ever change how much I care about you, Varg. I promise. I don't want to lose you either. It's just that I can't give you what you want. I'm so sorry."

He didn't believe that. He couldn't allow himself to believe that. He knew in his heart that she loved him. She could deny it all she wanted, but he knew the truth. He would not give her up. He didn't care how long it took; someday, she would belong to him, but for the moment, he would be patient. He was just grateful that she wasn't going to run away. At least she didn't hate him. He would rather have her as only a friend than lose her entirely, though he knew he would always want more. He couldn't help it.

He pulled back from her a little so he could look down into her eyes, and gently wiped the tears from her face. He had always hated to see her cry. He never understood why it bothered him so much when they were young, but now he knew.

"We should return to the den. I want Batsuba to see to your arm, and the gathering is about to begin."

She nodded in agreement, and then a terrifying thought occurred to her, and her eyes shot open.

"Varg! I forgot to perform a contraceptive spell," she cried and suddenly went deathly pale, and he was nearly overwhelmed by the smell of her fear and anxiety.

"Halea, it's okay. You're not fertile right now," he assured. She had passed her time of fertility several days ago.

"What? How would you know?" she questioned, clearly not convinced.

He laughed his deep laugh and smiled at her. "Don't you remember? I once told you I could smell when bitches are in heat."

Suddenly she did remember. She had no clue what he meant at the time, she was only a child, but it then occurred to her that maybe the lycan sense of smell could pick up on a female's subtle bodily changes that signaled her days of fertility. She felt embarrassed to be once again reminded of just how little was private when it came to lycans, and then she thought of something else.

"We smell like sex, don't we?"

He laughed even louder this time, and she groaned.

He took her in his arms again, surprising her a little, and he leaned in to whisper into her ear. "Let them smell it. I don't care anymore. I want everyone to know that you belong to me, and I don't give a damn if someone doesn't like it. I'm tired of keeping it a secret," he said as his lips began to nibble her ear.

He was making her heart race again, and he could detect the faintly renewed scent of her arousal.

134

Reluctantly she pulled away from him, leaving a disappointed look on his face. "I don't belong to you," she argued.

"It's only a matter of time," he replied matter-of-factly. "Haven't you already broken the rules for being a priestess?"

"I said I'm not allowed to love. I didn't say I wasn't allowed to have sex."

And she instantly regretted saying that as she watched a hungry predatory look come over him.

"Really?" he asked in a deep and seductive voice.

She blushed a little but held her ground.

"You behave yourself, you mangy wolf. You may be ready to brag about your conquests to your pack, but I'm not."

His face grew serious again. "It's not like that."

He could tell she was about to be stubborn, one of the few traits he was hoping she would have outgrown, but apparently not. Again, he had to remind himself that she was a human, and from what he had learned from her when they were younger, humans were far more prudish about sex than lycans were. He found it odd, but he had given his word that he would wait for her. He could only take what she would willingly give him, and if she wasn't ready to let him reveal his intentions towards her for his whole pack to know, he would have to respect that.

He sighed in resignation. "Fine, have it your way. There's a stream not far from here. We can wash up before we return, and there are plants that you can rub onto the skin to help remove and mask scents."

Much to his disappointment, she insisted they bathe separately. So, once he had given her the plants, which were easy to find, he waited out in the thick trees. When he first brought her to the den, his pack had been disturbed to discover their scents all over each other, but since hunting demons and sparring together, his pack had already come to accept the presence of her human smell. Her scent was all over the common area and the main fire pit, and she even left traces of herself on the many lycans she had healed with her purification powers. It bothered his people at first, but they no longer seemed to notice it. She didn't realize it, but they were already accustomed to her presence.

When it was finally his turn to bathe, he hated it. He hated washing her away. True, she wasn't his mate, and he had no idea how long he would be forced to wait, but that didn't mean he wasn't going to stake his claim on her. He didn't want any other males near her, and leaving his scent on her would serve as a warning that she was his woman and for others to stay away. Her scent on him would have the same effect for females, which he did not mind. He had no problem with letting it be known that he belonged to her. He would howl it to the heavens if only she would let him, but he had to tread carefully. She had not run from him, and she had not ended their friendship, but she could take that all back if he pushed too hard. It was so difficult for him as an alpha male; the instinct to claim and possess was almost unbearable.

~~~☼~~~

When they returned to the den, the sun was still up, and the other lycan warriors had not yet returned. They had heard no distress howls, so they knew no new tears had been found.

Despite all that transpired between them that day, she felt far less awkward in his presence now, even though she was still greatly troubled by his assertion that she would someday belong to him. It wasn't unusual for Varg to be so sure of himself, often smugly so. She had rather hoped he would learn a little humility with age, but apparently, he had not.

From now on, she would have to be careful not to tread beyond the boundaries of their friendship. She didn't want to encourage him with the idea that she could just drop everything to be with him. She had allowed it to happen already, and she had already hurt him. She didn't want to get his hopes up more than they already were.

Reluctantly, Varg had to leave her to prepare his pack for the arrival of the eastern wolves. It pained him greatly because he could smell her anxiety rising again at the thought of having to deal with a new and unfamiliar lycan pack. It would be like she was starting from the bottom all over again, and she remembered how poorly her presence went over the last time.

He left her in the care of Batsuba, who immediately went to work brewing herbs to ensure Halea's arm would not become infected and to reduce the pain and swelling. Halea could have done that herself, but the moment Varg mentioned to the old healer that the priestess had been injured, she sprang into action.

Batsuba had not missed the look of concern on her leader's face when he spoke of the priestess being injured. Had he not yet made his interests known? Perhaps he had, and the priestess rejected him? It was hard to conceive of any unmated female refusing an alpha such a Varg, but then again, Halea was human and a worshiper of the dragon deity. Varg's sex life, or lack thereof, wasn't really any of her business, but Batsuba couldn't help but be intrigued that the normally aloof male had finally taken an interest in someone and that that someone was so unusual.

They sat in the healer's tree-dwelling while Batsuba worked. Halea took off her robe and chanted a spell to remove the blood and close the new tear, and that was when Batsuba thought she detected the almost imperceptible smell of something familiar still embedded in Halea's garments. Perhaps Varg was successful after all.

Halea redressed and finished the last of her medicinal tea while listening to Batsuba discuss her healing arts when they both heard a commotion outside. The two women both went out to discover that all the excitement was because the eastern lycan pack had finally arrived.

Halea watched from the deck of Batsuba's tree as the common area flooded with excited lycans, welcoming the others like long-separated friends and family. Again, Halea felt a lonely ache inside.

Below she could see Varg approach another big male, whom she assumed was a fellow alpha, and they greeted each other warmly. Standing beside the eastern lycan leader was a particularly beautiful lycan woman, and Halea wondered if perhaps she was his mate until that same female threw herself onto Varg in a forward embrace.

Halea's jaw dropped. This female was obviously flirting with Varg, though Varg quickly pulled away from her and proceeded to occupy himself with greeting the other lycans from the eastern pack. Did he know her? Were they?

A painful thought crossed her mind. How could she have been so stupid? Lycans were so openly sexual; it was silly for her to believe she had been Varg's first. Varg had mentioned that his people took refuge in the east. He probably knew that woman very well. He probably knew many women very well. A strong, handsome, alpha male, without a mate, she could see how he could easily have any woman he wanted. Anger boiled within her, but she tried to push it away.

It would be better for Varg to forget her. It would be better for him to be with a woman of his own kind. Hadn't she wanted him to give up on loving her? Wouldn't finding someone else be the way? But suddenly, being faced with the very real prospect of him ever being with someone else made her heart ache with unbearable pain. She cursed herself for being so selfish.

Batsuba sensed the priestess tensing up beside her, and she looked in time to catch the unmistakable face of jealousy on the young woman.

"We should go down and greet them," said the healer.

Halea startled a little. "And get Varg into another fight?"

"They know you're here. That's why Varg sent for them. Your presence will be expected."

Halea groaned but nodded her head and began to walk down the spiraling stairs of Batsuba's home. Her stomach churned, and she stopped momentarily to take a few deep breaths. She had to remain calm and sure. She couldn't face that other pack reeking of anxiety. She couldn't afford to look weak or frightened at a time like this, especially not in front of that other female.

As she approached the outer crowd surrounding the common area, for a moment, she hoped she could just hang back and maybe go unnoticed.

"Halea," called Varg.

"*Damn him*," she thought.

He had been subtly looking around for her and noticed her when she and Batsuba came down to the common area. Everyone parted before her, and now she had no choice but to go to him.

Halea could feel the disapproving glares of the eastern lycan pack on her as she approached and went to stand beside Varg, her head held high.

"Ethelwolf, this is Priestess Halea. Halea, this is Ethelwolf, the alpha leader of the eastern wolf pack," introduced Varg, and Halea gave a polite half-bow. When she rose, she was surprised to see that the eastern leader did not seem at all perturbed by her presence, at least not outwardly so.

"Greetings, Priestess. You'll have to forgive my pack. Many were not alive when our lands last saw a convergence, but I've seen it for myself, and while I'm not particularly fond of your kind, I am aware of the necessity of priestesses to seal tears. When the lycan council gathers, you will have my support."

"Thank you. I will do everything within my power to keep the tears contained, and you can have my word that I mean no harm to you or any of your people. I only wish to do my duty."

The other alpha nodded his head in acceptance of her word, then turned back to Varg and began a more casual conversation. The two packs had formed a solid camaraderie in the years that the western lands were uninhabitable, and Varg was happy to see the old eastern leader again. He had been counting on his support in the lycan council and was relieved to know that despite his father's regrets, Ethelwolf's opinions on the necessity of priestesses had not changed.

Halea felt awkward. Why hadn't Varg dismissed her? She didn't need to be present for these pleasantries, and she had fulfilled her social obligations. That was when she again noticed the lycan female who threw herself at Varg was staring particularly hard in her direction. She quickly glanced back at the she-wolf and received a cold and scrutinizing glare as if she were being sized up. Halea had a feeling she wasn't going to like that woman at all.

After an agonizingly long amount of time, the evening meal was announced, and everyone began to gather around the fire pits. Halea thought it best to retire for the night and leave the lycans to themselves, but she didn't get very far when she heard Varg's voice.

"And where do you think you're going, Priestess?" he asked in a mocking tone, and when she turned back to him, he had a wolfish grin on his face.

"I assumed my presence would not be required at your feast tonight," she curtly replied.

"You assumed wrong. You will join me at my fire pit tonight," Varg said in a pompous and commanding tone. She shot him a fiery look, but his smile only widened.

Reluctantly, she followed him back to the common area. More than half of the pit consisted of eastern pack members. Varg sat in his usual place, and she thought perhaps she should sit away from him as Ethelwolf took his place to Varg's immediate left. As she turned to move further away, she felt his large hand grab her wrist, and silently he pulled her down close beside him on his right. She shot him another angry glare, but his smile of triumph didn't fade. It was then that she noticed the arrival of that female lycan again, and she instantly received a death stare from the she-wolf as she observed the human female sitting so close to Varg. Suddenly Halea was actually glad Varg had made her stay. Instead, the female lycan moved to sit on the other side of Ethelwolf.

Halea could feel disapproving eyes on her from the newly arrived eastern lycans, and a few even got up and left once they realized the human would be joining them. She tried not to let it bother her. It would probably only become even more awkward as the other packs arrived. She was certain they wouldn't all have leaders as agreeable as Ethelwolf.

One of the females from Varg's pack handed her a plate of food meant to appease her human palette. Varg's pack had already gotten over the shock of her strange human diet, but she could tell the eastern lycans were appalled as she sat there and quietly chewed her food.

Halea barely paid attention as Varg discussed lycan matters with Ethelwolf. She was exhausted, lost in her own thoughts, and still struggling to come to terms with what happened between her and Varg earlier that day.

Slowly lycans began to leave the fire pit after finishing their meal, and even Ethelwolf got up and wished Varg a good evening as another lycan came to escort him to where he would be staying for the night.

Varg finally had an opportunity to focus on Halea again, but to his displeasure, Otsana had not left with the others. Instead, she scooted closer to him on his left side as soon as her father was gone.

Varg tried to ignore her and turned to Halea, who looked distracted and had barely touched her meal.

"Was there something wrong with the food?" he asked, and Halea suddenly snapped out of it and looked up at him with wide eyes.

She was about to say something when the lycan female interrupted.

"Varg, I'm so glad to have you all to myself now that father's gone. I've missed you so much since your pack left the east."

Halea had been wondering what her relation to the eastern pack leader was, she had rather been hoping he was a mate due to them looking so close in age, but she had once again forgotten the eerie way immortals blended in with their own children.

Her blood boiled. *All to herself? He's not alone. I'm sitting right here!*" Halea thought bitterly and suddenly decided she didn't want to be there for their reunion. She moved to stand up when Varg grabbed her wrist again.

"You haven't finished your dinner. Stay," Varg asked, this time his tone sounding like a plea rather than a command. If not for that, she would have pulled away from him, but she relented and sat back down.

Halea chanced a glance past Varg, and the female lycan gave her a murderous glare.

"It's a beautiful night. Why don't we take a stroll where we can have a little more privacy?" asked the she-wolf.

"I am glad you're doing well, Otsana, but I'm going to be rather busy tonight. Perhaps you should ask Faolan or Aatu," Varg said, but inside he was dying to tell her to 'piss off.' Sadly, as a leader, he could no longer be rude when brushing her off. She was a guest in his den, and her father was the eastern lycan pack leader, though Ethelwolf had never done anything to encourage his daughter's behavior.

Otsana was about to protest when he quickly turned back to Halea, who was staring down at her half-eaten meal, looking uncomfortable. Was she angry about Otsana's behavior? He hoped not.

"Is it that bad?" he asked and reached out in an attempt to pluck a piece of fruit from Halea's plate, but she was too quick for him and instantly slapped his hand away, her face turning bright red in embarrassment.

Both women knew exactly what he had been trying to prove with his little gesture, and Halea was relieved when the she-wolf jumped up in a furious huff and stomped off.

Varg was doing his best not to burst out laughing, but he certainly couldn't wipe the grin off his face. Halea looked mortified.

She stood up, yanking her arm out of the way before he could snatch her back down again and accidentally sending a shock of pain to her injury. Varg noticed her flinch at the sudden movement, and he jumped up beside her.

"It's nothing. I'm just tired," she explained, trying to brush it off.

"I'm sorry, I'll walk you," he offered, feeling sorry for having caused her to hurt herself.

"You don't have to," she said in a sharp tone, but when she walked away, he followed her. She could tell people were watching them leave together, and she wanted to die of embarrassment. Once they were safely up the path that led to her private cave and further from the main gathering of lycans, Varg spoke to her in a whisper.

"Halea?"

"You don't have to babysit me. You can go visit with her," she said as quietly as she could.

Varg clasped the hand on her uninjured arm and quickly pulled her through the entryway of a cave she had never been in before and closed the massive doors behind them.

"Halea, are you angry about Otsana?"

"No! I don't care what you do," she snapped and suddenly regretted having said anything at all. It was clear Varg could smell her lying.

She tried to look away from him, but he wrapped his arm around her and gently tilted her face up with his free hand to force her to look into his eyes.

"Halea, she is nothing to me."

"You seem to be something to her."

He suddenly realized what had made her feel so threatened.

"Halea, I belong to you. I have always belonged to you, only you. Perhaps humans do things differently, but lycans are loyal. Even when I thought you were dead, there was never anyone else for me."

She wanted to believe his words, but it seemed so impossible. What if she had really been dead? What if she had never come back? Was she actually supposed to believe that he had held onto a childhood crush and hadn't moved on with this life?

Then she thought back on her own life. She had never felt for any man what she felt for Varg. Even when she believed he had died, she never had allowed herself to get close to anyone else. No matter how many men tried to tempt her into their beds, she had always turned them away, and she had never really understood why. Had she spent all those years being loyal to a ghost?

Rather than finding that comforting, she only found herself more troubled. She couldn't give him what he wanted, and the thought that he would be loyal to her and forsake finding happiness elsewhere hurt her just as badly as the thought of him succeeding in finding love with another woman. It seemed she was doomed to suffer no matter what happened. But for his sake, she had to set aside her petty jealousy and hope that he would let her go.

"Varg, you don't have to be loyal to me. You deserve to be with someone who can make you happy and…"

"You make me happy! No one else! I will not give you up! I would gladly spend a thousand ages alone for just a chance to someday make you mine. I would never settle for anyone else."

Her eyes began to tear up. This was so wrong. She regretted ever coming back. She could give him nothing but misery.

He clasped her tighter to him. He had to make her see how much he loved her. He needed her to understand that he would do anything to be with her. He gently wiped a tear from her face, then leaned down, and his lips came close to hers.

"Please, Varg," she said, turning her head and pulling away. "I'm sorry…I just…I need to go rest."

"You can sleep here," he offered, and she suddenly bothered to take notice of their surroundings. This cave was massive. It contained a minimal amount of items, but they were all lovely, and there was a huge comfortable looking bed. It was someone's living quarters.

"Where am I?"

"This is my private cave."

She was speechless. She had first seen the lycan den from a distance as a child. She knew that lycans could have beautiful homes and live comfortably, probably better than most humans, but she could never fully imagine what Varg's personal space would look like. When they were kids, she would have never assumed him to be one to keep a tidy room or even a room that looked like a room. This space was both rustic and elegant. The furniture was of solid wood, beautifully carved, and smoothly polished. There was a massive bed covered in soft, comfortable furs and a stone bath carved into the cave wall and fed with natural spring water. She noticed a bow propped up in the corner and assumed he must have taken up bird hunting. She wouldn't have expected it, but she couldn't deny that this living space did seem to fit him.

"Wow…it's nice. Nicer than I thought it'd be."

"What's that supposed to mean?" he asked with a slight tone of offense.

"Well, ya know, there's no pile of old chewed on bones. No muddy footprints all over the floor."

He gave her a cutting glare. "I'll have you know I throw my old bones way in the back where no one can see them, and I lick the floors clean at least once in a while."

She was trying hard not to crack a smile and failing miserably. "It is nice. Not too shabby for a mangy wolf, but I think I better go to my own cave."

He grabbed her hand as she moved away and pulled her close again. He leaned in and whispered hotly into her ear.

"Stay with me. I want you in my bed tonight. You can sleep, and I won't do anything…that is unless you want me to," he added with his usual wolfish grin.

She could feel an instant reaction in her body again as her heart skipped a beat and her breathing became a little deeper.

Varg missed none of this and was pleased that he could make her desire him so quickly. His lips softly brushed against her ear and moved down towards her neck, but again she pulled away from him.

"Would you behave yourself? I'm going to my own cave, and you can just cool off!" she scolded, then slipped away from him and out his door.

He was left alone in disappointment. He wanted her in his arms that night, if only just to hold her, but he knew one thing for sure, she had been jealous, and she had already given herself to him once. He knew she loved him. She could deny it all she wanted, but she was already his.

# CHAPTER 18 – ANOTHER HUMAN

Halea slept like a log, though her dreams had been troubled. When she woke, she couldn't remember her dreams, but they left her with a horrible aching sense of loss. She changed her bandage and noticed the wound on her arm had healed enough to where the stitches Varg gave her were ready to come out. She decided to ask Batsuba to help her remove them after breakfast, but as she was getting dressed to go outside, she heard a commotion.

The northern lycan pack had arrived, and when Halea went outside, Varg was already sitting around the fire pit with what appeared to be their leader as well as Ethelwolf.

Not wanting Varg to drag her into it again, at least not first thing in the morning, she decided to use a different path to reach Batsuba's tree-dwelling by skirting around the common area below. She ran down the mountain face and found a sturdy rope bridge that led into a patch of homes. Everyone was down in the common area greeting the northern pack, and so no one noticed her coming down from the tree-dwellings.

She wondered if Batsuba would even be in her home. As an elder lycan, she might be expected to welcome the others.

Halea walked casually around the outer areas of the main den space, and as she neared Batsuba's tree, she heard something strange.

"Psst…hey…hey, wait!"

When Halea turned around, she saw something that nearly dropped her jaw. A woman – a human woman!

The woman ran up to her without fear. She seemed a little out of breath, and Halea was panicking, wondering if she was a captive of the lycans. Why was this human woman coming to her?

"Are you a priestess?"

"Yes, my name is Halea, but who are you? Why are you here? Are you okay?"

To her shock, the woman laughed.

"Yes, I'm fine. My name is Jance. When they told us there would be another gathering because the council wanted to decide whether to let priestesses help with the tears, I asked Alf to let me come with him again. The last time we came, none of the priestesses had attended the gathering, and I was so disappointed. Lycans don't like humans, but they let you come to the gathering this time. I'm so glad! I haven't seen another human in decades! Oh, please tell me all about what's going on outside of the lycan world!"

Halea was struggling to get a grasp on the situation.

"Wait...but how are you here?"

Jance laughed again. "Sorry, my mate is a lycan. He's Alf. He's the brother of the northern pack's leader, Bertolf. I'm not a captive or anything, I swear. I'm here by choice. Don't look so worried."

Somehow Jance's explanation only confused Halea more. How was this possible? Did lycans really mate with humans? Where did she come from? How did she meet a lycan? Why didn't they kill her? They barely tolerated her, and she was a priestess, so how did this human woman manage to survive? Decades?

Jance could tell by the priestess's face that she had suddenly been thrown into a crisis of confusion. It was difficult for her not to burst out laughing at the poor priestess's expense, but her story was a lot to swallow all at once, especially for an outsider.

"Please come chat with me. I'll tell you everything," offered Jance, and Halea just dumbfoundedly nodded.

Jance and Halea walked until they found a quiet, abandoned sitting area where they made themselves comfortable.

"Want some cakes? I baked a whole bunch before we left. I'm sure you know what lycan food is like," offered Jance as she pulled open a full-looking shoulder bag and began removing and unwrapping several baked goods. "Nobody else here appreciates my cooking. Perhaps you will."

"Wow, they do look good," Halea appraised while accepting one of the cakes and taking a bite. It was delicious, and she was hungry that morning.

Jance could see her pleasure and beamed to know that the priestess liked her baking.

Once her mouth wasn't so full, Halea tentatively asked. "So how did you happen to end up with a lycan for a mate? I'm dying to know."

"Oh, maybe around twenty years ago, I lived in a small village far, far, in the north. It snows more often than not up there. My mother died when I was little, and my father was poor and wanted to marry me off as quickly as possible. I was pretty old to still be single, twenty-two at the time, and he didn't want to take care of me for forever, so he matched me up with a man from several villages over. He was awful. I hated him. He just wanted a woman to beat on and to be his slave. When the day arrived for him to come and claim me and take me to be married, I ran for my life. I had nowhere to go, and I didn't know what I was doing, but I just ran. I ran into the forest for three days, living on roots and berries and struggling not to freeze to death because it was fall and the snow was starting to come. Finally, tired and weak, I slipped down a ravine and fell very hard and broke my leg. I lay there for a day in agony, and eventually, I blacked out from fever.

That was when Alf found me. Alf's a wonderful hunter for our pack. He's one of the best northern warriors. He picked up the scent of my blood when he was out hunting by himself, and he found my poor broken mess of a body. Lycans will kill a

144

trespassing human, and I didn't know it, but I had wandered right into their lands. He was going to kill me, if only out of mercy because my broken leg was badly infected and I was on the verge of death, but he couldn't do it. He took pity on me. He confessed to me later that he often had a habit of sometimes letting prey go if he felt it wasn't fair to kill them, such as doe deer with nursing young to care for or other very young animals. Even creatures that fought so hard for their lives that he didn't like the idea of them losing the battle. If he was alone, and no other lycans were there to criticize, he would let them go.

He didn't know where I came from or how I got so far into their territory, but he could see that I was alone. He didn't smell any other humans. That was a problem, though. He couldn't even easily dump me back off near where other humans could find me. There was only him. He carried me off to a small cave, and while I was unconscious, he set my broken leg and put a splint on it. His mother had been a healer, which was fortunate for me. He found herbs to help heal my infection and bring down my fever."

She stopped and laughed.

"I remember the first time he brought me a dead pheasant, and I nearly threw up. Poor Alf, he had no idea what to feed a human. I had to help him cook it, and then he nearly wanted to throw up. He was a little short-tempered with me when I first woke up, and we started talking to each other. I was terrified of him at first, but I figured he could have killed me already if he wanted to, and though I had heard lycans were monsters, Alf was different. He stayed and watched over me for four days until my fever finally broke, and he was certain I wouldn't die, but he was still at a loss of what to do about my leg. A lycan would have been healed by that point, but I sure wasn't. I couldn't walk home to my people, and by that point, he didn't want to abandon me either.

He carried me on his back and took me to his den, where he asked Bertolf for his advice. Oh, what a mess I made for poor Alf. They nearly kicked him out of the pack; they were all so mad. Bertolf is a sweetheart, though, just like his brother. Oh, he was angry at Alf, but he was the first to forgive him. Eventually, most of the pack realized that I was harmless...helpless even, what with that broken leg. How could I harm anyone? And it was pretty obvious by that point that Alf and I were falling in love. He risked getting thrown out of his pack for me, but he never backed down.

By the time my leg was healed, we were in the thick of winter, and I prayed that spring would never come because I knew that I would have to leave and go back to my father and that awful man, and Alf certainly didn't want me to go. I'd have rather died than leave him. It was then that Bertolf went to meet with Bledig; he was the Wolf King at the time, Varg's father. Bledig nearly called a gathering over the whole situation but seeing as putting up with me was only up to the northern pack, who by that point had become like family to me, and they were okay with me staying. It was only up to Bertolf to get Bledig's approval. I wasn't there, but apparently, Bledig was pissed, and it took Bertolf over a week to finally get Bledig to relent on my being allowed to stay with the northern pack. He didn't like it, but he allowed it, which was all we needed. The moment Bertolf delivered the news to Alf, he asked me to be his mate. I was never so happy in all my life. We've been together ever since. I like lycans. Sure, they're assholes sometimes, but they can be nice once you get in with them. Once you're in, you're family."

Halea was left speechless. Did Varg know about this? Then something occurred to her. Jance looked almost her age. Around twenty years ago?

"How…how old are you now, Jance?"

"About forty-four, I think, no, maybe a bit less than that. Lycans don't use human calendars and I don't much bother keeping track since Alf made me immortal."

"*Immortal…*" she thought, "*but how*?"

Before Halea could ask, she heard an unfamiliar voice.

"You found one!" exclaimed a big lycan male, who wore a bright smile on his face as he looked down at Jance.

"Look! She's real! Another human at last! And she liked my cakes. Take that!" laughed Jance.

"Oh good, please give them all to her. I'm Alf; I'm sure you've guessed. My mate's done nothing but talk about wanting to see another human since this gathering was announced. I'm glad Varg allowed you to attend. Bledig wouldn't let priestesses in the last time, and she was so disappointed, she practically cried the whole way home."

"It's nice to see another human here for me too. And I am grateful for the food. I'm Halea."

Alf graciously decided to leave his mate alone with the priestess to enjoy her human companionship in peace while he went back to the other lycans. Jance immediately jumped into asking all sorts of questions about things going on in the human world, and Halea was quickly swept up in divulging every scrap of human news she could offer to the homesick redhead who hung on her every word.

"It's so good to finally talk to another human. I love Alf and my lycan pack, but I do get homesick sometimes."

Halea could see why Jance had such an easy time winning over her lycan pack; she was open, friendly, and naturally outgoing. She suddenly felt a little guilty for dodging Varg that morning, and she excused herself before making her way towards the common area. Varg was standing around with a large cluster of lycans, and she assumed he was assembling another hunting foray against the demons. The added numbers would be of great help to them.

She had another moment of hesitation, perhaps she would be intruding, but before she could worry about it much longer, Varg spotted her and immediately called her over.

"Halea, this is Bertolf, the alpha leader of the northern lycan pack," introduced Varg.

Bertolf resembled his brother in stature and face, but Halea could instantly tell there was something much more intense about him. He wasn't immediately as warm to her as Alf had been, but neither was he hostile.

"Greetings, Priestess. We came as quickly as we could. In the north, we have also seen an increase in demon attacks, and we currently suffer from an open tear plaguing our lands. I have promised Varg that I will speak on behalf of the servants of Tiamet at the council meeting, and in doing so, I hope you will send aid to our territory."

Halea's face washed with relief. So far, the gathering looked to be going in her favor.

"Once the council has made its decision, I will return to my Lord and High Priestess and report on demon and tear activity. If I can secure the safety of myself and other priestesses, then more will come, and we will fight until all the tears are contained and the demons eradicated. You have my word."

Varg couldn't help but bristle at the thought of Halea leaving, even if only temporarily.

Bertolf accepted her words graciously, and Varg and the other alphas began assembling their warriors.

"Where have you been all morning?" asked Varg in irritation the moment he could pull himself away from his duties of planning the hunt.

"I went looking for Batsuba. These stitches are ready to come out, and on the way, I got distracted. Did you know there's a human woman here? Her name is Jance, and she's mated to a lycan."

"I've known about her for a long time, actually."

"How long?" she asked, raising an eyebrow.

"We'll talk about it later. Did you find Batsuba?"

"No."

"See her before we leave. She's on the other end of the common area talking medicine with the other pack's healers. Don't be long. We're nearly ready to go."

Halea found Batsuba sitting in a circle with several other lycans, who all looked up warily at her approach. She could tell her presence made many of them uncomfortable except for a male lycan who sat beside Batsuba. When he looked up at her, his face lit up with a smile. He immediately jumped to his feet and approached her.

"Priestess Halea, Batsuba has told me of you. My, you are pretty for a human. I'm Marrok. I'm not a healer, but I am bothering Batsuba today while she works. Herbs make for such boring subject matter. Thank the gods you are here."

Halea was taken aback by this lycan's strange behavior. He was taller and more slenderly built than most other lycan males, and his face looked unusually youthful, but his eyes were particularly unnerving; they had the same characteristic as Batsuba's eyes. He had lived to see many ages. She could tell the moment he looked at her, Marrok was an elder.

"Sit down, you idiot! She's not here to entertain you! She's joining the warriors on the hunt," scolded Batsuba, who looked put out the whole time Marrok had spoken to Halea. "I take it you wanted me to inspect your arm."

"Yes, please," replied Halea as she watched Marrok sit down with a childish pout on his face.

147

Batsuba led her to the nearest place where Halea could remove the upper half of her robe in privacy and quickly removed the stitches that Varg had given her and applied an ointment and a light bandage.

"Don't mind Marrok. When you live as long as him, you get daft with age."

"Is that what you have to look forward to?"

Batsuba gave Halea a cutting glare and sent her off.

# CHAPTER 19 – THE BEAST

The lycans were battling all around her, and Halea could hear the screams of several being wounded by the dark weapons, but still, she focused all of her power on sealing the tear before her. Varg was close, fighting back every demon that attempted to stop her, and she was grateful that he was there. It was becoming clear that the need for additional priestesses was growing necessary. At last, she sealed the large tear, which left her feeling somewhat weakened, but her work wasn't done.

"Halea, are you okay?" Varg asked.

"That one took a lot out of me. I wish we had caught it sooner."

Normally, a tear that size would have taken two or three priestesses to seal. The tear had been discovered on the northeastern end of Varg's territory. The demons were spreading further, and still, there appeared to be no end to their numbers.

She watched as Bertolf transformed into his wolf form and swiftly eliminated the last of the demon stragglers. All around them, the other lycan warriors were attending to the wounded or running off after the few demons that had fled from the scene of the tear.

"Rest," commanded Varg.

"I can rest later. I have to help the wounded before it's too late."

He hated to see her pushing herself so much, and he prayed the council would come to a swift decision in her favor. He had hoped that by sending out more lycans, perhaps they could finally get the demons under control, but it was apparent the situation was growing more dire with every day, and he feared the worst.

Varg paced worriedly as Halea leaned over the injured, sweat beading on her brow and her face growing pale with each lycan she healed. He wanted to stop her, but he also needed her to help the others, and it was creating a terrible conflict within him.

At last, she purified the final wound and sat down and laid her head on her knees. He went to her and was about to put his arm around her when he heard her speak.

"It's okay, please."

Varg grimaced in frustration. She was preventing him from showing his affection for her before the other lycans, but he didn't care. He didn't give a damn if they saw. He scooped Halea up into his arms, and she let out a startled sound, but he did not put her down.

"Take the injured back to the den. The priestess can fight no more today," Varg ordered, and everyone began moving out. Bertolf looked back at him curiously in his wolf form but turned and left with the others.

Varg carried Halea and walked at a comfortable pace, allowing the others to get far ahead of them.

"I'm not crippled," she argued.

"Yes, you are. You're exhausted, and don't pretend to me that you aren't."

Halea sighed in resignation. Embarrassed, though she was, she was far too tired to bicker about it, so she allowed herself to relax in Varg's arms as he carried her back through the forest.

"Varg? Why are lycans so big when they change into their wolf form? I don't remember you being that big when you transformed when we were kids."

"That's because I was still a cub. You haven't seen my wolf form lately, now have you?"

She laughed in his arms, and he looked into her face to see what got into her.

"You were a puppy!"

He growled, and the rumble in his chest vibrated through her as he held her, but she didn't stop laughing.

"I was a lycan cub, not a puppy. I'm not a dog!"

"Show me what you look like now," she finally asked after somewhat managing to control her mirth.

"Why should I?"

"Is your fur soft like Ulas'? I touched her when she was a wolf to purify her wounds, and her fur felt so wonderfully soft. Is your fur like that?" He rarely transformed in front of her when they were children, and she had never dared to ask to touch him in that form, though she had thought about it at the time and always secretly wondered.

"How would I know? Like I can pet myself in that form," he grumbled, though the idea of Halea touching him in any form was appealing.

"Please?" she begged while batting her eyes at him.

Any semblance of remaining stern with her went right out the window. He was helplessly wrapped around her finger.

"Fine," Varg relented.

He set her down carefully on the forest floor, and Halea watched as he transformed before her eyes. Lycans could shapeshift in a matter of seconds if necessity called for it, but it seemed that he somewhat slowed the transformation so she could really see it. His face elongated, and his ears grew fur, and his hands changed shape, and she marveled as he grew to an immense proportion. When the transformation was complete, he was massive and menacing to behold, larger even than any of the other adult lycans she had seen transform, but she was not afraid.

In his wolf form, his fur was brown, and his eyes were the same shade of blue she had always known to be distinctly Vargs'.

150

He slowly approached her, hoping she wouldn't be put off by his true form, but he was relieved when she reached up and gently touched the side of his muzzle, and a bright smile illuminated her face like a sun. His heart soared.

He offered her his massive head in support as she stood, and she was grateful for the help as she leaned on him because she was still tired and faint. She explored his ears and where the fur grew thickest around his neck, and he closed his eyes as she ran her fingers through his pelt.

He transformed before she barely knew what was happening, and again, he was holding her in his arms.

"I prefer to be petted in this form," he said with a sly smile, pulling her in and tasting her lips. She softly returned his kiss, her heart thrumming in her chest. She couldn't help the way he affected her as she felt herself blushing again. She pulled back and rested her head on his chest and wrapped her arms around his neck.

"Varg, who injured you?"

"Injured?"

"There's a scar on your chest now. It wasn't there before. I thought therians healed." She had been dying to know about that mark and was also desperately looking for any excuse to distract him from making any further advances on her. She wasn't sure she could resist him.

"Oh, that. That was Lyall."

"What?" she shouted much louder than she should have because Varg cringed as his sensitive ears ached. "Oops, sorry."

He began walking again.

"It happened when I had to fight to become alpha. I told you."

"You told me you had to fight. You didn't tell me it was Lyall and that he hurt you like that. A wound like that could have been fatal. I didn't know he hated you."

Just when she was beginning to think better of Lyall, she found that he nearly killed Varg.

"Hate me? Far from it! Lyall was one of my father's closest friends. He's always thought of me as a son. He fought me because I needed to be properly challenged. An alpha can't just be handed his authority, it has to be won, or none would respect me as a leader, and nobody else was up to the task. If you think what he did to me was bad, you should have seen what I did to him."

"But the mark didn't go away?"

"If a therian injures another therian badly enough, it can leave a permanent scar where most other injuries would completely heal without a trace, but I don't mind. It's a mark of my trial and right to lead the pack. I'm actually very grateful to Lyall. He's harsh because he doesn't want me making my father's mistakes, but he means well."

Halea struggled to wrap her mind around this revelation. Lycan laws seemed so cruel and barbaric. She couldn't imagine willingly fighting someone she cared about to the point of nearly killing them, but for lycans, it was just their way of life.

A worrying thought suddenly gripped her.

If he was that badly injured just fighting a beta for the right to lead his own pack, what would happen when he would be required to fight against other alphas to be the Wolf King? She knew his father wanted him to be the next wielder of the Great Fang.

"Varg? Has anyone died fighting to be alpha?"

He was dreading where this conversation would lead, but he knew the subject would come up eventually.

"Yes, Halea. Many have died. It is somewhat less common when lycans are battling within their own pack to choose a leader, but it's far more lethal to battle for the right to be the Wolf King. The challengers are all alphas, and alphas, by nature, don't back down easy. Many choose to fight to the death."

He felt her grow still in his arms, and then he smelled it – fear.

"It's going to happen now, isn't it? This gathering. If I hadn't come, you could have had more time."

"Don't!" he ordered when he could smell her tears beginning to develop. He refused to let her regret returning to him – ever.

"Sooner or later, a Wolf King will have to be chosen. It doesn't matter when – I'm ready. I have always been ready. I will take the Fang, and I will see my people through this convergence. My father trained me for the day when I would replace him, and I will yield to no one."

That was precisely what she was afraid of, but she couldn't say it. It wasn't that she didn't believe that Varg wasn't powerful enough to win, but even the thought of there being the slightest chance he could die caused her heart to constrict in terrible pain. Was this how he felt for her when she spoke to him of the sacrifice?

Once they were finally near the den, she asked him to set her down. She was feeling much better after having been allowed to rest.

"Is something going on at the den?" she asked as they walked in together. The den had been packed since the northern lycans arrived that morning, but now she could hear a commotion that did not sound civil.

"Damn it, they're here," she heard him say, accompanied by a low growl.

They both ran towards the chaos that was erupting within the den. As soon as she and Varg appeared, a hush fell over the multitudes of gathered lycans, and Halea could see that yet another pack had arrived.

"So, it is true, you allowed a filthy human in among our people without first gaining the approval of the council. Even your father was not so foolish," snarled a large lycan male, whose eyes and hair was as black as night, and Halea felt uncomfortable the moment he cast his hate-filled eyes upon her.

Varg growled menacingly beside her. He could sense Rafe's intent to threaten Halea, and he would not allow it. Nor would he allow any to insult her in front of him. And he especially would not be disrespected in his own den.

A small amount of red began to seep into Varg's eyes, and suddenly the two males were charging at each other with claws ready to strike.

"Stop!" someone called in a booming voice, and when Halea looked, she saw that it was Marrok. She would have never expected such a powerful voice to rise out of such an unlikely person, but he, Batsuba, and several other lycans, whom she assumed to be elders, were emerging from the crowd. Everyone knew who they were and moved back to give them space.

Varg and Rafe skidded to a halt within close range of each other, both growling and staring each other down menacingly and refusing to break eye contact.

"This is a matter for the council to decide," interjected Batsuba in a powerful voice of authority.

"We are assembled at last. Let us wait no more. The alphas and council will now gather in the sacred cave, and there, we will decide the fate of the priestess," commanded Marrok, whose strange and youthful face subtly shifted to unveil the supremacy of his years.

Halea stood frozen. Her hope that things would go well for her in the council was starting to fade with the arrival of this new alpha.

"You will attend as well, Priestess Halea," commanded Batsuba, who came to snap her out of her stupor.

"A human bitch has no place in our council!" growled Rafe, and it took every ounce of Varg's self-control not to rip his throat out right then and there, but the elders had spoken.

"She will speak on behalf of her deity and her fellow priestesses. The council will hear her out," spoke Batsuba, as she locked eyes with the snarling alpha leader who glared down at Halea with hatred.

Alphas were leaders even above elders, but elders were valued for their wisdom, and though they were not leaders, they were always given great respect. Whether an alpha wanted to be respectful or not, an elder was not a lycan to mess with.

Halea had never felt so uncomfortable. Varg placed a hand on her arm as soon as Rafe had gone ahead with the elders in an attempt to comfort her.

"Everything will be okay," he promised her while leaning in and whispered into her ear. She merely nodded as they followed the others, leaving many lycans standing around in anxious anticipation as the alphas, elders, and the priestess disappeared deep into the mountain.

It was hard for Halea to see where they were going once they entered the mountain. She didn't have Varg's powerful night vision, so she held tightly to his hand and trusted in him to guide her through the long tunnel that led deep into their sacred cave. Suddenly she could see strange lights. She recognized them as a natural phosphorescence that glowed from the cave walls and ceiling. She was able to safely release Varg's hand when she eventually saw the soft glow of lanterns and fires ahead, and at last, they reached the sacred cave where the lycan alphas and elders assembled in a large circle.

The cave was massive. Varg's entire pack could have lived in that one space with room to spare. There were carvings of wolves within the stone of the mountain, as well as veins of gold that glittered along the walls.

Halea and Varg sat as far away from Rafe as possible, and they watched as Marrok stood before the council.

"As we have no king, allow me to bring order to this meeting. We of the northern, southern, and eastern packs have gathered here at the den of the western pack to decide on what must be done about the Chaos Dimension that appears to be again plaguing our lands. Demons are appearing in the south and east, and the north and west are suffering from tears, tears which cannot be sealed without the aid of a priestess who serves the Dragon Goddess. The decision to allow humans into our territories is not one to be made lightly. I am aware that some have misgivings about accepting the help of human priestesses since the last disastrous convergence, and that is why we must weigh our decision carefully. Here with us now is Priestess Halea, who will speak on behalf of the Dragon Goddess, Tiamet."

Halea took a deep breath and rose before them. The southern pack's leader glared at her with hatred so intense she could feel it like a charge in the atmosphere, but she refused to let him intimidate her. She had a mission to complete.

"I came to these lands to hunt demons and seal tears, but the demons are many, and every day new tears continue to open. I have been doing all I can within my power to seal these dimensional rifts since my arrival, but the situation is growing worse, and I alone am not enough. I must return to my Lord and my High Priestess and give news of tear and demon activity in these lands and request for them to send clerics and more priestesses to aid me. If the council grants for myself and other priestesses to fulfill our duties within these lands, we will work tirelessly to ensure that the demons are completely eradicated, and all the tears sealed. This situation cannot be contained by myself alone, nor can it be contained by lycans. Unless…"

"The human lies!" shouted Rafe as he jumped to his feet, causing Varg to also immediately jump up as well, but Rafe paid him no attention. "Priestesses promised their help the last time there was a convergence, but where were they when the great tear opened? The tears only began when the priestesses appeared. They are bringers of death and destruction. Humans have always warred against therians. They bring this curse to us because they want us dead, and they want our lands. They claim to possess the power to banish the great convergence tear, yet they did nothing to stop it the last time, and we paid with the blood of our people. Under no circumstance are humans to be trusted! The last time we trusted priestesses, our lands were invaded. And you, Varg, you have brought this filthy human into your pack, into your den, and if rumor has it, perhaps even into your bed. Even your fool of a father would have never stooped so low!"

Varg leaped forward, fangs bared. He was going to rip that bastard's face off when suddenly Bertolf threw himself in front of his fist. The northern alpha received the full brunt of his assault, which broke his nose with a sickening crunch and caused blood to gush forth. The force of the impact caused Varg to temporarily snap out of his rage. Bertolf shrugged it off, paying no attention to what just happened to him and instead focusing on breaking up the fight between the western and southern alphas. Rafe smiled in smug satisfaction, causing Varg to growl and attempt to charge again past Bertolf, but again Bertolf intervened.

"Don't let him provoke you. That's what he wants. He is here for only one thing, and you know it," spoke Bertolf as he tried to rein Varg in.

Bertolf was in no way defending Rafe; he had always despised the southern alpha. Varg was young and headstrong, and Rafe would try to exploit his rage and inexperience as a leader against him, both in battle and against the council. Bertolf knew that Rafe coveted the Fang above all else.

"Then let it be decided. I'm ready," Varg replied in challenge.

Halea watched as many wooden staffs were passed out among the elders, who began slamming them into the stone floor of the cave in a steady rhythm that drowned out the pounding of her heart. Marrok emerged carrying a long bundle wrapped in the fur of a wolf. He laid the object on a raised stone altar that stood before the statues of three stone-carved lycans, their bodies in humanoid shape, but their heads the heads of wolves, and she guessed they were likenesses of the ancient wolf gods. He carefully unwrapped the object, and there lay a gleaming sword with an intricate hilt that ended in a pommel in the shape of a wolf's head – the Great Fang.

Batsuba came forth holding a skull that appeared humanoid except for the protrusion of fangs from the upper row of teeth.

Varg, Rafe, Bertolf, and Ethelwolf removed all of their upper body armor and stood before the elder healer, and then each alpha reached into their own mouths and ripped out one of their lower canines and deposited the bloody teeth into the overturned skull.

Batsuba gently shook the skull and approached the altar and poured the alpha's fangs before the sword.

"First battle; Rafe against Bertolf and Varg against Ethelwolf. The gods have decreed it so," spoke Batsuba after examining the fangs.

Rafe and Bertolf were chosen to begin their match first, and Halea watched in horror as the two lycans squared off with such brutality that blood and sweat splattered everywhere around them. The fight ended when she heard a bone snap in Bertolf's left arm, and at last, he was forced to yield.

The pounding of the staffs continued, and it only served to heighten her anxiety. She wanted to go to Varg and beg him to make it stop, but she couldn't. She knew she couldn't. She could only watch and pray to Tiamet to protect him. She even dared to pray to the wolf gods, though she wasn't sure if they would heed the prayer of a human.

The battle between Varg and Ethelwolf was just as vicious. Ethelwolf was the eldest of the lycan alphas, the most experienced, and the most patient, and Halea cringed when Varg received a terrible slash down his back as the eastern alpha tore into him without mercy. Varg shrugged it off and counterattacked with all his might, hitting Ethelwolf furiously in the sternum and ribs over and over again until the eastern leader spat blood and dropped down on one knee. His battle was over.

"Varg and Rafe shall now battle; the gods have decreed it so. Only the strongest shall wield the Fang and rule supreme," called Marrok.

The pounding of the staffs continued as the two alphas were offered water and toweled off to prevent sweat from interfering with the battle, and some of their minor injuries were washed clean.

Varg looked over and saw Halea watching him with fear in her eyes. He went to her and leaned into her ear, the continuous pounding of the staffs drowning out his words to all but her.

"No matter what happens, I love you."

She looked up into his eyes and felt the overwhelming sincerity of his words, and she desperately wanted to reach out for him.

"Enough fawning over your human whore. Come and fight me, Varg," challenged Rafe with a vicious sneer.

That was all it took to send Varg into another furious rage, and everyone who watched the battle worried as they saw the faint tinge of red begin to seep into the blue of his eyes.

The two alpha males fought with such speed it was hard for even the eyes of the lycan spectators to keep up with their movements. Everyone could hear fists colliding with flesh and bone, and the scent of blood filled the air as they used their claws to tear into each other again and again. Rafe tried to pin Varg, but Varg was too fast for him, and in one quick movement, Varg had wrenched the southern alpha's arm from its socket. Rafe let out a vicious snarl but quickly recovered, and with a sickening snap, he forced his arm back into place and flexed his claws. Varg pounced while Rafe attempted to regain the use of his arm, and again they were tearing into each other, the sounds of their growls and snarls filling the cave despite the never-ending pounding of the staffs.

Halea cringed as Rafe pierced Varg's stomach with the four claws on his dominant hand and dug deep, causing more blood to spill around them, but Varg swung hard with a right hook and managed to send Rafe to the ground. Varg leaped for the southern leader, hoping to finally latch onto his throat, but Rafe was up again, and before Varg could move in for a strike, Rafe grappled him into a headlock and began bearing down on him.

Varg was struggling to break free of his grip when Rafe leaned into his ear where others couldn't hear over the sounds of the pounding staffs. "My first decree as king…that priestess will die."

Varg's eyes instantly turned blood red, and with immense force, Rafe was sent flying. The southern alpha impacted with the cave wall and crumpled to a heap on the ground. Suddenly the staffs stopped, and everyone jumped up and moved back. No one was safe when an alpha was in a blood rage.

Halea felt Batsuba grab her wrist and begin to pull. "Come away before it's too late," pleaded the elder healer, but Halea resisted, and that was when they both heard the vicious growling coming from the fallen southern alpha.

Rafe jumped to his feet. His eyes also had turned blood red, his claws and fangs had grown longer, and his face contorted with rage and hatred, and that was when he cast his eyes on Halea and charged.

Varg sprang forward, tackling Rafe to the ground where the two began tearing into each other, and Halea couldn't even follow them with her eyes, but she could see blood flying and spraying the cave walls and floors red. Even her human ears could hear the sound of flesh tearing as the two alphas raged against each other.

At last, Batsuba managed to pull the horrified priestess further away from the warring alphas, though she never looked away from the carnage. The other alphas and many of the elders were quickly evacuating the cave.

Rafe swiped at Varg, slicing along the edge of his jaw with his claws, fueling Varg's instinctual rage further and causing him to lunge forward and grapple the southern alpha, pinning him to the ground. His hands managed to grasp Rafe's neck, squeezing the life out of him with every strangled breath. Rafe punched and sank his claws into Varg's chest and sides, but Varg would not release his grip. The harder Rafe struggled, the tighter Varg squeezed as his claws pierced into Rafe's throat, perilously close to his jugular.

At last, the southern alpha blacked out, but still, Varg would not let him go.

Halea watched in frozen horror as Rafe went limp beneath Varg.

"Varg, stop!" she shouted, breaking free of Batsuba's grip and running towards him.

"Halea, don't!" shouted Batsuba, but she dared not run after her.

Varg turned his head, never releasing Rafe, and fixed his burning red eyes on Halea, who stopped running as soon as she was closer to him.

"Varg, please, don't. You don't have to, please," she begged.

His eyes regarded her dangerously, and a threatening growl rumbled through him.

"Varg, it's me, Halea. Please come back."

Slowly he loosened his grip on Rafe's throat and rose to his feet before her. His body trembled all over, and the growling never stopped. Every muscle was taut, and she could sense that anything could make him snap at any moment, but she couldn't turn away.

His whole body was covered in gashes that oozed blood that dripped in pools at his feet, and his face was covered in bruises, and she could see the beginning swelling of a black eye. Rafe looked no better as he lay motionless on the ground, and she had no way to tell if he was even alive.

Slowly, timidly, she walked closer to Varg, causing his growls to grow louder with every step.

Batsuba wanted to look away. She didn't want to see her alpha kill the priestess. She didn't want to watch him tear her limb from limb. The woman was a fool, but there was nothing she could do to stop it now. She could only witness as the priestess lived her final moments.

Varg remained motionless as, at last, Halea stood before him.

"It's all right. I'm here, Varg. I won't leave you. Please come back to me," she pleaded while slowly raising her hand and reached out to touch him. She wasn't even sure where she could touch him, he was so badly wounded everywhere, but she had to try.

In one imperceptibly fast motion, his arm shot out, and he gripped her around the wrist. She winced in pain as his fingers tightened around her, but suddenly something shifted within his eyes. He loosened his grip and pulled her into him, causing her to crash against his body and staining the front of her robe with blood. He growled against her, and his other hand gripped her hip tightly as he stared down at her with burning red eyes.

"It's okay. Everything is okay," Halea whispered softly, and he deeply breathed in her scent. "Varg, I need you, please," she added while reaching up and softly nuzzling her nose into one of the uninjured areas of his neck. She could feel his heart hammering in his chest, but the moment she touched him, he released her wrist and wrapped both of his arms tightly around her. There was tension throughout his whole body, but she was no longer afraid. He warned her not to trust him, but she knew in her heart, Varg would never hurt her because he loved her. He ran his nose softly down the side of her face, gently grazing his lips and fangs along the edge of her jaw, and she knew that he wanted her to submit to him, and so she leaned her head back, exposing her throat before him. His growl deepened, and she closed her eyes as he ran his tongue along the pulse of her throat, his sharp fangs digging into her flesh but never breaking the skin.

"Halea…" he breathed in a voice both deep and unnatural as his beast called out for her. He had fought for her and would let none threaten what was his. No one would take her from him. She belonged to him. The alpha within him roared with desire. She had come to him. She had offered herself to him. She had chosen him, and he had chosen her, and every instinct within him was howling that she should bear his mark.

"Varg, please come back. Please come back to me," she pleaded again, and as she spoke, the red slowly receded from his eyes. She leaned in and gently kissed his bloody lips, trying only to touch him softly, knowing that every inch of him was probably in pain.

But he needed so much more, and he hungrily delved into her mouth, ignoring everything but her.

Batsuba looked on in amazement. At first, she had assumed Varg was only in lust with the human priestess, but now she knew, there was no denying it - he was in love with her. No one could get that close to a blood raged alpha and survive unless it was his mate or one chosen to be his mate. Varg had chosen. But, she couldn't believe it. How was it possible? Lycans did not fall in love so quickly, and he barely knew this woman. How could they have formed such a powerful bond so soon? It was time she discovered the truth.

# CHAPTER 20 – WOLF KING

Halea watched in fascination as the bruises slowly faded and the smaller cuts and scrapes on his flesh shrunk and disappeared. Varg slept peacefully beside her, and she allowed herself to gaze upon him. He would undoubtedly have many new scars, but to her, he would be no less beautiful.

There were so many serious wounds that needed to be cleaned and stitched that Batsuba had reluctantly agreed to let her help tend Varg's injuries. Normally, the old healer preferred to work alone when she had no apprentice. She especially didn't like friends or family hanging around her patients when she was busy tending to their medical needs. They often only got in the way. But when she suggested that Halea leave so she could tend to Varg, the alpha let out such a terrible growl, even she dared not disobey him. Instead, she chose to put the priestess to some useful tasks. The human did seem to have a knack for such work, which helped the old healer feel a little better about allowing her to stay with the patient.

Batsuba was dying to have a word alone with her leader, but even after all his wounds were sealed and bandaged, he refused to send Halea away, even when she had sternly warned him that he needed to rest.

Halea was afraid to touch him for fear of hurting him in any way, but when she tried to scoot over to give him a little space, he grabbed her hand and pulled her in beside him. They were alone in his private cave, but once the medicine kicked in, he quickly fell asleep.

Sleep would not be so easy for her. She couldn't just brush aside all that happened. She couldn't forget the way he looked at her when he told her he loved her or how terrified she had been for his life.

She loved him.

She loved him more than anyone in the world. She had always loved him, but it didn't change the fact that she wasn't supposed to be in love with him. She had sworn an oath. Just as he had a duty to his people, she had her duties as well. No matter what she felt in her heart, she couldn't just throw away everything to be with him, even though she secretly ached to do just that.

It just couldn't be.

All she could do was lay there next to him, listen to him breathe, and watch as his wounds slowly healed before her eyes while holding his hand, and enjoying being near him for as long as she could.

By morning Varg was much better, though many of his deeper wounds were still raw and not yet fully healed. His black eye was gone, and most of the minor cuts, scrapes, and bruises had disappeared, and he could also feel his bottom fang slowly regrowing in his jaw.

"I'll bring you something to eat," Halea offered when he tried to sit up and winced a little in discomfort. Even a lycan could only heal so fast, and she didn't want him reopening his serious wounds.

"No. I have to go out there. They're waiting. I can hear them."

The moment they emerged from Varg's cave and looked down the mountainside, every lycan below fell silent and stopped in the middle of what they were doing and looked up. Then, one by one, they all dropped to their knees and bowed their heads before Varg.

"Come," he said to her, and Halea nervously walked down the path with him until they reached the common area, but still no one rose, no one spoke, they were all waiting for Varg.

At last, one lycan came forth, Marrok, and he carried a long, wrapped bundle in his arms. He approached Varg but did not come too closely until Varg acknowledged him by nodding his head in permission. Marrok got down on one knee before Varg and unwrapped the bundle, revealing the Great Fang.

Marrok bowed his head in reverence and held the sword up towards Varg, who reached out and grasped the hilt.

Suddenly Halea heard a howl, and then another, and another, until everyone was howling.

The Wolf King held up his sword.

~~~~⋄~~~~

Halea felt out of place again as everyone vied for Varg's attention, but he would not dismiss her, and he kept her close beside him at all times. Many congratulated him and swore allegiance. Others wished to discuss his plans for dealing with the demons and tears. While Varg recovered from his battle, the council had reassembled and voted in overwhelming favor of allowing Halea and other priestesses the ability to enter lycan territories to fulfill their duties. All that was needed was Varg's vote, and no one doubted what his decision would be.

The lycan council's purpose was to offer advice and wisdom to the Wolf King and vote on matters that affected their people as a whole and to make their opinions known. A Wolf King will usually abide by the council's wishes, but he does possess the power and authority to act against the council's decision, but to do so is to risk losing respect and damaging alliances with the other packs. If Rafe had won the right to be king, he could have decreed for Halea to be executed and barred all priestesses from ever entering their lands, despite the council's objections. Many on the council were relieved when Varg was able to defeat the southern alpha. A good king would be one who would act with his people's best interests at heart, even if it wasn't always a decision he wanted to make.

Halea noticed that Rafe was nowhere to be found and assumed that he was off somewhere licking his wounds.

Halea slipped away for a little while to clean her robe, which was still covered in Varg's blood from the previous night's battle. When she returned, a large party of warriors was preparing to leave for another demon hunt.

"Where do you think you're going?" she asked Varg as she noticed him preparing to leave.

"To lead the hunt, where else?"

"Absolutely not! Your wounds aren't healed yet. Batsuba wanted you to rest. You at least need one more day before you go exerting yourself again," she argued.

She could tell he was about to argue when again she stopped him.

"I'll go with them. They'll need me to seal tears anyway."

"I am *not* sending you to battle demons by yourself!" he barked. Rationally, he knew she fought demons alone all the time, at least before she came back to him, but he didn't like it. Lycan mates often fought side by side, protecting each other's lives at all costs. The thought of her being anywhere where she could be in any form of danger, where he couldn't be there to protect her, was almost unbearable for him. And what was worse, he hadn't told her about what Rafe had said the night before. Rafe wouldn't dare openly defy him now that he was the Wolf King, but that didn't mean it felt safe for him to leave Halea out of his sight. His instincts were warning him not to trust the southern alpha, and he wasn't so sure about the rest of the southern pack either. He simply didn't feel comfortable letting her out of his sight, but he wasn't sure he could explain himself without frightening her.

"I won't be by myself! I'll stay close to Faolan and Aatu if it makes you feel better. It's not like you aren't needed here. Please, Varg. Please rest for just one more day. I'll be safe, I promise. You don't have to worry about me. You know I can take care of myself," she pleaded.

He emitted a grumbly sort of growl but stopped protesting, and that was about the most she could hope for. She knew enough about Varg's pride to know it was probably killing him on the inside not to be joining the rest of the warriors, even if it was only for one day.

He did manage to stay busy the entire day the warriors were out. It seemed every elder and just about every other lycan who hadn't joined the hunt wanted some of his time. He did have a responsibility as supreme alpha to do more for his people than just fighting for them all the time, though he certainly preferred the fighting part.

Even though he was there, most of his people noticed he was on edge and distracted, constantly listening for any sound in the distance. He was listening for howls of danger, and the fact that at any moment, Halea could be out there in trouble, set his nerves on edge.

The sun was beginning to set when Batsuba finally managed to steal a moment of Varg's time for herself. She asked to speak with him in his cave, where they would be less likely to be heard.

He would have much preferred to stay outside and stare into the distance, waiting for the warriors to return, but he had a feeling he knew what Batsuba wanted to talk to him about. It was time to come clean.

"You seem quite fond of that lovely little priestess. In fact, if I didn't know any better, I'd say you were in love with her," the old healer directly stated the moment they were alone.

"Yes, I love her," he freely admitted.

As alpha, he didn't have to tell Batsuba anything he didn't want to. He was her leader and now her king. Batsuba was a respected elder, the healer of his pack, but she also valued her because there was always something motherly about the old woman. She was the closest thing he had to a mother since his own died. He thought he even remembered hearing his father once saying that she had been a Wolfmother, but that would have been impossible.

"How? She is a human, and you've only just met her! Forming such a strong bond so quickly, even with another lycan, would be nearly impossible, and yet you expect me to believe that you have already made this strange human priestess your chosen?"

The old woman was furious, not about his choice, but because there was something she didn't know, and she hated it. Batsuba had lived through several ages and was one of the wisest lycans, perhaps the wisest, and it infuriated her that there could be something she wasn't able to understand.

Varg offered a sly smile before speaking.

"Seems you don't know everything after all," he teased, and he thought he could see fire in her eyes at his provocation.

If he wasn't her alpha, she would have slapped his face, but instead, she struggled to control her anger.

"Do you remember when I once came to you as a cub and asked you to teach me how to make scent masking potion?" he reminded.

A knowing look of revelation seized the healer's face.

Suddenly everything fell into place. She had assumed Varg's constant time away from the pack in his youth was only due to his father's grief and the loss of his mother, yet Varg had usually seemed very happy despite all that. It had never occurred to her that he would ever dare to secretly meet with a human. Even now, the idea seemed almost inconceivable, but yet, somehow, it had happened.

For once in the old woman's life, she was speechless.

Varg smiled again. Nobody to his knowledge had ever pulled the wool over Batsuba's eyes, yet he had, and he was a cub when he did it. He couldn't help but savor the elder's reaction.

"Yes, it was her. It was always her. We were only children. Innocent. Lonely. And then the convergence came and tore her away from me. I thought I'd lost her forever. I thought she died, but she's alive. My Halea has returned to me, and I won't let her go this time."

Batsuba recalled all the years of his adolescence when she couldn't understand why he had shunned the attentions of the females who practically threw themselves at his feet.

"Varg, she is a priestess…"

"I don't give a damn what she is! She is mine! We belong to each other. You know my choice is made."

He was right. The choice was made. There could be no changing it now. Nothing she could say or do could ever sway him otherwise, but she couldn't shake the dread on his behalf.

"Then why haven't you marked her yet?"

She asked the one question that managed to cut him and the one he couldn't bear to accept.

"I know she loves me, but she's trapped by her oath to the Dragon Goddess. I would give anything in the world to make her my mate right now, but she has only barely begun to be a priestess, and I gave her my word. No matter how long it takes, I will wait for her."

"And what if she never comes to you?"

Again her words cut him like a knife, giving voice to all of his deepest fears. He couldn't allow her to shake his resolve. Halea loved him; even though she had never proclaimed her love for him, he knew it. He needed to believe, more than anything, that the day would come for them to be together.

"She will come to me, and she will be my mate. There can be no one else! And when that day comes, I will make her immortal, and I know you know how to do it."

Batsuba recalled the day he came to her asking questions about the human woman Jance, and again she cursed herself for having been so blind.

"Yes, through blood magic. She would have to drink a special potion…as well as your blood. You would bind her to your life-force. She would share your own immortality and your healing power, but if you should die, then the sands of time would flow for her again, and eventually, she would grow old and die."

"If she gives up being a priestess, she will lose her immortality anyway. I would gladly share my life-force with her to keep her alive – to keep her by my side."

"So be it," replied the healer.

Outside his cave, Otsana listened with her ear to the door, she had only arrived in time to hear Varg's intentions towards the human, but it was enough to make her seethe with rage.

# CHAPTER 21 – WALKING AWAY

They had successfully slaughtered many demons that day. No new tears were found, and Halea was starting to hope that perhaps they were beginning to get the situation under control. When she returned that evening, she found Varg waiting for her. He had missed her and worried about her that whole day, but as he reached out to hold her, she shied away from his embrace.

"Varg, please," she said, still feeling embarrassed by his open display of affection before so many of his people.

But he was having none of it, and before she could pull away again, he grabbed her towards him and silenced her protest with his kiss.

A few looked on uncomfortably, particularly those from the southern pack, but most others chose to mind their own business. Varg was their supreme alpha; only a fool would anger him now. Besides, everyone already knew the truth. Rumor had spread like wildfire that the human priestess was able to soothe him out of a blood rage, and that meant only one thing.

Some were shocked and appalled, but there were also quite a few who were indifferent, and even many who approved.

Varg had been a good leader to his pack since the death of his father. His people had their misgivings at first because he was so young and inexperienced, but in the years since becoming their alpha, he had restored their lands to them, helped them rebuild their homes, provided food and protection to all, and they had quickly grown to respect their young leader.

Pack was everything to a lycan, and all pack members were family, whether they were blood-related or not, and Varg, despite his youth, had become like a father to his people. They looked to him for guidance and protection, and they loved him for all that he did on their behalf. Lycans were not an unappreciative people.

Everyone in his pack was used to their alpha being somber and aloof, and they had always attributed it to the loss of his parents, the devastation of the convergence, and the heavy burdens of leadership. The human priestess brought out a side to their leader that many, except for the oldest of his childhood friends, had never seen. He laughed and smiled when he was in her company. They could see that her presence soothed his volatile alpha temper and made him easier to approach.

A pack needed a strong alpha, but an ideal leadership came from an alpha pair; a male alpha for protection and a female alpha for nurturing, a father and mother figure to the whole pack, and they had long been without a Wolfmother.

Halea, while not a lycan, and being clearly ignorant of many of their ways, had earned their respect. She had fought beside them and saved countless lycan lives, and many still felt indebted to her, but if she were to become a member of the pack, they would feel less uncomfortable in accepting her help. But most importantly, she made Varg happy, and his pack wanted to see their alpha happy, even if his choice seemed strange and unexplainable. Yes, they would have preferred him to choose someone of his own people, especially as supreme alpha, but it was too late now. It was clear the choice had been made, and all they could do was to come to terms with it.

That night a feast was held in honor of the gathering and Varg's victory. All the packs had assembled because of a deadly crisis, which was still unresolved, but such a celebration was necessary to reaffirm the bonds between all the packs, to help raise spirits in dark times, and to give friends and family a chance to socially reconnect that may not see each other very often otherwise.

Halea sat silently next to Varg. All the other alphas gathered together around their new king, including Rafe, who had greeted Varg with grudging respect. Halea could still feel animosity towards her from the southern alpha, but Varg watched him closely to ensure he wouldn't try anything.

If anything, Rafe hated the priestess even more. He would have preferred to be defeated and slain in battle with honor than to have a filthy human intervene on his behalf. He would offer her no gratitude or indebtedness. He seethed with rage when he awakened to learn what she had done and that she was Varg's chosen – his supreme leader's chosen, which meant should she become Varg's mate, she would be an alpha over him as well. That thought alone filled him with murderous hatred. He was powerless at that moment, but he swore that someday he would have vengeance. He would bide his time.

Ethelwolf was mostly indifferent. He disliked humans as a general rule but could also see that having a priestess as a pack member might hold some benefit. Their powers were quite useful. Ultimately, he decided it was none of his business.

Bertolf couldn't help but see the irony in the situation. Varg's father had staunchly opposed his brother's union to a human female at first, and when he at last relented, he still made it abundantly clear that he did not approve of such unions, yet here was his own son, with a human for his chosen. Bertolf had wondered if there was any truth to the rumors, but in the end, it wasn't any of his business who his supreme alpha chose for a mate. He had given his brother's mate a chance, and she had made his brother happy. He was not opposed to giving the strange human priestess a chance as well.

Halea was distracted with her own thoughts again. She had not wanted things to happen the way they did. Everyone was talking about her and Varg, and she was so embarrassed she wished the ground would open up and swallow her. She already felt bad enough that Varg was coming to believe he could have more from her than she could offer. Now she feared his people were expecting them to be together as well. What would it do to him when she left? Would she have embarrassed him in front of his people? She didn't want to make things worse than they already were.

Varg could sense her distraction but assumed it was because Rafe was making her uncomfortable. At last, she rose and excused herself. He wished to follow her, but he couldn't walk away when the other alphas were addressing him, so he was forced to wait.

Halea returned to the lake where she had once sparred with Varg, and just remembering that night made her heart flutter, but she chided herself for allowing such feelings. She desperately needed to regain control over the situation, and now that the lycan council had made their decision, it was time.

She sat under a large tree and watched the full moon's light dance over the rippling water.

"Halea?" Varg called for her.

"I'm over here," she replied.

"I'm sorry Rafe was making you uncomfortable. You don't have to worry about him. I wouldn't let anyone hurt you."

"It's not that," she said and stood back up. "Varg…it's time for me to leave."

Guilt stabbed her as pain, and perhaps even panic, washed over his face.

"Leave? Why?"

"I made a promise to the council, remember? I said I would bring back help, but to do that, I have to return to Antherose. I have to report all this tear activity to Lord Anshar."

"But, you'll come back then?"

She turned to look away from him. He was the last person in the world she wanted to hurt.

"I don't think I should, Varg."

He grabbed her arm and turned her to face him, forcing her to look him in the eyes.

"Why? Why are you saying this?"

"Varg, please. I can't give you what you want. Every day I stay, I'm making it worse. It would be better if I didn't return with the other priestesses, at least for a while. I'm not saying I never want to see you again, please, believe me, that's not it. It's just that…everything's been happening so quickly…I just…need time."

She could see him struggling to contain his anger and pain at her words.

"Tell me you don't love me," he commanded.

"*Damn him*," she thought. He knew she couldn't lie to him.

"Varg…"

"Say it!"

But before she could even think of any way to protest his order, she was trapped as he pinned her against the tree. His hard body pressed firmly against hers, and she worried he might be harming his injuries, but he paid them no mind. She opened her mouth to gasp, but he sealed her lips with a deep and hungry kiss. His hands grasped her hips as he pressed himself against her, and she could feel his hardness between them. A moan escaped her before she could even stop it, and he growled in satisfaction.

166

He could already smell her arousal in the air, and it was driving him insane with need. He slowly slid his hands up to cradle her full breasts and released her lips and began gently sucking and nipping at the soft flesh of her throat, sending even more heat flooding into her core. She weakened in his arms as she grew wet from his touch, which was both rough and gentle.

She should have told him to stop. She should have been the rational one, but she couldn't. She couldn't help how much she wanted him. She couldn't help how he made her feel inside. She couldn't help the complete power he seemed to have over her, and at that moment, she didn't want to stop it.

His tongue worked magic over the skin of her collarbone, and his hands slid down and grasped her bottom, pulling her tighter to him and causing her to gasp and dig her fingers into his thick, dark hair as his straining need brushed up against her.

He slid his hands back up the front of her body and pulled open her robe. She cried out when he slipped his fingers into her undergarments and gently stroked her wet fold, causing jolts of hot pleasure to shoot through her body and make her knees grow weak. He removed his hand only long enough to reach up and remove his upper body clothes and armor, then he leaned back into her and seized her mouth once again.

She allowed her hands to explore his powerful chest and biceps, being careful to avoid his more severe wounds as he ground his need into her, nearly causing her to cry out.

She heard fabric ripping as he used his claws to shred her undergarments from her body, and she could feel him opening the front of his trousers as he pulled himself out.

"Tell me you don't want me," he breathed hotly into her ear, giving her one last chance to refuse him, but she couldn't. She knew it was wrong to use him so, but she couldn't deny how much she wanted him.

When she refused to deny him, he pressed her firmly against the tree and lifted her thighs around his waist. He forcefully pushed himself inside of her, stretching her with his impressive girth and making her cry out in ecstasy. He growled in pleasure to feel how warm and wet she was for him, how much she needed him, wanted him. She was his. Her body knew what it wanted, and it wanted him.

His need was primal as he moved inside of her, and she wrapped her arms tightly around him even though she knew he would never drop her.

"Halea...say it...tell me that you don't love me," he commanded again as she began to writhe in his arms. She was gasping for air, and he buried his face into the side of her neck, breathing her in as deeply as he could and slowly trailing his fangs across her flesh. He could feel the red bleeding into his eyes, the instincts taking over, the beast fighting to be released, to claim, to possess, but he couldn't allow it. He would never allow the wolf in him to harm her. He needed her to come to him of her own choice, or the bond would never hold. He needed her love.

"Varg..."

"Halea, I love you...please."

She was so close, but he was slowing down on purpose, denying her the release she so desperately craved, and he knew she couldn't tell such a lie.

She gently pulled back on his hair, encouraging him to look into her eyes. She could see him silently pleading with her, begging her, and she couldn't resist him anymore.

"Varg, I love you."

He crushed her lips in a deep and hungry kiss and growled with pleasure as he moved faster against her.

She loved him, and nothing else mattered to him at that moment except for her. He could feel her coming undone in his arms, her walls clamping around him and sending him over the edge with her. He let out a primal growl as he released his seed inside of her, his fangs growing as the beast within fought to take over and claim its mate. He let go of one of her thighs and sank his claws into the tree, the wood splintering behind her as he struggled to rein in his beast.

They were both panting and spent, and slowly he withdrew himself from her body, and they sank to the forest floor beneath the tree. He held her tightly to him and softly stroked her hair as they struggled to catch their breaths.

He gently ran his fingers along the edge of her jaw and gazed into her eyes.

She was trapped in his eyes – lost. She could see his love pouring through into her very soul, and she felt like a monster. She had made everything worse for him. So much worse.

"You're mine, Halea, you know it. You know you belong to me. We belong together. We've always belonged together. Halea, I need you. Please, be my mate."

She closed her eyes and cursed herself. Why was she so weak? She wanted to say yes to him. She wanted to be his. She wanted to be in love with him and for him to be in love with her. She wanted to be by his side for the rest of her days, but she wasn't supposed to want any of those things. No matter how much she wanted to, she couldn't keep him.

"Varg, I love you, I do, with all my heart. I've always loved you, and I know I could never love anyone as much as I love you, but that doesn't change the fact that I'm not supposed to fall in love. I can't be a mate or a wife or anything. Please don't ask this of me," she pleaded as tears formed in her eyes. Her heart tore to shreds as overwhelming pain and sadness clouded his face - and then anger.

He pulled away from her, leaving her feeling bereft.

"Yet, you would choose some faceless Goddess over me. There isn't anything I wouldn't do for you, Halea, nothing I wouldn't give, and yet you still turn me away," he spoke coldly while gazing at her with hurt and anger in his piercing blue eyes.

"Would you abandon your people and your duty as alpha for me?" she asked, and he hesitated at her words.

"There are things we can't just walk away from. Our world is being torn apart! Another convergence is coming; it has to be. Nothing has been right since the last one happened. I watched my home be destroyed. I watched the city burn and be swallowed into the sea...my mother was there! Even countless lycans were slaughtered. For years I thought you were one of them. How many more will die?

How can I rest when I hear the call of the Goddess begging me to help put an end to this? I don't need to see her face to know our world is in danger. You told me that my friendship would be enough. You told me you would wait for me."

She was right. He had promised himself and her that he would wait for her, no matter how long it took. He hadn't meant to lie to her, but every day he longed for her more, every day the beast within him begged for her, howled for her, and it was tearing him apart on the inside because the idea of being separated from her again was eating into his very soul. He didn't want to wait for the world to be healed. What if it never happened? What if nothing ever changed? What if they were all doomed to die? He couldn't help wanting to spend, what could be their last precious moments, together.

"I would give up everything for you…everything…because nothing means anything to me without you," he replied, then he grabbed his clothes and left her alone.

She broke down and sobbed uncontrollably, burying her face in her hands.

# CHAPTER 22 – ALL THE POWER I HAVE

Varg could feel the soil beneath his paws and the wind whistling past his ears as he ran through the forest. The moon was bright above, but within him was only darkness.

After reaching their old childhood forts, he shifted back into his humanoid form and stared up at the trees where they once played, and his heart constricted with pain.

He had pushed her too hard.

While shouting to the heavens in frustration, he took out his rage by smashing his fists into trees until they were pulverized and his knuckles were left torn and bleeding, but he didn't care.

He was convinced she would leave him and never return, and it was all his fault. Why couldn't he wait? He said he could. But saying and doing were two very different things, and he had been weak. She had made him weak.

He collapsed beneath her tree fort and stared up at the moon in the stillness of the night for hours, struggling to think of what he could do to keep her from leaving him forever.

"Varg? There you are. I've been looking for you all night," said Otsana as she walked into the clearing.

He was so wrapped up in his tortured thoughts he hadn't paid any attention to her scent. It had been faint because she was downwind of him and lycan, so not a scent he associated with a threat. She had followed his scent to find him.

"Return to the den, Otsana. I am not in the mood," he commanded, trying his best not to growl at the she-wolf who was trying his patience.

"Oh? Are you sure you're not in the mood?" she asked while coming closer and shedding all of her clothing onto the forest floor.

~~~✧~~~

Batsuba sat alone by the dying embers of a fire pit, sipping a cup of relaxing herbal tea and waiting for Varg to return from wherever he had disappeared to. It was time to change his bandages and probably remove most of the stitches she had given him. She had an inkling as to where her leader had gone and wasn't about to go looking for him.

She watched as Halea returned to the den – alone. The young priestess was disheveled, and it was evident by the stale scent of tears and the look on her face that she had been crying. Batsuba could distinctly tell that she had only just recently been intimate with their leader.

This wasn't good.

Halea tried to make her way up the mountain path toward her private cave without being noticed, but it was no use.

"Halea, come with me to my home, child," offered Batsuba.

Halea could tell that Batsuba was genuinely trying to offer her her kindness, and it would probably be unwise to refuse such an offer, so reluctantly, she nodded her head and followed the old healer to her tree-dwelling.

Once inside, Halea sat down, and Batsuba started a fire and began boiling water to make tea for her guest. It was clear she could use something to help her relax.

"He told me about you," said Batsuba, and Halea looked up at her in surprise.

"Oh, yes. I know all about you. It seems you two have been acquaintances for much longer than I would have originally expected. He thinks he's pretty sly by having deceived me all those years. He's a smug asshole and way too cocky for his own good!"

Halea couldn't help but crack at least a little bit of a smile at Batsuba's astute observation.

"But, he's a good man and a good leader. You never knew his father, but he was a good man too. I helped to bring Varg into this world, and I don't want to see him hurt. I take it by the smell of dry tears that there is discord between you now."

Halea nodded sadly and stared into the cup of tea that Batsuba had just given her.

"I love him, but I'm not supposed to. Priestesses aren't allowed such attachments, and I have my duty. I don't think he understands," she confessed.

"He's not a fool, but he is a fool for you. That is just the way lycans are when they are in love. I don't know how much about us you truly understand, but there is something I need to make very clear to you, when we lycans choose who we love, we love without doubt, with complete loyalty and devotion. Once our intended mate is chosen, then we mate for life. If a chosen refuses the lycan who loves them, that lycan can't just simply get over it, not if they were truly in love. Perhaps humans can deal with a broken heart quickly because you are mortal and your lives are so short, but a lycan can take decades, centuries, even ages, to heal from such a wound. But as long as the mating never happens, at least there's a chance to heal, a chance to move on and perhaps love another."

Suddenly Halea remembered what Varg said after he had first confessed his love for her.

*"I can't forget you or just stop loving you. It doesn't work that way, not for us."*

At the time, she had just assumed he was being dramatic, but now the full weight of his words came crashing down on her.

She had tried so hard to convince herself that if she just left, he would eventually get over his heartbreak and move on. Perhaps he would meet a lycan woman who was worthy of him and find his own happiness, but now Batsuba was telling her that if she broke his heart, he would suffer for much longer than she could have ever imagined.

Batsuba watched as fresh tears flooded the young priestess's eyes.

171

"It isn't that he doesn't understand, Halea. It's that he can't help himself. You are his chosen, whether you want to be or not, he has given you his love, and he can't just take it back."

As if she hadn't already felt completely wretched for having hurt him, now she felt even worse.

~~~◇~~~

Varg wasn't entirely surprised by Otsana's forwardness. Perhaps he would have felt sorry for her if he had any reason to believe the she-wolf's feelings were genuine, but there was no bond between them, and there never had been.

"Perhaps you should save that for an alpha that gives a damn," he told her.

Her eyes flashed with rage. "And you would pick some filthy human whore over one of your own kind? She isn't worthy of an alpha, and especially not a Wolf King!"

Varg jumped to his feet and struggled to keep his temper under control. He wanted to strike that bitch for insulting his Halea.

Otsana could tell she was on dangerous ground by disrespecting her Wolf King's chosen, but she couldn't help the rage that burned within her. She struggled to believe how it could be true. How could any lycan alpha ever truly love a pathetic weak human? Such a creature was utterly unworthy, and she had convinced herself that if Varg only gave in to her temptations, perhaps she could prove he wasn't really in love with the human female and that it was just a fleeting lustful infatuation.

"And you think I would have you? You don't love me; you just want to be an alpha's mate!"

"But, Varg, we could learn to love each other if only you'd give me a chance," she purred, trying to put on the charm once again as she moved closer to him.

"No, thanks," he said as he moved away from her and dashed off into the forest, leaving her behind.

Otsana let out a furious howl of rage. She would not give up so easily. She would prove to him that no human was worthy to be his mate.

~~~◇~~~

Halea was still sitting in Batsuba's tree-dwelling. It was late, and she had already been tired before drinking Batsuba's relaxation tea. She was about to leave and get some rest when she heard screams of terror followed by the howls of distress.

Both Halea and Batsuba ran outside to see what the commotion was and looked up in horror to see that a massive tear had appeared close to the den, far larger than any that had appeared yet, and demons by the hundreds were spilling out.

Halea wasted no time, leaping down from Batsuba's tree and charging with her spear blazing. Everywhere around her, lycans were running for their lives while the warriors sprang into action to help defend the den.

~~~◇~~~

Varg was nearing the den when he heard the howls. They were under attack! He raced with all his speed until he met with the chaos. Lycan warriors from all packs were rallying to hold back the demons that continued to spill forth from the tear.

"Varg, they keep coming!" cried Aatu, who slashed down demons left and right. All around them were the screams of death.

Varg quickly joined the fray and began tearing into demons with a fury that almost sent the red into his eyes. He had to find Halea. He fought his way closer to the tear until, at last, he saw her. Her spear glowed like a bolt of lightning in her hand as she slew demons all around her.

"Halea!" he shouted for her.

"Varg…I can't reach the tear…there are too many!" she shouted over the sounds of battle all around them.

His hand gripped the hilt of the Great Fang; he had no choice.

"Take cover!" he shouted in a voice that managed to boom over the din.

Lyall was fighting near and heard Varg's order and passed the message on until all the warriors were running as if to escape the battle.

Varg moved in close to where Halea was fighting and drew his sword.

"Stay behind me," he called to her while holding up the blade, which flashed forth a blinding light that caused the eyeless demons to shriek and shrink back.

He aimed as far from their dwellings as possible and brought down the sword, which released the mighty force of its power, blasting through hundreds of demons in a single strike and leaving a wake of devastation.

Something about the blast disrupted the tear, and demons ceased emerging from the dimensional rift while the remaining servants of Chaos ran in terror.

"Stop them! Don't let them escape," Varg called, and the lycan warriors who ran to avoid the Fang reappeared and re-entered the battle.

With the demon forces diminished and no further activity from the tear, Halea turned her attention to closing the dimensional rift.

This tear was massive. It should have required four or even five priestesses to seal it, but there was no one else. The sounds from within were warning her that Varg's sword would not hold them back for long. She had to seal it.

"Tiamet, hear my prayer, please give me your strength, I beg of you!" She raised her hands to the swirling purple light and concentrated with all her power. Her hands glowed white, and the tear began to shrink, but the strain was almost too much. "Please, Tiamet…help me," she pleaded again, as her power sprang forth with an intensity she had never known before as her whole body glowed from the force of her purification.

Varg continued to slay demons around her as she used her powers against the tear.

"Defend the priestess, now!" he ordered, and every able-bodied lycan surrounded Halea and battled back the demons that were charging in to prevent her from sealing the tear.

With a deafening roar like thunder, the tear snapped shut, and the few remaining demons let out a wail of despair and turned to escape, but almost all were caught and destroyed by the many lycans who pursued them.

Halea was sweating and trembling all over, everything around her was spinning, and then the world went dark.

~~~☼~~~

She woke up to the sun shining in her eyes and a pounding headache.

173

"Halea!" Varg exclaimed, and she realized he had been holding her hand.

"What happened?" she asked in a weary voice. She could hear wailing and screams of grief somewhere outside. She was in Batsuba's tree-dwelling again, though Batsuba was not there.

"You fainted after the tear closed. I was so worried when you wouldn't wake up."

"How long was I asleep? What's that noise outside?"

"It's almost noon. You slept through the night. I tried to be here with you as much as possible, but they've needed me too. We lost many lycans last night, almost a hundred, and many more are gravely wounded. Everyone is in grief."

"Oh, Varg...I'm so sorry," she cried as tears streamed down her face. If any lycans had been injured with dark weapons, it would have been an excruciating death, and she had not been there to help purify the wounded.

"Take me to the injured. If there are any still alive, I might be able to purify their wounds."

"Halea..."

"I'm okay. I know I was drained last night, but the rest has helped me. Please, Varg, I don't want anyone else to die."

They went outside, and Halea squinted as the bright noonday light caused her headache to pound, but she refused to mention it to Varg at that moment.

All around her, the dead were being laid out on shrouds for burial, and families were weeping in each other's arms. As they walked past the devastation, she recognized one of the bodies.

"Oh no, Varg...it's Ula," cried Halea as she began to sob at the sight of the fallen female lycan. She turned and wept into Varg's chest as he held her in his arms, and he tried to soothe her as best as he could while cursing himself for having let her see that.

He led her away from where the burials were being prepared and towards where Batsuba was working tirelessly to attend to the wounded.

Many who were injured by the dark weapons had already met their agonizing fate, but there were a few who were still struggling to hang on to their lives when Halea arrived.

"Halea, you're awake," cried Batsuba in relief. Even her skilled medicine was powerless against the weapons of Chaos.

Among the gravely injured was Faolan. His body was wracked with pain, and he shrieked as the darkness closed over his eyes. Halea spread her hands over his wounds and called upon the Goddess, and as her light flowed into the injured male, his agonized thrashing began to cease, and he lay back, gasping for air as if coming up from water.

She used her purification to heal everyone she could but cursed herself for not being strong enough to help everyone when it all began. If only she had been stronger, Ula might have lived, and fewer families would have been devastated.

While finishing up with the last of the injured, she overheard someone reporting to Varg.

"Four have chosen to join their mates among the gods; two have young ones, so they'll not join the dead today. I'm sorry, Varg," reported the male lycan.

"What of the other packs?" he asked.

"The eastern pack was hit the hardest. Many mates will die when the news reaches their den. Northern pack lost about twenty; the southern pack only lost five."

Varg scowled at the news. He could have counted on Rafe not to be so willing to let his own pack take the brunt of the battle. Undoubtedly his pack would be the first to leave the gathering as well.

Varg looked over to see Halea had finished healing the wounded and was regarding him with a questioning and worried look in her eyes.

"Varg, what does he..."

"It's nothing. What's done is done. How are you feeling?" he asked, desperate to change the subject.

"A little tired, but I'll be fine. Faolan will live, as well as the others. I need to speak with you, alone," she told him, and he felt a wave of panic at her words.

They walked until they were out of hearing distance from most of the den.

"Varg, I have to leave - now. I can't wait anymore. That tear was too much for me. Your people need help, and if I don't go soon, even more lives will be lost. It's time."

"Halea, I'm sorry. I didn't mean to push you. If you need time, I'll give you time. I swear it! Just don't leave me...not like this," he begged, and the look of anguish in his eyes broke her heart.

It was too late. The damage had been done, and there was no taking it back. Not for him, and not for her. She didn't want to lose him either.

She reached up and gently caressed the side of his face, and he couldn't resist leaning into her for comfort. His heart was racing.

Fear.

He had never been afraid like this before in his life. The one thing that mattered most to him was about to slip away, and he was powerless to stop it.

"Varg, I'll come back."

For a moment, he felt as if his heart had stopped beating, and he could only hear his pulse pounding in his ears.

"I'll return, and I'll bring help. I'll come back for you because I love you, but that doesn't mean I can stay forever when I do return. This is just until I have fulfilled my duty, and then I will have to leave...and I can't tell you when I'll be back after that...if I'll be back."

His moment of relief was laced with pain, and he cursed himself for again wanting more. He should be grateful that she was returning at all with the way he acted. But he had given his word, and this time he would not break it.

"I'll wait for you," he promised while enveloping her in his embrace.

# CHAPTER 23 – THE CHOOSING

It was evening the next day before Halea reached Antherose. She had run non-stop, even forsaking sleep, just to arrive as quickly as possible. Every minute that she was gone, lives could be at stake. They were all counting on her to return with help – Varg was counting on her, and she could not fail.

She bowed before the High Priestess who greeted her upon her arrival at the castle.

"I must report to Lord Anshar. It's bad news," explained Halea.

"You as well? Many priestesses are flooding back to the castle with tales of tears beyond number."

"Is Mama Dragon here?" asked Halea.

"No, she hasn't returned from her mission yet, but she should be here soon. We are expecting more arrivals by tomorrow."

High Priestess Maven led Halea to Lord Anshar's study and escorted her before the Lord, who was seated at his desk poring over maps, and Halea could tell he was tracking the tears.

"You are dismissed, Maven," commanded Lord Anshar, and Halea could sense the High Priestess's hesitation to leave, but without argument, she turned and left them alone.

Lord Anshar couldn't escape the mixed feelings within him as he looked up from his desk at the young priestess who stood before him. He had missed her. He couldn't explain why. He never missed the presence of any of the other priestesses, but he also hadn't poured as much effort into their training as he had with Halea. He had allowed her to come closer to him than any other, and when she was away, he often found himself thinking about her, but now he wished she had not come back to Antherose. He knew why she had returned without her even having to say a word.

Halea moved to bow before her Lord, as High Priestess Maven had often chided her for not being reverent enough. It felt awkward to lower herself before Lord Anshar, as she never used to bow before becoming a priestess.

When she knelt next to where he sat at his desk, he noticed it – her scent. His eyes narrowed as he looked down at her, where she waited with her head bowed.

"Speak," he commanded.

She was startled when she looked up into his face and saw something in his eyes she had never seen before. It shook her a little, but she tried to brush it off. Lord Anshar was dealing with the coming burden. Perhaps she caught him at a bad time.

"Lord Anshar, I have just returned from the western lycan territories. I regret to report that tear activity is far greater than expected, and demons have been appearing in astounding numbers. I was able to secure safe passage for myself and other priestesses from the current Wolf King and the lycan high council, which will allow us to safely perform our duties within all lycan territories. Please, Lord Anshar, I need help. I gave my word to return with more priestesses. I've sealed many tears, some very large, and recently, one that should have taken several priestesses to close. They will be slaughtered if more help isn't sent as quickly as possible, and it's too much of a burden for me to bear alone. Please grant me clerics and more priestesses to aid me in this battle."

Lycan. Yes, he knew that scent, though it had been many years. But he also detected more.

"You have done well, Halea," he spoke in a cold and detached tone as she looked up at him expectantly. "Tell me…who is he?"

Halea's eyes widened in shock, and Lord Anshar could hear her heart speed up.

She had allowed herself to forget that Lord Anshar's senses were just as powerful as any lycan. She had hastily washed a little in a stream on her way to Antherose but hadn't realized Varg's scent, and the last time they made love, was still present in her robe and hair.

But why would he ask? Priestesses were not forbidden from bodily pleasure. To her knowledge, Lord Anshar had never concerned himself with the activities of the other priestesses.

Still, she had to tread carefully.

Halea fought the urge to look down at her hands in shame. If she turned her eyes from Lord Anshar, he might misinterpret her behavior as being deceitful.

"A lycan," she practically whispered, and Lord Anshar's face hardened.

"Who. Is. He, Halea?" he asked again, breaking the words apart to emphasize that he was not to be defied.

"His name is Varg. We grew up together before the last convergence. He was once the only friend I had. We each thought the other had died. He is the Wolf King," she confessed.

Lord Anshar's face betrayed nothing as she spoke.

"Are you in love with him?"

She didn't need to answer. Lord Anshar could hear her heart pounding and see the flush of heat rise into her face. The scent of her anxiety spiked and nearly overwhelmed him.

"I dedicate myself only to Tiamet," Halea replied.

Anger burned within him as she avoided answering the question, but at the same time, it didn't matter - he already knew the truth.

"I will give you as many priestesses as can be spared. You will report all tear activity to your grandfather, and tomorrow the signs will be read. Go," he ordered.

As Halea turned to make for the door, she heard Lord Anshar's voice behind her.

"You made an oath, Halea. Do not forget."

Halea knew his final words were a warning and merely nodded her head in acceptance before closing the door behind her.

Maven watched as Halea walked hurriedly from Lord Anshar's study. She waited patiently for a few more moments before deciding to speak with her Lord about Halea's request, when suddenly she heard the sound of something heavy smashing loudly from inside Lord Anshar's study, followed by a yell of anguish that shook the castle all around her.

～～～☼～～～

Halea was alone in her old bedroom. Her grandfather was at a late cleric's meeting, so she had let herself in. She sat by the open window and stared up at the night sky.

What did she do to make Lord Anshar so angry? Was he afraid that she would break her oath for Varg? Maybe he felt she betrayed him.

*"He devoted so much of his own time to help train me. Perhaps he's angry that I would throw it all away so soon?"* she thought.

Was she throwing it all away? Just because she loved Varg didn't mean she had turned her back on Tiamet.

Her mind was confused and tormented as she grappled to understand what went wrong.

She thought of her mother, and her heart ached in a way that formed tears in her eyes. At that moment, she longed for her mother as though she were still a child. She so desperately wanted someone to talk to, someone to confide in, someone who understood her. Her mother was the only person she had ever told about Varg, and while she hadn't approved at first, in time, her mother had accepted their friendship, even encouraged it. She wondered what her mother would think if she were alive, to know that her daughter had grown up to fall hopelessly in love with that same lycan that had once been her childhood friend. Somehow Halea believed that her mother would have understood because her mother always put her happiness first, and her mother had never really wanted the life of a priestess for her.

Halea lay on her bed and cried herself to sleep.

～～～☼～～～

Varg watched as the elders said prayers to the wolf gods and performed the funeral rights. The other packs would take their dead home to be buried in their own sacred burial grounds, but they all still attended the funeral of his pack members as a sign of respect and for those who knew the dead to express genuine grief and condolences.

The western pack's burial grounds were high in the mountains that bordered the northeastern part of their territory.

Once the elders were done, and everyone was spreading earth upon the dead in one final farewell, Rafe approached Varg and bowed his head. Varg reluctantly nodded, allowing the other alpha to speak his mind.

"I will obey the council's decree and your order to allow the humans into our pack's territory, but should they fail us or endanger the lives of my people in any way, I will see every last one of them dead."

Varg bristled at Rafe's threat and struggled not to tear the southern alpha's head off. Rafe's words trod too close to defiance, and he knew it, but he couldn't fault an alpha for putting the safety of his pack first. He didn't doubt that if the priestesses were anything like Halea, they would do everything within their power to subdue the tears. Halea trusted the other practitioners of her faith, and even though he knew no other humans or priestesses, that was good enough for him. If the priestesses did their job, Rafe could not harm them without openly defying him, and if he tried anything that would break their agreement of safety for the Tiamet worshippers, he would make Rafe pay with his life.

Rafe knew all this, but he felt confident that the recent battle would have opened Varg's eyes to the dangers of trusting his pack's safety to humans. He wasn't convinced that Halea's presence wasn't why the tear had shown up in the first place. It appeared that she had let many die before bothering to save them with her witch-like powers to purge the evil of the dark weapons. Perhaps she was a witch and had cast some dark spell over their king to blind him to her true evil intentions. How else could he have loved her so soon? He would much rather believe that than believe his new king was a fool and a filthy human lover.

As far as Rafe was concerned, Varg was doomed to relive all of his father's mistakes, but worse. He would watch the day come when Varg would rue his choices, just as he had watched Bledig regret his. Unfortunately, the price would be the blood of their people, and for Rafe, that was unforgivable.

"I respect that the safety of your pack comes first, and I hear your concerns, but if you break the agreement, I will personally tear you limb from limb. Now, go! Take your pack and return to the south," commanded Varg, and the southern alpha retreated with a glare.

Varg wandered high up the mountain face until he found the two graves that he always visited when his duties as alpha brought him up into the mountain. He knelt beside the graves and felt the cold hard soil beneath his hand. He had never fully understood his father before, but now he knew, and his mind wandered to Halea.

It had only been a couple of days, but it already felt like an eternity, and he couldn't shake the nagging dread that perhaps she had changed her mind and would not return, but he tried to banish such pessimistic thoughts. Halea said she would return, and she would. But it was hard to be patient. It suddenly felt strange to sit at the fire pit for meals without her beside him. He dreaded the idea of leading his warriors on a demon hunt without her fighting alongside them. He missed her comforting scent and the warmth of her skin. He closed his eyes in anguish at the thought that even when she did return, soon again they would be parted and that he could be separated from her for years, decades, or even centuries, but he refused to believe for forever.

He was bound by his word. He would wait for Halea until she was ready, no matter how much it hurt.

~~~☼~~~

Uro was pleased to see his granddaughter again. He had missed her, though the news she brought of the tears was greatly distressing. He had been in many meetings discussing these occurrences, and with Halea's recent report, he was certain that it was time to present the facts to the High Priestess.

Uro was sitting at the kitchen table. They had just finished breakfast, and Halea was washing dishes. Even though she wasn't a little girl anymore, her grandfather still expected her to do chores whenever she visited him, and truthfully, she didn't mind. He was getting on in years.

What little was left of Uro's hair had grown even whiter, and his glasses were thicker now and the lines on his face more numerous and deep. Halea felt an ache in her heart as she looked over her shoulder and observed him nodding off where he sat at the table. He must have been exhausted from staying out so late at the cleric's meeting, and she scooted his teacup over so he wouldn't spill it if he jolted out of his sleep.

She had been his last acolyte. He was too old now to train any more priestesses, and that was a hard fact for him to swallow because finding and training priestesses had been his greatest joy as a cleric. Now, his function was strictly research. Uro was one of the most learned clerics, and he was greatly respected.

Halea pulled out a chair at the table as quietly as possible and sat with her cup of tea next to her grandfather, and studied his sleeping face. He looked so weary and frail. He always seemed so stern before, and she remembered how strict he had been with her. As a child, she always resented it, but now as an adult, she realized how much he had always loved her. Though he expressed that love differently than her mother, it was no less real.

She wondered how many more years he had left and fought the tears rising in her eyes. It was natural for grandchildren to outlive their grandparents, and she understood that, but she had been made immortal. She couldn't shake the dread that was creeping up from the inside; that watching people grow old and die before her eyes would be something she would have to deal with for the rest of her days.

She thought of Varg and found peace in knowing that at least the sands of time couldn't take him from her.

A sudden knock at the door startled her grandfather out of his sleep, causing him to jerk in reflex. Halea smiled, knowing that if she hadn't moved the tea, he would have made a mess everywhere, and she wondered how he managed when she wasn't there.

Halea opened the door and found High Priestess Maven and Mama Dragon.

"Halea!" cried Mama Dragon as she threw her arms around her and nearly squeezed the life out of her.

Maven ignored her colleague's display of affection and addressed herself to Uro.

"You are needed at the castle. I trust Halea has debriefed you."

Uro nodded his head gravely.

Maven and Uro went ahead in a carriage, but Halea chose to take her time and walk to the castle with Mama Dragon. It was a beautiful day, and she had missed the motherly priestess.

"Has anything exciting happened on your recent mission? Kalee is here. She apparently got involved in a bar fight on her last assignment," Mama Dragon asked in her thick foreign accent and laughed.

"Men were fighting over her again, I'm sure," replied Halea with a smile.

"If you didn't take such rural assignments, men would be fighting over you as well."

"There was someone," she replied quietly, but Mama Dragon had not missed it.

"Halea! How wonderful! I'm so happy for you! Was he handsome? Tell me everything!"

"He…um…well you see…he's a lycan."

Mama Dragon stalled in her steps and regarded Halea with a shocked expression. Halea cringed. She suspected Mama Dragon wouldn't understand, nobody would, and she instantly regretted saying anything at all.

"Halea, you weren't forced…"

"No! No, it wasn't that. I wanted to be with him. We were…well…are...friends, and…things just happened."

Halea couldn't help but feel insulted that Mama Dragon would assume the worst, especially about Varg, but she had to remind herself that where Mama Dragon came from, therians only took women for pets or slaves, and they had a particularly bad reputation.

"Friends? But how?"

Halea took a deep breath and started from the beginning. She was hoping to have at least one person to confide in, and Mama Dragon was the closest thing she had to a mother since the loss of her own.

<hr>

Lord Anshar stood before the dark mirror and stared into its unfathomable abyss. Every time he looked beyond the faint reflection, he felt a terrible sense of foreboding. Tiamet had entrusted it to him and him alone, but in all the ages that he guarded the mirror, he was no closer to understanding the secrets of the dimension that lay beyond its surface.

He heard a knock at his study door, and quickly covered the mirror.

"Enter."

"The High Priestess Maven, my Lord," announced the servant as the High Priestess entered and bowed low before him.

Maven couldn't help but notice that his desk was missing, and there was a large dent in the wall as if something massive had been smashed against it, and again she wondered at what she had heard that night before Lord Anshar snapped her out of her musings.

"Is it so?" he asked.

"Yes, my Lord," she replied while looking up into his face, her pupils dilating as she feasted her eyes on him.

"We can't understand how it can be, but it's true. The convergence is coming, soon, very soon! How?" she cried.

"It is because I failed, and now many will pay with their lives," Lord Anshar replied grimly.

"Lord Anshar, that isn't so! You have never failed us! You have saved our world countless times, and I know you will again."

He should have been flattered by her faith in him, but instead, he found it insulting. Maven could not see the truth. He was not some perfect godlike being.

"This is my fault, Maven. I let my emotions get in the way of my duty, and the wrong priestess was sacrificed. That can never happen again. Nothing can go wrong this time. Demons have been assembling in the ruins of the holy city. What have the clerics found?"

"The clerics believe they are waiting for the coming of the convergence, but it is odd that it would happen in the same place twice. Nothing is as it was before."

"And nothing may ever be the same again. It's time. There must be a choosing, and this time the ritual must not be interrupted. I will allow no other priestesses or clerics to be present for the sacrificial ritual…"

"But, my Lord!" cried Maven. She had never been excluded from a ritual. It was always something they had all assembled for. Witnessing the miracle of The Blade That Cuts Through Worlds was a sacred rite for the worshippers of Tiamet.

"That is an order, Maven. The last time they knew where we would be, they knew how to attack us, and many of our order were slain. I will not allow anyone else to be put in the path of danger this time."

This time he would allow nothing to come between him and the sacrifice and ensuring that no others would be in danger was the best way to do it. This time there could be no room for mistake.

"We must proceed with the choosing," he continued.

"I have convened with the clerics and senior priestesses. The choosing shall be between Denji and Halea."

Lord Anshar felt a wave of anguish wash over him.

"*Not her. Please, Tiamet, not her,*" he prayed.

~~~◇~~~

Somehow Halea knew this day would come. She had always been strong, too strong. She had sealed that massive tear on her own, and there was no denying the will of Tiamet that flowed through her.

She walked silently behind Denji toward the castle chapel. It would be between her and the noble beauty from across the sea.

The two priestesses entered and walked towards Lord Anshar and High Priestess Maven and dropped to their knees, their heads bowed low.

Halea heard the metallic sound of Lord Anshar unsheathing the holy blade.

He held the sword horizontally between his two hands and looked down upon the priestesses, his heart pounding.

"Call upon the Goddess. It is she who will choose," he spoke.

Halea and Denji began to pray in the ancient language, calling upon Tiamet to lend them their power, offering themselves as worthy of her blessings. When at last they both felt their purification powers burning within them, they looked up as Lord Anshar held out the blade.

He looked into Denji's resolute eyes and nodded for her to proceed first.

Slowly the priestess reached forth her hand and gently laid her fingers upon the cool steel of the sword.

Nothing.

Lord Anshar gritted his teeth so hard he could nearly feel them cracking. The clerics had to have made a mistake. Perhaps there was another.

Halea reached for the blade, and her light poured into the holy weapon causing it to glow so brightly that it illuminated the entire chapel.

There had been no mistake. She had been chosen.

# CHAPTER 24 – MINE

Uro clutched his chest in pain and collapsed when news that Halea had been chosen reached him.

"He's suffered a very mild heart attack," the healer explained to Halea as she sat next to her sleeping grandfather in the castle's infirmary.

"Will he be okay?"

"He'll be fine. We'll keep him here tonight for observation, and tomorrow he can return home, but he must get more rest, and he will have to take medicine regularly for his heart from now on."

"See that a nurse goes home with him when he is discharged. I want him to have around-the-clock care," ordered Lord Anshar, who had just entered the infirmary, and he winced to see Halea holding her grandfather's hand with silent tears streaming from her eyes.

He wasn't sure if Uro could survive Halea's sacrifice with his advanced age and failing health, but he owed it to her to do everything within his power to ensure her grandfather's comfort and care. It was the least he could do.

"Halea, I'm sorry to interrupt, but I wish to speak with you before you leave."

She nodded her head and followed Lord Anshar into the hall outside of the infirmary.

"Thank you. I wish I didn't have to leave him, not now, but I also know he would understand," she said.

The exact time of the convergence was still unknown. The clerics could only say that it would be soon, but that could be days, months, or even years. Halea would have to continue with her duties until needed, but she couldn't roam far. She needed to be close enough to the ruined city to reach it within a few hours should the convergence begin, and while Lord Anshar didn't like sending her back to the lycan, it was the closest assignment.

The demon activity around the ruined city led him to believe without a doubt that the convergence would happen in the same place again as if it were planned. Ages of clerics trying to discover the mysteries of the Chaos, and still, they were no closer to understanding the nature of the dimension that sought to destroy their world.

"Samesa and Kalee will accompany you into the western territory, as well as forty clerics. I have no hope that the situation will be brought under control with the convergence coming so soon. It will get worse. We haven't regained our numbers since the last disaster, and that's the best I can give you for now. More priestesses and clerics are returning to the castle every day. I will send as many as I can spare to report to you so that you may send them on to the other lycan territories. I am entrusting you to lead this mission."

"I will fulfill my duty," she replied and bowed her head.

"The wrong priestess will not suffice this time. Halea…you can't back out now. It's too late."

She merely nodded her head, but he could smell tears renewing within her eyes.

He turned his back to her, not wanting to see her pain.

"Halea!" shouted Mama Dragon, who was running up after her.

Halea had said her farewells to her grandfather, who cried bitterly to see her leave again so soon after learning she was destined for the blade, but he could do nothing to prevent what was to come. For the first time in his life, he regretted pushing her to become a priestess.

Halea shouldered her replenished travel bag, and with spear in hand, she was making her way to meet with Samesa, Kalee, and the clerics who were waiting on the city outskirts when she heard Mama Dragon calling for her.

"Halea, is it true?"

"Yes."

Mama Dragon began to weep. For the past eight years, she had grown to love Halea like a daughter. Though she had always been motherly towards all of her fellow priestesses, it was with Halea that she became closest. She reminded her of her own daughter, and when the news spread that Halea was chosen for the blade, she had been devastated.

She had not particularly taken the news of Halea's entanglement with a lycan very well. Though she had not outwardly objected, she didn't necessarily approve either, and she had seen Halea's disappointment.

"Halea, please don't leave without saying goodbye."

"I looked for you. They said you would be stationed at the ruined city. I thought you had already left."

Mama Dragon had been a falconer in her home country, and her skill had proven most valuable to their cause since her conscription. She would send news of demon activity from the ruined city. Lord Anshar would soon be joining her. Since the last destruction, he had ordered the Citadel to be rebuilt, and while it was far from being complete, it would serve as his base of operations until the convergence came.

"I'm sorry," blurted Mama Dragon as she grabbed Halea into a hug. "Love whoever you want. As long as they love you, I'm happy for you."

Halea pulled back in surprise. Mama Dragon's initial disapproval had broken her heart, but to finally hear the motherly priestess give her blessing brought tears of joy and relief to her eyes. All she had wanted was for someone to understand.

"Thank you," she replied and returned Mama Dragon's embrace.

Halea remained mostly silent while leading Samesa and Kalee through the forest. Their clerics were trailing far behind because mere mortals could never keep up with the speed of priestesses, but they knew in which direction to travel.

Halea wasn't sure what she would say or do if Varg found out that she had been chosen.

*"He'll go crazy, that's for sure,"* she thought bitterly.

She had already made Samesa and Kalee swear to not bring up the choosing before any of the lycans. Thankfully, she didn't expect they would spend much time socializing with them. Varg had a way of prying information out of her, and her only way to avoid arousing his suspicion was to keep busy with their mission and evade the topic at all costs.

She promised to return, and she had, but she had her duty to lead the mission, and the other lycans would not suffer the rest of the priestesses and clerics anywhere near their den.

A strong breeze whipped up, and the trees rustled.

*"Well, that did it,"* she cringed as she felt the westerly wind.

Even with her average human ears, she could hear the sound of a howl in the distance, and she stifled a groan. She should have expected he would post sentries to send out an alarm the moment their presence was detected.

Samesa and Kalee exchanged nervous glances and readied their spears. It had been many years since they last entered lycan territory, and they had not exactly been treated with a warm welcome.

Halea ignored their paranoia and watched for movement through the trees. It didn't take long.

Samesa and Kalee stood firm as three large lycan males appeared through the trees as if materializing out of thin air, and they marveled at their therian speed.

"Halea!" exclaimed the bigger male, who, to their utter shock, grabbed Halea in a tight embrace.

Their first instinct was to fight him off her, but when they realized Halea was returning his embrace and smiling up at him, they just stood there with their mouths gaping open.

Varg had spent the past few days in great anxiety. Halea had promised to return quickly, but it seemed to be taking far longer than he originally imagined, and he was beginning to seriously worry that she wouldn't come back. Leading demon hunts had not been the same without her, though he still had the support of the eastern and northern lycan packs that had yet to return to their territories.

He desperately wanted to taste her lips, but he forced himself to be restrained. The other priestesses were watching, and he didn't want to cause problems for Halea with her own kind.

"What took you so long?"

Halea had prepared herself for this question.

"I'm sorry. I was able to get help. This is Samesa and Kalee, and Lord Anshar has granted me forty clerics, but it will take them time to catch up with us. They should be here by sundown, though. Is there somewhere we can make camp?" she explained, as she intentionally avoided answering his question.

For a moment, she thought he was onto her, with the strange look he gave her, but she was relieved when he finally spoke.

"Yes, there's a good spot not far from here, a clearing big enough to accommodate your people."

Varg quickly cast a glance over the two priestesses, who looked as nervous as they smelled. This was his first time seeing any human priestesses other than Halea this close-up, and he could tell by the postures of Faolan and Aatu that they were equally on edge about the new arrivals. They had only just barely acclimated themselves to Halea's presence, and now they had to deal with new humans in their territory.

"Thank you. We'll set up our camp, and we can meet with you in the morning."

"*Uh-oh,*" she thought when he gave her an angry glare.

Samesa did not quite recognize any of these lycans from her last encounter. The one that appeared to be their leader looked familiar, though. He resembled the one that was in charge the last time, except this one's eyes were a vivid shade of blue, and she wondered if they were related somehow.

It was clear to her that Halea had managed to successfully forge a friendly alliance with the alpha lycan, but she was at an utter loss as to how she had managed to pull off such a feat.

"I wish to speak with you in private," Varg said to Halea in a low and commanding voice.

"*Oh gods, here it comes,*" Halea thought with dread, but she nodded her head in agreement and waited as he ordered Aatu and Faolan to escort the priestesses to their designated campsite.

Her two friends shot her worried glances, but she gave them a nod to signal that she was fine and to follow the two lycan males.

"Meet with you in the morning? The other humans will be fine without you. You are coming back to the den with me," he said in clear command.

"Varg, you have your pack, but this is mine," she said in a low tone or warning, trying to explain it to him in terms she was hoping he would understand. "Lord Anshar put me in charge of this mission. I am not leaving my people! Besides, we'll see each other tomorrow. I'm not that far away."

"I don't care! I want you with me!"

She sighed loudly. It was clear she wasn't going to get through to him with argument, so she switched tactics.

"Varg, please," she pleaded while leaning into him.

He instantly knew what she was up to but decided to hold out to see what concessions she had to offer.

"I'll still make time to be with you, just the two of us. It's not like we have much privacy back at the den anyway."

"*Damn it, she's doing it to me again,*" he thought while recalling how she had flirted her way into seeing his wolf form. He softly stroked the side of her face and drowned himself in her scent, and she reached up on her toes to gently kiss him, and he was instantly a goner. He returned her kiss with an intense, hungry need, and he couldn't help sliding his hands down her body.

They were both breathing heavily when he finally broke their kiss and he stared down into her eyes.

"I've missed you so much. I'm greedy, and I don't care. I want every moment I can have with you."

Halea's heart ached. She knew Varg envisioned an empty life without her, but he had no idea how few and precious their last moments really were, and she struggled not to cry. He could never know the truth.

"I want to be with you too, but they need me. I can't just run off any more than you can. Please, Varg, I'm begging you to understand."

He made a sound halfway between a growl and sigh, and she knew that he had relented.

～～～☼～～～

Otsana watched from the shadows, waiting downwind until the priestess was left alone, even though she had been sure to mask her scent. She boiled with rage to hear their words, but today she would prove no human was worthy of a lycan alpha.

She stalked silently as the foolish woman made her way towards where the rest of the humans would be making their camp. She had to intercept her before she reached the others.

"So, you want to be with him, huh?"

Halea stopped in her tracks as she heard the familiar female voice and turned as Otsana emerged from the trees.

"You're not good enough for him. You're just a stupid human."

Halea's eyes narrowed as she regarded her rival.

"And you're a fool. He's made his choice. You're a lycan; you know he can't change it now."

"You're a witch! No alpha would ever sink so low. You did something to him! He doesn't even know you! You expect me to believe he fell in love with a pathetic human whore so quickly? Well, I'm not going to let you control him like that."

Otsana had overheard Varg express his desire to mate the human wench, but she had not heard his explanation to the healer of how they truly met.

Halea watched as the angry she-wolf took a fighting stance before her.

"Have it your way," Halea said while tossing her spear and travel bag aside. As much as she hated this woman, she wouldn't enter an unfair fight by using a weapon. A lycan's claws and fangs were as good as a weapon, but Halea wasn't the slightest bit intimidated. She was going to put that bitch in her place.

Otsana wasted no time charging at her, and Halea quickly sidestepped the slash of her claws and sharply turned to elbow the she-wolf in the face.

Otsana staggered from the impact and stopped to spit blood out onto the ground.

"You bitch, you're going to pay for that!" she growled. She had not expected the human to be so fast.

Halea jumped forward, and using her fiercest offensive hand-combat maneuvers, she forced Otsana to put up her defenses to fend her off. The she-wolf quickly went in for the attack and managed to knee Halea hard in the stomach, nearly causing her to double over. When she moved again to finish her winded opponent, Halea dodged in time to plant a round-house kick to Otsana's chest. That was when Halea noticed the slightest tinge of red bleeding into the edges of Otsana's dark blue eyes.

Otsana leaped upon her and tackled her to the forest floor, and Halea cried out as the she-wolf's claws sliced down the side of her ribs while she managed to forcefully hold back her other hand, which was trying to dig into her throat.

With a hard upwards push and a fierce kick Halea managed to throw off the she-wolf, but she could barely get back on her feet again before she was forced to defend herself from Otsana's claws. She gritted her teeth in pain as Otsana swiped out and tore down her forearm.

<hr />

Varg was walking back towards the den at a leisurely pace. He wasn't particularly looking forward to the evening meal around the fire pit if Halea wasn't going to be with him, and he wanted time alone to think when he detected the scent of something on the wind that caused his eyes to flash red.

<hr />

The two females were tearing into each other, but neither would surrender the fight. Halea stumbled as Otsana landed several successful punches into her face.

"You could never be his mate. You are weak! Why would he ever want you?" shouted the she-wolf, and that was when Halea snapped.

Before Otsana knew it, Halea had her pinned and was punching her in the face over and over again with pure hatred in her eyes.

"You. Stupid. Jealous. Bitch!" Halea shouted while punctuating each word by smashing her fist into the female lycan's face. "He doesn't love you. He chose me! I'm his mate, not you, and you better get over it, or I'll fucking kill you! He. Is. Mine!" she shouted into Otsana's bloody face and punched her once more with all her might, knocking the she-wolf unconscious.

Halea gasped for air. She released the unconscious lycan from her grip and rose on trembling legs.

"Halea?" she heard Varg's voice call, and she looked up to see him staring at her with a mixture of love and worry.

She froze and instantly broke into a cold sweat. How much did Varg hear?

"I came as soon as I smelled your blood on the wind."

Varg was immediately by her side, and Halea could see red forming around the edges of his eyes as he surveyed her many bruises and gashes.

"I'm okay. It's all right," Halea offered, trying to calm him, and she was surprised at how quickly the red faded from his eyes. Perhaps it was obvious that Otsana had already been taught a lesson.

"Halea…is it true? Do you really want to be my mate?"

How could she tell him no? She did want to be with him. She knew it in the depths of her soul. They had so little time left. The convergence could come to snatch

189

her away at any moment. She wanted to spend every last day she had in his arms. Maybe her final days were the most she could ever give him. Shouldn't she at least offer him that much? Her duty was to defend the lycan territories until the convergence came. Maybe she would be spared a few more years.

At last, she nodded her head before looking into his eyes. "Yes. I want to be yours. I love you."

It felt as if his heart would explode with joy. She wanted him to be her mate. She had fought for him and claimed him, and now she had finally agreed to be his.

He swept her into his arms and seized her lips in a passionate kiss, and despite the burning pain of her bloody wounds, she couldn't think of anything but him. His touch. His warmth. His undying love.

When he finally broke their kiss, she was limp and panting in his arms, and he couldn't stop smiling.

"When?" he asked, and a moment of panic gripped her.

"I...I don't know...I need a little time...but...I haven't much...I just...need a little time," Halea stammered, desperately trying to get a grip on what she was doing. What if she was making a terrible mistake? Well, it was too late now! She didn't know anything about what it took to be mated, and though time was against her, she wasn't exactly prepared to do it *right away* either. She needed to think. She needed someone to talk to.

The only thing she knew was that mated or not; eventually, he would lose her, and at that moment, the least she wanted to do before she died was prove to him how much she loved him, to offer him the last days of her life. It was all she could give him.

# CHAPTER 25 – THE FACE OF MADNESS

"What in the name of Tiamet did he do to you?" cried Kalee when Halea finally arrived covered in noticeable claw marks and bruises and with her robe nearly shredded to tatters and covered in blood.

"Calm down, you two. He didn't do anything to me. I was attacked."

"A demon?" asked Samesa.

"Uh...yeah," replied Halea, being thankful that humans couldn't sniff out lies the way therians could. They came because they had been assured safety from the lycans, and she didn't want this one incident to reflect badly on Varg or the rest of his people. "A bunch of them," she added, knowing they wouldn't believe she couldn't handle herself against just one demon. "Don't worry. I made them pay." She tried to conceal a wicked grin as she recalled how Varg had to carry Otsana back to the den like a sack of potatoes over his shoulder. As angry as he was with the female lycan, he couldn't leave her unconscious in the forest with demons around, even though she certainly had it coming.

Halea tossed her travel bag down by the fire her friends made and began rummaging for medical supplies.

"I knew it. I knew we shouldn't have left you alone. Lord Anshar ordered us to protect you, and already we're messing up," grumbled Samesa as she ran to fetch the waterskin to help Halea wash her wounds.

Varg had wanted Halea to return with him to the den, at least long enough to have Batsuba tend to her injuries, and it had taken her quite a while to calm him down and assure him that she and the other priestesses would be fine managing on their own.

"What do you mean 'protect me?'"

"You can't die...before..." explained Kalee as she helped Halea out of her damaged robe.

Halea's eyes narrowed in irritation.

"I see. And here I thought Lord Anshar trusted me to at least not get myself killed between now and then."

"It's not that he doesn't trust you. You're the most powerful priestess alive, but that doesn't mean accidents can't happen. You're lucky he let you out on a mission at all after what went wrong the last time. It's a testament to how much he does trust you that he'd let you complete this mission when your life is literally the only thing between Chaos and us," defended Samesa.

"In fact, our first mission is to protect you, and our second is to deal with the tears. You're the important one now. So don't go getting yourself killed," said Kalee as she helped Halea clean and bandage her wounds.

*"Great, first Varg being overprotective, now them,"* Halea thought bitterly, but she had to admit, they did have a point. She really couldn't take any chances with her life. No one could replace her now that Tiamet had chosen her, and they could not afford another failed ritual. The demons that killed Ami only knew to target her because they had attacked in the middle of the ritual, and she had borne all the marks of a sacrifice. Whatever intelligence lurked behind the Chaos, it had no way of yet knowing who the chosen priestess was, and that afforded Halea at least a little safety.

They managed to get Halea cleaned up and bandaged and her robe repaired before the clerics arrived. None of these clerics had ever been in lycan territory before, and few had seen therians besides Lord Anshar. Halea was worried by the fact that so many academic clerics were included in their numbers. All clerics knew how to fight because they were expected to train new priestesses. Priestesses didn't have time to train; they were too busy fulfilling their duties to drag rookies along. Many clerics preferred to devote themselves to worship or studying demons, tears, and the mysteries of the Chaos Dimension. There were very few well-rounded clerics who were adept at both fighting and academics. Halea was fortunate that her grandfather was so skilled in all aspects of being a cleric. It was clear some of these clerics spent too much time behind scrolls and not enough in the field.

Samesa and Kalee were disappointed as well but tried not to show it. Since the failure of the last convergence, they had not been able to recruit and train as many new priestesses and clerics as they truly needed, and they knew they had to be grateful for whoever they could get.

"We hope we didn't keep you waiting," said Codeon.

Halea recognized most of these clerics. Codeon was from a faraway land, and her face was pale with dark eyes of an exotic shape, fair skin, and flowing silky black hair. She was in her late thirties and primarily a scholarly cleric, but she was also a powerful spellcaster. Halea was familiar with her enough to know that she would be useful in the field. She wasn't the best fighter, but she was capable.

With her were her two usual companions Favion and Edmond, and a new cleric who looked very young, perhaps in his late teens or early twenties.

"Have you met Dean?" asked Edmond, who introduced the new cleric.

"Greetings, Priestess Halea. I'm honored to meet you," Dean said while offering her a sweaty handshake. Halea had a bad feeling about this new guy. He looked rather frail. His hair was blond and wispy, and he had wide green eyes and a nervous smile.

"We're happy to have you," Halea offered, again being thankful that she was among humans and not lycans.

"Hey baby, did you miss me?" Favion asked Kalee as he sat down next to her at the fire.

Favion had been one of Kalee's lovers in the past, but she had to cut it off when he became too clingy. Favion had rusty red hair that was somewhat long and pulled back in a low ponytail, his eyes were dark, and he had a short goatee. Favion had a thing for priestesses, any priestess. He enjoyed the casual encounters, as he generally preferred not to get attached, but that didn't mean he wasn't always up for as many casual encounters as he could get, and he had always been particularly fond of Kalee.

"Who are you again?" asked Kalee, as she struggled to keep a straight face.

"Still trying, I see," commented Samesa to Edmond, who looked embarrassed to see his friend's behavior, which Halea thought was odd because he certainly should have been used to it by now.

"Trust me, I'd have loved to have left him behind," replied Edmond, who knew all too well that despite Favion's shortcomings, he was one of their best fighters.

Edmond was a sensitive soul, who tended to favor the more scholarly side of his devotion to Tiamet, but he did actively strive to be a better fighter, and Halea appreciated his effort. He had dark brown hair and eyes and dark tanned skin. He was a little thin but stronger than he looked, and he had recently completed training his first priestess. Both Favion and Edmond were in their late twenties, but they were shaping up to be valuable clerics with more time and experience.

"I heard you did well as a master," commented Halea. She didn't know Favion and Edmond as well as Samesa and Kalee. To her, they were casual acquaintances, but Edmond had always struck her as a friendly, likable person who took his position as a cleric very seriously.

"Yes, I was honored when Lord Anshar assigned me an acolyte. More than I can say for Favion, I don't think Lord Anshar trusts him around young impressionable priestesses."

"What? I'm a saint! I would never lay a single hand on an acolyte," defended Favion. "Besides, I prefer my ladies more experienced," he added while wiggling his eyebrows at Kalee, who was doing a poor job at not smiling and encouraging him.

Halea sat by herself away from the campfires that night as all the clerics were socializing. The next day they would begin the hunt, and they would be busy the whole day, and she couldn't wait that long. She needed to speak to someone right away before meeting with Varg again. She looked over her shoulder to make sure that no one was watching before slipping into the woods to search for the herbs to make scent masking potion in the moonlight.

~~~◇~~~

Varg ran through the moonlight. He couldn't contain his joy in his humanoid form, and so he ran as the wolf. Halea had finally agreed to be his mate, and he had never felt his spirit soar so high.

He stopped halfway up a mountain slope that bordered the northern edge of his territory and gazed down at the valley below and breathed deeply of the cold high elevation air.

While he was thrilled that Halea had finally agreed to be his, he still couldn't shake a deep unexplainable worry. Had she really given up being a priestess? It seemed so unlike her. He wondered if she intended to serve her Goddess until completing her mission in his territory and then abdicate being a priestess to be with him. That would mean he would have to wait until they subdued the tears and demons in his lands, but how long would that take? Perhaps that was why she was so reluctant to be mated right away.

He told himself to be patient when she refused him, but now that she had agreed, he struggled against the beast within. She was so close to finally being his, and every instinct inside of him was clawing, howling, demanding that he complete the ritual that would bind her to him for the rest of their lives.

He had to keep the beast under control, but it was tearing him apart.

Still, he couldn't ignore the nagging feeling that something was wrong.

Was it wrong to take away her purpose in life? Was he wrong for expecting her to abandon everything she had ever worked for just to be with him? What if she regretted it later? Lycans never regretted their mate, but Halea was not a lycan. Maybe she could regret. Maybe she would resent him for dissuading her from her calling. He didn't want to make her unhappy. He didn't want anything to come between them. If she were a lycan, he wouldn't have such concerns. Lycans knew without a doubt that the one they wanted for a mate was their true chosen. While he knew Halea loved him, he couldn't help wondering what had made her change her mind.

~~~✧~~~

Halea sighed in relief to see the soft glow of light within Batsuba's tree-dwelling. She worried the old healer would have been asleep, as it was late at night. Thankfully, lycans didn't need sleep as much as humans.

Batsuba was surprised to see Halea standing in her doorway. She heard someone climbing up but detected no scent.

"Come in, Priestess," she invited. It was apparent by the look on the young woman's face that something was ailing her. Gossip had spread like wildfire when Varg appeared and dropped off the unconscious eastern she-wolf, only to disappear into the night again without so much as an explanation. Though, it was clear by Halea's scent and blood on Otsana that the female lycan had picked a fight that she had not won.

"I agreed to be Varg's mate," Halea blurted.

Batsuba's dark eyes regarded her with deep concern.

"Something is wrong?"

Halea had counted on Batsuba being able to see directly through her. Why else would she show up at her home in the middle of the night to announce such news?

"I was chosen."

Batsuba's eyes shot open with an instant look of understanding. Batsuba had lived through many ages and many convergences, and she knew of the blood sacrifice.

"No...stay away from him," Batsuba finally growled in a low and angry voice.

"Why? I know it was foolish of me, but whether we're mated or not, he's going to lose me. I just wanted to make him happy. I didn't know what else to do."

The old healer was seething with rage, but she struggled to keep her temper under control. She had to remind herself that Halea was human. She did not understand their ways.

"Listen to me carefully, Priestess. You know that Bledig, Varg's father, is dead. Did Varg tell you how he died?"

Halea shook her head. "He…said he just walked away one night and never came back."

Halea had wondered how such a powerful being could die but never dared to bring it up with Varg. Discussing his mother's death had caused Varg anguish in the past, and so she had buried her curiosity about his father.

"It had been a hard winter, and the snow was deep, but at last, with the coming of spring, we were able to send a search party up into the northeastern mountains, our sacred burial grounds. It was there that they found him, his frozen remains, lying on top of *her* grave. He lay there until death finally reunited them, and it was beside her that we laid his bones to rest."

Halea dropped to her knees and trembled as tears streamed down her face.

"You understand now. You cannot be Varg's mate. He will follow you. He will follow you into the next world. If the mating bond is never made, he will suffer to lose you, but at least someday, perhaps he would have a chance to go on. If you mate with him - he will die."

Suddenly Halea understood why Varg's father had always been so cold and distant after the death of Varg's mother. He had lived only long enough to see his son grown, and then he had gone to join his mate.

"But…it can't be like that for all lycans…it can't be…"

"It is! Once we are mated, we are bonded by blood and spirit. Our mate becomes a part of us. Only death can break that bond, and without it, we cannot go on. Since the dawn of our race, there has only ever been one lycan, only one, to survive the loss of their mate. And there is not a single day that I do not long to join him in the next world."

Halea looked up in shock.

"If you truly love Varg, you must stay away from him."

~~~✧~~~

That morning, howls of warning announced danger. The devotees of Tiamet immediately sprang into action as soon as Halea explained what the calls meant. She had heard lycan warning howls enough to have grown familiar with them, though she was far from understanding their nuance.

A small party of lycan scouts had tracked the fresh scent of demons passing through the northern forests of their territory until they discovered the massive tear. It appeared mostly inactive, with only occasional demons trying to come through the dimensional rift.

Varg led his warriors as well as several volunteers from the northern and eastern packs to the tear after they had announced the distress call, and they immediately surrounded the purple vortex to prevent any demons that might spill out from escaping. Their sensitive ears began to hear sounds coming from within the tear. Soon, more demons would appear.

"Where are they? Aren't they supposed to be the ones tracking these things down?" asked Aatu nervously as the sounds within the tear grew louder.

"What makes you think Halea even knows what our howls mean?" asked Daciana, who stood close to Hemming as both listened to the sounds of the coming demons but did their best to avoid looking directly into the tear.

"Don't they have bad hearing? We're probably on our own," grumbled Lyall.

"She's been on enough hunts with us to know what the distress calls mean, be patient. We'll hold off the demons as long as we can," replied Varg.

The tear pulsed, and a quick glance confirmed, it had just grown larger, and then all hell broke loose.

The lycans were quickly overwhelmed by their sheer numbers, and the sound of battle filled the air. The foul scent of demon blood polluted their noses, but they continued to hold their ground.

That was when the flashes of white light appeared, and suddenly the humans were fighting alongside them. The priestesses in their white robes and the clerics in their blood-red uniforms, each possessing different weapons based on their individual skill sets.

Bertolf, having transformed into his wolf form, was tearing wraiths apart. A bipedal demon was about to leap on his back and slice into him with its razor-sharp claws when a human cleric sprang forth with two flashing blades that caused the beast to burst into a flame of white.

Favion was nervous to fight so close to a giant wolf, but he had to remind himself that the lycans promised safety. He readied his blades which bore the ancient language carved into their handles, spells for purification, and quickly went to work in slaying demons all around. The large wolf eyed the human cleric briefly before leaping back into the fray, and Favion was glad he had moved on.

Codeon was chanting spells that sent short bolts of purification into the air and lobbing sutras which instantly purified every demon they came in contact with. She had already erected a small personal barrier that allowed her to cast spells safely from where she stood.

A young cleric male was thrown to the ground and about to be pounced upon when Faolan tore into the attacking Wraith, ripping it in half. The young cleric regarded the lycan with fear in his eyes. Dean had very little firsthand experience battling demons and he was trembling all over as he watched the lycans shred the demons until their black blood soaked the ground.

"Get up, Dean! Come on, we need you!" shouted Edmond, but Dean would not move.

Edmond moved in closer to the younger cleric, hoping to buy him time to recover himself as he slew any demons that came near with his rune-carved staff.

Varg tore into demons without mercy as he struggled to find Halea. She had to be close, but there was so much chaos all around. At last, he spotted the gore-stained white robes of the three priestesses as they positioned themselves next to the tear.

Kalee was the defender of their formation, slaying demons all around with her spear, which glowed with the charge of her purification powers; she guarded over Samesa and Halea as they worked. Halea had already begun to pour her power into sealing the tear; her hands raised high as white light collided with purple. Her eyes were closed as she focused on calling upon the Goddess for her strength. Around her, Samesa chanted and focused her power on creating a barrier. Once the barrier was complete and the three priestesses safely within, Samesa and Kalee both turned and joined Halea to concentrate their power on the tear before them, being careful not to look directly into the dimensional rift.

Dean watched the three priestesses from where he crouched as they worked together in perfect discipline to seal the tear.

The tear.

It seemed to be calling to him. That strange purple light, and suddenly, he couldn't look away.

He stared deep within the vortex that opened into the realm of Chaos, and there he saw it.

It instantly gripped his mind, and at that moment, he saw and felt the fabric of time and space disintegrate before his eyes, and before him lay the vast expanse of nothingness.

Edmond heard Dean let out a horrible blood-curdling scream that rent through the air at such a high unnatural pitch that even the many lycans turned their eyes to watch as the young cleric gripped his face in a frenzy as his eyes rolled up into his head and blood poured forth from his ears, eyes, nose, and mouth.

"No, Dean. Don't look into it!" shouted Edmond.

But it was too late.

The young cleric fell to the ground, twitching, and writhing, and screaming incoherent gibberish.

Suddenly the tear snapped shut, and with it sealed, the priestesses turned and stabbed their spears through their barrier to slay any remaining close demons. The lycans and clerics made short work of any remaining forces from the Chaos until, at last, their work was done.

Bertolf, though he hated to admit it, was impressed. Priestesses were allowed into his territory before the last convergence after the council had agreed to it, but he had never brought his pack to fight alongside them. Whenever there was a tear, he had just left it to them. Very few lycans seemed to have been seriously injured, despite the overwhelming numbers, and the ones that were wounded by black blades were already being healed by the priestesses once they emerged from the safety of their barrier.

"Halea!" called Varg, as soon as he could break away from seeing that his pack was safe, and their injuries tended to.

"I'm sorry it took us so long. We did hear the call. Clerics are slow but useful," Halea explained with a weary smile while wiping the sweat from her brow with a dirty hand and only managing to smear more mess across her face.

Varg was suddenly reminded of the day he first met her. A messy-faced little girl, all alone in the forest; the day she changed his life forever.

She was never more beautiful to him than at that moment.

Before Halea could even register what was going on, she was trapped within his embrace, and her startled cry was swiftly silenced by his deep kiss. She quickly fell slack in his arms as the intensity of his love poured into her very soul, all reason washing away in the tidal wave of his intense passion.

The other lycans simply averted their eyes. It was no secret to them that Halea was his chosen, and they all knew that if they valued their own lives, they'd mind their own business. The humans, on the other hand, stared in utter shock as Halea was passionately kissed by the lycan male, and it was pretty clear that she was not objecting.

"Well...that's new," whispered Kalee as she stood next to Samesa.

Samesa only narrowed her eyes. To her, Halea was playing a dangerous game, and she wasn't exactly sure what was going on.

The shrieking and thrashing of Dean eventually drew Halea out of her daze, and at last, she pulled back from Varg, who reluctantly loosened his hold.

"I need to help him," she said while breaking away to join the circle of clerics gathering around the young man who thrashed and writhed on the forest floor.

Halea crouched beside the young cleric as several others held onto his limbs to keep him from hurting himself.

"He has looked into the face of madness," spoke Codeon, who began chanting a prayer over her companion as he babbled and drooled incoherently.

Halea placed her hands on both sides of Dean's head and called upon Tiamet to give her strength. The white light flowed from her fingertips into the shrieking cleric, and slowly he began to still, until at last, he lay motionless and completely silent, staring up into the sky above with blank eyes.

They all bowed their heads in sadness. It would have been better if he had died. To look into the Chaos and live was a fate worse than death. No one ever came back once they stared into the face of Chaos - no one. Purification could soothe the initial shock, but there would be no coming out of it. Dean was lost.

"I'll take him," spoke Edmond at last. He felt an all-consuming guilt. Clearly, the young cleric had been frightened and overwhelmed. He had not been ready yet, and Edmond cursed himself for not being able to stop Dean when he had the chance.

"I'll go with you. It'll take at least two of us to get him all the way to Weldison," offered Codeon. Her husband lived in Westvear city, and she was not opposed to seeing him again with a convergence so close at hand. Seeing Dean as he lay there drooling silently, staring into nothingness, only made her more aware of how precious life truly was, and she would regret it if she didn't remind her husband how much she loved him. As a cleric, any day could be her last.

Halea wiped tears from her eyes as Codeon and Edmond helped Dean to his feet. He could walk if they guided him, but he responded to nothing and no one and only stared ahead and drooled pathetically. The two clerics led their lost friend into the trees, and then they were gone.

"What will happen to him?" asked Varg.

"He will live his life trapped within his own mind...until the day he dies. There is nothing anyone can do for him. He'll sit in Weldison for the rest of his days. It's a hospital...an asylum...for those who have been driven to madness by looking directly into Chaos. Lord Anshar is the patron of the hospital. He founded it long ago and sees that all who suffer from Chaos madness are cared for until their lives finally expire."

"There is no hope at all?" Varg asked, shocked and horrified. The mere idea of having to live out one's entire existence in such a state seemed worse than hell, and he wondered if it wouldn't be kinder to just put them out of their misery.

"Occasionally some improve a small amount; maybe speak a little again, though nothing they say makes any sense. They usually don't recognize anything or anyone, though."

Varg wrapped his arms around Halea, and she buried her face in his chest as he comforted her.

Samesa watched as Halea and the alpha lycan displayed their affection publicly again. She was going to have to talk with her friend.

# CHAPTER 26 – PRISONER OF YOUR LOVE

"Halea, what is going on with you and that shifter?" asked Samesa as she pulled her friend aside later that evening at their campsite.

"Don't call him that!" Halea barked. She wasn't about to stand there and let anyone use such a derogatory term towards Varg.

Samesa only stared back at her friend in confusion and worry.

"Look, don't worry about it. I'll be dead soon anyway. What I do now doesn't matter."

"Doesn't matter?" Samesa cried, raising her voice louder than even she realized. When she saw the disapproving look on Halea's face, she lowered her tone. "Halea, it's none of my business who you, or any priestess, get involved with…normally…but this…this isn't natural. He's not even human. He's an animal! My gods, what are you thinking?"

Halea burned with rage. She was perilously close to putting her fist in her friend's face.

"Look, not all therians are monsters. Lord Anshar isn't! Neither is Varg! I don't give a damn what you think, and before you go ratting me out to Lord Anshar, he already knows! I know my position, and you don't have to worry about it. I'm still going to die. For you. For them," she said, waving her hand generally back towards the campsite. "And for him. So don't worry about how I spend my last days living."

Samesa's eyes watered up with hurt and sadness, and suddenly Halea felt a little sorry for being so harsh.

"Look, you're my friend. Varg would never harm me. I'm in absolutely no danger, at least not from him. I've known him since we were kids. We grew up together. Yes, I know he's a lycan. It didn't matter to me then, and it doesn't matter to me now. Please…just try to understand…this is the last happiness I'll ever have."

Samesa embraced her friend and sobbed on her shoulder. "I wish it weren't you. I wish it weren't anyone, but especially not you."

~~~☼~~~

Varg waited on the outskirts of the den, staring into the distance, and occasionally sniffing the wind. At last, he detected Halea's scent and ran out to meet her.

Halea's heart was beating fast, and she hoped Varg would just assume it was because she had been running. Batsuba's words were still on her mind from the night before, and she didn't have nearly enough time to think of what to do. He couldn't know the truth, and she knew patience was not one of his virtues.

"Sorry, I'm late," she said as he rushed up to greet her, and without a word, he snatched her into his arms and nearly kissed the life out of her. His kiss was intense and full of need as he thrust his tongue into her mouth, and she could feel the pounding of his heart against hers. He let his hands run down her body and cup her ass, pulling her tighter against him and causing him to let out a low growl of desire. She couldn't help digging her fingers into his thick, dark hair as she allowed herself to let go and enjoy the intensity of his love. She needed to feel him this way. She needed to savor every second.

She was gasping for breath and a little dizzy when he finally broke their kiss.

"I've missed you. The den hasn't been the same without you," Varg said while softly caressing the side of Halea's face, and he noticed that her wounds from her fight with Otsana appeared to be almost entirely gone. He was surprised but relieved that that bitch hadn't left any permanent scars.

"I noticed the northern and eastern packs were with you today," Halea mentioned, trying to steer the conversation in a safe direction.

"The eastern pack is leaving tomorrow. Otsana has been too ashamed to show her face since a puny human kicked her ass, and I'm sure she begged her father for them to leave. Ethelwolf was furious that she dared to attack a priestess after the council's decree, but I assured him that her transgression had not harmed our agreement with your people."

"Not so bad for a puny human," she laughed as they walked back towards the den hand-in-hand.

"Rafe took his pack and left after the funeral. He will obey and allow priestesses into his territory, but he left with a warning. If your people fail him, he will make them pay with blood."

"I'm not worried," she said to reassure him. She wasn't at all surprised that the southern alpha would say such a thing. She wasn't concerned about his threat against her people, they wouldn't fail in their duties, but deep down, she couldn't shake the lingering fear that Rafe might try to do something to Varg.

"I'm not very worried either, after what I saw today. I've always wondered how just a few human priestesses could subdue a tear and a whole horde of demons when it seemed to take my entire pack to keep them off you while you worked when it was just you."

"Well, most of the time we spend between convergences, tears, and demon appearances aren't nearly as bad as they have been here, but when they do get this bad, it does take several of us to do the job."

"Is it coming?" he finally asked.

Halea cringed, and he instantly saw.

"It is, isn't it?"

She finally nodded and prayed he wouldn't ask the one question she dreaded most.

No such luck.

Varg stopped them before they reached the den and grasped her shoulders firmly with his hands and stared down into her eyes.

"Who?"

"Who, what?"

"Don't act like you don't understand me! Who was chosen?" he growled, and Halea could tell he was deathly serious.

She trembled beneath his hands and squeezed her eyes shut. He could hear her heart beating faster than he had ever heard it beat before as tears began to flood down her face.

"Halea, look at me!" he shouted while shaking her, forcing her to finally look at him – and then he knew.

"No," he finally spoke with a low growl. "You will not."

"Varg…"

"No! Do you hear me? I said '*NO!*' You're going to be my mate. Let some other priestess die, but it will not be you!"

"Varg…no one else can do this. The last time the wrong priestess was sacrificed, the convergence just came back in far less time than it should have, and countless people lost their lives. It's too late."

"You said you wanted to be with me. You said you wanted to be my mate, and now you want to die!"

"Forgive me…I didn't know. I didn't…understand," Halea tried to explain while sobbing uncontrollably. "I just wanted to be with you…for my last days alive…I wanted to be yours…if only for a little while."

Varg trembled with rage, his grip on her shoulders growing painfully tight.

"If you think…for even one moment…that I'd let you die," he growled.

"Varg…"

But suddenly, he snatched her spear from her hand and cast it into the distance, and before she could protest, he threw her over his shoulder and was racing into the den. He moved with lightning speed until, at last, they were at his private cave, and she cried out as he roughly tossed her onto his bed.

"Varg…wait!" she cried, but he refused to listen as he turned and went back to the entrance. He pulled the iron brace from the inside of the doors, then went outside.

She jumped up and tried to stop him, but he had slammed the heavy iron doors shut, and she could hear him securing the brace from the other side.

"Varg! Varg, what are you doing? Open this door!" she shouted while pounding on the heavy door with her fists.

"You two, get up here, now!" he commanded down to Faolan and Aatu, who had watched their alpha carry in the priestess. The two betas ran up to where their leader waited on the mountainside.

"Guard this door. She does not come out. No one goes in except for me. No matter what she says or does, you keep her in there."

Halea jumped up and pried open the small window above the door.

"Varg, stop this! You can't do this. Please!" she begged.

He only glared back at her with a look of finality, then turned to walk away.

202

"Varg, if you do this, the world will be destroyed. There is no other way!"

"Then let the world be damned," he said as he walked away.

# CHAPTER 27 – THE WOLF AND THE LAMB

Halea slammed against the iron doors with all her might, causing them to shake violently and another dent to appear, but still, they would not budge.

Outside, Aatu and Faolan kept watch as Varg had ordered, and they cringed every time the priestess charged the doors, causing the iron to groan. No matter how much she shouted for them to release her, they could not.

Aatu wondered what had come over his alpha to do such a thing. Wasn't she his chosen? Why was he keeping her locked up? But he had seen the look of anger in his leader's eyes, and he was not about to ask questions.

Faolan struggled with a mixture of guilt and duty. Halea had saved his life. She purified his wounds when he was on the brink of death. He owed her his life, but if he disobeyed Varg, his life would be as good as over anyway, and so he stood there silently and tried not to listen as she shouted from within.

Halea crouched on the floor and clutched her shoulder in pain. It was no use. The window above was too small for her, and Faolan and Aatu would be in her way. It was time to use brains instead of brawn.

Standing back, she looked at the iron doors.

Metal.

She reached out and placed her hands on the cool surface and closed her eyes.

"Tiamet, please," she asked, and a rush of power flowed through her body and began to charge the doors.

Faolan and Aatu jumped in shock as the doors began to glow as if they were on fire.

"What is she doing?" asked Faolan in fear.

"I don't know! Maybe we should call for Varg?" But just as Aatu was about to howl for his leader, the glow slowly faded.

"Damn it!" swore Halea, as she was unable to hold the charge, and she finally relented as the sweat dripped from her brow. The doors would conduct, but to what purpose? Charged weapons were usually used to strike opponents. The doors just sat there and absorbed her energy but did nothing.

She collapsed to her knees, defeated.

~~~☼~~~

Kalee rolled over and opened her eyes to see the smoldering remains of their campfire from the night before. She stretched and yawned and noticed that several clerics were already up and about.

"Bout time," remarked Samesa with a smirk as she appeared and tossed more wood onto the dying embers.

"Where's Halea?"

"Well, she said she'd be back in the morning. I thought she'd be here by now," Samesa replied.

"You don't think?"

They both had the same concern. What if that lycan harmed her? What if Halea was wrong and he wasn't to be trusted? Lord Anshar would be furious if they let any harm come to her.

Samesa cast Kalee a worried look.

"I hope I wasn't a fool for letting her go off."

"Maybe we should go look for her?" suggested Kalee.

"Let's give her a little more time. Perhaps she's on her way. If she's not here in an hour, I'm going."

~~~☼~~~

Varg stood on top of the vantage point, the same place where he had once taken Halea to look at his den. He stared into the tree line at the border of their hunting grounds.

They would come. They would come to take Halea away from him. And if he let them, eventually, they would kill her, and he was *not* going to allow it.

Varg seethed with anger. He had given his word that Halea's people would not be harmed on lycan territory, but if they came to take her away, he would break the agreement. He hated going back on his word. It violated every code of honor he was raised to value, and what's worse, some of them were people she considered her friends.

*"Pft, some friends. With friends like that, who needs enemies?"* he thought bitterly. Perhaps he could run them off without having to kill any of them. It all depended on how far they would be willing to go to defy him on his own territory. He could only hope it wouldn't come to that, but no matter what, he would keep her alive by any means necessary.

~~~☼~~~

Halea woke up as the sun's rays began to glow through the small window above the doors. It was hard for her to determine what time it was because it was a western-facing window.

"Where's Varg?" she asked, not bothering to raise her voice. They could hear her perfectly fine.

There was a moment of silence before she finally heard Aatu's muffled reply. "We're not sure. He hasn't been back, but I'm sure you'll be the first to know when he's here."

Halea sighed when suddenly it occurred to her exactly where he was, and a wave of panic seized her.

*"Varg, please don't hurt them,"* she prayed.

~~~☼~~~

Samesa looked up at the sun rising in the sky. Everyone was thinking the same thing, and nobody liked the possibilities. Clerics and priestesses fought demons, not therians. Their weapons weren't even effective on therians, and the clerics wouldn't have a prayer against the superhuman speed and strength of the lycans.

"She's not here," whispered Kalee.

"I know," replied Samesa.

"Maybe it was demons. She was attacked the other day. Maybe it wasn't the lycans. They did give their word we'd be safe. What reason would they have to hurt or kill Halea, especially if she said she was friends with their leader? They need our help; surely they saw that after yesterday."

"Maybe they got hungry?" interjected Favion, who was quite nervous about the entire situation.

Neither probability was very comforting, but despite her fears, Samesa did want to give the lycans the benefit of the doubt. She still remembered the look in Halea's eyes when she spoke of Varg. Maybe she was safe and fine and had just lost track of time, or something else unpredictable could have happened. Perhaps she was somewhere wounded or killed by demons. If that were the case, it'd be wrong to blame her disappearance on the lycans.

"Spread out. We're going to search the forest for her, at least make sure she's not somewhere close before we go jumping to conclusions. If we don't find her...I'll go, and I'll get to the bottom of this."

⁓⁓☼⁓⁓

Thunder cracked in the distance, and Varg looked into the west as a massive dark cloud rolled in from the sea. The wind began to pick up and shake the trees. It was odd to see such a storm in the summertime, and how had it developed so quickly? That was when he saw it, a strange purple light glowing in the distance.

He had seen that same purple light once before when he was a cub.

It had begun.

⁓⁓☼⁓⁓

They had all been searching for quite some time when the sound of thunder shook the ground. Samesa quickly climbed the highest tree and stared out into the west, and terror gripped her heart.

⁓⁓☼⁓⁓

Halea sat at the foot of Varg's bed and silently wept until she thought she heard the faint rumble of thunder followed by muffled screams of terror coming through the doors.

She pushed a heavy wooden table against the doors to get a better look out through the small window. Howls warning of danger filled the air as Lycans ran everywhere in panic when one howl rang out louder than all the others, and everyone stopped. Halea could barely see below, but she heard Varg down in the common area shouting orders.

"Stay calm. Take only what you can carry. I want everyone to evacuate into the mountains," Varg commanded.

206

"Varg, the den?" asked Lyall, who hated the idea of giving up on their home without a fight.

"I'll stay. If their numbers aren't so great this time, perhaps I can use the Fang to hold them off. Last time too many lives were lost because we waited too long to get everyone to safety."

"Then I will stay as well. I will fight by your side," Lyall declared.

Several other lycans from Varg's pack offered to stay, but he refused to accept the help of those who had mates or young children.

"But, Varg, I can fight!" argued Hemming.

"Not this battle, Hemming. Your family needs you."

"We wish to fight as well," offered Bertolf and Ethelwolf.

"No, lead your packs to safety, this is my den, and so my pack will watch over it. May the ancient wolf gods be on your side."

⁓⁓✧⁓⁓

"Lord Anshar, the barrier is in place," reported Mama Dragon.

Lord Anshar sat upon the rubble of the ruined city, his sword clenched tightly in his fist as he cast a quick glance up into the sky. The convergence was still forming, and the demons had yet to appear, but soon the barrier would be their only protection. It came far earlier than he had hoped. He had been biding his time in the ruins of the Citadel that were slowly being reconstructed, and the moment the convergence manifested, he suited up in his armor and red cloak and went to the ruined city.

"Shall I send Rufus to fetch Halea?"

"No, she will come. I know she will. Wait at the edge of the forest until she arrives, then send the falcon to notify me, and I will begin preparing the ritual site. After that, take cover, get as far away from this accursed place as you can, and pray."

"Yes, my Lord," replied Mama Dragon with a bow before racing into the distance.

"*Hurry, Halea,*" Lord Anshar thought bitterly as he listened to the roar of the Chaos and the howling of the demons within.

⁓⁓✧⁓⁓

In the end, Varg selected only a small group of warriors to stay behind. He wanted to risk as few lives as possible. He didn't have the heart to tell them that theirs would be a hopeless battle.

The worshippers of the Dragon Goddess would have to sacrifice some other priestess or let Chaos take the world, but he would never let Halea die. If the demons were too many for them to hold back, he would take Halea and the remainder of his warriors and retreat into the mountains.

The alpha in him wanted to stay and fight to the end, but he had to think of Halea and his pack.

Varg stood beyond the edge of the den and watched as his people evacuated their homes and his heart constricted. Why were they cursed to live in such a cruel world?

Suddenly a scent reached him on the wind, and rage burned within him.

⁓⁓✧⁓⁓

"Varg, let me out! Please!" Halea shouted while pounding on the iron doors as tears streamed down her face. She turned and pressed her back into the cool metal and sank helplessly to the floor. Time was running out, and the ritual would fail if she didn't find a way to escape, and that was when she looked up through bleary eyes and saw it – Varg's bow.

*"Yes!"* she thought as she picked it up and began looking for arrows. All she needed was a projectile with some metal, and maybe there was a chance.

But she couldn't see a quiver anywhere. Quickly she began tearing apart Varg's cave, overturning furniture, and ripping open anything she could find, until at last, in a heavy wooden chest of drawers, she discovered a single arrow.

The fletching was in poor shape, but its point was made of steel, and accuracy wasn't important, which was good because she had absolutely no experience with a bow. She had barely ever used any weapons outside of her spear, but she had seen clerics use bows and knew enough to be able to properly nock the arrow. All she would have to do is release it.

~~~~☼~~~~

Samesa broke into a nervous sweat, which trickled down her back. One of the few times in her life that she had actually felt too warm since coming into the northern lands. Before her was the lycan den, and she could see thousands of lycans evacuating.

She walked towards the den with her head held high, and when she was within a few hundred meters, she stopped and waited.

Soon, a lone lycan came out to meet with her, and as he came closer, she tried to suppress a tremble. It was their alpha, Varg.

"It is time you leave these lands," he told her in a stern tone the moment he was within a comfortable speaking distance, and she could hear him giving her a low growl of warning.

"I'm not going anywhere without my friend. Where is she?"

~~~~☼~~~~

Halea pulled back on the bowstring with all her might and focused all of her energy along the shaft of the arrow.

"Tiamet, hear my prayer, please. Give me strength, Great Dragon Mother, you who have chosen me. Lend me your power," she prayed as the arrow glowed with a blinding white light, and the Goddess's power coursed through her veins.

The arrow shot forth like a bolt of lightning, exploding the doors from their hinges with such force that Faolan and Aatu were struck and knocked down the mountainside.

Halea raced to the entrance and looked down to see the two males lying unconscious far below, and she prayed she hadn't killed them.

"Forgive me," she said before turning and running for the rope bridge that led into the tree-dwellings.

Very few lycans seemed to be left in the den, and the few who remained paid her no mind. Most were still running for their lives.

Once she reached the trees, she was about to descend when she heard a woman's voice.

"Halea?"

Halea turned and found herself face to face with Batsuba.

"I'm going. I have to. There is no other way."

The old healer's fathomless eyes grew moist as she regarded the priestess before her, and she nodded her head.

"Tell Varg…I'm sorry, and that I love him." Halea removed the blue crystal from around her neck and placed it into the she-wolf's hand, and then she ran down the spiral steps and disappeared into the forest.

~~~☼~~~

Faolan opened his eyes, and his head throbbed horribly. Aatu was groaning in agony beside him. With great difficulty, he rose to his feet, and the world lurched beneath him as blood trickled down the side of his face.

"Varg…I have to tell Varg."

~~~☼~~~

"Halea is safe. She is safer with me than she is with you. Now leave," Varg ordered again with another growl.

"I want to see her. I'm not leaving until I do."

"No. Halea is not yours, and I will not let you or anyone else take her life from her. You'll have to go through me."

"Halea is chosen. Her sacrifice is so that all may live, including you and your people. If you interfere with the will of Tiamet, then the whole world will be destroyed!"

"My people will endure this. We are not weak like you pathetic humans. I would fight all the demons of Chaos and Hell before I'd let anyone take her away from me."

Samesa twirled her spear and entered a fighting stance.

"I am not afraid of you. Set. Her. Free!" she demanded while staring down the lycan alpha.

She had challenged him; there was no avoiding it now. The beast within him demanded blood.

"Varg!" someone shouted, though he could barely focus on anything but the priestess he was about to destroy. He could feel the red begin to bleed into his eyes.

"Varg, Halea's gone!" he heard the voice shout above the raging wind of the convergence storm. Varg's head snapped in the other direction, where he saw Faolan running towards him with blood smeared down the side of his face.

Samesa could barely hear the words of the beta male over the sound of the raging Chaos in the distance, but something he said drew the alpha's attention, and she could have sworn she heard Halea's name. Without another word, the alpha took off at lightning speed, back towards their den.

"What happened?" she shouted to the other male, who stared after his leader.

"She got away," he shouted back with a shrug.

A bright smile accompanied her laugh of tremendous relief.

"*Atta girl*," Samesa thought.

When Varg made it to the den, he immediately began searching for Halea's scent. He had to follow her trail. He had to stop her.

"She is gone, Varg," he heard Batsuba say.

"When? When did she leave?" he demanded.

"Varg, you cannot prevent this. This is her destiny."

"No. You're wrong! I am her destiny."

Batsuba opened her hand and revealed the blue crystal to him.

"She truly loves you," spoke the healer as she placed the stone in his hand.

Tears formed in his eyes as he squeezed the stone in his fist.

"And that is why I will never give up."

# CHAPTER 28 – FOR YOU

Halea raced through the forest. She had to make it to the ruined city before the demons escaped through the convergence and blocked her ability to reach Lord Anshar. She could see the dimensional rift growing in the distance as the wind caused every tree to bend with the force of the raging storm.

When at last she reached the edge of the forest she heard someone calling for her.

"Halea!" shouted Mama Dragon, who ran to meet her. Her falcon flapped its wings as it struggled to stay steady on her arm against the winds.

"Halea, thank the Goddess that you're here. Where is your spear?"

"I…lost it."

"Here, take mine. Now run! They're coming," Mama Dragon cried while handing her spear to Halea and raising her other arm to launch Rufus into the air.

The demons were surging forth from the convergence tear.

~~~☼~~~

Varg ordered Lyall to lead the remaining warriors who stayed to guard the den with strict orders to retreat if the situation became hopeless.

He charged through the forest at his fastest speed until, at last, he reached the edge of the trees. He had never gone beyond that point before. He had never set foot in human territory, but he would not stop until he found her.

~~~☼~~~

Mama Dragon took cover at the edge of the forest and erected a barrier around herself for protection when she saw a lycan race through the trees and make his way towards the city.

"*A lycan…why?*" she thought.

A sudden realization struck her - it was him. It could only be him. He had come for Halea.

~~~☼~~~

The moment Lord Anshar saw the falcon in the sky, he felt a wave of both anguish and relief wash over his heart.

~~~☼~~~

Demons were pouring out of the tear like a swarm of locusts as Halea ran through the city, following the falcon that was leading her to where Lord Anshar would be waiting. She raced through the barrier which Lord Anshar opened just enough to allow her to enter and quickly sealed again once she was safely within.

She struggled to catch her breath and as the demons swarmed around the barrier, crashing into it like ocean waves upon a rock. All who touched the barrier were instantly purified, but still, they desperately tried to fight their way in.

"It is time," Lord Anshar said while handing her the bowl of ink he had prepared.

~~~☼~~~

As Varg followed Halea's scent through the ruined city, he came face to face with an enormous horde of demons who moved straight for him the moment they saw him. Varg drew the Fang, and with a heavy swing, a massive burst of power shot forth, cutting down demons by the hundreds. He raced through the pathway that he cut, but the demons were soon swarming all around him.

This was it. He couldn't hold back, and that was when he let the beast within take control.

~~~☼~~~

Halea painted her body with the sacred symbols and runes as she chanted the words for the ritual. It was hard to focus as the roaring demons continuously threw themselves against the barrier and burst into the white light of purification.

She wondered if Varg had found out that she escaped. Surely, he had by now. She prayed he wasn't out there with those demons.

Lord Anshar could sense her distraction. "Concentrate, Halea. Call upon your power."

He cursed himself for being so hypocritical. He wasn't exactly focused either. In a matter of moments, he would have to kill her. He would have to look into her eyes for the last time, and her blood would forever stain his hands, and for what? Even if the ritual were successful, there would always be tears, there would always be demons, there would always be death and destruction, and in two hundred years, it would only return. He was so sick of the cycle, so weary with the knowledge that his only purpose was to fight the Chaos over and over again. He could never hope for anything else.

A loud blast caused them both to look up and witness a flash of white light, followed by the shrieks of countless demons being slain.

"Varg!" cried Halea. There could be no one else. He was using the Fang to reach her. Another flash caused the ground to shake all around them.

Lord Anshar growled, a sound Halea had never heard from him before, and she thought she saw the shape of his pupils grow elliptical.

"We begin the ritual. Now!" he commanded.

*"So, you've come for her, have you?"* Lord Anshar thought bitterly. He could allow nothing to interrupt the ritual, not even Halea's lover.

Halea knelt before Lord Anshar and bowed her head. Her heart was pounding in her chest. Varg was in danger, and there was nothing she could do. Her time was up.

"Halea, you have been chosen. Will you give your life for Tiamet? Will you sacrifice your blood so that all others may live and that evil may be banished?"

212

She looked into his eyes, and a stab of agony shot through his heart. Her eyes were filled with tears that streamed freely down her face. The overwhelming sadness mixed with her hopeless resignation cut into the very soul of him.

"I will die willingly," she said.

It was his turn to look at her with pity in his eyes. He knew she did not want to die, and anguish consumed his beautiful face.

~~~✕~~~

Varg had finally reached the barrier. His eyes were burning red, and the blood of countless demons covered him, but at last, he could see her. There was another male with her. He had to hurry.

He charged into the barrier with all his might and growled in agony as the pain shot through him with an intensity that almost sent him to his knees. He grit his teeth until some of them cracked, but still, he forced himself into the barrier.

~~~✕~~~

Halea rose and began to chant in the ancient language. As she performed the many poses of the ritual, she drew a circle around herself in the dirt with the tip of her spear before inscribing the runes of sacrifice at her feet.

At last, she stopped and looked into Lord Anshar's eyes again. "Let my sacrifice be consecrated with blood."

He slowly drew his sword, The Blade That Cuts Through Worlds, and she could hear her own heart beating; it seemed to drown out all the sounds of Chaos and madness around her. There was nothing but the beat of her heart and the gleam of the blade.

Lord Anshar heard the barrier being disrupted, and he turned in time to see Varg breaking through.

He quickly raised his sword, but before he could strike Halea, the lycan tackled him to the ground.

Halea cried out in shock as Varg and Lord Anshar tore into each other. Varg's eyes were red with rage as he slashed with his claws and managed to cut into Lord Anshar's armor, spilling blood. Lord Anshar's eyes turned elliptical as he too entered a blood rage.

He would make the lycan pay.

He slashed at Varg with The Blade That Cuts Through Worlds, but Varg quickly blocked him with the Fang, and soon they were clashing swords. Their weapons, each powered by the gods of old, blazed as they fought, and each clash was like the sound of thunder.

"Varg, stop, please," Halea begged, but neither male could hear her as they attacked each other again and again.

Varg was not as skilled with a sword as Lord Anshar, only his speed, strength, and the rage of the beast within him was keeping him alive. No matter how hard he tried, he could not make a successful strike against the dragon therian.

Lord Anshar carved a deep slice down Varg's side, causing him to roar in pain, and then he struck him with all his might, causing Varg to fly into a ruined building with such force that the entire structure collapsed on top of him, burying him in the rubble.

"Varg!" cried Halea, and that was when Lord Anshar turned his elliptical eyes on her.

Lord Anshar walked towards Halea, sword in hand, and she closed her eyes.

A loud crash preceded the other sounds of disorder all around her. When Halea opened her eyes, she saw that Varg had emerged and thrown Lord Anshar into the side of a building, knocking the structure over in a cloud of dust and debris that caused the ground to shake beneath her feet.

But the shaking didn't stop, and Halea could tell that Lord Anshar was still alive, and that was when she saw the glow of two large elliptical eyes rising from the dust of the ruins. A massive, winged beast let out a roar that shook the ground, and she knew she was looking at his true form – the dragon.

Varg showed no fear and charged with the Fang in his hand and leaped into the air to attack the beast.

Halea watched in horror as the dragon easily swatted Varg from the air and was quickly on top of him, crushing him with its massive claws. Even she could hear the bones snapping and crunching as the white dragon tore into Varg, who yelled in agony as the beast's claws pierced into his chest and lungs, then suddenly he went still.

"Varg! Stop! Stop it, please!" she screamed as she ran and threw herself at the dragon's feet.

"Don't kill him. Please, don't kill him. I'll die. I'll die willingly, I swear. Just don't kill him."

Lord Anshar released Varg from the grip of his claws and shifted back into his humanoid form. Halea crawled closer to Varg and wept bitterly to see how severely injured he was. No matter how she tried, he would not move.

"Varg! Varg, please don't die. I'm so sorry," she cried while throwing herself over his body.

Lord Anshar looked down on Halea as she lay over the lycan's body, and his heart constricted as he watched her suffering. She had thrown herself in front of his true form just to save that lycan. Suddenly he found himself wishing he knew what it felt like, if only for one moment, to have that kind of love.

"His heart still beats. Halea, it is time."

Halea gently caressed Varg's face one last time, then rose and stood before Lord Anshar.

He looked into her eyes. Her sorrow overwhelmed him, and his hand shook as he raised his sword. He could see into the depths of her soul as she stared back up at him. She wasn't doing this for the world. She wasn't doing this for Tiamet. She was doing this for her fallen love. Her sacrifice was for him and him alone.

And that was when he knew.

Lord Anshar lowered his sword and reached out with his other hand to touch Halea's face. Her tears felt warm beneath his fingertips, and he leaned down and kissed her.

Halea was shocked and frozen as she felt his lips against hers, but she never closed her eyes. A rush of power flowed through her in a swirl of light, and, at last, he pulled away from her.

Her immortality was gone.

"Be happy," he said, and for the first time, she saw true peace within his eyes.

He turned and passed through the barrier, effortlessly cutting his way through any demons standing in his way. He ran towards the great tear that loomed in the sky and threw himself into the Chaos Dimension. Thunder cracked the air, and all the demons shrieked as a flashing light forced her to shield her eyes.

When she looked up again, the convergence was gone.

# CHAPTER 29 – BLOOD MAGIC

The demons scattered in all directions, but Halea paid them no mind.

"Varg? Varg, please wake up," she pleaded while kneeling beside him, her tears falling on his face.

He was lying in a pool of blood that continued to spread, and she didn't even have her medical supplies. She quickly tore the sleeves from her robe and applied pressure to try and stop his bleeding.

"Someone, help me, please!" she shouted, but there was no one.

She heard the cry of a falcon, and when she looked up, Rufus was perched high on the remains of a half-collapsed building.

"Rufus! Rufus, get Mama Dragon, hurry, please!" she cried out to the bird, which took off into the air and flew towards the forest.

"Hold on, Varg. Don't die," she whispered next to his face. "Stay with me."

~~~⌂~~~

Mama Dragon watched as the demons converged on the city. She had braced herself for them spreading into the surrounding area while the great tear was still open, but they seemed intent on focusing all their might on the city, and she knew their primary mission had been to stop the ritual.

She watched in shock as the convergence vanished in an unusual flash of blinding light, but concern laced her relief – something wasn't right.

Mama Dragon readied herself as suddenly hundreds of demons rushed past her and scattered in all directions. Many seemed to ignore her; others were instantly purified against her barrier as they leaped in to attack. She wished she had her spear to stab through the barrier and take down more of the evil creatures, but all she could do was wait.

Eventually, they grew to ignore her presence, daunted by her barrier and directionless without the convergence. That was when she heard Rufus cry out as he flew above her, and she couldn't wait anymore. Something had gone wrong, and she was needed in the ruined city.

Quickly she removed her barrier and raced with all her speed, dodging demons that lashed out as she ran. Few gave chase, and those that did were slain with the purification from her bare hands.

At last, exhausted, Mama Dragon reached the barrier that she and Lord Anshar had created together, and she couldn't believe her eyes. Halea and her lycan lover were inside, but Lord Anshar was nowhere to be seen. Mama Dragon raised her hands and called upon her power, opening the barrier just enough to get inside.

"Halea? How? How are you here? Where is Lord Anshar?"

"Oh, Mama Dragon, help me, please. Lord Anshar is gone. He disappeared into the Chaos."

Mama Dragon's face took on a look of absolute horror. Lord Anshar, gone? How? Why?

"I need your help. Varg is dying," Halea cried, snapping Mama Dragon out of her stupor.

The older priestess had never treated a lycan before, but she was skilled with medicine and could tell by the look on Halea's face that she was frantic with worry. She removed her travel bag, and together they set to work.

As they worked, Halea recounted everything that happened, though she avoided mentioning the kiss. They reset Varg's broken bones and treated and sealed his more severe wounds. Before they were even halfway done, they had already used all of Mama Dragon's emergency medical supplies.

"If what you say is true, Lord Anshar is gone forever. We can only pray that his sacrifice has finally brought an end to the convergence."

"He once said he wanted to find another way."

"We've slowed the bleeding. He's lucky he's a therian. No other could have survived such wounds, but he's not out of danger yet. He needs more help than we can give him. He needs a healer."

Halea looked around; demons were occasionally still lurking beyond the safety of the barrier, waiting to prey on them.

"We need to take him to the den."

Mama Dragon rose to her feet and picked up her spear that was lying on the ground. "Leave it to me," she said before disappearing through the barrier.

Halea waited anxiously, cradling Varg's head in her lap. "I'm so sorry, Varg. I'm so sorry. Please hold on just a little longer."

At last, Mama Dragon returned with two long and sturdy wooden rods and a bundle of canvas salvaged from a derelict building within the city. Together, they quickly assembled a litter and gently moved Varg.

"They're still swarming out there. We can't fight while carrying him. We're going to have to run for it."

Halea nodded. She hated to jostle Varg in his fragile condition, but there was no other way.

As soon as Mama Dragon disabled the barrier, they ran, dodging to avoid demons at every turn. Thankfully with their speed, they were able to stay ahead of their enemies, and before long, they were racing through the forest. The fastest wraiths were chasing after them, and Halea prayed they could make it to the den before being caught.

~~~✧~~~

Lyall was relieved when he saw the tear disappear in the distance, but his relief was short-lived when hundreds of demons began swarming into their territory. The lycans slaughtered all that came too close to the den. Their numbers weren't as bad as the last convergence, but there were still too many, and Lyall feared he would soon have to call a retreat when suddenly he saw small flashes of light in the distance.

The humans were still fighting.

Samesa and Kalee had erected a barrier around themselves and the clerics, and they were doing their best to strike down any demons they could reach with their weapons from their point of safety.

"*If they can make it, then so shall we,*" thought Lyall with determination.

A howl rang out in the distance, and he quickly rushed back to the den, expecting to find Varg, but what he found instead made his blood run cold.

Halea and another priestess were gently setting down a litter carrying Varg, who looked deathly pale and completely lifeless. Several lycan warriors had found them at the border of their hunting grounds and fought back the wraiths pursuing them. Batsuba quickly rushed in and shoved aside several other lycans who were in her way.

The old healer had chosen to stay instead of fleeing into the mountains with the others. She had waited to see if Varg would return and was dying to know how Halea was still alive, but her curiosity would have to wait. It was clear that Varg was in terrible condition, and the hard trek through their territory had not been good for him. She quickly went to work. Halea helped her to the best of her ability, and this time Batsuba was grateful that she was there.

"What happened?" asked Lyall.

"There will be time for that later. They need you, hurry," barked Batsuba in clear command.

All around them were injured lycans, many suffering from the wounds of dark blades.

"I will help," offered Mama Dragon.

Batsuba wanted to argue, but she couldn't focus on saving Varg and everyone else, and there was nothing she could do for the wounds of dark blades. At last, she nodded her head in agreement, and Mama Dragon quickly went to work.

The two priestesses and the healer worked through the night as they heard the shrieks of demons being slaughtered all around them, but at last, as the sun began to rise, most of the demons seemed to have vanished or been slain.

~~~✧~~~

Varg opened his eyes as the sun began to irritate them and absently wondered why he had left his doors wide open, but as his eyes came into focus, he realized his doors were missing entirely. That was when everything came back to him all at once, and he jolted upright only to experience horrendous pain all over his body.

"Varg, don't move," he heard Halea say.

Halea had lain curled up beside Varg for the last two days, barely leaving his side. Batsuba occasionally came to check on the progress of Varg's recovery and to assure Halea that he would live.

Rufus flew until he found Mama Dragon, and she had sent him back to Antherose with a message for High Priestess Maven. That morning they had received High Priestess Maven's reply that they were all wanted back at the castle

218

immediately, but Halea merely shook her head when her fellow priestesses came looking for her.

"I've made my choice, and Lord Anshar knew it. That's why he took my immortality away. I'm not one of you anymore. My place is here," she explained as the priestesses wiped tears from their eyes before hugging her one last time.

"You were the last to see Lord Anshar. High Priestess Maven will want to speak with you," said Mama Dragon.

"She'll have to wait. I'm not leaving Varg right now."

As the priestesses were about to leave, Halea ran to catch up with Mama Dragon.

"Wait!" she called. "Please tell my grandfather that I love him and that I'm okay."

The motherly priestess agreed to send her message, and Halea was left to watch them disappear into the trees.

When Varg finally awoke and heard Halea's voice, he turned to look at her, ignoring the pain, and he could scarcely believe what he was seeing.

Was this heaven?

"Oh, Varg, I'm so glad you're finally awake. I was so worried. Everyone's been worried. Lyall keeps coming to ask how you're doing. I don't think he likes being in charge of this place," she explained with a smile.

He reached out and softly touched her face, his eyes growing moist with unshed tears.

"Halea…you're here. Are we dead?"

When she smiled, he knew he had to be in heaven, but she shook her head 'no.'

"Everything is okay now. The convergence is gone. I'm here. I won't leave you."

"Ever?"

"Never," she replied and leaned down to kiss him.

~~~☼~~~

It took nearly a week for the last of Varg's broken bones and injuries to completely heal, and he carried many new scars, but Halea didn't care. He was alive. They were both alive, and they were finally going to be together.

She stayed by his side throughout his recovery, and Varg cursed that he wasn't his usual self because there was nothing he wanted more than to finally claim Halea as his mate.

Halea thought about telling Varg about her final moments with Lord Anshar, but the last thing she wanted to do was get him all worked up and angry when he needed to rest and recover. It wasn't that she intended to hide the truth from him; it was just that she wanted to wait for a better time. Besides, Lord Anshar was dead. He had sacrificed his own life to save her, and she carried his final words in her heart.

One night while Varg was sleeping, she went into the forest alone to weep. She would miss Lord Anshar. He had always been good to her. He had saved her life more than once. He had been a friend to her, and she prayed to Tiamet that wherever he was, his soul would finally be at peace.

~~~☼~~~

"Up and about, I see," said Batsuba when Varg entered her tree-dwelling.

The last of their pack had just returned home from the mountains. Varg had sent a runner to give them the news that it was safe to come home. Lyall and the small band of warriors that remained had eradicated almost all of the demons that strayed into their territory, and the few that had eluded them would eventually be found and eliminated.

Aatu had even found Halea's spear and returned it to her. Halea felt terribly sorry for hurting Aatu and Faolan when she escaped, but they didn't harbor any hard feelings. In fact, they were impressed and had developed a newfound respect for her.

Halea didn't seem angry with Varg for having locked her up for her own good, but he suspected she would chew him out for it once she was done fretting about the state of his health. He, on the other hand, had no regrets about his decision. He had only done it to protect her and would gladly suffer her wrath when the time came.

Varg worried that Halea was sad to no longer be a priestess, though aside from the loss of her immortality, she seemed the same in all regards. He knew she wanted to believe that with the dragon therian's sacrifice, perhaps the world would no longer need priestesses, and that thought seemed to comfort her. He could only pray to the ancient wolf gods that she was right. He wanted it to be over and for their world to finally be rid of the plague of the Chaos Dimension. He just wanted to live his life with her in peace, and at last, the time had come.

"It is time. Prepare the potion for the blood magic ritual," he said to Batsuba.

~~~☼~~~

Halea felt nervous, and she was sure she reeked of anxiety to him.

"Are you sure, Halea? There can be no doubts. This can't be undone," Varg asked, and he prayed that she was still set in her decision.

To his relief, she didn't hesitate.

"I'm just nervous. I've never done anything like this before."

"Well, part of it, you have," he said with a wolfish grin that immediately caused her to blush.

She had already painted the ancient rune for the contraception spell onto her left wrist. She wasn't quite ready to leave everything up to Varg's senses.

"Not that! I mean, being mated. I imagine it's what women, human women, feel like on their wedding day. I want this, Varg. I want to be your mate. I love you…it's just that…I hope I'm enough. I'm not a lycan. What if I'm not good enough to be your mate?"

He gave her a stern look as he pulled her into his arms.

"Yeah, you're a puny human, so what? I'm only a mangy wolf, remember? I don't care about any of that. I only care about you. You own my heart and soul, don't ever doubt that you're not good enough because no one in the world can ever mean as much to me as you do. I love you, Halea. I've always loved you, and I'll love you until my last breath and beyond. You're all I want."

He gently tilted her head back so he could seize her lips, and his heart pounded against his ribs as she opened her mouth, allowing him deeper access. He explored her heatedly with his tongue, savoring her taste, her touch, her warmth, her scent that was already making his blood boil with desire.

She slowly ran her hands down his hard chest, and he growled with pleasure as she softly traced his scars with her delicate fingers. He could never get enough of her touch. He reached behind her head and slid his fingers into her silky hair, pulling her even tighter against his kiss as his tongue thrust into her mouth. His other hand roamed down her hip and pulled her closer, and she moaned as his hard length pressed against her. Already he could smell the scent of her arousal, and he fought to keep the red from bleeding into his eyes as the beast within wanted only to mount her, claim her, mark her, but he wanted to savor this moment. He wished to remember this night for all eternity, the night she became his mate. He intended to please her in every way and wouldn't rest until she was screaming his name.

He scooped her up into his arms and carried her to his bed – their bed.

His recovery had been absolute torture, not because of the pain, but because the most beautiful woman in the world was beside him, loving him, and he could barely hold her in his arms in his weak condition. Now that he was healed and whole again, he would finally possess her.

He laid her on their bed and ran hot kisses down her jaw and throat, sucking and nipping the flesh along the way. Her pulse quickened beneath his lips, and he struggled to keep his fangs from growing. Not yet.

Halea slid her hands over his chiseled stomach and down even lower until she was stroking him through his trousers, and he nearly exploded at her touch.

He sucked in air with a groan of bliss as she worked her hand over him.

"Varg…let me touch you," she breathed in his ear, and he damn near sunk his claws through the bed as his grip tightened.

She opened the front of his trousers, and he let out a pleased growl as she freed his excited member and gently worked her hand along the length of his shaft.

"Halea," he breathed before capturing her lips again and allowing one of his hands to cup and squeeze her breast.

"Varg, lay back," she said, and he was not about to argue. Whatever she wanted of him, he would gladly give.

He removed his trousers and lay down and watched as she slowly crawled her way up his body. It was almost too much. She was so beautiful. A Goddess. A queen. His queen.

She reveled to see him breathing so heavily beneath her, and she grew wet with excitement. Oh, the things she wanted to do to him.

She straddled his hips, and he had to fight the urge not to thrust upwards, and he felt frustrated that she was still wearing her robe.

As if she guessed what he was thinking, she untied her robe, and he was both surprised and pleased to see that she wore nothing beneath it, nothing except for the crystal he returned to her. He wanted her to keep it.

She leaned forward and pressed her soft lips to his, and he reached up and filled his hands with her breasts, teasing slow circles around her nipples with his thumbs.

221

She moaned against his lips, and again he wanted to just dive inside of her, but whatever sweet torture she had in store for him, he was not about to interrupt.

She trailed her lips along his jaw and towards his ear, where she played with his earlobe, and he nearly lost it when her tongue ran over the length of his long, pointed ear.

Varg's entire body rumbled as he growled in excitement, and Halea smiled wickedly while slowly kissing down his throat and scraping her blunt human teeth along his skin.

"*Oh, gods, if she…*" he thought, and then she did. He felt her bite him where his throat met his collarbone, and he growled, the furs tearing to shreds beneath them as he sank his claws into the bed while losing control in the most delicious way. She hadn't bitten him very hard, hadn't even bruised his skin, but it was enough to excite him to the point of frenzy. Lycans usually left love bites on their mates, and she had left him wanting her in the worst way.

But she wasn't done with him yet.

Fire burned in his veins as she slowly moved her mouth down his chest, and he growled again as she ran her tongue across his nipple. She slid her hand down his thigh and slowly back up again to softly caress his balls before grasping his length.

She could feel the heat radiating off his skin as he continued to tear into the bed with his claws while she slowly worked her hand up and down his hard shaft. He was so beautiful to her, and she loved feeling him in her hand. His skin was soft like velvet, but beneath it felt like solid steel, and she marveled at the size of him. As she trailed her kisses down the chiseled plane of his stomach, a small droplet formed at the head of his member. Before he could register what was happening, her warm tongue slid over the head of his cock, and it took all of his strength not to burst inside of her mouth.

"Halea," he breathed as she took more of him into her mouth. Her tongue was doing things to him that he had only ever dreamed about, but the reality was so much better. She stroked the base of his shaft as her warm wet mouth moved languidly over his head. If he didn't stop her soon, the ritual would be spoiled.

"Halea, I want to be inside of you," he begged, and she smiled as she released him and slowly crawled her way back up his body.

He watched, hypnotized, as she slowly lowered herself onto his throbbing member.

"Gods, Halea, you feel so good," he growled as she took him in. She was so warm and wet and tight, and he was losing his mind.

She gasped at the way he felt inside of her as she slowly rode him. His hands tightly gripped her bottom as she worked against him, a grip so firm she was sure he would bruise her, but she didn't care; she wanted his hands on her body. She wanted him to take her, and soon she was growing closer to the edge.

She cried out in shock and disappointment when he pushed her off of him but knew when he reached beneath the pillows and pulled out a vial that it was time.

"Sure this isn't going to kill me? You know I'm not a lycan," she asked with a smile as he opened the vial and handed it to her.

"Don't worry, it's made just for puny humans," he said, and she drank the contents of the vial.

As soon as she drank the potion, he was on top of her, and she ached to feel him inside of her again. To her relief, he wasted no time opening her legs and positioning himself at her entrance. He bit his lip and drew blood that spilled onto his chin, and she knew what she had to do. He brought his face down to meet hers, and she slowly lapped the blood from his lips which she sealed with a deep kiss, and that was when he plunged deep inside of her, and she nearly came as his growl shook her entire body.

"Oh, Varg," she cried out in bliss to feel him within her once again. "I love you."

He was losing control, but this time he wasn't holding back, not this time. He let the beast take him. Allowing his instincts to possess him, the red flowed into his eyes as he thrust inside of her with wild abandon. He could feel her walls tightening around his shaft, and she was almost his.

She cried out his name while writhing in ecstasy beneath him, her blunt nails scratching down his back, and then with a growl, he sank his fangs into her throat just above her collarbone as he released inside of her.

She screamed in both pain and pleasure as he left his mark and another wave of release washed over her, and she trembled as lights danced before her eyes.

He lapped the blood from her neck as the red slowly receded from his eyes. They were both trembling and gasping for breath, their bodies glistening with sweat, but they could both feel it. She now shared his life force - his immortality. The bond had been forged.

He had never felt her this way before, and she could feel him as well. They both experienced the deep, overwhelming love they each possessed for the other as if they were one heart, one soul.

"Varg…"

"Halea, I love you," he said before smothering her with an intense kiss. When he finally broke the kiss, he stared into her beautiful eyes, eyes that he would now be able to lose himself in for the rest of their lives. "You're mine, Halea. You belong to me. You're a part of me, and I belong to you."

Tears formed in her eyes. Normally there was nothing in the world he hated more than to see her cry, but because of the bond he could feel, she was crying because she was happy. His Halea was happy - happy to be with him.

~~~✶~~~

Far in the north, across the snow-capped mountains, lightning cracks the sky.

A new tear is formed.

~~~END~~~

NOW AVAILABLE!

Blood Bound

Book two of Convergence

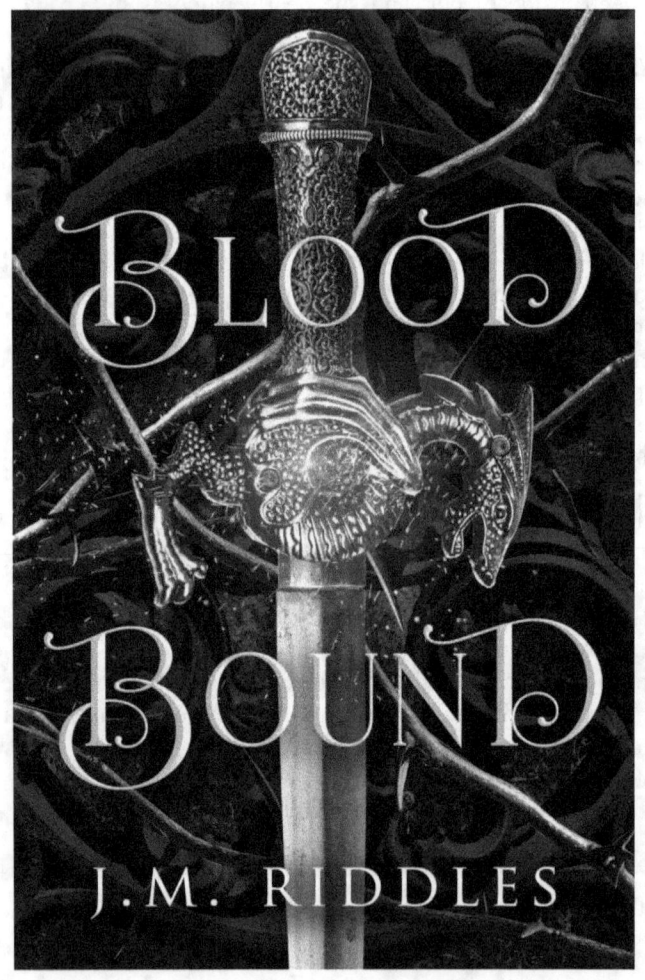

J.M. Riddles (aka Your Humble Author, aka J) is an avid fantasy and science fiction lover. Some of her writing also features romance, paranormal, horror, and surrealism. Some of her interests include heavy metal, food, art, makeup, nature, and all things nerdy. For other writing projects, social media links, and additional information, you can visit her at

jmriddles.com